"Fast paced, surprising, and madly compelling."
Rosie Fletcher, Total Film

"A great, imaginative, gripping read…"
Nev Pierce, Editor-at-Large, Empire

"Joshua Winning could well be on to a winner with this unsettling but entertaining icebreaker; hopefully Nicholas and this trilogy will mature nicely together."
Claire Nicholls, SciFiNow Magazine

"Don't think you've read this before in the Harry Potter books, Sentinel sets a darker, grittier tone. The action is fast and violent, the monsters, including a seductive vampiress, are memorable."
John Wyatt, The Sun

"Written poetically, with carefully-drawn characters, this is an extremely promising YA debut by a young author."
Kate Whiting, Press Association

"Winning's eminently readable style, coupled with some strong characters and a pace that nicely rounds out the book make this a cut above the vast majority of the young-adult fiction market that tries the same approach."
Daniel Benson, HorrorTalk

"One for fans of Terry Pratchett, Edgar Allan Poe and Tolkien. Joshua Winning's Sentinel has everything fantasy readers could want: action, mystery, gore, magic and an orphan with wacky relatives."
Lizzy Fry, Culture Fly

"Adventure, twists, demons and mystery abound in this spellbinding tale of a hidden earthly underworld."
David Estes, author of The Moon Dwellers

"Sentinel first hooks you with a cadre of compelling and appealing characters, then before you know it, you're trapped in a nightmare of intangible forces that become more and more threatening, more and more clever, more and more inescapable. You definitely reach a point where you can't put the book down."
D.A. Metrov, author of Falcon Lord

"A well-crafted, sharply honed novel that creeps into your subconscious, settling deep before springing a few surprises upon the unsuspecting reader. You won't want to put it down, and you probably don't want to read it on your own in an empty house!"
Sarah McMullan, The 13th Floor

RUINS

First published in 2015 by
Peridot Press
12 Deben Mill Business Centre, Melton,
Woodbridge, Suffolk IP12 1BL

Copyright © Joshua Winning 2015

The right of Joshua Winning to be identified as the Author of this work has been asserted by him in accordance with the Copyright, Designs and Patents Act 1988.

All characters in this publication are fictitious, and any resemblance to real persons, living or dead, is purely coincidental.

All rights reserved. No part of this publication may be reproduced, stored in a retrieval system, transmitted in any form or by any means, electronic, mechanical, photocopying, recording, or otherwise, without the prior permission of the publisher.

ISBN: 978-1-909717-28-2

Set and designed by Theoria Design
www.theoriadesign.com

Visit: www.thesentineltrilogy.com
Follow: @SentinelTrilogy
Like: facebook.com/SentinelTrilogy

JOSHUA WINNING

RUINS
BOOK TWO OF THE SENTINEL TRILOGY

Rules for survival

1 Don't make friends
2 Don't talk about your past
3 Don't tell anybody what you can do
4 Don't show weakness
5 Don't let the monsters see you

- Anon.

PROLOGUE

TEN YEARS AGO

SIRENS WAILED IN THE NIGHT AND the sky was a blood-red inferno of fire and ash. People gathered in the street to stare. They huddled in slippers and dressing gowns, transfixed by the burning house. Some offered reassuring murmurs. Others scrutinised the shadows, fearful that whoever had done this was still nearby.

"It was her. She did it."

"Keep your voice down."

The girl hugged her knees, teetering on the edge of the kerb. She was only five years old, but her scowl made her look older. The fire danced in her eyes and her pink pyjamas were flecked with cinders.

Across the street, smoke belched from a house torn apart. The building had been bisected and the girl could see her bedroom through a smouldering fissure. It was blackened and burnt. A nest of broken memories.

Her foster parents stood with their backs to her, arm in arm, watching the blaze. Her foster mother glanced over her shoulder and the girl trembled, caught in the woman's accusatory glare.

"What are we going to do?"

"Let's wait for the authorities to arrive."

"What are we going to do about *her*."

The girl screwed up her fists and shuddered at the keening of the approaching sirens. Her heartbeat quickened. Nobody was watching her anymore. She got to her feet, her eyes trained on her foster parents' backs.

As she turned to run, arms snapped around her and she was hoisted from the ground.

"Don't go anywhere," her foster father warned in her ear.

The girl thrashed and growled and angry energy flushed through her. The air shimmered with heat and her foster father dragged her into a neighbour's garden.

"Stop it," he said. "Breathe."

He crouched down, holding her at arm's length, his forehead creased with concern.

She couldn't. Her insides churned. The garden wall trembled and the grass rustled as if disturbed by the wind. She'd dreamed the house was collapsing around her, and when she'd woken up, the dream hadn't ended. She wanted to sob, but she didn't. She bit the emotion down, clenched her fists until they hurt. And still the rage roiled inside, causing sweat to trickle down her temples.

Across the garden, a tree erupted in flames.

Her foster father jumped and squinted fearfully at her.

Through the dreadful churning in her belly, she heard the pad of determined footsteps behind her.

"Elizabeth, no—" her foster father began.

Something struck her in the back of the head and the girl felt the grass whisper against her cheek.

The last thing she saw was fire and ash in the night sky, and she knew it was all her fault.

CHAPTER ONE
The Festival Of Fire

Present day

"You've been out hunting again, haven't you?"

Sam Wilkins sucked his cheeks and gave the doctor as much of a surprised look as he could muster.

"Don't know what you're talking about," he grunted, hearing the falseness in his tone. At seventy-one years old, he really should be able to come up with a decent little white lie. He had one of those honest faces, though. Everyone told him that. The nervous smile and hooded eyes always gave him away. He ran a hand through his thinning silver hair as Dr Geraldine Adams glared at him over the rim of her glasses.

"Your blood pressure's not so much through the roof as swooping about with the sparrows," she said sternly. She was in her early sixties, crinkled around the edges, but fiercer than ever. She had been a savage Sentinel in her day, wily and ruthless as a coyote, but like many older Sentinels, she had forgone hunting in favour of her day job. A loss, Sam thought, but at least he could still rely on her in a pinch. And she remained formidable; spectacles magnified her eyes and they were inescapable.

Dr Adams removed the apparatus from his arm and dumped it on the desk, pausing to slip an escaped strand of her own silvery hair back into the neat pile pinned atop her head.

Sam rolled down his shirt sleeve and said nothing. He was glad Dr Adams' check-up hadn't involved removing his shirt. He'd never be able to explain the still-yellow mottling of his skin; slow-fading bruises from the fight in the temple beneath the cemetery.

"You know you're gambling with your health, Sam," Dr Adams persisted, tapping notes into a computer. The office was small but light, slatted blinds letting in fingers of sunlight. A framed photo of a puffy, toothless child rested on her desk. A scrap of A4 paper was pinned to the wall. Chubby handprints had been eagerly pressed into multi-coloured paint.

"Samuel Wilkins!"

The elderly man nodded and returned the doctor's stare, twisting the battered grey fedora in his hands.

"You should be taking it easy," Dr Adams said. "Let the youngsters do the hard work, it's their turn now. You should be enjoying retirement. Get a dog. Play chess. Learn French. Forget about monsters."

Sam didn't tell her that sounded like his idea of hell.

"Would that I could. There's bad stuff coming, worse than we've seen in our lifetimes. You don't just sit back and let that happen."

"But you certainly don't go out looking for it," Dr Adams told him. She knew him too well. Softening, she touched his liver-spotted hand. "I'm begging you, stop. It'll be the death of you."

Sam held her gaze. It was now or never – the real reason he'd submitted himself to Dr Adams' scrutiny.

"Ever heard of a Dr Snelling?" he asked.

She removed the hand. "Why'd you ask?"

"He worked somewhere here in Cambridge."

"Smelling?"

"Snelling," he corrected her. He checked his pocket watch. Two pm. He would have to hit the road soon.

"Doesn't ring any bells," Dr Adams mused. "Should it?"

"Nothing important," Sam assured her. "Though, there is something."

"I'm not going to help you on any monster hunts. You should know better, and frankly–"

"Just... a nod or a shake of the head," Sam interjected. "Has anything ever crossed your path, you know, anything regarding possession and the such? I'm asking you as a professional, of course. I don't want to know what you get up to outside of work hours."

Dr Adams shot him a look that would have left his left cheek glowing if it had been a slap. "Samuel Wilkins—"

Sam raised his hands and got to his feet, backing toward the door. "Don't mind me, just an old fool with an overactive imagination," he said, opening the door.

"Snelling," the doctor said suddenly.

Sam paused. "Sorry?"

Dr Adams bit her lip. He'd never seen her do that before. "There was something, back in the nineties," she muttered. "Now what was it? No, I can't think." She glared at him, jabbed a pen in the air. "And you shouldn't be rooting around in anything of the like."

"I'd best be going," Sam said. "If you happen to think of anything, drop me a line, won't you?"

She was sterner than ever. "No more hunting."

He assured her, as convincingly as he could, that he would do nothing of the sort. Even as he said it, he knew he had no intention of stopping. What else was there? If he went to his grave fighting, that's the way it had to be. He was born a Sentinel and it was his duty to protect people from the dark things that prowled just out of sight, unnoticed until it was too late. He supposed ignorance was bliss.

Dr Adams prescribed him some pills for the blood pressure and Sam begrudgingly fetched them from the pharmacy. He'd never remember to take them.

The walk home was balmy, the sun heavy on his shoulders as he hurried down the street. The fedora clung to his forehead and the heat made him nervous. The snow had melted the day after that terrible night in the mausoleum, when he'd discovered that even more Sentinels had been turned against them – had become Harvesters. The cold evaporated like a bad dream and the sun blasted apart the lingering clouds.

Sam shuddered. So sudden a change in the weather didn't bode well. It was a diversion; a distraction from what was to come. How could spirits buoyed by the return of bright August mornings ever imagine the darkness that awaited?

He surveyed the street. Cambridge was different in the wake of that night. True, it had always been subject to demonic activity, that was the reason he was stationed here. The demonic activity had stepped up in recent weeks, though. Ever since Anita and Max Hallow were killed in a train crash and the demon Diltraa picked its way through the city's child population. Diltraa was banished, but still Sam worried. There were others, and the Harvester population was only swelling. And then there was Malika, the red-haired witch. There had been no sign of her since Diltraa's demise, but Sam suspected she was merely licking her wounds before leading a fresh assault.

When he got home, he double-bolted the front door and wound string from the handle to the radiator. The string was lined with little bells that tinkled when he plucked it. He was taking no chances. After checking the back door and downstairs windows, he fixed himself a late lunch. A cup of tea and a few slices of toast. He took them upstairs and climbed the step-ladder into the attic, ignoring the ache in his right knee as he went.

The attic was as he'd left it the day he and Liberty had found the message on the Ectomunicator, the old typewriter-like device that the Sentinels had once used to message one another. He hadn't been up here since that evening; he couldn't face it after what had happened at the church. The guilt sat like a stone in his stomach. Immovable and constant. Richard. Vince. Jack. He'd killed them all. They had been Sentinels, but something had turned them; transformed them into bloodthirsty Harvesters whose sole desire was to kill Sentinels.

There was only one thing he could do to stop himself succumbing to the gnawing guilt – he had to find out why. What had turned them? And who was behind it? Somebody was assembling an army. He had to stop them.

Liberty was doing what she could in-between looking after her daughter. Though she was a handy person to have around – Liberty was a Sensitive and attune to psychic activity – Sam was relieved she was focussing on family. He was loathe to drag her into this again, especially so soon after she had been used by Malika to open a portal into Hallow House. The trauma of that nasty ordeal had nearly killed her and, five days later, Liberty was only just starting to resemble her old, sarcastic self.

No. He wouldn't bother Liberty. The weight of responsibility rested on his shoulders alone.

With a sigh, Sam seated himself at the desk at the back of the attic. He clicked on the lamp and a circle of light fell on the Ectomunicator. Wearily, he drew the dust cover over it and retired the contraption to the back of the desk, making way for his meagre lunch.

He sipped the tea, crunched the toast unenthusiastically, popped one of Dr Adams's blasted pills, then opened a drawer under the desk and took out a clunky old laptop. He powered it up, hoping he could remember everything Max had taught him – he hadn't used it in some time. The little lines in the corner of the screen told him he was connected to a wireless network, so he opened a browser and started typing.

He wasn't sure what he was looking for – there was no information regarding Sentinels or Harvesters on the Internet beyond the ramblings of the conspiracy hounds. He tried a few random searches. Nothing useful came up.

Sam leaned back in his chair. It had all started with Richard. Richard and Dr Snelling. Sam had tried to call Dr Adams when Richard was attacked, but she had escaped the snow for two weeks in Mauritius with her husband. Sam wished she'd been there to see Richard. Maybe she could have figured out what Snelling had done to him. She could have helped Sam save him.

He remembered those cold, accusatory eyes boring into him from the kitchen floor and shuddered.

"Snelling," he muttered, shaking the image off. He typed the name into the browser, which returned over seven million unique results. Sam puffed in exasperation and clicked through the first few links. Most of them were useless. Building companies, some scientist called Snelling who didn't seem relevant, and reams of other unrelated news stories.

He paused, his hand hovering over the mouse pad. Sam squinted at the website he'd opened.

"How interesting," he murmured.

★

The book made a satisfying *thwack* as it hit the wall and thumped to the floor.

Nicholas Hallow grunted, disappointed it hadn't smashed through into the next room – at least then he wouldn't have to look at it. Instead, the book sprawled on the carpet. The way it had landed, he could still read the silver words along its spine.

The Sentinel Chronicles – August 1997.

He'd found the book on his bedside table five days ago, the morning after he'd fought Diltraa. It was the one book in the Sentinels' extensive records that he'd been unable to uncover. The book's absence from the library had aroused his suspicions because he was born in that very month. And then suddenly there it was, as if the room had coughed it up, taunting him with the promise of answers.

Every page was blank. Every single one of them.

The disappointment thudded in his chest.

Another dead end.

Nicholas couldn't help feeling he was the punchline to a particularly stupid joke. Jessica Bell, the leader of the Sentinels, had revealed something that even now made his skin crawl, as if he'd shrunk inside of it. Almost sixteen years ago, he'd been born in the village of Orville, less than a mile from here. His birth had almost destroyed the village and every single person living in it. They were all killed, their souls frozen in time.

"*They're dead*," Jessica had said, "*but they continue to live undead lives, caught there for all eternity.*"

Remorse wrenched at his insides and Nicholas glared at the book. There had to be a way to find out how he'd caused such destruction. And there had to be a way to fix it. Jessica had been so busy since the night in the garden, though. That was five days ago, and he'd barely seen her since. They'd burned Diltraa's remains together; the Garm's, too. Pounded the bones into ash, and that was the last of it.

Nicholas suspected that he was still being protected from something. He wished they would just be straight with him. He'd survived a demon – what could be harder than that?

"Not a fan of the ending?"

Nicholas jumped. A cat peered at him from the door. Isabel's fur was black, zigzagged with silver. The fact that she could speak was as unremarkable to him now as the fact that all other cats couldn't.

"You're getting good at being stealthy," he remarked. "I didn't hear you at all that time."

The cat regarded him coolly. "Or perhaps you were too busy daydreaming, as usual."

"I need to find out what happened in Orville," he said, shoving a hand through his dark, curly hair.

Isabel couldn't help. Technically, she'd been dead when he was born, her spirit trapped in the pentagon-shaped room on the ground floor of Hallow House. She was as clueless about the town as he was. She'd taken the time, though, to explain certain things to him. He'd learned words like 'Harvester', which were Sentinel-killing bounty hunters, and he'd overheard conversations as Jessica met with visiting Sentinels. A mad man with a katana had rampaged through the streets of Manchester, killing twenty people; a chemical plant had a meltdown, incinerating hundreds of workers; thousands of dead fish washed up at Beach Rock in Norfolk.

Isabel had uttered the word that nobody else dared.

"*Apocalypse.*"

"There's plenty of time for that later," Isabel said. "They're about to start. Come."

In a blink she was gone.

Casting a final look at the book, Nicholas resisted the temptation to give it one last kick and hurried after her, plunging through the empty corridors of Hallow House. When he'd arrived here two weeks ago, the never-ending warren of hallways had given him a headache. Now, he knew the house inside out.

By the time he arrived at the entrance hall, the cat had vanished. Instead, he found Sam waiting for him.

"Come on, lad, let's not miss it, eh?" the elderly man said. Nicholas noticed rings under his eyes and Sam seemed thinner than usual. His grey suit was practically baggy.

"How are things?" Sam asked as they left the house.

"Oh, you know. Paying the bills by killing demons. It's a grind but the kids need new shoes."

Sam chuckled. He could always count on a chuckle from Sam, no matter how poor the joke.

Together, they trudged into the countryside. The evening air was warm, but Nicholas shivered. He noticed orange flickers as they approached the forest and he looked at Sam nervously, hoping they were safe out in the open.

A ring of poplar trees bordered a wide clearing. The sky was a cheek-blushing pink, and at the clearing's centre, a large crowd had already gathered. Nicholas's insides leapt when he realised every one of them must be a Sentinel. He could count the number of Sentinels he'd met on one hand, and he scanned the horde keenly, discovering Sentinels of all shapes and sizes. They looked utterly normal. Supermarket people. The fear that he was under-dressed in shorts and a T-shirt – summer clothes Sam had fetched for him from Midsummer Common – quickly evaporated. Aside from the odd raven feather or silver pendant, the others were completely unremarkable. He couldn't help feeling a twinge of disappointment.

A breeze stirred and Nicholas couldn't help trembling. "Is it safe? Out here?"

"Oh yes," Sam said. He pointed to the trees. "Don't you see them?"

Nicholas peered at the band of poplars and noticed that a figure stood between each trunk.

"Sensitives," Sam told him quietly. He winked.

Nicholas's eyes widened. Sensitives. Like him. If that's what he was. After his parents' deaths, he'd become aware that he could sense things before they happened. In one of the library's books, he'd read that Sensitives could do that, too.

Sam led him further into the clearing and they joined the crowd. The Sentinels had gathered for a memorial ceremony. After they had dealt with Diltraa's remains, Jessica told Nicholas about what had happened in Cambridge in his absence. Sentinels were attacked and turned, including one of Sam's friends, Richard. A lot of people had died in a tomb beneath a cemetery, and Nicholas was relieved Sam wasn't one of them. No wonder the old man looked so tired.

His insides squirmed when he thought about Malika and her demon master, Diltraa. They had orchestrated a plan to break into Hallow

House and they'd succeeded, almost killing Jessica. A swell of pride briefly stilled the squirming anxiety. He'd been responsible for chasing Malika away. He'd used his powers to buckle the witch's defences and even glimpsed some of her own dark thoughts.

He frowned at the memory. He'd seen Malika huddling naked in a corner of the Pentagon Room. The image felt old, like a piece of the past, and he still didn't understand what it meant.

Meanwhile, Diltraa had been slain by Esus, the silver-masked phantom who guided Jessica.

Shaking off those troubling thoughts, Nicholas contemplated a crude wooden structure at the centre of the dell; it was a platform with a set of steps. The Sentinels crowded in front of it eagerly, though they were disarmingly solemn. Firelight filled the clearing; night had yet to fall, but a number of wooden posts had been driven into the ground and set ablaze. They reminded Nicholas of Guy Fawkes Night.

A sudden murmuring rippled through the Sentinels. Nicholas saw that the crowd had parted and people were craning forward, straining their necks, clawing at the rows of shoulders in front of them to get a better look at something. At first, he only glimpsed silver and black as somebody approached. Then he saw Jessica and his breath caught in his throat.

The leader of the Sentinels glided like a scythe through the congregation. In the firelight, her skin was mercurial, her eyes dark and enchanting. Stiff black feathers were fastened in her golden hair and fanned about one shoulder. A silvery-white dress – cut at an angle to expose one gleaming shoulder – swept the ground behind her. Perched on her bare shoulder was a raven, and the bird assessed the crowd with uncommon interest.

The Sentinels dipped their heads.

Every nerve in Nicholas's body hummed, as if Jessica's presence had forced them to spring awake.

He scowled. Behind her, swaggering with the aloof manner of an alligator, stomped a brute of a man. His boots were the size of cement blocks, his hands, strapped in brown leather, as large as dinner plates. A powerful chest strained against the confines of a leather bodice. His face was like a Cubist painting; a botched nose had clearly endured numerous blows and his squashed mouth was forever contorted in a sneer.

This was Lash. A stupid name, in Nicholas's opinion, but fitting given his position as Jessica's new bodyguard. Though Diltraa and Malika's infiltration of Hallow House was being kept a secret for now ("There would only be panic, and what use is that in a war?" Isabel had told him), Lash had moved into the manor to ensure Jessica's safety. Nicholas had only encountered him a handful of times, none of them pleasant.

Jessica swept between the adoring masses, then steadily mounted the platform. While Lash took his place at the side of the stage, Jessica revolved to address the crowd. The voice that rang over their heads was clear as the starry heavens.

"There is a darkness abroad and we are the thing it covets," Jessica called. "It swells with each cycle of the moon and already great numbers have succumbed to its suffocating embrace."

The tiny hairs on the back of Nicholas's neck prickled. The woman before them was a formidable creature. Proud and defiant. When he'd first met her, Jessica had been waiting for him at the house with an impish smile. He'd seen a tear in that facade, though, the night Diltraa invaded the manor. Jessica had been reduced to a sobbing child. Nicholas found that hard to believe now.

Was this bold new image a ruse? A performance to inspire faith in her followers? Or had something happened that night in the gardens? Something that had changed her? Peering up into her heart-shaped face, he couldn't decide either way. Whatever Jessica was doing, though, it was working. Every Sentinel had fallen under her spell.

"For your losses, I am sorry," Jessica continued. "Those who died did so fighting the cause that their fathers and mothers fought before them. It is a proud death, though one not free from sorrow."

At these words, Jessica's gaze rested on a short blonde woman whose eyes were glistening with tears.

"They must be honoured," Jessica said. "Their labours remembered. No death will ever be in vain, no spilled blood forgotten. That is the reason we are collected here today, to–"

"Tell me why my son died!"

A voice erupted from the crowd. Shocked gasps bristled through the clearing and Lash squinted, a hand sliding to the dagger strapped at his belt.

Silence fell.

"Peter Carmac," Jessica said, barely moving. The raven at her shoulder glowered into the throng, the black balls of its eyes impossible to read. "If you wish to speak, speak."

All faces turned toward one man. He was in his late fifties, Nicholas guessed, skin toughened by years of hard labour, a blobby nose riddled with burst capillaries. He gripped a cap in his hands but shoved his chin up at the stage.

"My son, he was one of them found at the church, St John's," Peter Carmac called in a voice bitter with grief. "He'd went missing a few days before, not like him at all. He was a good boy. Then he turned up dead, shot in the face. I couldn't even…" His voice quavered and a tear-stained woman who Nicholas assumed was his wife put a trembling hand to his shoulder. He shoved it off. "I couldn't even recognise my own boy! And I want to know why!"

Carmac. Nicholas didn't recognise the name, but he assumed Peter Carmac's son was one of the Sentinels who had been turned in Cambridge. He felt a surge of compassion for the man. Sentinels were confronted with death more than the average person – they were demon hunters, after all, and their lives were fraught with risk. Many of the faces in the crowd bore the tell-tale signs of hardship and loss.

Jessica clasped her hands before her. Her skin was like marble.

"On the night of the 21st August," she began slowly, "an Ectomunicator message was sent to every Sentinel posted in Cambridge. It requested their urgent attendance at St John's Baptist Church. This message was sent by an imposter. It was a trap for Sentinels. Those who answered the call were mercilessly slaughtered. Later that night, their bodies were discovered in the chambers beneath the church." She paused, absorbing the expressions of grief and horror stretched across every face. "It is our belief that Harvesters were behind the attack. They are gaining in strength and number. We believe they are uniting with a common goal. Gone are the days when they hunted alone. To that end, a ban has been placed on all Ectomunication."

"But my son..." Peter Carmac's voice rose, cracked.

Jessica's expression was sorrowful. "There is much we do not know. The one thing we can say with absolute certainty is this: the days of peace are behind us. War is coming and we must prepare. But that is talk for another day. Let us proceed with the festival and honour those who are no longer with us."

Nicholas looked up at Sam and saw that his face had crumpled. He wondered if he'd known the victims. With a start, he remembered Isabel. What had happened to her? She certainly wasn't with Jessica, and she couldn't be among the crowd, she'd be crushed. He scanned the clearing, then spotted a sinewy shape in the limbs of a poplar tree. Isabel's whiskers caught the firelight and she looked wild.

There was movement on the stage. Jessica swept noiselessly down the steps, Lash clumping behind. She moved around the side of the platform and the crowd spilled after her.

"Where we going?" Nicholas asked.

"You'll see," Sam said, resting a hand on his shoulder.

Elbowed forward by the Sentinels, Nicholas followed the current around the platform. It was strange being among them. He didn't feel part of their world. It was as if he was intruding on something private and painful. Nobody acknowledged his presence, though, nor challenged it. He attempted to make himself as small as possible, shrinking away from the elbows that prodded him.

Waiting for them on the other side of the platform was an immense iron cauldron. It coughed smoke that strove eagerly into the pink sky. Jessica stood to one side and waited for the crowd to settle.

"Death is forgetting," she said at last. "The dead forget, but they will never be forgotten. Let us show them that we remember, and always will."

With that, the raven leapt from her shoulder. It took to the air and dropped something into the cauldron. A rush of sparks and smoke mushroomed up to meet the heavens. High up now, the raven wheeled through the air, tracing the curve of the poplars.

Jessica smiled kindly at an elderly woman to her right and Nicholas noticed that a queue had formed by the cauldron. The old woman clutched something in her gnarled hand. A slip of paper. She hobbled to the cauldron and dropped it in. A flash of flame briefly lit her face, then nothing. She wiped her eyes with a silk scarf as she shuffled away.

Nicholas watched as, one by one, the Sentinels approached the cauldron and dropped in slips of paper. He felt a nudge at his side.

"Here," Sam said quietly. Nicholas looked down as the old man pushed something into his hands. A square of paper folded roughly in half. Confused, Nicholas unfolded it. Two names were scribbled there.

Anita Hallow.

Maxwell Hallow.

His parents.

"Go on," Sam said, his face expressionless.

Nicholas swallowed. His heart was suddenly beating very fast. He joined the queue. More slips of paper were consigned to the cauldron and the line dwindled until finally Nicholas was by Jessica's side. She gave him the same benevolent half-smile she'd bestowed upon the other Sentinels and returned her gaze to the cauldron.

His insides trembling, Nicholas moved closer. He looked down and saw that he was clutching the folded note so tightly that he'd almost crushed it. Forcing himself to take a breath, he raised his hand and cast the paper into the flames.

"On this night, the Trinity are with us," Jessica called. "They share our grief. Accept their comfort."

She tapped the rim of the cauldron lightly and it hummed like a bell. Glowing embers flurried up with the smoke.

Nicholas staggered back.

The smoke snaked into the crowd, but nobody spluttered. Nicholas felt it whisper about him and where it thickened above the cauldron, flaming figures pirouetted. In golden flashes they pranced and flickered, at once bright as the sun, then hazy as candlelight.

Nicholas was rooted to the spot.

He looked around to make sure everybody else was seeing the same thing and, with a start, he found that he was alone. The other Sentinels had vanished.

The air grew melancholy. Transfixed, Nicholas watched the flaming figures bow and flex. They danced out of the smoke, twirling in front of him. They grew wings, became birds, skittered high into the air, then set the trees aflame. Nicholas gasped as the clearing transformed into an inferno. Prickling heat raged through him.

Where was everybody? Even as he thought it, he caught a glimpse of something silvery between the trees. Had Sam and the others gone into the forest to continue the ceremony? No, the forest was burning. They couldn't be in there.

Something drew him into the trees anyway. In a daze, Nicholas stumbled toward the flickering silver. Though the voice in his head warned him against it, his legs didn't listen. He passed into the forest, which was no longer aflame, though the trees were blackened and steaming.

Attempting to suppress the panic wedged in his throat, Nicholas fumbled onward. He didn't dare call out.

Branches shook and he heard a rush of wings.

Snelling? No, Snelling was dead.

A dark shape bowled toward him and Nicholas only just caught sight of the raven before it crashed into his face. He threw his arms up and hit the ground.

Caaaw!

The raven swept up and away, then bowled toward him again. Nicholas cried out as black smoke erupted in the air and a masked figure emerged where the bird had been. It swung a sword at him and Nicholas tried to shuffle back, but it was too late. He squeezed his eyes shut as the blade plunged for his neck.

CHAPTER TWO
The Trinity

There was no pain. Nicholas waited, his heart hammering, ready for the agony of the blade thrusting into his throat. Instead, he heard something heavy land in the dirt beside him. He opened his eyes and stared up into Esus's silver mask. The sword clasped in the phantom's gloved hands pressed coldly against his skin, but went no further.

"Do you wish to die here?"

Esus's voice gave Nicholas goosebumps. It vibrated in his head and he wanted to throw up. He knew little about Esus, except that he was Jessica's guide and adviser.

"Do you?"

Nicholas's insides spasmed and he fumbled for an answer, but he couldn't think with the sword probing his flesh.

"Well?" Esus demanded, increasing the pressure on the blade.

"Of course not!" Nicholas yelled.

"Then fight."

At first Nicholas was confused, but then he saw that another sword lay beside him. Esus removed his blade, remaining crouched, his black robes rustling about him. The merciless orbs of his eyes glinted through the mist.

"I don't know how–"

The phantom swung the sword again.

Not thinking, Nicholas seized the other weapon and brought it up to shield his body. Metal clashed against metal and a painful juddering shook his bones. He gasped and tensed against the ground.

"Weakling," Esus snarled.

Shame and anger boiled Nicholas's stomach and he drew on all of his strength to force Esus's blade away. The phantom's sword left his and Nicholas scrabbled to his feet.

Esus is the raven, he thought again through the pounding in his skull. He'd spotted the bird in the weeks following his parents' deaths. It seemed to follow him everywhere he went. It was the symbol of the Sentinels, but he didn't know why.

Esus prowled between the trees and an image of him fighting Diltraa flashed before Nicholas's eyes. Esus had hacked off the demon's head using the Drujblade, the bone dagger that Isabel had given to Nicholas. He felt queasy at the thought of Esus repeating the trick with him.

He raised the sword, his hands shaking. What was Esus doing? The few times he'd encountered him, Esus had been elusive and forbidding. Why would he save Nicholas from Diltraa only to kill him now?

"What's going on?" he asked.

Esus whirled at him, slashing the sword in a silver arc. Nicholas raised his own and they clanged together. Esus swung at him again and again, pushing Nicholas through the trees. His back struck a trunk and the swords clanged again, but Nicholas lost his grip and his weapon thudded to the earth.

Esus hissed and slashed above Nicholas's head. A decapitated branch clattered to the ground.

"Again," he ordered.

"What are you?" Nicholas panted, retrieving his sword. It felt heavier than before and he trembled, clasping it before him. He grit his teeth as the swords clashed once more. He moved sideways, away from the trees. He could barely see the blades as they moved. He responded to Esus's spars impulsively. Breathlessly, he staggered, his shoulders aching, pleading with him to drop the sword.

Esus dealt another blow and Nicholas's sword sailed out of his hands. A boot struck his chest and Nicholas thudded to the forest floor, Esus's sword slicing down.

"No!" he cried, hot fear overcoming him.

The blade went into the ground by his head and remained there.

"Again."

"I can't."

"How do you expect to fight the emissaries of the Dark Prophets when you cannot fight me?"

"I don't even know what emissaries means," Nicholas shot back between pants.

"The demon nearly claimed your life," Esus spat. The memory of Diltraa's blazing white eyes leapt into Nicholas's mind and his cheeks burned. He stared at the emotionless mask hovering above him and attempted to see through it. He had used his powers to get into Malika's head; that was how he'd driven her away. Perhaps he could do the same with Esus.

He pushed, striking out with his mind, picturing a sword thrusting into Esus's skull.

All he saw was a black void. A nothingness. A buzzing like insects screamed in his ears and Nicholas winced, pushing harder, sensing an alien presence. Something angry. A seething, boiling, formless entity.

Esus. He could sense him. Nicholas didn't know exactly *what* he was sensing, but it was something physical, deep within the phantom. His soul? His darkest secrets?

"Good," the phantom rasped. "That is how you will fight."

Was he aware of what Nicholas was doing? What *was* he doing?

Esus turned and peered into the forest.

The connection snapped and Nicholas shook his head, the buzzing gone, replaced with a crashing headache – and the sound of somebody approaching. He was sweaty and weak with fatigue, but he also felt oddly elated. He'd done it again. He'd tapped into the power within him.

Jessica appeared. Isabel scampered at her feet and Lash the bodyguard lingered behind.

"Well?" the cat asked.

"The boy is weak," Esus replied tersely. "Green. His training must begin at once. Show him."

Darkness crowded in around him, as if the phantom had drawn on every shadow in the forest, and he was gone. Nicholas heard wings beating above their heads.

Esus is the raven, he thought again.

"What just happened?" he demanded, shakily getting to his feet. Esus had called him weak, but he had a feeling he'd done something right. The phantom had pushed him. The sword fight was to scare him. The real test had been what he'd done to defend himself.

"Are you injured?" Isabel asked.

"Just my pride."

"That doesn't count."

"Didn't think it would. What did he mean by training?"

"Nicholas," Jessica said. "It's time we talked." Her calmness unnerved him.

"No kidding," he said. "Where is everybody?"

Jessica was already gliding between the trees, spectre-like in her silver and black attire, and he hurried after her. He assumed she was leading him back to Hallow House, but he couldn't be certain of anything anymore.

"They have departed," Jessica explained. "The Festival of Fire is over. You'll have to excuse Esus. His methods are somewhat unconventional. He wanted to catch you off-guard."

"Well, he succeeded," Nicholas muttered.

An uncomfortable sense of foreboding squeezed his ribcage. What had Esus meant by training? *Sentinel training?* The squeezing intensified. Were the secrets of the Sentinels finally going to be revealed? Did Esus expect him to fight? And if so, who was going to teach him?

"What is Esus?" he asked, slowing his pace as he tried to catch his breath.

"This way," Jessica said. She saw his hesitation and smiled mischievously. "Esus was a wild thing when the Trinity came upon him. Savage as nature itself, prowling the woods; half mad, half feral. In his breast, the Trinity sensed a fearsome instinct. An unflinching bloodlust. And, perhaps, unfaltering loyalty to any who bested him in battle. They couldn't fathom what he was. He was of two worlds; part of this one, part of another. He could change form at will. Snap his bodily chains and become something else entirely."

The Trinity. Nicholas had seen them mentioned in books, too. The Sentinels worshipped them like gods.

"The Trinity tamed him to a degree," Jessica added. "Wrestled with his spirit. His fire. Taught him words. But they didn't integrate him into civilised living. They needed his wildness, his innate violence."

They reached the house. The windows glimmered, casting distorted shadows to the ground.

"And The Trinity?" Nicholas asked.

"Come," Jessica said, opening the front door. "Let me show you."

Nicholas held his tongue. He didn't dare hope that Jessica was finally ready to answer his questions. Silently, he followed her through the house, traipsing down the dusty corridor that led past the Pentagon Room. Finally, they came to the garden at the heart of Hallow House. It had yet to reclaim its former glory. Great patches of bare earth gaped like wounds yet to heal. But here and there, budding foliage had appeared, bright green toes wriggling out of the ground.

"That will be all, Lash," Jessica said to her guard.

The brute eyed Nicholas distrustfully and Nicholas resisted giving him a rude hand gesture. Acknowledging her command, Lash nodded at Jessica and strode back the way they had come.

"You'll have to forgive him, too," Jessica said. "He takes his appointment very seriously."

Nicholas nodded. "As the grave."

"Like the garden, we're still recovering." Jessica led him between the flowerbeds. Isabel scurried after them and Nicholas watched her pause periodically to scrutinise a new scent. Despite her caustic nature, she seemed to have made peace with her feline predicament. For now, at least.

"I'm grateful for your actions that night," Jessica continued. "Without you, I'm not sure Diltraa would have been defeated." Nicholas didn't say anything. He couldn't take any credit for that. It was Esus who had lopped off the demon's head.

"What did you think of the Festival of Fire?"

"It was... different."

"The Sentinels are a proud people. They were raised as fighters and it takes a lot to shake them. I must offer my own apology, also. The book I left with you, the blank *Chronicles*. It was not meant to anger you, but illustrate how much of a secret that period truly is. If you come with me now, I'll explain everything."

Jessica knew he'd been angry? He wondered if there was any privacy whatsoever in Hallow House.

They came to a clearing. A rough circle of flat earth with a curious pit in the centre. Nicholas recognised it as the spot where the willow tree had stood. He and Jessica had used it to hide from Diltraa and the demon had ripped it from the ground, leaving the tree's agonised roots exposed.

"There's a reason Diltraa targeted the garden," Jessica said.

"It said something about the Trinity," Nicholas recalled. The memories flickered, felt half-glimpsed. He had cracked his head against a tree and it was still sore.

"It wanted to know the whereabouts of the Trinity," Jessica said. She laughed and Nicholas watched, confused, as Jessica strode into the circle of earth.

"It had no idea how close it came," she said, reaching into the ground, into the ugly hole at the clearing's centre. Nicholas was surprised to see a stone slab buried there. Jessica pushed against it, then moved back.

"Careful," she cautioned.

There came the sound of stone striking stone and loosed earth spilled into darkness. The ground trembled faintly under their feet, then was still.

"Is that what Malika wanted, too?" Nicholas asked. The red-haired witch had appeared to him as his mother and tried to persuade him to kill Jessica. Malika wanted Jessica dead, but why? Because she was the leader of the Sentinels? Or was there more to it?

"Come," Jessica urged, ignoring his question. It seemed there were limits to what she would tell him. She approached the opening in the soil, stepping into it and vanishing. Nicholas hurried over. The stone slab had gone. In its place, a set of rocky stairs coiled down into the earth.

"Stop dithering," Isabel called as she, too, disappeared.

Nervously, Nicholas followed. The air was damp and his nose itched. His footsteps echoed ahead of him, but the staircase quickly widened and he could breathe without succumbing to the fear of being buried alive. A light gleamed somewhere below. It illuminated the craggy walls, which were inscribed with crude pictures and words that he couldn't understand. He felt very young in a very old place.

Just when he thought the steps would never end, he reached the bottom.

They were in an unremarkable stone room. The walls were rough-hewn, the ceiling so low that Nicholas was forced to stoop. Jessica stood before a simple stone entranceway, the cat beside her. She shot a look over her shoulder.

"Ready?" she asked Nicholas.

"For what?"

Jessica smiled and eased open the rocky door.

Nicholas glimpsed gold. And more stone. Jessica and Isabel went inside and Nicholas tentatively followed. Candlelight wavered across the floor of an ancient tomb, pinching the shadows. Stubby candles were pooled everywhere – on little shelves, in shallow bowls, even on the floor itself – and the wax had melted to form wan rivers. Roots pushed through cracks in the stony ceiling and clung to the walls. And there was gold etched into the walls, still glimmering faintly.

"Come in," Jessica said, her voice echoing. She stood by three glass casements in the centre of the tomb. They were coffin-like, but infinitely more ornate, resting side by side on stone slabs.

At the back of the chamber, a carving of a bird presided over all.

Nicholas shivered. He was sure the bird had blinked.

"This is most hallowed ground," Jessica murmured, watching him as he took in his surroundings. "Few have been permitted entrance here. Isabel–" She broke off, noticing that Isabel was perched atop one of the glass coffins. "Get down! Shoo!" She swatted at the cat.

Isabel shrieked and hopped onto the floor.

Nicholas approached the coffins and touched the one at the centre. He gasped and the hairs bristled along his arms. An image flashed before his eyes.

A woman. Her hair is white silk, her skin coffee-coloured, her eyes blue as the ocean. She possesses a wiry intelligence.

Nicholas yanked his hand from the coffin, the image fading. He was unsure if he'd imagined the woman. She'd felt so real.

"They're full of water," he said, peering into the coffins.

"They have always been," Isabel's voice rang. "But where are the sleeping maids? What of them?"

"They have passed into memory," Jessica told the cat, who had seated herself on one of the candle-bearing shelves.

"Maids?" Nicholas asked. "What is this place?"

"It is the Trinity's sleeping chamber," Jessica said simply. "This is where they retired from the world, tiring of its horrors. They slept here for thousands of years. Now they are gone, returned to the earth that birthed them." Shadows danced across her face as she scrutinised him. "Let me tell you a story."

She went to the far wall and brushed dry roots from it. "Many centuries ago, there were two sisters and a brother. The boy was called Thekla. The girls were called Athania and Norlath. They were nomadic warriors, their skin dark mahogany, hair white as snow. They were the most feared and loved of the land. In that time, the world was known as *Ginnungap*, and it was a bleak place of death and devils. The Dark Prophets were seated in the wastelands of the west, and their insidious will stretched across the land. Only the iron-willed survived. Iron-willed and iron-boned. Thekla, Athania and Norlath were known as the God Slayers, because that was what people believed demons were – angry gods whose black hearts had been corrupted by their hunger for power.

"One day, Thekla received a message from the town of Nilhands. It was under siege. A monstrous creature had torn the heads from seventy soldiers and used them to fashion a nest for itself in the uppermost quarters of the castle. Riding out, the God Slayers stormed the castle and battled the beast. When the beast was slain, Thekla and his sisters were offered all the riches they could carry with them. But Norlath wanted no riches, no reward save one thing – the bravest women and men of Nilhands would join them, become their companions in the battle against the foul things that corrupted the innocent.

"It was quite a request for unassuming townspeople, but Norlath's expectations were modest. Five men and two women allied themselves with the God Slayers that day, and together they rode from town to town, exorcising evil everywhere they went. Each town they visited, so more recruits were enlisted, until their army was a formidable thing, always headed by the God Slayers, whose skills on the battlefield were unmatchable."

Jessica had made it halfway round the room. Nicholas listened raptly. It seemed even the drowsy candlelight had fallen under Jessica's enchantment.

"Eventually, the time came for the God Slayers and their army to confront the Dark Prophets. War raged for thirteen months. Both sides suffered huge losses, but finally the God Slayers emerged triumphant. They cast the Prophets out, drew on powers that nobody knew they possessed to rent open a seam in reality. The Prophets were banished to the darkest regions of Hell.

"When the remaining beasts were gone," Jessica continued, "having either retreated to their own realm below the earth or been wiped from Ginnungap altogether, the God Slayers built a town. Hyperion. They forged their own mighty fortress, and the townspeople affectionately called them the Trinity – the three who had saved the world from monsters.

"What the townspeople did not know, though many suspected, was that the Trinity were divine beings. Their veins ran with sacred blood. As the Dark Prophets were the ultimate in depravity, so were the Trinity the ultimate in purity. The name God Slayers was entirely accurate because that's exactly what the Trinity were – Gods birthed by the very soil of Ginnungap to restore balance to the world. Now that the world was cleansed, it did not need them anymore."

"What happened to them?"

"Thekla, Athania and Norlath retired below their fortress in three water-filled coffins, where they would wait until they were needed again. Their army became the Sentinels. Each generation that followed knew of the Trinity and what they had done, and watched the world for signs of evil's inevitable return."

Jessica stopped. Her hair fell across her face and she seemed sad. She perched on a step behind the coffins.

"But where are the Trinity now?" Nicholas asked. "They're not in the coffins."

"They slept for so long that they lost form," Jessica said. "I watched them grow transparent as water, and one day they were simply gone. Reclaimed by Ginnungap. Perhaps we left them too long. We should have roused them sooner."

"And Esus?" Nicholas asked. He wandered to the stone bird atop the throne and touched it. A new image flickered behind his eyelids.

A raven soars above a battlefield. It plunges through the ranks and sweeps toward three shadows. The sun glimmers, dancing about the figures, who wear silver armour and raise blood-stained swords.

Gasping for breath, Nicholas released the statue. He couldn't tell if his powers were growing, or if the magic in this chamber was so potent it was heightening them. A rush of exhilaration rippled through him. He'd never been able to summon images on command.

"When they first bested him in battle, Esus became the Trinity's eyes and ears," Jessica explained. "And when the time came for their retirement, Esus became the first *Vaktarin*, the first to guard them in their slumber. But as the years bled into one another, even mighty Esus wearied. Men came, fearsome conquerors, and a great battle took place over the town of Hyperion. Afterwards, all that remained was a smouldering ruin. The Trinity's castle was devastated. In the wake of much bloodshed, Esus entreated a family of Sentinels to rebuild, to create a residence above the Trinity's subterranean chamber and guard it in his stead."

"The name of that family was Hallow," Isabel put in importantly. "They guarded proudly when Esus could not."

Nicholas's head was spinning. Jessica had drawn a vivid picture of Sentinel history that he'd been unable to glean from the *Chronicles*. It went back further than he could have imagined. He thought about everything he'd learned at school. Darwin. The industrial revolution. Nazis. That history was familiar, accepted. This, on the other hand...

"This is mental," he breathed.

"It's a lot to take in." Jessica smiled kindly. "Now you see why we have been hesitant to burden you with too much information. I say 'burden', because that is what it can invariably be. Can you imagine what would have happened had we spoken of this all when you first arrived?"

"I'd have called the local nuthouse and told them one of their patients was on the loose," Nicholas said.

Still might, he thought ruefully, recalling Jessica's fragile mental state.

Jessica laughed and the sound glanced off the walls. "And now?"

"I still think you're all nuts," Nicholas said. He couldn't deny what he'd seen, though. How had those images jumped into his head, if not by magic?

"You'll just have to accept it." Isabel tutted, glaring at him from her alcove.

"Man has his history," Jessica added more tactfully. "We have ours. They're intertwined. Ours just happens to be, shall we say, less well publicised."

"And for good reason," Isabel drawled.

Jessica seemed to understand that he was struggling.

"Think of this," she suggested. "This is the history your parents knew. They kept it from you, and that was their choice. But this was their world. And it is yours, too."

Nicholas looked at the coffins. The inscriptions on the walls. His ears rang. Jessica's stories clashed with what he already knew about the world. It was like trying to push a square peg into a circular hole. But this room, this *tomb*... it had a feeling. The kind of feeling that usually existed inside a church, or an old house. A feeling of time and pride and wealth.

And he'd seen demons. There was no denying they existed.

"So how did you come into all this?" he asked Jessica. "You said before that you weren't a Sentinel."

"No," Jessica replied. "However, ordinary people have been welcomed into the Sentinel fold for centuries. Those with particular talents. That's why I was brought in. My Sensitivity meant that Isabel was training me to become a Sentinel, though she didn't tell me that at the time. When she died, leaving none to take up residence in Hallow House, I became the *Vaktarin*."

"Esus saw the potential in her," Isabel said. "He had watched her since she was a child. I suspect he thought she was somebody else."

"And I have protected the house ever since," Jessica explained. "It is my magic that shields the house from external forces. For five hundred years, a barrier has enclosed the house – a barrier that you punched through when you pulled Raymond Snelling inside."

The guilt was a blow to the gut, but Nicholas saw that Jessica wasn't reprimanding him. Understanding shone in her eyes. Perhaps she knew how isolated he'd felt since moving here; that he knew things were being kept from him. Could that be the reason she was telling him all of this now?

"The barrier has been reinforced," Jessica continued, no doubt attempting to prevent Isabel from adding her own commentary. "What happened with Snelling won't happen again."

Nicholas felt dizzy with all that he'd learnt. "Well..." he began. "That just leaves me. How do I fit into all of it?"

"You're an emissary of the Trinity."

The new voice boomed into the cavern. It set Nicholas's teeth on edge.

Esus.

The mood in the underground chamber changed as the phantom emerged from the shadows.

Nicholas wasn't sure if he'd been there all along, listening to them talk. The silver mask caught the candlelight and pitch black eyes flashed like polished pebbles.

"What does that mean?" Nicholas asked, refusing to be intimidated by the figure, despite what he'd just heard about him. He couldn't fathom how ancient Esus was.

"Restrain from using big words, they confound him," Isabel drawled and Nicholas shot her a glare.

"You were born with certain gifts." Esus's voice drummed hollowly. "You were chosen by the Trinity even as you slumbered in the womb, but a seed of a man. It was you they chose, you they imbued with a drop of their heavenly power – and you who can revive them again."

"Revive them?" Nicholas began. "What do you–"

"The knowledge resides dormant in you. It is your duty to unlock it by any means necessary."

Nicholas was dumbfounded. This was what was expected of him? This was the reason he posed such a threat to Malika and the Harvesters? He didn't want to believe it. He felt a delirious impulse to laugh, or demand proof. And he would have if it wasn't for the three pairs of eyes fixed on him. He swallowed, his mouth dry.

"Why would they choose me?"

"It was not you alone. There was another," Esus continued. "A girl.

The Trinity chose two. You were raised within the Sentinel fold by Sentinel parents, but she is lost to us. You must find her, return her to us. The Trinity chose the two of you for a reason. Only together will you be able to rouse the Trinity and banish all that ails the world. Without her, it's possible we are all doomed. If the agents of the Dark Prophets should find her first..."

Nicholas wasn't sure how to defuse the pressure building in his head. Perhaps this really was why Jessica had kept things from him. He imagined steam blasting from his ears.

"We have reason to believe that she is in Bury St Edmunds," Esus intoned.

Nicholas knew the town. It wasn't far from Cambridge. He'd been there when he was younger.

"Which is precisely where Mr Wilkins is headed," Jessica added softly. "A curious coincidence. So curious, in fact, that it can't possibly be one. The time has come for you to leave Hallow House. In your brief stay, the climate has changed – both literally and metaphorically." She winked at him. "Consider this your training. Your gifts are a vital asset; you must learn how to use and control them. Only by doing so may you unlock the knowledge that the Trinity hid within you."

"You must become a Sentinel," Isabel added.

"But train how? By finding this girl?" Nicholas asked. Somehow he doubted he would be getting a lightsaber out of it. "Who is she? What's her name?"

"That, too, eludes us." Esus's tone was like wind rushing over a grey expanse of ocean. "The name she was given at birth has been discarded. Lydia Green was her birth name, but that is no longer the case. She has been running for a very long time, but you have a connection. With your gifts, you alone are capable of finding her."

As if to balance the phantom's solemnity, Jessica added: "Isabel will be there to help you."

Nicholas couldn't tell if the cat was happy about that or not – she always looked miserable. He liked to think she had puffed herself up importantly.

He shook himself. "Sam. Why is Sam going to Bury?"

"Mr Wilkins has a, what do you call it? I forget the terms... A 'lead' on the Harvester who called himself Raymond Snelling," Jessica said. "It seems there's a house in Bury St Edmunds registered under his name. You'll help Mr Wilkins with his investigations, familiarise yourself with the Sentinel way. You may even be of use to him. You've proven you can handle yourself when it's required. I think this will be good for you. And Isabel."

"Snelling," Nicholas breathed. The name sent shivers down his spine. He'd watched Snelling being incinerated by a fiery portal; Snelling had been screaming madly when he died. Nicholas imagined a screaming ghost returning to haunt him and shuddered.

"Yes," Jessica nodded. "Tonight you rest. Tomorrow, you and Mr Wilkins will visit the home of Raymond Snelling."

CHAPTER THREE
Dawn

Six months ago

Dawn Morgan awoke to the sound of screaming. Darkness crowded in around her and for a moment she thought she was still asleep. But the screaming was real and it was close, splitting the night apart. She sat up with a start and listened, holding her breath.

It was coming from somewhere in the village. Perhaps two houses up. She'd never heard anything like it.

"Dad?" she whispered. Her voice sounded tight and small, like it belonged to a child instead of a teenager. No answer came. Her parents should be asleep on the other side of the guest hut they were sharing, but she couldn't hear their usual soft snores.

Just the screaming.

The Cambodian heat, unbearable even at night, even at this time of year, was suffocating and Dawn wrestled with her blanket.

Fumbling out of bed, she hurried to her parents' mattress. Nothing. The blanket had been pushed to the foot of the bed and her parents were gone. Normally that wouldn't have concerned her. She was fifteen and her parents could do whatever they wanted, but something was definitely wrong.

The screaming continued and, panic lodging in her throat, Dawn rushed to the door, throwing it open. She stared out in shock.

The hillside village was on fire. People were shrieking and running. There were twelve huts, six on either side of a dusty road, and every one of them was ablaze. Dark-skinned figures flitted through the night like terrified birds, some clutching small bundle-like children, others returning from the river with slopping buckets of water.

In a daze, Dawn staggered between the villagers. Dust and grit stuck between her toes but she felt as if she were floating. Still asleep. She frowned, looked down.

An ash-like substance was on the ground. It was piled in a peculiar mound. Dawn stepped back and felt like she was going to be sick.

The ash was in the shape of a person.

Somebody had been burned, rendered ash, lying in the dirt like an animal. And she'd just stepped in the remains. What had done this?

"Mum?" she called. "Dad?"

She scanned the village, seeing half a dozen similar ash-figures on the ground. Some were curled into balls. Others were on their knees, as if pleading.

A figure stumbled into her and Dawn grabbed the man's arm.

"Sovann," she said, recognising one of the villagers. "What's going on?"

He looked at her as if he didn't recognise her, as if they hadn't been staying in the village for the past five weeks and Sovann and his wife hadn't cooked dinner for them that very night. His face was pinched with fear, his skinny frame slick with sweat.

"Sovann," she repeated, squeezing his arm.

"Fire," he gasped desperately. "Fire."

He freed himself from her grip and hurried away toward one of the burning buildings, a bucket in his hand. Dawn stumbled further into the village. The heat was unbearable. She was only wearing thin pyjamas, but even they felt heavy.

And no matter what the villagers did, the fires blazed on, consuming the wooden huts. The Khmer Loeu were a gentle people and they had never faced such a scourge before. She knew that they wouldn't be able to overcome it.

Dawn realised that Sovann was the only man she could see. The rest were women. Some huddled in groups at the end of the road, away from the fires. Others fought to control the blaze, desperately using great, dry leaves in an attempt to strangle and suppress it.

"Mum," Dawn gasped.

Finally she saw her. Dawn hadn't recognised her at first, she was so dusty. Her mother crouched in the dirt at the far end of the road, where the first hut marked the border of the village. Her dark hair was plastered across her face.

"Mum," Dawn said, reaching her at last. She stopped.

Her mother was sobbing over an ash figure.

"What happened?" Dawn asked. She wouldn't let herself consider that the ash figure was her father. It couldn't be. He was here somewhere, helping the villagers fight the fire.

Her mother didn't respond. Dawn grabbed her shoulder and pulled her away from the thing on the ground.

"Tell me what happened," she said, but her mother's expression sent shock shuddering through her. Her eyes were wide, her face a mask of anguish. She didn't seem to be able to speak, instead emitting a terrible, guttural wail like the sound a baby makes when it's hungry or tired. Only worse. Far worse. Because it was coming out of her mother.

Dawn looked around for somebody to help her and froze.

A figure was watching her from the other end of the road. He lingered outside the guest hut; the hut she had just fled. He wore a camel-coloured jacket and dark jeans. His pale skin gleamed as it reflected the firelight, blond hair greased back, angular cheekbones protruding. Even from here, she could see the fire dancing in his dark eyes.

She knew him. They'd had dinner with him the previous night. *Samnang*, they called him. *Good fortune*. But he wasn't Cambodian. He was a wanderer. A guest. He'd stumbled into the village a week ago, dehydrated and exhausted, and the elders pitied him. Fed him. Gave him shelter. When he recovered, he entertained them all with rope tricks and card games. He was handsome and charming.

Dawn shuddered. Samnang was looking straight at her. His square jaw clenched and his top lip tugged into a sneer.

"Mum, get up," Dawn urged.

Samnang paced leisurely toward them.

Dawn hoisted her mother to her feet.

"No!" Her mother screamed suddenly, thrashing for the ash figure. "JOHN! NO!"

She wriggled like a rabbit in a trap and Dawn grabbed her mother's arms. She was stronger than her peers, both in body and mind, and she had to draw on all of her strength to hoist the flailing woman away from the ash figure.

"Mum, come on!" she yelled. Samnang was getting closer with every passing second.

"RUN!" she commanded, shoving her mother ahead of her into the forest. Her mother sobbed and wailed, but Dawn pushed her in the back and together they ran. Dawn hated running, but she had to now, even if her knees creaked and her toes snagged painfully on the undergrowth.

Samnang set the fire.

She'd known it the second she saw him watching her with that look on his face. He'd set the fire, and he'd done something to her father. Killed him. Turned him into... whatever it was he was now.

A pile of ash.

Batting leaves away and swallowing down the terror that threatened to consume her, she tore through the forest.

★

PRESENT DAY

Dawn ran. Her lungs were on fire and her calf muscles felt as if they were tearing, but she didn't stop. The mud track was baked hard by the sun and every panicked footfall reverberated up into her skull, making her head pound. The sound of the dual carriageway was engulfed by her own scratchy gasps and she batted at the nettles that lay at the fringes of the field.

Undeterred, Dawn raced on, her mousy brown hair – the tips still purple from an earlier dye job – flapping like miniature flags.

"HEY!"

A voice struck at her back.

"You can't run forever!"

Dawn ignored it. Her hair was plastered to her forehead and her throat felt full of chalk, but she didn't stop. Rounding a corner, she almost crashed into a startled couple.

Squeezing between them – an accomplishment given her chubby figure – she tore on, barely catching the man's disgruntled barks as she retreated.

The path wove between trees and finally she caught a glimpse of the park on the other side of the river. A bridge appeared and Dawn clambered over it. The Abbey Gardens opened up before her in a sea of green. She staggered past the play area and up over a high grass bank, scrabbling on all fours until she was perched – panting and sweating – in the exposed roots of an oak tree.

From here she could see the whole park. It rested in the evening half-light and if she'd been somebody else, the kind of person who painted watercolours, she'd probably admit it wasn't bad. Instead, she surveyed the gardens watchfully.

Somebody clattered onto the bridge she'd just crossed.

Dawn shrank back into the shade of the tree, certain that her pursuer couldn't see her. The sweat was cooling on her brow, making the skin taut, and her backpack bit into her shoulders.

The other girl came to a halt where the bridge met the grass. She was tall and had dark skin. She seemed to peer right at her and Dawn held her breath, refusing to move a muscle. The girl held her stare for a moment, then hurried away from the play area, vanishing into the bowels of the park.

Dawn collapsed breathlessly against the tree trunk.

This was her favourite spot in Bury St Edmunds. The old town wasn't a place for teenagers. Though it had grown in recent years, added to piece by piece until it was almost as bustling as nearby Cambridge, there was little for her here. The cinema was somewhere she could be easily cornered, and she never had any money to spend in the shops. The bustle of restaurants only made her stomach rumble and she was nervous she'd bump into local families who'd glare at her the way they always did whenever they occasionally caught sight of her in the street. They didn't like out-of-towners.

The Abbey Gardens were different. Though busy in the summertime, there were plenty of craggy corners she could wedge herself into, and the park hummed with a sense of history. Years ago, back in the days of Henry VIII, it had been a monastery. Those walls had long crumbled away, leaving flinty ruins that struck up from the earth, dagger-like. Kids often climbed them before an adult dragged them away bawling.

"Enjoying the view?"

Every muscle in Dawn's body tensed. She resisted turning toward the voice. Maybe if she stayed perfectly still she could become invisible.

A shadow fell across the tree roots and Dawn had no choice but to look up. The pink sky dazzled behind a lofty figure. Her pursuer had found her.

"Should've picked a better hiding place," the black girl spat. Dawn guessed she was fifteen, too, though she had the demeanour of somebody older. The hardness in her voice was mirrored in her pitiless eyes and she was rough around the edges. Not *grubby*, but sort of frayed. Abrasive.

Dawn struggled to her feet. Her muscles – tight after the run – felt ready to snap, but she had to get away.

"Going somewhere?" the other girl asked.

Dawn tried to ignore her. She turned to start up the hill, but a hand flashed out and pushed her. She staggered backward, tripping over the tree's roots and hitting the ground. The air left her lungs in a painful huff.

The other girl was an outline in front of the setting sun. "You're not going anywhere until you tell me why you've been following me," she snarled coldly.

Tears sprung to Dawn's eyes. She couldn't catch her breath. Couldn't get up. She wanted to curl into a ball and disappear.

"Who are you?" the other girl demanded. "Why you following me?"

Dawn struggled, remembered how to push her hands against the ground, heaved herself up.

A foot buried itself in her shoulder and she was forced back into the dirt.

"Please," Dawn mumbled.

"HEY!"

A voice rang over the park. Dawn strained to find its owner and spotted a man by the play area. The park's caretaker.

"She's okay!" the other girl called airily. "She tripped, but she's okay!"

She grabbed Dawn's arm roughly and dragged her to her feet. "You weigh a ton."

Dawn tried to get away, but the other girl's grip tightened. She drew Dawn closer; she smelled like incense and something fusty. "I catch you spying on me again, you're dead," she whispered in her ear. Then she let go.

Dawn staggered away. She pulled the straps of her backpack tight at the shoulders and hurried over the grass before the other girl could change her mind.

Could've been worse, she thought. *At least she didn't spot the camera.*

CHAPTER FOUR
Downstairs

THE MORRIS MINOR RUMBLED DOWN THE country lane. Nicholas peered out the window as if seeing the countryside for the first time. Green fields rushed by in a dazzling blur and Nicholas thought this must be how people felt when they'd been released from jail or hospital. He'd been cooped up in Hallow House for what felt like so long, he'd almost forgotten there was more to the world than a crumbling old mansion.

Summer had returned in all its suffocating glory. Even in just shorts and a T-shirt, he was boiling. He'd slept restlessly, Jessica and Esus's words somersaulting in his head. Could everything they'd said be true? That he was meant to resurrect the Trinity? And could some mystery girl really help? Nicholas felt like something had taken a bite out of him.

His present discomfort was nothing compared to Isabel's, though. He smiled faintly, watching the cat in the rear-view mirror. She clung to the back seat, ears flat against her skull.

"Just go easy on the upholstery there," Sam said to the animal's grumpy reflection. Isabel's eyes narrowed into slits.

"Just think of it as a cart being drawn by invisible horses," Nicholas told her.

"How does it move?" Isabel demanded.

"Magic," Sam and Nicholas replied in unison.

"Infernal contraption," Isabel muttered, stumbling as they turned a corner.

Sam flipped the visor down to shield his eyes from the sun. Nicholas did the same and peered at the old man. He'd barely seen him since all of this had begun. They'd not had time to talk after the festival. The last time they'd talked properly was on the bus, and that hadn't exactly gone well – especially as Sam had evaded all of his questions.

"Sentinels, huh?" Nicholas murmured.

Sam concentrated on the road. He nodded.

"And demons."

Nothing.

"And her." Nicholas jabbed his thumb at the creature fixed rigidly to the backseat.

"Yes," Sam breathed.

"Would've been nice to have had a head's up," Nicholas said.

"Nicholas–"

"I know, I know. I get it. Big secrets and blah blah blah. Still can't get my head around it, though. My parents. They... they were, you know..."

"Indeed," Sam said. "Just as their parents were before them, and theirs before them before that. It's a birthright. We know things that other people don't and it's our duty to keep them safe."

"They all looked so... ordinary," Nicholas said, recalling the Festival of Fire. "Last night. All the others."

"Ordinary!" Isabel snorted. "The gall of it. *Ordinary* people do extraordinary things every day. What were you expecting? Suits of armour?"

Sam chuckled. He winked at Nicholas. "But more seriously, that's partly the point. We're supposed to look ordinary. When a Sentinel comes of age, she or he has two options: enlisting with special operations based on a particular skill, or being assigned to what's commonly called the mortal sector. We couldn't exactly go unnoticed there if we looked like what's his name, Arnold Schwarzenegger. Mortal sector workers like me and your parents are, for lack of a better term, ground-level spies. Your father was a publisher, but he also served as a Sentinel, watching for signs of emergent evil. You'd be surprised where the cracks appear."

Nicholas nearly scoffed at the idea of his parents as spies.

"And the special operations?" he asked.

"There are Sensitives," Sam explained. "Or those particularly adept at research. There are experts on the Trinity and mythological profiles. The most physically capable often become part of an elite set of Hunters. Our friend Lash is of that crop."

"Don't remind me," Nicholas muttered, glowering at the mention of Jessica's new bodyguard. What about Jessica, though? She'd been the leader of the Sentinels for five-hundred years. Had she ever left Hallow House? She'd said it was protected by her magic. Perhaps that prevented her from leaving; she couldn't abandon ship. *She's not exactly stable, either*, Nicholas thought. Was Jessica confined to Hallow House for her own safety? Or was the world a safer place with her locked away in there?

He shook himself free of his thoughts. "Wouldn't it make more sense just to get it out in the open? Let the world deal with demons and all that bad stuff? Surely having the army on your side would be a bonus."

"You're assuming it's never been attempted," Sam said.

"It has?"

"Of course. On many occasions." Sam squeezed the steering wheel between liver-spotted hands. "There are those who believe it should all be out in the open."

"Preposterous," Isabel spat.

"It has been tried," Sam continued. "The last time I know of was in 1980. A town in North Yorkshire. There was something in the water. A dead *jaruka* demon was rotting in a reservoir and contaminated the water supply. Hundreds fell ill. The authorities were called in and the cadaver was discovered by the national health body, aided by local Sentinels who had infiltrated the water company. Instead of revealing the *jaruka* and causing an international catastrophe, the authorities stamped on the story. It never leaked to the press and it was never recorded in any official documents. The body was destroyed and the authorities moved on." Sam paused, his blue eyes shining. "Oh, there are people in the know. People high up. There have been far too many occurrences for them not to be aware. But they've enough on their plate as it is. As long as *somebody's* dealing with the problem, that's good enough for them. Fewer dirty hands and *far* less paper work."

Nicholas's head felt like the whirring drum in a washing machine. "But... that's nuts! Why didn't anybody try again? Who did they speak to? It doesn't make any sense that they'd just ignore evidence like that."

"That's the way it is."

"Child." A feline voice probed from the backseat. "Man is a creature twisted into knots by fear. If a blind eye can be turned, you can rest assured it will be. Never was there a being more self-serving than Man. Nor quick to bury a truth too difficult to bear."

Sam laughed. "To put it lightly."

Nicholas slumped in his seat. "I'll never understand any of this."

"In time," Sam said. "Once we begin training..."

"That's another thing," Nicholas interrupted. "What exactly is this training going to involve?" He couldn't even begin to imagine. Was he going to have to jump through flaming hoops and track demons? Shave his head like they did in the army and navigate back from some remote spot using only the sun's position in the sky and his own wits?

"Your training has already begun," Sam said. "Or it will today. Best way to learn is by doing. You'll help with the Snelling investigation."

"You think investigating Snelling will help you find out what happened to the Sentinels in Cambridge? The ones who got turned?" Nicholas asked. Just saying the name made him want to spit. The shopkeeper he'd befriended in Orville – the one he'd assumed was another Sentinel – had been nothing but a duplicitous fraud. Nicholas was glad he was dead. He rubbed his chest, remembering the concussive blast that had barrelled into him, unleashed by the strange metallic gauntlet that Snelling had wielded as a weapon.

"It's a start," Sam said. "There may be something useful in the house. We know he was working with Malika and Diltraa, but where did the gauntlet come from? And if you hadn't stopped them, what would they have gone on to do?"

"Malika." Anger rumbled in Nicholas's chest.

"Other Sentinels are attempting to track her down. The Hunters are out there tracing her scent. We may find that our paths converge. If she's allied herself with somebody new, she must be stopped."

Nicholas brooded on that thought. He doubted Malika needed new allies. She seemed perfectly capable of wreaking havoc on her own.

"What about the girl?" he asked. "How am I supposed to find her?"

"We'll get to that," Isabel said.

They trundled through the countryside and conversation turned to brighter things as Sam recalled his boyhood years in Bury St Edmunds. "It's a special place," he said. "You'll see. Full of history. Did you know witch trials were held there long before they happened in Salem? Or that there are tales of a huge network of ancient tunnels beneath the town? Or that Edmund The Martyr himself is said to be buried there, hence the town's name? Legend has it that a wolf still guards his severed head."

Nicholas had heard some of the tales before, but he hadn't visited Bury since he was young.

"You sure you want me tagging along?" he asked.

"Why ever not?"

"Our track record isn't exactly great. Especially when it comes to things with wheels. I'm a bit of a demon magnet, if you hadn't noticed."

"I'm sure we'll cope," Sam said evenly. If he was nervous about having Nicholas at his side, he wasn't letting on.

They chugged on, passing through one quaint village after another. Nicholas was surprised by how similar they were to Orville. Every one seemed stuck in time. These villages didn't give him the creeps the way Orville had, though. Orville was a cursed place, and he was the reason for that curse. Another thought to push away.

"Ah!" Sam exclaimed, relieving Nicholas of his guilt-ridden thoughts. "Almost there."

A sign on the dual carriageway announced BURY ST EDMUNDS – 3 miles. A train ran alongside them momentarily before swerving to the other side of a field and disappearing. On the horizon, twin caterpillars of white vapour crawled lethargically into the sky, emerging from an ugly concrete monolith. The sugar beet factory, Nicholas recalled.

They left the dual carriageway and drove into the town. The roads were narrow, busy and old. Sam steered the car down a particularly grubby street and parked at the kerb.

"Welcome to Bury St Edmunds," he said, popping open his door and shrugging on a satchel as battered as his fedora.

Nicholas didn't remember the town being quite this rundown.

They were on the outskirts, he supposed. When he'd visited with his parents, they'd never strayed much beyond the town's bustling centre. He stepped out onto the street. To his surprise, Isabel scrabbled out after him and leapt onto his shoulder. She wasn't as heavy as he'd expected.

The cat didn't say anything, but her whiskers quivered. She coiled her tail about his neck, and Nicholas felt oddly comforted, despite the heat. It was like she'd been doing it for years.

Sam locked the car and strode purposefully down the street. Nicholas followed him around a corner, wondering why they'd parked so far away from their destination. A Sentinel trick, he imagined. As if reading his thoughts, Sam winked at him.

"Never be placed at the scene of the crime," he said secretively.

The house was a workaday semi-detached with a front garden that had gone wild from neglect. The sullen midday sun exposed windows that were blackened with chipped paint like so much parched earth, and the roof had holes pecked in it as if by some monstrous beast.

Sam paused at the gate, eyeing both the house and its dilapidated neighbour. Neither showed any signs of life.

"What a dump," Nicholas muttered. He nudged the fence with his foot and it creaked drunkenly. "Shouldn't be surprised considering who owned it."

Sam said nothing, instead pushing the gate inward. It crashed from its hinges.

"Delightful," the old man murmured under his breath.

Isabel jumped noiselessly from Nicholas's shoulder and was the first to reach the door.

"And how do you propose we make entry?" she asked dourly.

Sam gave Nicholas a look and he shrugged.

"She has a point," he said. "How are we going to get in?"

Sam approached the door, ran his hands down the flaking wood and pawed at the brass lock thoughtfully.

"Just you keep a look out," he said to the cat, rummaging in his satchel.

"You're not going to do what I think you're going to do..." Nicholas began uncertainly.

Isabel looked up from the doorstep as the old man set out a leather pouch on the nearest windowsill and drew a shining brass instrument from it. It looked like a tool for removing debris from teeth after a meal.

"I'm fraternising with a criminal," the cat muttered, but she didn't blink as she watched Sam insert the metal stalk into the lock.

Nicholas scanned the neighbour's house. There was no movement behind the net curtains. No slinking shadows. The street was deserted, too. This was a part of town that he suspected most people avoided. Just down the road, he glimpsed the unmistakable tableau of red bricks and satellite dishes that signalled a council estate. He hoped they'd be gone by dark. Demons were one thing, but he didn't fancy going up against a band of knuckle-cracking teenagers.

You fought a demon and lived, he told himself in an attempt to settle his nerves. But he couldn't lie to himself. *You survived, but only just.*

Click.

"There," Sam breathed. He sounded relieved. Nicholas wondered how long it had been since that particular skill had been put to the test. Nicholas felt far from relieved, though, especially when Sam pushed the front door open and he spied what lay in wait.

The hallway was dark as a tomb. The stench of burnt wood and plastic lingered. Nicholas instinctively put a hand to his mouth as they crossed the threshold.

"Jesus," he muttered. "You think he actually *lived* here?"

"One way to find out," Sam said, returning the leather pouch to his satchel. He ushered Nicholas inside and pushed the front door to, stopping short of shutting it completely.

A bare bulb dangled from the ceiling and it, too, was black on the inside, as if somebody had blasted it with a blowtorch. At some point, a fire had raged within these walls. When that might have been, Nicholas couldn't guess, but the stench of that gutting inferno festered and poisoned the house's every pore. The house was sick with unease.

"What do you think?"

Sam was talking to him.

"About what?"

"You know," Sam said, waving a hand at the air. "Are you getting anything?"

"Other than a headache?" Nicholas said. He saw from Sam's

expression that now was no time for jokes. "No," he added, assuming that Sam wanted to know if he could sense anything about their surroundings – other than the obvious. "Nothing."

Some of the tension left Sam's shoulders. His pupils were large in the dark, like a bird's, and the shadows the fedora cast made him appear oddly menacing. Nicholas had always seen Sam as a jovial spirit. Recent events had definitely changed that.

"We'll take it one room at a time," the old man uttered softly. "At no point do we enter a room alone. Keep an eye out for anything... unusual. False walls, drafts, cold spots. Snelling could have hidden something here." He paused and reached round to his back, exposing his teeth briefly in a grimace, as if the tendons in his shoulders had pulled. His hand returned clutching a small pistol. "Precaution. Get behind me."

Nicholas followed the old man's back through the house. He'd been right; it was a dump. Every room was black and burnt. Desolate as a fatigued hearth. Graffiti was scrawled here and there. Distended pink letters that must mean something to somebody. An empty vodka bottle lay in the fireplace. The kitchen was full of leaves and there was a sleeping bag abandoned by the sink. Upstairs, every room was empty. There wasn't so much as a mattress or a toothbrush. The house had been picked clean long ago. Even the toilet had been removed.

Sam knocked on every wall. He pulled up floorboards and peered into the cobwebby recesses. But there was nothing other than skittery spiders, which Isabel chased into corners. Nicholas would have laughed at the cat, but Sam's desperation filled each room with a dark cloud blacker than any of the walls.

Back by the front door, Sam scratched his forehead. "Nothing," he muttered to the floor. "Not a blasted thing." The frustration bunched up his jowls. He seemed to have pegged everything on this, but he'd been chasing ghosts. Snelling was dead. The trail ended here in an infuriating, burnt-out full-stop.

Nicholas looked away, anywhere but at Sam, and noticed Isabel dabbing at something down the hall. A door under the stairs.

"What about there?" he asked, nodding in Isabel's direction.

"There's a draft," Isabel noted, scurrying out of the way when Sam paced up to the door. *His boots must look like elephant feet to her*, Nicholas thought.

Sam tugged the little door open and peered down a set of concrete stairs. There was a faint light.

"Basement," he said gruffly, checking his pistol. "Stay close."

Together they descended. For some reason, the flames that had engulfed the rest of the house hadn't touched here. When they reached the foot of the stairs, Nicholas was grateful for the stink of must; it was preferable to the stench upstairs. He peered around.

It was more of a cell than a basement. A tiny cement square with an even tinier, grime-caked rectangle meekly filtering sunlight inside. It was filthy. The floor was covered in dust, and by the far wall there was a curious dark shadow that looked like—

"Blood," Isabel announced, her nose hovering centimetres above the stain.

"Fresh?" Sam asked.

"Relatively," Isabel said. She dabbed at the mark daintily. "It is dry."

Nicholas lingered by the stairs. His head buzzed. At first he thought it was the fetid air, but now he wasn't sure.

Sam wandered to the far wall and scrutinised the exposed bricks. Just above the bloodstain, holes had been drilled and there was a metallic residue lightly dusting the brickwork. The floor, too. There were strips where the cement floor was darker, as if something heavy had once rested here.

What sort of object would make marks like that? Nicholas thought.

"Something was here," Sam murmured, easing himself to his knees. "Something was here and it's been taken."

Nicholas frowned. The buzzing intensified. Something was needling at him, tugging at his insides like a fish hook. Before he knew why, he asked: "You knew one of them, didn't you? One of the people that was turned?"

Sam's concentration broke. He cast Nicholas a fleeting look then puffed out a breath, straining to get up from the floor. "It happened just after you left," he told the wall. "Snelling. He attacked a friend. A good friend..." Sam paused and Nicholas could see that this was difficult; this was the reason, perhaps, for the old man's desperation. "He turned

Richard against us, somehow. He became indistinguishable from a Harvester. And he wasn't the only one."

"What happened to him? Richard?" Nicholas asked. "I mean, did you find out how to get him back?"

Sam's answer fell like the lid of a coffin.

"No."

Nicholas didn't hear him. His head had started spinning. His stomach roiled and churned. That awful but oh-so-familiar feeling had returned; the feeling that normally meant nausea was about to be the least of his problems.

"Uh, Sam," he began, but Sam's gaze had already darted to the ceiling.

Had there been a noise? A faint footfall? A breath or a whisper?

Nicholas tensed. Listened. Isabel squashed herself up into the space where the wall met the floor, ears cocked.

Nicholas's stomach cramped and he suppressed a groan. Sam looked at him and his face set to stone.

"Blast," he muttered. In what seemed like a single step, he was beside Nicholas, then jabbing the air with a finger. *You. Follow me. Upstairs.*

Nicholas sucked in a breath and nodded.

Sam set a boot on the bottom step, then crept up the staircase, pistol raised. Nicholas followed with Isabel at his heels. He didn't know what the house was trying to tell him. Whatever it was, it was making him want to empty his stomach right here on the stairs. This feeling. It was a warning. Like that day on the bus just before Malika had attacked. But what was the warning this time? He tried to focus on breathing, not vomiting. Not imagining what kind of monster might be laying in wait just upstairs.

He bumped into Sam. They'd reached the top of the stairs. Sam put a finger to his lips and eased the door open. He stuck his head through.

Nicholas waited. Isabel pressed to the side of his leg, her tail coiled about his calf.

Sam disappeared into the hallway and Nicholas stood motionless, listening.

Silence. Nothing.

Nicholas realised that he was holding his breath and he released it slowly. A faint sound came. A shuffle, perhaps. Maybe just a dry leaf skating across the floor.

Nicholas edged into the hall. Then froze.

Sam stood facing the front door, not moving. He had become a living statue.

Nicholas frowned and moved closer. The sick feeling had gone, but there was no relief. Only concern. The look on Sam's face was terrible. He'd gone deathly pale and his lips trembled.

"Sam?" he ventured. "What is it?"

It took Sam a moment to register Nicholas's question.

"There was somebody there," he croaked eventually, barely talking above a whisper. His eyes were fixed on the front door, the pistol shaking.

"Who? Who was it?"

Sam looked like he'd seen a ghost. Whatever the older man had seen, it had stuck him to the spot, and unease prickled hotly through Nicholas.

"Sam? Who was it?"

Before Sam could answer, an almighty crash resounded from upstairs. *More than just a crash*, Nicholas thought. *A detonation*. The ceiling rocked above them and a mixture of dust and ash cascaded in delicate swirls. The blast sent a shock through Nicholas's bones.

Sam was at the front door in an instant, jerking the handle.

But the door didn't open. Somebody had locked it from the outside.

Another deafening roar and this time half the ceiling collapsed. A burst of orange briefly lit the stairwell and Nicholas fell against one of the walls, staring up in horror. Charred carpet lolled though the hole in the ceiling like a dried-out tongue and chunks of burnt wood littered the floor.

Nicholas's mind went blank. He couldn't feel the wall against his back or the floor under his shoes. His ears rang and he barely noticed Sam hurry into the kitchen, then dart back into the hallway just as the room behind him erupted in a maelstrom of flying debris.

"DOWN!" Sam yelled.

But Nicholas merely stared dumbly back. What was happening?

DOWNSTAIRS

There was nobody else in this burnt-out tomb, but now the tomb was collapsing around them and they were going to be buried in the wreckage. Hundreds of tons of wall and wood and brick were going to crash onto them, smash their bodies, crush out every last breath.

It took a sharp prick in his leg to snap Nicholas to his senses.

"The house is falling apart!" Isabel shrieked. "If you don't move we'll die!"

That did it. Nicholas plucked the cat from the floor and raced over to Sam, who was holding open the door to the basement. As Nicholas dashed inside, he just had time to appreciate the full force of another bone-shaking detonation that took out the living room.

Knocked from his feet, he tumbled down the final few steps and only just caught himself as he hit the floor.

"Damn," he croaked, appreciating how close he'd come to cracking his skull open on the concrete. An even more desperate thought seized him.

Sam!

Coughing up dust, Nicholas raised himself from the ground. A hand reached out and helped him and Nicholas saw that Sam had made it down just before the blast. They were both covered in grey filth; the innards of the house all over them.

"I thought–" Nicholas mumbled, but Sam had already limped over to the tiny, cell-like window, appraising it quickly. He seemed to comprehend that they'd never fit through it. They'd torn down into the one room that seemed safe, only to find there was no way out again. Nicholas cursed, extricating himself from the floor.

A cacophony of explosions erupted above their heads. Nicholas had no idea how long they had before the entire house collapsed. He tried not to think about it, instead staggering over to the wall that had been drilled with holes. Sam was already there, touching every brick, jabbing and pushing like it was some kind of medieval slot machine. Nicholas did the same, assuming they were looking for a loose brick, a chink in the wall's armour that might yield and release them from this prison.

Debris crashed through the cellar door and there were flames now, lapping eagerly over the ceiling. The heat assaulted them in waves and Nicholas began to sweat all over.

Then one of the bricks moved.

It shifted inward under the weight of his hand and he shoved it harder. The brick grated against its neighbours, complaining with every centimetre, but then it was through. Nicholas heard it hit the floor on the other side.

A broken rectangular hole grinned at him.

"Hurry," Sam urged, seeing what Nicholas had done.

Together, they seized at the bricks framing the gap and wrenched with everything they had. Mortar crumbled and the book-sized blocks came away in grating protests to be dashed to the floor. Above them, the ceiling started to sag and the flames lashed closer, eager orange tongues straining for them.

"Isabel," Nicholas called, and the cat was at his side, the blacks of her eyes like little inverted moons. "Can you fit?" he asked.

Isabel squinted at the hole in the wall and launched silently at it, rippling into the shadows beyond. Nicholas and Sam continued to wrench at the wall. Finally it gave. Shoulder to shoulder, the duo staggered through into the welcoming blackness.

The cool against Nicholas's skin was like an eskimo's kiss. He reached out his hands to prevent himself from blundering into anything.

"There is an exit," Isabel's sharp tones rang, and Nicholas had never been more grateful for her ability to see in the dark. "To your left. It's up in the corner, two wooden panels like a trapdoor."

Nicholas stumbled against Sam and together they edged through the darkness. The sounds of carnage from Snelling's house were still audible, and Nicholas wondered why nobody from the neighbouring houses had come to help. Perhaps they had tried, but found no way of getting inside.

"There," Sam said. There came a rattle, the sound of Sam grunting with effort, and then the world opened up to them like a box of chocolates.

The sky was pink and raw, something out of a comic book, and they rushed up into it, gasping at the clean air.

Weakened by the heat, Nicholas and Sam staggered into the parched back garden and collapsed onto the grass.

Nicholas wiped the mixture of soot and sweat from his forehead, staring up in horror.

The house was ablaze. Thick black smoke streamed upward, a jagged scar in the coral-coloured sky.

"There was nothing in the house," he murmured, coughing up cinders. "We looked. There was nothing in there that could've done that."

Sam took out a handkerchief and mopped at his brow.

"Somebody came in after us," he muttered, folding the grimed handkerchief in half and dabbing his upper lip.

"Who? Who was it?"

Sam was transfixed by the burning ruin.

"If only we knew," the old man said softly.

Sighing, Nicholas sagged against the grass and listened to the approaching sirens.

CHAPTER FIVE
New Arrivals

"Here," Sam said, handing Nicholas his suitcase. It felt like it was stuffed with rocks.

They'd managed to evade the police, rounding the corner just as the first blue and red lights tumbled across the tarmac toward Snelling's house. Sam had driven them into the centre of town, muttering something about finding a place to stay, and Nicholas had felt too beaten up to argue. He coughed, tasting smoke, and he could still feel the heat against his skin.

Together, they crossed the narrow street. At the end, a sandstone tower craned over the surrounding buildings. The Norman Tower looked like a giant chess piece. Just one of the peculiar, ancient buildings that populated Bury's older quarters.

Sam led them down an even narrower alleyway that was lined with pretty doorways. The sign read Angel Lane. He stopped halfway down and rapped at a red door. Even his knock sounded exhausted.

After a moment it drew open and a woman appeared.

"Samuel!" she exclaimed.

"Aileen," Sam said cordially.

Aileen resembled an old dinner lady. Her face was round and jolly. A tissue was crammed under the strap of a slender gold watch and her elbows had all but disappeared into a supple mound of doughy flesh. She wore a long, pleated brown skirt and a short-sleeved blouse, over which a flowery tabard had been fastened. It barely covered her ample bosom.

"What a pleasant surprise!" the woman exclaimed. She primped at her purplish hair in dismay, the flesh under her arms wobbling. "Look at me, I'm a mess. Whatever must you think?"

Nicholas suppressed a smile.

"It's a pleasure as always, Aileen," Sam said.

"I wasn't expecting anybody," Aileen trilled. "We're completely empty and nobody called ahead for you. But, my! You're looking well. Haven't aged barely a day." She beamed brightly at the elderly gentleman. The fact that he was covered in ash didn't seem at all unusual to her.

"Yes," Sam coughed. He seemed uncomfortable, perhaps because of their appearance. "This is Nicholas," the old man continued, gesturing at Nicholas.

"And Isabel," Nicholas added.

The woman's smile slackened at the sight of the cat on Nicholas's shoulder. "Ah," she began. "House pets. Thing is, we don't normally allow them. Rudy's friendly as anything when it comes to people, but other cats…"

"We don't want to cause a problem," Sam interjected.

Aileen's gaze softened as it returned to him and she flapped the air with podgy hands. "No bother, no bother. I'm sure we can arrange something."

The chatter subsided.

"Could we–?" Sam entreated, crooking an elbow at the door.

Aileen threw her hands up again and dabbed delicately at her forehead. "Look at me, blathering on and I've not even invited you in. Yes, yes, come in, come in."

The hallway was busy and dated. The yellowing wallpaper was distractingly fussy and a string of oval-shaped frames lined the walls. A doily-covered table by the door supported an ancient telephone with a dial. Beside that was a framed photo of a tabby cat with a protruding fang. The patterned carpet, paired with the scent of bleach, made Nicholas woozy.

"Come in, come in," Aileen insisted, leading them through the house. "It's lucky I cleaned this morning. You should've seen the state of the place just yesterday, you'd have called for Aggie and Kim in a moment's breath."

For some reason, Nicholas doubted Aileen's house was ever anything other than spotless.

They passed an equally antiquated living room, where yet more doilies were draped over the backs of every chair, and a steep staircase, then went into the kitchen. Nicholas felt as if he'd stumbled across a set from an old sitcom. Everything was a lurid shade of green. The cupboard doors. The plates fixed to the wall. The bustling wallpaper. The only thing that wasn't green was the linoleum floor. It was orange.

Nicholas looked at Sam, but the old man didn't seem to have noticed.

"Just a minute," Aileen said. She foraged in a drawer and retrieved a rudimentary wooden carving of a woman. It had twigs for hair and cut-stone for eyes.

"You don't mind, do you?" Aileen asked, turning to them.

"By all means," Sam said, taking the effigy. He held it for a few seconds and then handed it to Nicholas, whose bemusement must have been clear. Just who was this woman?

"Only a precaution," Aileen explained brightly. "It screams bloody murder if you're a bad egg. Can't be too careful what with everybody coming and going around here. I'm not one for rumours, but better safe than sorry, I always say. Ah, lovely." She took the totem back and threw it into the drawer. "You'll be wanting your rooms first. And then I'll put the kettle on." She opened a lime green door to what turned out to be a pantry.

"The beds will need making up; it's been a while," Aileen quavered as she went inside, talking more to herself than either of her guests. Nicholas noticed she was playing with a set of keys. What was she doing?

Sam followed Aileen into the pantry and beckoned for Nicholas to do the same.

At the back of the storeroom rested a full set of shelves, all of them crammed with food. Tins. Fresh vegetables. Little herb containers. It was as if Aileen was expecting an air raid any moment and she'd be blown if she was going to let any of her guests starve if that happened.

Their host brandished an old key and foraged between the shelves for something. Nicholas saw her flabby arm jiggling, then heard the *click* of a lock. Aileen pushed a shelf and the wall swung inward.

"Didn't I mention?" Sam said to him, knowing full well that he hadn't. "Aileen runs a Sentinel safehouse."

"Safehouse?" Nicholas asked.

"They're dotted all over the place," Sam told him. "You can never be too careful. The house itself is a false front for the real house, which resides behind. A quite clever idea, I have to say. Very Dutch. Who'd ever suspect Aileen?"

The old man winked at him.

Aileen had disappeared up a flight of stairs and Nicholas heard her humming to herself animatedly.

"Sentinels and their secret doors," he muttered, hurrying after Sam.

Upstairs looked like a completely different house. A long, bright landing was broken up by numerous flights of stairs that led off in different directions. They followed the sound of humming and came to a small room that was sparingly furnished, but preferable to the finicky décor downstairs. A single bed with crisp white linen. A beige armchair. A sink.

"Here," Aileen said to Nicholas, "this'll be yours. I'll put Samuel in across the hall."

She left the room and Sam trudged after her.

Nicholas went to the window. The sun hung over the town and he admired the golden view. They were high up and he could see over row upon row of neat rooftops. An old stone building that looked like a watchtower peeked above them. Nicholas remembered it was the entrance to the Abbey Gardens.

"Looks alright," he said, "different to how I remember."

It was strange; Bury resembled a compressed version of Cambridge. Almost like a toy town imitation. The Market Square contained most of the shops, and the cobbles of Abbeygate Street led from there to the Abbey Gardens. It was a small town with quirky lanes and not a single skyscraper, not counting the spire of St Mary's Church.

As he eyed a flinty shape within the Abbey Gardens, Nicholas felt a pang of... what? Grief? The last time he'd been to Bury, he'd come with his parents. He must have been about seven. The thought unsettled him, reminded him of the loss. The thought that, one day, he'd be without his parents would never have occurred to his seven-year-old self. He wished he could be seven again.

"It's a park," he murmured, his eye drawn to the watchtower-like edifice. "They turned the Abbey ruins into a park for kids."

Isabel hopped onto the windowsill.

"A strange township," she mused. "Whatever possessed them to turn ruins into a park?"

"People like them," Nicholas said. "Makes them feel, I don't know... Part of something, I guess."

He noticed the cat peering up at him. The depths of her eyes sparkled like gems. Nicholas remembered there was a crystal called 'tiger's eye', and thought the name apt. Then, in a flick of her ears, she was staring out of the window again; had dismissed whatever she'd been thinking.

Nicholas gazed longingly at the freshly-made bed and wanted nothing more than to collapse into it. His stomach grumbled and he decided he'd offer Aileen a hand in putting some of her air raid supplies to good use.

Downstairs, a kettle whistled on the hob and Aileen bustled about, crashing crockery onto the kitchen table and mopping up with a green dishcloth. She even performed a little hop as she went from the table to the sideboard, humming as she went. Nicholas thought of Tabitha, the neighbour who'd looked after him after his parents died. Aileen and Tabitha would probably get along famously.

"I'm sorry about your son," Sam was saying.

Aileen nodded, busying herself at the counter.

Something had happened to Aileen's son? When the landlady offered no further response, Sam lowered himself into a chair at the kitchen table. Nicholas noticed that the top button of his shirt was undone. It struck him immediately because to Sam, unbuttoned shirts were for youths and tramps. It was hot in here, though. The temperature seemed to have risen again and Nicholas felt weak with the heat.

As he joined Sam at the table, he caught movement out the corner of his eye. An immense shag of tabby fur unfurled in a basket on the windowsill. A squashed, fanged face surveyed them. It was the ugliest cat Nicholas had ever seen.

When the creature spotted Isabel, who was sitting by the pantry, it emitted a bleak hiss.

"Rudy, stop that," Aileen said in a horrified whisper. "Excuse him, thinks he's king of his own castle."

"I was just informing Aileen of the reason for our visit," Sam told Nicholas, ignoring the cats.

"Never heard of a Snelling," the landlady contributed from the hob. The kettle sang and she plucked it from its perch, pouring their tea. "I know most names in Bury, but that's a new one."

She eased herself into her chair. Her bosom rested on the tabletop as she daintily stirred her brew.

"No," she mused. "Definitely never been a Snelling around here."

"We're not sure if that was his real name," Sam explained. "But there's definitely a house here owned by a Snelling." He gave Nicholas a wary look. "Or, at least, there used to be."

A bang resounded as the front door slammed. Nicholas and Sam both jumped.

"Dawn?" Aileen called to the ceiling. "Dawn is that you? Come and say hello!"

A shadow appeared on the wall in the hallway. Large and long. Nicholas just caught sight of a purple-clad elbow before the shadow disappeared and he heard heavy footsteps on the stairs. Whoever it was had gone upstairs – not to the hidden safehouse through the pantry, but to the first floor of Aileen's garish home.

"Dawn!" Aileen called again, an edge of annoyance in her voice. "We have company!"

A door slammed upstairs.

"She's not been the same since..." Aileen murmured apologetically, sharing a look with Sam. She seized her tea cup and sipped through pursed lips that, now Nicholas thought of it, seemed to have acquired a fresh application of rouge since Aileen left them to their rooms.

Recomposing herself, the landlady added: "What's this Snelling got to do with anything?"

"We've yet to find that out," Sam said. "Harvester, perhaps."

Aileen sucked in a breath as if he'd sworn.

"You've heard about the school," she said.

"School?" Sam ventured.

Aileen was on her feet again. She went to the recycling box by the back door and fished out a newspaper. *The Bury Free Press.*

"It was a couple of days ago. Made the front page. Terrible business." She slapped the paper down in front of them.

SCHOOL MASSACRE HORROR.

Nicholas craned across the table to get a better look.

"Seven teachers, all butchered in a classroom," Aileen surmised for them. "And the headteacher's missing. Meredith Fink. They think she did it, though I don't see how; she was almost seventy. I had to have a lie down after I heard about it. Poor Vicky was a teacher there. Dreadful business. Dreadful."

"Vicky was..." Sam ventured.

"One of ours," Aileen nodded.

Nicholas detected a familiar glint in the old man's eye. He had a feeling they wouldn't be leaving Bury for a while.

Another low hiss resounded through the kitchen. Rudy had taken to the floor. The cat hunched low and stared intently at Isabel, its hackles raised. There were barely three feet between them.

"If you continue to stare I shall be forced to teach you some manners," Isabel said tartly.

The other cat growled deep in its throat.

"Cretinous nuisance," Isabel spat. She swiped a paw at the tabby. "Be gone!"

Rudy yowled and his tail doubled in size. He scuttled out of the kitchen and disappeared down the hall.

"Where were we?" Isabel asked.

*

Rae Walker flipped through a magazine she'd read a hundred times and tried to ignore the grumble in her belly. The magazine was water-damaged and brown, like everything in Retro Threads. Tossing it aside, she surveyed her empire. The old boutique had been condemned and the windows were boarded up. The mannequins struck poses under transparent plastic sheets and monster cobwebs swayed in the corners.

Condemned buildings were notoriously difficult to break into, but somebody hadn't done their job properly on Retro Threads. Rae had easily pried away the board covering a small latch window in the alley. Now it was her home and despite the stink of mould, the shop was cosy. It was exactly what she needed after the year she'd had. A cave to swallow her up. A place to forget.

She checked the shop to make sure she was alone, then she retrieved a crumple of white tissue paper from her pocket. Carefully, she extracted something silver from the paper and held it up.

The power had been cut when Retro Threads closed, so she relied on the candles that she'd pinched from the market for light. The silver pendant in her fingers glittered. The raven figurine spun lazily on its chain and Rae studied it intently. It was the only thing she had of her mother's; the only thing they had left her with. Something about the necklace weakened her. Confronted her with the fact that her parents were long gone and she would never know them. She didn't even have a picture. Perhaps that was for the best. Better to leave them as insubstantial phantoms; things that were never flesh and blood to begin with and couldn't be again.

Rae heard a shuffling sound and stiffened. She stuffed the pendant back into her pocket just as a scruffy shape scrabbled through the latch window and dropped silently to the floor.

"Where you been?" she asked.

"Out."

Twig was small for a twelve year old, but what he lacked in stature, he made up for in wiles. He moved like a fox; sharp-boned and wide-eyed. From what she'd gathered about his past, he'd been on the streets for even longer than she had, and she often teased that he was half feral. The grubby pair of school shorts and green hoody only completed the look. Twig refused to wash in the sink in the back office, which still had running water. She didn't care. He could do what he wanted.

"You stink," Rae said, noticing that a pungent stench of garbage had followed Twig into the shop.

"Hats saw me lifting these," the boy said, chucking a small box at her. "Had to hide in a bin."

Rae examined the sandwich box. From the look of the bread, the sell-by date printed on it had long gone. She'd not checked a newspaper in ages.

"Welcome," Twig said, stuffing his sandwich into his mouth.

Rae glared at him.

"Just cos you've got a new set of togs doesn't make you any better'n me," Twig chewed out between mouthfuls.

She looked down at her baggy jumper and tight-fitting jeans. Retro Threads had served her well, providing her with shelter and a new set of clothes. The shop didn't have any boy's things, though, so Twig had to make do with the shorts and hoody he'd been wearing for the past six months. She'd never seen him in anything else, but he didn't seem to mind. They were like a second skin now.

"Don't pretend you didn't try on the skirts," she shot back.

Twig merely gulped down the sandwich in response. Rae's stomach grumbled loudly and she tore open her own box.

"I've decided," Twig said, standing by a mottled mirror trying on silly hats. "I like this place better'n the last."

The last place had been London. That's where Rae had found Twig. A territorial street gang called the Cronies had set on him and she had saved him. She hadn't meant to, but she had a soft spot for the underdog. There hadn't been time to consider what might happen if she helped him out.

He shadowed her for a week. For a week she ignored him. She had a set of rules to live by. The first was *Don't make friends*. When her attempts to ignore him failed to shake him loose, he'd offered her an overripe pear and she'd accepted it. They were together from then on.

It had worked so far. He was good at stealing. She was good at finding shelter. London had been overcrowded, though, and after the run-in with the Cronies, they'd snuck onto a late-night train and woken up in some town called Bury St Edmunds.

Rae watched Twig as he tried on a lady's hat with a peacock feather. Sometimes he had nightmares. She didn't sleep much – she was used to being on the street, half-dozing, always alert – and she'd heard him calling out for somebody called Mark. She didn't ask him about it.

That was rule number two. *Don't talk about your past*. It was the only way to survive. Secrecy was her armour.

They'd made a home in Retro Threads, but Rae was restless. She'd not stayed in the same place for more than a year, and she was moving more frequently. They'd been in Bury three weeks and already her feet were itching. She couldn't sit still. Couldn't relax.

"Who was that girl?" Twig asked.

Rae threw the empty sandwich box into a pile of rubbish in the corner and rested her back against the shop's glass counter. *The girl.* The chubby one with purple hair who'd been following her. At first, Rae had thought she was imagining it. Bury was small and you saw the same faces every day. The girl was good, too. It was five days before Rae realised she was being followed. She tried to tell herself that she didn't care why, but the question nagged, making her insides twitch.

Hopefully she'd scared her enough in the park to shake her off.

"Dunno," Rae said.

"She know you?"

"No."

Rae wanted to change the subject. Or not talk at all. She liked quiet. She rested her head against the counter and closed her eyes.

"What's that?"

She barely felt Twig's fingers brush her pocket and then he was holding the pendant up to the candlelight. Rae jumped to her feet.

"Give it back," she yelled.

Twig gave her a mischievous look and hopped onto the glass counter. "Where'd you get it?" he asked. "D'you lift it?"

Rae swiped at him, anger bubbling through her, but he easily dodged her blows. "Give it back!"

Twig cackled and skipped over the counter.

"S'pretty," he said. "We could sell it."

Rae felt the rage churning dangerously inside. If she let it build any further, they'd be in trouble. She told herself to breathe; to settle the volatile churning. It wanted to be unleashed. She felt it edging at her mind; a strange, seductive probing that was desperate for her to let go.

"You scrawny rat," she shouted. "Give it back!" She clambered onto the counter and hurled herself at him. Twig yelped and they both toppled to the floor. Rae landed on top of him and for a moment, she saw red. The heat pleaded to be released and she wanted to release it.

It was only the look in Twig's eyes that subdued her. She drew a sharp breath and snatched the necklace from him. On her feet, she shoved it back into her pocket and climbed up to the latch window, pushing her way through.

The reedy evening light afforded Bury St Edmunds a ghostly quality that she'd grown accustomed to. The streets were surprisingly empty and she paced them feverishly, clenching her fists and attempting to calm down. She'd been wrong to let Twig tag along; she should have left him in London. He wasn't her responsibility. It was better when she was alone. She couldn't hurt anybody that way.

She had to move on. The thought of spending nights out on the street again, though, filled her with dread. Retro Threads wasn't exactly a palace, but it was preferable to a cardboard box in a traffic tunnel.

An image of Kay flashed in her mind and Rae felt sick. She tried to blot it out, to think of something else, but she couldn't. Kay'd had the same look on her face as Twig. The surprise. The sudden fear.

A reversing lorry emerged from a side street and she jumped out of the way.

"Watch it, love," the driver called down from his cab. When he saw her, his frown brightened into a cheeky grin. "Wouldn't want to steamroller a face like that, eh?"

Rae ignored him and stormed down another cobbled side street. Was everybody an idiot? This town seemed to be full of them. She felt caged. They had no idea what life was really like. They wouldn't last a week on the streets. Hell, she'd like to see them try a day.

Renewed hatred prickled through her and she kicked a dustbin, scattering the contents across the pavement. She went up Abbeygate Street. As the sun began its gradual descent, the rooftops made peaked shadows rotate across the tarmac. Restaurants were only just opening their doors and putting out signs in preparation for the evening punters. The smells were a divine torture. The stale sandwich sat heavily in her stomach and she wondered what real food tasted like.

In the market square, the Moyse's Hall Museum clock chimed and Rae looked at the flint-stone building. Resting at the end of a row of high street shops, it seemed out of place. Out of time. One of the last vestiges of a world that no longer belonged in Bury St Edmunds. Small stained glass windows squinted out onto the market square and there was a high bell tower with a double-peaked roof shaped like a witch's hat.

Rae frowned.

A man was locking up the museum. He was tall. Blond. Attractive, though he was of course ancient. At least forty. He pocketed his keys, then he turned and looked directly at her. Her stomach shrivelled up. It was an alien feeling; an uncertain nervousness.

The man smiled as he strolled down the pavement. "Evening," he said, pausing on his way.

Rae nodded, squinting at him.

"You ought to be getting home, I'd say. It'll be dark soon."

"I'm not afraid," Rae said. He was even more alluring up close. Those eyes. A strong jaw bristled with fair stubble. He laughed and he had perfect teeth.

"I'm going this way," he said. "If you want to walk next to me that's fine. Don't want anybody taking advantage."

Rae considered him. He was smart in a midnight-blue jacket and dark jeans. His skin was like satin. He wasn't offering to walk her home, but near enough. She didn't want him to know where she lived. Not because she was ashamed, though she was, but because there was something dangerous about him. This perfect specimen.

"Alright," the man said, seeming to note her unimpressed expression. "G'night."

He raised his hand in a little wave – an effeminate gesture that he somehow managed to make look masculine – and walked off down the street.

Rae wondered if he expected her to follow him. She'd encountered plenty of guys just like him. The cities were full of them and she'd seen her share of those. No, he was different. There had been a whiff of danger intermingled with his aftershave. Despite his friendliness, he couldn't hide the hardness in his eyes.

She watched the museum man go. Most guys were easy to read, but she couldn't read him at all. She had a feeling that he had his own games – and if she attempted to play him at them, she might just lose.

CHAPTER SIX
Seeing

Sentinel training officially commenced that evening. Nicholas felt battered and bruised after the incident at Snelling's house, but his eyes were agleam as he sat with Sam at a round table in Aileen's cosy study. Isabel positioned herself on the tabletop among the books, scrutinising them like a snooty librarian.

"A Harvester won't hesitate to strike," Sam said darkly. "A Harvester exists only to eradicate Sentinels. It won't stop until it sees blood, and perhaps not even then."

"Are all Harvesters just Sentinels that have been turned?" Nicholas asked. Sketches of nasty-looking weapons filled the page in front of him. Curved daggers with serrated edges, a crossbow, even a razor-sharp ball and chain.

"That's a new wrinkle," Sam admitted. "Though we know little about Harvesters, we believe they used to be recruited. Anybody could be a Harvester. The fact that Sentinels are being turned is merely an insidious new torment concocted by the agents of the Dark Prophets. The good news, if you can call it that, is that they're human, and therefore fallible. But most spend their entire lives training, fighting and killing. A Harvester knows at least a hundred spectacularly violent ways to kill you, if not more. They're deadly and adaptable."

Nicholas thought of Snelling, the only Harvester he'd encountered. Snelling had posed as a shop owner, calling himself Melvin Reynolds and preying on Nicholas's naivety to gain access to Hallow House. Harvesters weren't just killers, they were lethal manipulators. He couldn't believe how naïve he'd been. It was only a week ago, but Nicholas felt like a completely different person. His eyes were open now. He couldn't imagine ever trusting anybody that readily again.

"How do you spot them?" he asked. "I mean, they look like normal people, right?"

"There are no tell-tale signs," Sam admitted. "That's what makes them so dangerous. The man who stops you in the street to ask for directions could be a Harvester. Or the woman who sits next to you on the bus."

"So you pretty much don't know until they've got a knife in you." It wasn't a comforting thought.

"That's why Sensitives are invaluable in the fight against Harvesters," Sam said, clearly attempting to instil some hope in what seemed like a hopeless situation. "They're able to sense what others cannot. In time, you should be able to do so."

"But only if you train," Isabel put in.

Nicholas ignored her. Sam pulled a book towards them and began talking about battle strategies. There were more than Nicholas could have ever imagined. Sieges, coercion tactics, charges, counter-attacks... Then there were things called tactical objectives and attrition warfare, plus different types of battles – offensive and defensive, even counter-offensive.

They spent over an hour going through it all. Sam drew up theoretical battle plans and asked Nicholas to do the same, offering suggestions for ways to improve them.

"Who taught you all of this?" Nicholas asked, his head swimming.

"My parents," Sam said. "All Sentinels are trained by a parent or guardian. There's no Sentinel school beyond the lessons passed down through the generations. A Sentinel learns on his or her feet, in the trenches, mired in the chaos of battle."

Not for the first time, Nicholas felt a yearning for his own parents. He wished they'd trained him and explained how the world really worked. Instead, they'd shielded him from that life. After his talk with Jessica, he finally understood why. She had said he was chosen by the Trinity. If his parents hadn't hidden him away, he'd have spent his whole life being targeted by abominations like Snelling, Malika and

Diltraa. He probably wouldn't have made it to his sixth birthday, let alone his sixteenth.

Still, he felt robbed of the opportunity to talk to his parents about all of this.

The study door opened suddenly, snapping him from his thoughts.

"Oh," a figure in purple uttered, freezing in the doorway.

"Hello young lady," Sam greeted her pleasantly. "You're Dawn, yes? Aileen's granddaughter?"

Dawn nodded, biting her lip. She was chubby, her mousy brown hair dyed purple at the ends, and her gaze darted between them.

"I didn't mean to interrupt," she said softly, her voice barely above a whisper.

"Plenty of room," Sam said. "Please, come in."

"I'll come back later," the girl said, and like that she was gone, the door clicking shut.

Nicholas didn't know what to make of her.

"This is all great and interesting," he said, gesturing at the books. "But when do we get swords?"

"Swords?" Sam asked.

"Yeah. I thought you were going to teach me how to fight."

"The boy desires to fly before he has even peered over the edge of the nest," Isabel commented dourly.

Nicholas shot her a look. "If I'm going to end up in more exploding buildings, I at least want to be able to defend myself." He couldn't end up in the dirt the way he had when Esus attacked him in the forest. If Esus had been a Harvester, Nicholas would be dead now. He'd been lucky so far, but his luck wouldn't last forever.

"You're right," Sam said, surprising him. "Perhaps that's enough book learning for today. Follow me."

Excitement fizzing through him, Nicholas hurried after Sam. The old man descended the steps into Aileen's kitchen. The landlady was out and the house was quiet. Dawn must have gone to her room.

"Here," Sam said, heading out the back door into the garden. The sun was sinking behind the rooftops, casting a flagstone courtyard in mottled light. A vine crept up the back wall, towering over potted plants.

Sam plucked two cushions from the garden chairs and faced Nicholas. He beat them together in front of him.

"We start with the basics," he said. "No swords. Basic defensive manoeuvres will toughen you up and teach you how to minimise damage during an attack. Then we move on to the more complicated stuff."

Nicholas hesitated. It looked like Sam expected him to hit him, but he couldn't punch an old man, even if he was asking for it.

"Stagger your stance," Sam said. "Hands up. Always keep them up or you'll find yourself with a black eye or a fat lip. And always keep one shoulder to me."

Uncertainly, Nicholas did as he was told, balling his fists before him.

"Good. Now use one fist to protect your face and punch with the other."

"You want me to—"

Sam beat the cushions together once more. "Do it," he urged, as if daring Nicholas to defy him. Taking a breath, Nicholas threw a punch, battering the soft pad with his knuckles.

"Good, but harder. What are you, five? And keep moving. Stay on your toes."

Nicholas wobbled onto his toes and threw another punch, frustrated that it was weaker than the first.

"Keep going," Sam encouraged him.

Nicholas jabbed again. They circled about in the courtyard.

"The *visectus* demon goes for the eyes," Sam said. He held the cushion higher and Nicholas pounded it. "Good! Take its eyes before it takes yours."

Nicholas was already gasping for breath. He hadn't realised how hard this would be. He didn't stop, though, exhilaration pumping through him. His shoulders ached and sweat coated his face, but he grit his teeth and pushed on, throwing everything he had into the punches.

"The *svartulf* is low to the ground," Sam said, lowering the cushions to his side.

Nicholas pummelled them.

"Visectus!" Sam yelled, holding the cushions up. "Svartulf!" he hollered again, lowering them. "Visectus! Svartulf! Visectus!"

Nicholas punched high and low, panting, his ribs crying out.

"We're going to that school tomorrow," Sam puffed, still circling. "If something's waiting for us, you need to be able to knock it back, keep it at bay. Two this time."

Nicholas slammed his fists into the cushions one after the other.

One, two. One, two.

"Hands up!"

He hadn't even noticed they were dropping. He wiped his perspiring forehead and raised his fists again, burying them in the cushions as Sam dodged and wove about the courtyard. Nicholas couldn't believe how agile the old man was. He supposed that was a benefit of being trained from birth. It was second nature to Sam. The most exercise Nicholas had ever done was at school, and his life hadn't exactly depended on it then.

"Thirty seconds," Sam told him. "Non-stop. Come on. Show us what you've got."

Nicholas was flagging, the strength draining from him. His mouth was chalk dry, the rest of him drenched in sweat. He clenched his jaw and summoned every last scrap of power left in him. He hurled punches as fast and hard as he could.

Jab, jab, jab, jab.

"Four! Three! Two! One! Enough!"

Sam lowered the cushions.

Panting, Nicholas bent over and rested his hands on his knees. His whole body hummed with pain and triumph. Sam slapped him on the back.

"Good lad," he said breathlessly. "You'll be a demon hunter in no time."

"Barbarians," Isabel muttered from the back door.

★

As night drew in, Nicholas sat in his bedroom at Aileen's safehouse, encircled by books. The room was small and had no desk, so he'd spread numerous volumes of *The Sentinel Chronicles* out across the floor.

They were all from Aileen's study. He hoped she wouldn't mind that he'd borrowed them.

"What are you doing?"

Nicholas nearly jumped out of his skin.

Isabel's voice had rung right in his ear. He was poring over the volumes so diligently that he hadn't noticed her uncurl on the edge of the bed and crane over his shoulder.

"Jesus," he said. "You've got to stop doing that."

Isabel stared intently at him. The lamp light brightened the silver flecks in her black fur and her whiskers bristled. It was over a week since she'd taken over the body of the cat he'd rescued in the countryside and she was behaving more like a wild animal every day. She began preening her fur.

"You're almost convincing as a cat when you do that," Nicholas said without looking up from the book.

Isabel stopped. She squinted at him and sniffed.

"You could do with one yourself," she told him. "It's already starting to smell like my father's hunting cupboard in here and we have only been here for one evening."

Nicholas shrugged.

"What are you reading?"

Nicholas raised the book over his shoulder so she could see. *The Sentinel Chronicles – September 1997.*

"Riveting, I'm sure."

"It's useless," Nicholas said, not even trying to conceal his annoyance. He dumped the book on the floor. In the days that followed the defeat of Diltraa, he'd been attempting to go through every instalment of the *Chronicles* from 1997 to find out what had happened in the months surrounding his birth. But there was no mention of him. Nor Orville. Nor the things that had happened there. It was like the Sentinels had turned a blind eye to the events that had taken place in that spooky little village. Whether it was out of disinterest or guilt he wasn't sure.

"You're trying to find out what happened in Orville," Isabel noted.

"So?"

"It is only natural," the cat said. She wrapped her tail around herself, as if to keep her toes warm. "You discovered that everybody in the village died because of you. That's a heavy burden."

"Why *did* they die?" Nicholas demanded.

"There's a power in you," Isabel told him. "It came into this world with you, and it blasted through that forsaken place like a storm of arrows."

"And they're dead, but not dead," Nicholas said. "They're, what, frozen?"

"They're dead, as far as I could tell," Isabel said. "But their souls are trapped. Pinned to that place like butterflies."

"Like you were in the Pentagon Room."

"Quite so. After my death, that room was sealed off, and me with it," Isabel explained. "No doubt Jessica hoped one day she would resurrect me, and that meant preserving my body in the exact state of its demise."

"You came back," Nicholas mused. "So that means the villagers have a chance, too."

"Possibly," Isabel said. "If somebody discovered a way. Until then, there's nothing we can do."

"There must be something."

Nicholas rested back against the bed with a sigh. He'd also been scouring the *Chronicles* for clues about the girl Esus wanted him to find, but that search had been equally futile.

"This girl... Lydia," he murmured. "How exactly are we supposed to track her down?" They had nothing to go on apart from a name that the girl apparently wasn't using anymore.

"Let's see," Isabel said. She hopped down from the bed and padded across the carpet, peering at a velvet box that rested among the books. It was the box that his parents had left him; the one that he couldn't open. He'd found it in the study behind his parents' bedroom wall, along with the box that contained the raven pendant. The pendant was in his pocket.

"Ah," the cat uttered, sounding pleased. "You have this already. This should help immensely."

"What are you talking about now?"

"The box," Isabel said. "Open it. We'll continue your training now."

"I'll fetch my crash helmet."

"Your what?"

Nicholas sighed. "It's locked. Can't open it."

"What a delightfully defeatist attitude you possess. It's a wonder you even bother to get out of bed in the morning. Here, take it and I'll tell you how to open it."

Nicholas grabbed the box and turned it over in his hands, just as he had the first time. It was about the size of a flat jewellery box. But it was useless. There was no way to open it. That didn't seem to faze Isabel, though. Could she really help him uncover what was inside?

"It is yours," the cat said, sitting upright. "Nobody else has control over it. You alone may open it."

"It was a birthday present," he said. "It's my birthday next week."

I'll be sixteen, he thought.

"I'm sure your parents wouldn't mind if you opened it early."

"They'd kill me," Nicholas said.

"All the same. Now, shut your eyes."

"You going to do funny things to me?"

"Take this seriously," Isabel snapped.

Nicholas closed his eyes, feeling ridiculous.

"Now visualise the box. Every detail of it. The smooth corners. The soft material. The weight of it. Build a picture of it."

"Yes, master," Nicholas droned.

"Have you done it?"

Nicholas took a breath and pushed aside his self-consciousness. He tried to imagine what the box looked like. He'd had it in his hands a few moments ago. It wasn't heavy, but it wasn't light, either. And the velvet felt soft, almost like rabbit fur.

"Yes," he said quietly.

"Now imagine where it is, here on the floor. Imagine it sitting before you, just as it is."

In his mind, the box was now sitting on the carpet.

"Picture it there," came Isabel's voice. "Now reach out – no, not with your hands. Reach out with your insides, with your guts, and open it."

"But–"

"Just. Do it."

Nicholas huffed and pictured the box again. He reached for it as the cat had instructed, pushing his will on to it. He saw himself picking it up and there, where nothing had been before, was a little silver catch. He flicked it.

There came a snapping, creaking sound and a soft thud.

Nicholas opened his eyes. The box lay open on the floor.

"Did I–?" he marvelled, pulling the box nearer to inspect its contents. There was wood. And metal. And something shining cold and purple. It was some kind of apparatus, nestled in the soft cushion of the box's interior.

"Well don't just stare at it," Isabel said.

Nicholas swallowed, his throat dry. Gingerly, he pulled the contraption from the box and unfolded it. Two wooden legs slotted into a flat panel that formed a base. Suspended on a silver thread was a purple disc that looked like it was made of amethyst. When it was put together, Nicholas thought it somewhat resembled a mechanical metronome; he'd seen musicians using them to keep time.

"It's a seeing glass," Isabel told him, as if she had known all along what was in the box. "Many Sensitives use them to begin with; it helps them to hone their skills. This is a particularly fetching specimen."

"What does it do?" Nicholas asked.

"It helps you access what's already there, inside you." She blinked at the seeing glass. "You set the crystal swinging and it puts you into a trance. It relaxes you so that you can concentrate solely on seeing and sensing beyond what's in front of you."

"So it's going to hypnotise me?"

"Not exactly," Isabel said. "Let's try it."

Nicholas eyed the instrument unsurely. Accessing that part of himself, the part he didn't understand, made him nervous.

But it might help him find the girl.

"Set the crystal going," the cat instructed. "Send your thoughts out into the spirit planes. Ask the question you need answered. Ask for the whereabouts of the girl."

Trembling slightly, Nicholas tapped the purple disc and it began to swing from side to side. He reclined against the side of the bed and shook out his arms and legs to dispel any nervous energy. He followed the crystal as it swung. Whenever the small disc reached the mid-point of its arc, it caught the light and flashed.

Swing. *Flash.* Swing. *Flash.*

Nicholas felt both heavy and light, like he was suspended in water. That familiar prickling sensation stirred deep in the pit of his stomach.

Swing. *Flash.*

Flash. Swing.

Nicholas's eyes began to droop.

"*The girl,*" he commanded in his head. "*Show me the girl.*"

Flash. Swing. *Flash.* Swing.

His stomach knotted. The light in the room softened, darkened, until all he saw was the flash of the little purple disc.

Flash. Flash. Flash.

Fire. People running, screaming. A man with a cane stalks the streets. Something monstrous screeches inhumanly and tumbles from the night sky.

Nicholas heard himself panting. He tried to slow the images down, but they wouldn't be curbed. They poured into his mind like lava and he felt himself drowning.

A red triangle sizzles. Three large objects like pods simmer in a nest of embers. Elvis Presley grins. A woman sits in a classroom and something wet slithers out of her. A silver raven pendant glimmers. Moonlight edges over the lip of a well. Malika emerges from a pool drenched in blood...

"Nicholas!"

He retched into the carpet. His mouth and nose were full of something tangy. Blood. He was only vaguely aware of somebody pawing at him.

"Deep breaths," a voice said. "Deep breaths."

He tried to breathe and slowly the room came back into focus. The seeing stone was still. The books seemed to crane up from the floor to see what all the fuss was about.

"There you go. Are you well?" Isabel rested her paws on his knee.

Nicholas wasn't embarrassed anymore.

"Malika," he choked in horror. "She was... there was blood everywhere..."

CHAPTER SEVEN
At School

As the sun rose over bury St Edmunds, a peach-coloured sky provided an optimistic backdrop for the neat rows of peaked roofs. The shadows slid back and dissolved and the sun's rays trickled into widening puddles that warmed every cobble and tile. Nosily, it pushed in at windows. One high window confounded it, though. Curtains were drawn to block out the world, and the sun was forced to peek through at the edges.

The birds woke Nicholas early. He slept deeply for a few hours, exhausted by what had happened at Snelling's house, not to mention his troubling encounter with the seeing glass. When the unfamiliar squawking roused him, though, his mind quickly began whirring again. Who had Sam seen at Snelling's house? Who had attacked them? What did the school massacre have to do with it all, if anything?

Breakfast consisted of eggs and bacon. Sam attempted to help Aileen at the hob, but she quickly established her authority over all things food-related.

Nicholas smiled weakly as, defeated, the old man seated himself at the kitchen table. He ached from yesterday's training and he felt sick to his stomach. The image of the dead woman in the classroom burned in his mind. Was she one of the teachers from the school massacre? And then there was Malika slithering out of a vat of blood...

"You're going to think a hole through the table-top any second now."

Nicholas realised Sam was speaking to him.

"How you feeling? After yesterday?" the old man asked.

"Fine," Nicholas said. "Bit achey." He told Sam about the vision from the seeing glass, watching the elderly man's face cloud with concern.

"Lad, if it's too much—"

Nicholas wasn't having any of it. "I need to do this." He thought back to the conversation he'd had with Reynolds – Snelling – in the back of his shop. Reynolds wanted to know what motivated Nicholas to fight. Nicholas's answer remained the same – he had to. It was what his parents would have wanted. Now that he knew about the dark forces in the world, he couldn't just ignore them. He had a responsibility, one that his parents had stepped up to, as had their parents before them.

He couldn't stop thinking about the images from the seeing glass. They didn't make sense. What did Elvis Presley have to do with tracking down the girl? And the raven pendant? He reached into his pocket and felt his own necklace there; the other gift from his parents. He carried it with him everywhere.

Isabel wasn't any help. She'd never even heard of Elvis Presley. She said one interesting thing, though. "The triangle is sometimes used in summoning incantations."

Summoning. He was expected to find a way to summon the Trinity... Nicholas's head ached and he couldn't wait to get out of the house.

"It's all going to pot," Aileen muttered as she poured herself a cup of tea.

"Aileen?" Sam asked.

"Safehouse in Manchester was attacked last night," the landlady said, her usual cheeriness absent this morning. "Harvesters. And there was an incident at a hospital in Cardiff. Fifty people dead."

"What happened to them?" Sam asked.

Aileen eyed Nicholas.

"Aileen?" Sam prompted.

"They were all turned inside out."

Nicholas's stomach contracted in horror and he attempted to control the anxiety that wriggled through him, but the look of concern that Sam and Aileen shared only made it wriggle harder. Things were worsening out there. Awful things were happening all over the country. What next, Europe? The rest of the world?

He couldn't help feeling responsible. Esus had made it clear that if he didn't find the girl and figure out how to resurrect the Trinity, they could all be doomed.

Nicholas grit his teeth. He had to find that girl.

"Last I heard, Esus was tending to the survivors in Manchester," Aileen continued, but Nicholas was too caught up in visions of bodies ripped apart to catch anything else the landlady said.

An hour later, he, Sam and Isabel stood together scrutinising a squat, grey building. It was dry-baking in the sunlight, appearing to harden with every passing second, like a fried toad.

Royal Birch Primary School was a twenty minute walk outside the town centre. A petrol station down the road was its nearest neighbour and the school field at the back blended into rolling fields.

Nicholas remembered what the paper had said happened at the school. Seven teachers, all murdered. Ripped apart. One of them had been called Vicky; she was a Sentinel. Unease pinched his temples and he tried to shake it off. The heat was drying him out, too.

Isabel's tail curled around his neck, and despite the suffocating warmth, Nicholas was glad she was there. He couldn't let his nerves overwhelm him. He had to be strong for Sam. And Isabel.

He'd almost convinced himself that Diltraa's attack on Hallow House was the end of it. He'd survived that confrontation, and the one with Snelling, and he was quite finished with the supernatural, thanks very much. If anything, though, things were snowballing. If they carried on the way they were...

"Remember what I taught you yesterday," Sam said. Nicholas nodded and thought he caught pride twinkling at him from beneath the old man's fedora, but he couldn't be sure because then Sam was striding towards the school, his satchel over one shoulder.

Police tape criss-crossed the double front doors. Blue and white. Almost festive. Flowers lay in bundles, too. Dried to a crisp by the sun. The written notes were already bleached and illegible. As Nicholas scanned the flowers, an image needled into his mind.

Bodies in chairs. Blood slides across the floor. A fist clenches in agony.

AT SCHOOL

He was sensing something from inside the school. Had using the seeing glass opened something up that couldn't be closed again?

He took a breath and focussed on Sam.

The elderly man had taken out his lock-picking kit. His hands weren't as jittery as they had been at Snelling's house, and it wasn't long before they were standing in the reception hall.

"Wait," Sam said, drawing the doors closed behind them. "After what happened here, we're going to have to be very careful. Who knows what foul things were summoned in this place. If we disturb anything, it could prove fatal."

"There is a foul stench," Isabel added, her finer senses picking up what they couldn't.

"Just give me a moment," Sam said. He rummaged in his satchel, setting it on the front desk and retrieving a black feather, a Zippo lighter emblazoned with a skull and crossbones and a tightly-bound package of dry twigs. He removed his fedora and Nicholas watched Sam as he lit the herbs.

Dark smoke and the musty scent of cedar wafted up from the bundle. Sam took the feather and, elbows crooked, used it to waft the smoke purposefully before them. He stroked the air in one direction, then another, before finally turning and wafted it directly at Nicholas.

Nicholas coughed.

"Hey—" he began, but Isabel dug a warning claw into his shoulder and Nicholas fell silent.

When the twigs had burnt out, Sam returned the objects to his briefcase.

"What did you just do?" Nicholas asked.

"For protection." Sam shrugged. He replaced the fedora and pushed open a pair of double doors. Nicholas followed him into a long corridor.

"You didn't do that at Snelling's," he said.

"I have a bad feeling about this place."

Nicholas was glad he had the Drujblade sheathed at his hip. Esus had used the bone dagger to kill Diltraa, which offered Nicholas some small comfort.

Colourful displays adorned the walls, and under the whiff of cedar, Nicholas caught that undeniable school bouquet – a chemical mix of bleach and pencil shavings. He had been out of school for a couple of weeks now, but it felt like a lifetime. If his friends knew what he was doing at this very moment...

Their footsteps resounded loudly. They sounded like prison wardens. Or victims in a horror film. Nicholas loved horror movies, but he'd seen enough of it for real. And he and Sam were behaving exactly how stupid characters in those films behaved. Who else would look into what had happened at the school, though? Besides, they were Sentinels.

Sentinels.

It sat a little easier now. He had a name for what he was; what his parents had been. The name gave him a purpose. While his friends would go back to school in September and struggle to figure out what they were going to do with their lives, Nicholas knew what he had to do with his. Of course, Maths and Science exams were a little easier than the tests that Sentinels underwent. Chances are you wouldn't be skinned by a demon while taking your Maths A-Level.

Isabel's fur bristled against his neck and Nicholas was overcome with a tingling heat. He was only wearing shorts and a T-shirt, but it was unbearable. Sweat clung to his top lip.

Sam removed his fedora and mopped at his own brow with a handkerchief. Clearly the heat was affecting them all.

"Did somebody forget to turn the heating off?" Nicholas asked.

"This isn't a natural heat," Sam said.

They reached the end of the corridor. A doorway was covered in black plastic. It was tacked all around the doorframe like a shroud.

"This is it," Sam said under his breath. "The staff room. Hold this."

He placed the satchel in Nicholas's arms and opened it again, this time removing a box-cutter. With great care, he sliced through the plastic, dragging the blade from top to bottom. It yielded as easily as warm butter.

Nicholas stood, still holding the satchel as Sam peeled the plastic back and peered through a small window.

Nausea punched Nicholas in the stomach and he doubled over in pain.

Eight chairs. Arranged in a circle. An old woman observes, smiling as dark things swarm about the other teachers. Lecherous claws grasp for them. Open them like meat packets. Blood spills. And a pair of cold blue eyes watch dispassionately as the teachers are gutted.

Nicholas attempted to steady himself. The ground seemed to be tilting beneath him and he felt as if he was about to hit the floor.

"Boy," came Isabel's voice.

Her voice brought him back to the corridor. A hand seized Nicholas's other shoulder, and he found himself peering into Sam's wizened face.

"Don't look," the old man said, though it came out as a barely-controlled choke. Their eyes locked and Nicholas saw that Sam was worried. Scared, even. He couldn't help trembling.

"I've already seen," Nicholas said softly. "They were sacrificed in there. Something cut them all open."

Sam dropped his gaze, still clutching Nicholas's shoulder.

"A sacrifice," he said. "This place has been desecrated."

"For what?"

Laughter punctured the air. A child, perhaps. Or a woman. A filthy, high-pitched snigger.

"Samuel. Nicholas. Isabel. Welcome."

It was an inhuman sound that reminded Nicholas of Diltraa. The guttural rasp that had come from the demon's throat. The voice skittered over the floor and penetrated his heart.

"Don't listen to it," Sam said.

"What's here?" Nicholas asked, his blood running cold as a face appeared in the window behind the black plastic. A withered, pale countenance like a skull. Lips peeling into a leer. Dark smudges for eyes. It was the old woman from his vision; the one who had watched the teachers being butchered.

"It's her," Nicholas said.

By the time Sam whirled to look, the face had vanished.

"The headmistress," Nicholas said. "She killed them all."

"Harvester," Isabel spat.

"Let's go," the old man said, seizing the satchel from him. "Come on." He marched away from the door. Nicholas hurried down the corridor alongside him.

"Leaving so soon? Won't you stay? I'm sure we can find ways to entertain you."

"Ignore it," Sam barked.

The heat was unbearable. Nicholas felt clammy and leaden. It was as if he was wading through cement. He grabbed the Drujblade from its sheath and clutched it tightly. The corridor ballooned out before him and the exit was impossibly far away. The colourful paper on the walls shivered. Nicholas's gaze snapped up to the ceiling. Something was there. A gathering pool of darkness.

"They've fed, but they're still hungry."

The corridor was watching him.

A buzz of electricity shuddered through the air and the strip lighting blazed. Nicholas threw a hand up to shield his eyes. White light battered him. Finally, darkness collapsed back in around him.

Red and yellow spots simmered in Nicholas's vision and he wasn't able to see. He stumbled blindly. Just as he began to grow accustomed to the dark, the lights turned on full blast once more. Above his head, the drone of electricity throbbed and then, one by one, each of the lights emitted a *crack-pop* and shards of glass rained down.

Nicholas squeezed the Drujblade. He staggered away, crashing into the wall. His hands felt slick with sweat. No, not sweat. As his vision cleared, he saw that they were red. Red with blood. The walls were bleeding.

His heart hammered in his chest.

"Sam?" he yelled. "Sam, where are you?!"

He couldn't feel Isabel, either. She was gone from his shoulder.

The blood was everywhere. It dripped from the ceiling and dribbled warmly down his cheeks.

Something swooped and Nicholas instinctively ducked. He cast about in confusion. Whatever had bowled at him hadn't made a sound, had swept as noiselessly as a kestrel, but he'd felt an odd flush as it whisked past.

"Isabel?"

Another movement, and this time Nicholas caught it as it rippled across the wall. Fangs stretched wide and snapped shut. Bony claws snaked over the wall.

A living shadow with horns and awful cut-out eyes.

It was red against the bloody wall, then grey on the floor.

It watched him for a moment, then frantically lunged.

Before Nicholas had time to react, the shadow tore through him, drenching him in heat, and he gasped in shock. Within seconds there were more of them. Undulating in waves, the monsters surfaced through the shadows, fixing their cut-out eyes on him before thrashing in his direction, clawing from the floor and walls, any surface within reach.

Nicholas slashed the Drujblade, but it had no effect. He keeled from one wall to the next, attempting to evade their blows.

The shadows towered over him; immense, distorted, alien things that writhed from the ceiling. Barbed claws snatched at him, erupting from the floor to seize his legs.

Nicholas twisted and pulled, but there was no escaping them. They held fast.

One of the shadows pressed a claw to his chest. He felt a wrench inside his rib cage. A horrendous pulling. The monster was inside him, feeling for his heart, attempting to rip it free.

He collapsed to the floor in agony.

A liver-spotted hand seized his shoulder and Nicholas peered up. As light broke across Sam's face, though, Nicholas cringed away in fear.

The old man's eyes were gone. Ghastly, bloodied hollows gaped blankly at him and Sam's face contorted into a mask of hatred.

"*Nicholassss,*" the old man hissed. "*Join us. Join ussss...*"

"ENOUGH!"

Sweet relief came in an instant. The shadows tumbled away, as if dragged by an invisible tide. Just like that, they were gone, along with the horrible vision of Sam.

Gulping for breath, Nicholas peered down. The red was still on him. The blood. Already, it was congealing on his clothes, his skin, in his hair. He fought the urge to vomit.

Light returned to the corridor and he spotted Sam leaning against a wall, panting for breath. His eyes were back to normal. His satchel was further down the corridor, near the exit.

It wasn't Sam who had bellowed, though. It took Nicholas a moment to process the fact that the voice had been female.

It had been Isabel.

Nicholas searched for the cat, finding her at the centre of the corridor. She looked double her normal size, her fur had puffed up so much. The cat stared intently at a figure lingering outside the staff room. A scrawny woman. All bones and wrinkly flesh. Her hair was pinned atop her head and her hands were mittened claws.

The headmistress, Nicholas realised with a start. *The one from the paper. Miss Fink.*

It was the face he'd glimpsed peeking through the window. Aileen had said the headmistress was seventy, but she looked almost twice that, as if the Dark Prophets had drained her of all life, leaving her little more than an emaciated corpse.

"*The Tortor will rise,*" the hag hissed. "*The Tortor will rise and you will all perish writhing in agony.*"

"Your parlour tricks hold no power over us," Isabel spat. "You will desist."

Nicholas blinked at the cat, not believing what he was seeing.

Golden fire flickered in her eyes and a shadow towered over her. It was the shadow of an old woman, attached to the cat's paws. The shadow raised an arm and pointed toward the staff room. The fire in Isabel's eyes flashed.

"DESIST!"

There was a moment of tension. The air crackled. Then, without saying a word, the headmistress was gone.

Peace settled over the hallway.

"You'll have to forgive Miss Fink. She has the manners of a stray dog."

Nicholas tensed. Another figure had appeared in the headmistress's place. A man with blond hair and high cheekbones. He was broad-shouldered, his voice low and arrogant.

"No," Sam murmured beside him.

"Samuel Wilkins," the newcomer drawled. "What a pleasant surprise. What's it been, fifteen, twenty years? Time really is a thief, isn't she? You haven't changed a bit. And you've brought a young novice with you." The man winked at him. "Did you enjoy Miss Fink's little show? She's a touch dramatic, but she gets the job done."

"Stay back, Laurent," Sam growled.

Laurent? Sam knew this man?

The stranger held his hands up. "Such suspicion," he scoffed, sounding hurt. "Are you not pleased to see me, old chap? I've got the kettle on if you fancy a catch up."

"Whatever you're up to, Laurent, I entreat you to stop," Sam said.

The other man considered them. He wore a dark blue jacket and his chin jutted confidently. Was he a Harvester? Nicholas wanted to get away from him as quickly as possible.

"Stop?" Laurent mused. "Yes, that would make life a great deal easier for you, wouldn't it? Sadly, it would make things a great deal less entertaining for me." He flashed perfect white teeth. "Don't worry, I have no use for you yet. Go now. Rouse the ranks. It will be for nothing. Tell them all that Laurent Renault has returned and he wants blood."

Nicholas felt Sam clutch his arm. He pulled him down the hall, away from Laurent.

"See you soon," the man called.

Together, Nicholas, Sam and Isabel wordlessly retreated. They stumbled out into the baking sunshine, exhausted and trembling, and Sam led them away from the school, his expression grim.

"I'll need to speak with Esus," he said softly. "The school will need to be guarded. The sacrifice was just the beginning. That hag was a Harvester, she couldn't be anything else. One of Laurent's pawns. He is planning something terrible for this building."

"Who is he? What were those things that attacked us?" Nicholas asked.

"In my time we called them murklings," Isabel said. "Officially, they're called *nillumbra*. They're usually invisible to humans. They must have gained in power. The sacrifice..."

"The sacrifice gave them a boost," Nicholas murmured, finishing the thought for her. "Great." He frowned. A girl stood a little further down the street. She looked about his age. Tall and dark-skinned. A little scruffy. She raised a hand to shield her eyes from the sun and stared intently at the odd trio scuttling away from the school.

When she saw him looking, the girl lowered her hand and hurried away.

★

Nicholas showered and watched the drain devour the bloody water. When he'd scrubbed every inch of himself until he finally felt clean, he stood in front of the bathroom mirror.

He was paler than ever. His mop of dark curls was a tangled mess. He thought he looked older already. It was less than a week until his sixteenth birthday, but he looked even older than that. He'd wised up, maybe. Life wasn't the carefree cruise he'd always taken it to be.

He rinsed a glass in the sink and gulped down some water. A girl had been watching them outside the school. Could she be the one he was looking for? It seemed like too much of a coincidence, but he was starting to believe that everything happened for a reason.

If she *was* the girl, had she stumbled across him by accident? Or was she looking for him, even as he attempted to find her?

Nicholas spat in the sink. It didn't matter; the girl had vanished.

He trudged down the landing.

"You alright, lad?"

Sam stood outside his room.

Nicholas nodded. "I didn't know blood could smell that bad."

The old man grunted. His forehead was creased with concerned. There were only a few specks of red on him from the school, but his crumpled attire was far more alarming. Nicholas had never seen Sam looking dishevelled.

"Anytime you want to go back to Hallow House, just say the word," the elderly man told him.

"I'm not going back."

As disturbing as it was to be almost buried alive and then covered in blood, Nicholas had to see this through to the end. Even if it meant more attacks, which were all-but guaranteed. What else could he do? Cower with Jessica in the mansion? Let others fight instead? Let them die in his place?

Darkness crowded into the landing and Nicholas put a hand to his head, which had begun to pound. A figure materialised at the top of the stairs.

Esus stood observing them, gloved hands clasped before him.

"Samuel," the phantom intoned. His voice rumbled behind the silver mask and inside Nicholas's skull.

"Thank you for coming," Sam said.

"You have news?"

"Laurent Renault is in town," Sam said. "He's the one responsible for the slayings at the school. I have a feeling that was just the beginning. Laurent's up to something."

"You know of his plans?"

"Not yet."

"Uncover them," the phantom ordered. "And you boy, find that girl."

The darkness swelled and Esus vanished.

"I do love when he drops by," Nicholas muttered, his headache clearing. He was glad Esus hadn't stuck around. "Who is Laurent?"

Sam regarded him wearily. "Laurent is a very dangerous man. But then, you don't need to be told that. I've only encountered him twice; neither time was pleasant."

"And?"

"The first time I met him, he was the talk of the Sentinel community. He was nineteen years old when he slaughtered his entire family. Not just his parents, but his brothers, cousins, nieces. He wiped out his entire bloodline, and nobody knew why. He... well, I'll spare you the details. I was there when he was caught and taken into custody. He was to be punished for his crimes. He was taken to a safehouse in Leicester, and I was one of the senior members sent in to question him. It was one of the worst afternoons of my life."

Sam looked down at his hands.

"There's nothing quite so terrifying as a man whose poisonous convictions are wrought in iron. And Laurent's convictions were as poisonous as they come. He showed no remorse for what he had done. He was perfectly rational about the whole affair. His family had to die, he said, and so he had killed them." Sam's features became drawn as he recalled that dark time. "We deemed him fit to stand trial. Though his actions seemed insane, he was in fact quite sane. He possessed a formidable intellect. Before the trial, Laurent escaped the safehouse. He left a trail of bodies in his wake, and then he was gone."

"He was a Sentinel?" Nicholas asked.

"A Sentinel corrupted. Not like my friend Richard, though. Laurent's hatred stemmed from a far more human place, as far as I could tell. He was the youngest of a large family, easily overlooked and often forgotten. In short, he was an attention-seeker. Golly, but he found a way to make people take notice."

"Are we safe here?" Nicholas asked, suddenly feeling trapped on the tiny landing. "I mean, he was a Sentinel. Does Laurent know about this place?"

"Aileen's only been here for five years," Sam reassured him. "Before that, she was in Cambridge. That's how we know each other. If I were a betting man, I'd say we're in no danger at Aileen's as long as we're careful."

Nicholas didn't feel comforted. "Okay. But what happened the second time you met Laurent?"

Sam levelled his gaze at him.

"He attempted to bury us in the ruins of Snelling's house."

"He was the one at Snelling's? The one you saw?"

"I didn't want to believe it," Sam uttered. "I had hoped Laurent's blood-lust had either been sated, or he'd met with his own sticky end beyond the boundaries of the Sentinel community. Sadly, it seems he has only gained in strength."

"The Harvester at the school said something about a Tortor," Nicholas said.

The Tortor will rise.

"I've never heard that word before," Sam admitted. He rubbed his neck wearily. "Perhaps that's something you could look into while I attempt to find out what Laurent's up to. Esus will have stationed a number of Sentinels at the school. They'll stop anybody going in, or anything coming out." He gave Nicholas an encouraging shove. "Chin up, it's not over yet. While you were in the shower, I called a friend of mine. Liberty. I've asked her to stop by this afternoon. She's like you. If anybody can help you with your search, she can."

"What about Laurent?"

"I still have a few contacts. I'll touch base with them and see what they know. Don't worry, lad, we're obviously doing something right."

"What do you mean?"

"A viper only attacks if it feels threatened. We're applying pressure in the right places. Now we just need the courage to force the vipers out of their nests—"

"And chop off their heads," Nicholas finished for him.

CHAPTER EIGHT
Cobbles

Rae cast about the market square. She only just caught sight of Twig's scarecrow hair as he disappeared beneath one of the stalls. The job was on. They were using the oldest trick in the book – Twig called it 'looky, looky, I got a cookie' for no apparent reason. She distracted the stall workers while he lifted a couple of apples or a loaf of bread. Once, they'd managed to get away with a side of ham and feasted until their stomachs cramped.

They'd done it a hundred times, but Rae was uneasy. She'd not spotted the chunky girl who had been following her again, but she couldn't shake the feeling that somebody was watching her. More and more, the town was suffocating her. She'd made up her mind. Tonight, she'd leave. She'd wait until Twig was asleep and she'd hitch a ride out of town.

The thought of abandoning Twig wrenched at her. An unfamiliar brew of guilt and something else. An ache deep inside her ribcage. In some twisted way, he'd become family. He felt like a little brother.

He's not your brother, she reminded herself. *He's better off without you.*

A peculiar whistle snapped her from her thoughts. Twig was waiting for her to make a move. She eyed the stall they'd picked. It was laid out with an assortment of pies and meaty delicacies, all shielded from the baking midday sun by a colourful awning. They cost a fortune, no doubt baked by the heavy-set fifty-something overseeing them. He was aided by a bored-looking, pock-faced teenager who Rae assumed was his son.

Easy money.

She strolled over, peering at the pies. The smell caused saliva to flood her mouth. She swallowed and focussed on the task. Out of the corner of her eye, she noticed the teenager watching her and she moved up and down the stall, taking care not to look at him. The fifty-something was busy serving an old lady.

"They're, uh, home-baked."

The pock-faced teenager had taken the bait. Rae smiled inwardly. Always best for them to make the first move. Less suspicious. She looked at the boy and widened her eyes.

"Really?" she asked, sounding impressed. "My mouth's watering already."

Always lie with the truth.

She added coyly: "You make them?"

"Well, uh, I helped," the teen said. She could swear he'd stood up a little straighter, puffed out his chest like a baboon. Boys were so predictable.

Not the boy at the school. Rae found herself thinking about what she'd seen earlier that day. She'd been walking through town when she found herself at the school where the teachers had been killed. And there had been a boy covered in what looked like blood. She was sure she'd imagined it, but she'd felt something. A prickling in her gut.

"Hello?"

She looked at the teenager. "Huh?"

"I asked if you wanted a sample. I'm allowed to give those out." He seemed confused by her sudden lack of interest and he was making up for it with freebies.

"I, uh–"

"Hey!"

An angry shout drew her attention away from the teenager. The heavy-set baker's face had bruised scarlet and he was staring at something. Twig was frozen at the back of the stall, stuffing his pockets with pies. He blinked at the baker, then at Rae. She could see his fox brain whirring, then he darted away beneath the stall.

"Damon, get him!" the baker barked.

The pock-faced teenager scrabbled after Twig.

"Hey, that free sample still going?" Rae called desperately, but Damon wasn't listening. He was already out of the stall and chasing Twig through the market.

"Do you know that little pest?" the baker demanded. Rae found herself caught in a furious glare. She cursed. Not waiting for the baker to grab her, she sprinted after Twig and Damon. For an awful moment she worried she'd lost them, but then she saw the flash of the teenager's trainers and Damon disappeared into an alleyway.

"Thieving little—"

Rae found them on the ground in the alley. Damon was on top of Twig, pummelling him with bony fists. She grabbed the teenager's hair and dragged him away. He squealed and squirmed free, facing her.

"Stupid cow, you're with him?" he panted.

"Don't call her that!" Twig yelled, on his feet again. He tackled Damon and they crashed against the wall. Damon dealt a blow to Twig's jaw. Rae's insides contracted in horror as he crumpled to the cobbles and Damon went for him again.

Heat coursed through her. "Get off him!" she shouted, clenching her fists.

The cobbles rattled like loose teeth beneath them. The air shimmered and boiled. Damon didn't stop.

"I said *stop*!"

Cobblestones erupted from the ground one by one, as if the alley was spitting at the sky.

Damon froze. He and Twig peered around in confusion, suddenly aware that something strange was happening. The stones continued to rattle and pop. The boys turned to Rae.

"Get out of here," she growled.

Damon took one look at her and fled.

"Freak!" he yelled, vanishing back into the market.

"What just happened?" Twig wheezed as she helped him to his feet.

"Let's just go," she said. Already the heat was skimming away and she felt exhausted. She wanted to get back to Retro Threads and shut herself away. Sleep. If she was asleep, she couldn't think about what she'd just seen. What she'd just done.

Beside her, Twig grinned and blood oozed from his cut lip. "Look," he said, pulling a squashed pork pie from his pocket. Rae couldn't look at him. Her gaze was fixed on the other end of the alley.

A dark form watched them. A man. The light behind him obscured his features. The figure turned and strolled away.

Somebody had seen the whole thing.

★

Piano music trickled through the bar, skipping over wine glasses and flirting with the wooden fan overhead. Undulating through the candle-lit atmosphere, the music swooped towards a man perched on a plush barstool. His eyes were closed; all the better to savour the twinkling notes.

Laurent could almost imagine he was somewhere else. Not Bury St Edmunds, where people crawled insect-like through life. Rome, perhaps. He missed Rome. A place of culture and vitality. He hadn't even minded being so near to the Vatican. The power festering there was too old to have any effect on him and he'd made many useful contacts in the city. Funny how evil was always attracted to places of great beauty.

As the music trembled, Nathan's face surfaced unexpectedly in his mind, as if he'd broken through the suffocating bathwater. But Laurent knew he hadn't. Nathan was dead. He'd drowned him. An unfamiliar feeling prodded at Laurent's belly. Not guilt or grief. Sadness. Melancholy. The feelings confused him and Laurent brushed them away.

Nathan was a momentary lapse, nothing more. Laurent had grown bored in Cambridge waiting for Diltraa to fail, and he'd needed some entertainment. Nathan provided just the entertainment he was looking for. It was Nathan's own fault if he'd started developing feelings. Laurent had done the right thing getting rid of him.

When the piano piece ended, he let out a euphoric sigh and raised a beer to his lips. Frédéric Chopin's 'Nortune in C-sharp minor'. He adored it not only for its beauty, but for its insidious power. In 1943, a concert pianist called Natalia Karp had played the piece to SS Captain Amon Göth while she was incarcerated in a Nazi concentration camp.

Göth was so moved by Karp's playing that he spared her life.

Laurent scoffed. Though he adored music, he'd certainly never let anything as useless as emotion stay his hand. Göth had been weak.

Nathan had drowned.

As he sipped his beer, Laurent caught a flash of eyes in the mirror behind the bar. A woman sat in the far corner, contemplating his brooding reflection. This was the kind of establishment that attracted only the wealthy – the price list had seen to that – and the woman was bloated with riches. Laurent doubted she could breathe, her dress was so restrictive, and her flabby face sagged with years of gluttony. Fifty, Laurent guessed. Fifty and lonely. And, it seemed, quite taken with him.

Laurent ignored her. He stared into his own blue, reflected eyes.

He wanted to savour this while he still could. The stench of wealth. The opulence. It wouldn't be long before it was all gone.

He could feel the woman's lustful gaze boring into him. With a twang of irritation, he saw her considering heaving herself out of her chair to join him. To heap flattery at his feet, no doubt, in the hope that Laurent would go home with her. Make her feel something. Rescue her from the pit she'd fallen into.

The thought disgusted him. Where some might pity such a wretched creature, Laurent felt only revulsion; a vague burn of bile. She should be put down. If he could find her pulse in the flaccid folds of that neck, he'd squeeze it until it stopped.

There was a flutter of red and Laurent snapped out of his thoughts.

A woman had entered the bar.

Laurent watched her breeze across the marble floor as if she owned the place. She wore a slip of a red dress; a fashionable, figure-hugging specimen that caressed her hips and trailed off at her knees. Her auburn hair coiled atop her head, fastened with a silver pin.

As she passed a young couple, she drew the attention of a man. His eyes widened and he seemed to forget the woman sitting opposite him. He received a glare and a terse word across the table.

"You never could resist making an entrance," Laurent said as Malika slid onto the stool next to him.

"First impressions," Malika cooed. "More important than even the prettiest face."

The bartender approached nervously.

"White," Malika told him. "Dry." The bartender opened his mouth and she added coyly: "Large."

The bartender's cheeks reddened and he fumbled with a wine glass.

"You're in a playful mood this afternoon," Laurent observed.

"And you're breaking hearts again."

He couldn't help an indulgent glance in the mirror. The fifty-year-old stalker looked crestfallen. She comforted herself with her wine. Laurent sneered.

"This town is even more depressing than the last." Malika sighed, running her finger around the rim of her wine glass. "At least Cambridge had variety. This place is just... dull."

"Not for long," Laurent pointed out, though he agreed. He had been in Cambridge when the snow storms swept in, transforming the city into a forbidding ice sculpture. The very bones of the city had trembled, and the destruction wreaked there fed his own grumbling appetite for carnage. Diltraa destroyed young innocents. Harvesters hunted and killed Sentinels. Malika herself rearranged the Fitzwilliam Museum to her own liking. Through it all, Laurent patiently waited, knowing his time would come.

When the Dark Prophets returned, he would become their General and share in their glory.

"How could anything so important possibly be hidden here?" Malika derided. "They're so privileged. It's all I can do not to start ripping out throats."

Laurent noticed that the bartender was listening. He turned his dark brow on him and the bartender hurried away, busying himself with the dishwasher.

"Soon," he said.

"What's happening with the girl?"

"She's here. I've seen her."

"And?" Malika asked.

"She's going to be a challenge. She's not as moronic as other teenagers."

"What's she calling herself these days?"

"Rae," Laurent grunted. "Rae Walker. Unconventional name for an unconventional person. She'll come around. We just have to wait for the right moment."

"You sound like *him*."

Diltraa. Laurent knew he was nothing like that loathsome hellbeast.

"Patience, my ruby-red rubra," he soothed, baring his immaculate teeth. "She's like a volcano; she'll erupt at any moment. All we have to do is wait."

"Let me guess, you'll be there to catch her when she falls?" Malika teased. She still hadn't touched her wine.

"It's more than that," Laurent said. "She needs me; she'll realise that. She's tough, but she's scared. She has no idea what's happening to her."

"Poor little mouse."

"We found her first, that's the important thing. The school has been prepared. It won't be long."

The piano music continued to tinkle. Laurent watched the young man sitting behind the grand piano, momentarily mesmerised by his dancing fingers. Fine, long fingers. Laurent felt his thoughts drifting and he attempted to rein them back in. He couldn't be distracted; not when everything he had so carefully planned was at stake. The pieces were moving into place. It wouldn't be long.

"And the Hallow boy?" Malika murmured. Laurent detected anxiety from her, which surprised him. He wondered what was setting her on edge. Something to do with the boy. Her own failure to recruit or kill him?

"He has something," Laurent mused, recalling the skinny teenager from the school. "He definitely has something... A pity you weren't able to deal with him when you had the chance." He couldn't resist pouring a little salt into the wound.

Malika responded just how he expected.

"Diltraa." Her shoulders rose like hackles. "He ruined everything. All his talk of biding our time... Then he attacked when he had yet to regain his strength. They cut him down like a weed. He deserves to be back in the fiery pit."

"Not the way I'd expect you to talk about your maker," Laurent observed casually.

"He's gone. He was never going to make it; they're all the same. They cleave to their grand plans but they're unable to see them through."

"Especially when their own Familiars are turncoats."

Smash.

Malika crushed the wine glass in one hand.

The bar fell silent. Dozens of eyes blinked in their direction.

"Temper, temper," Laurent tutted.

The pianist began playing once more and a hum of voices returned. The bartender hurried over to clear away the broken shards.

"Leave the boy to me," Laurent said coolly. He pondered the dregs of his beer. "I'll deal with him."

"Bad boy," Malika purred, licking a drop of blood from her finger. "We should go."

Laurent set his glass down on the bar. The thought of returning to the hotel left him feeling hollow. Unsatisfied. He could afford to stay in any hotel the town had to offer. Funds weren't a problem. There were always rich idiots eager to bankroll his activities if he fulfilled his pledge to bring about the apocalypse. Doom-hounds were always flush; perhaps they'd sold their souls to attain their wealth. He didn't care. It was a perfect business arrangement. They felt important and had something to brag to their friends about, and he could practically print his own money.

Still, a cold, impersonal hotel room was nothing compared to the vibrations of a lived-in home. And he would need to commune with the Prophets again soon, which meant he needed blood. Lots of blood. Why not kill two birds with one stone? A night of entertainment that also furthered his goals?

He peered into the mirror behind the bar and scanned the patrons. Where would he go this time? Whose charity could he exploit? His sly gaze drifted to the fifty-year-old in the corner. She was staring miserably into her wine glass. No, not her. Too easy. He turned to the piano player. Their eyes met and Laurent raised his glass, nodding his appreciation.

The pianist smiled.

★

The Nutshell pub was heaving, though it didn't take much for it to fill up. It was, after all, the smallest pub in Britain – just fifteen by seven feet. The décor was as eccentric as the handful of patrons. Exotic, crumpled bank notes tiled the ceiling. An aeroplane propeller hung on one wall and a stag's head – currently sporting a fashionable tie – kept watch from behind the bar. Most curious of the pub's accoutrements was the mummified cat suspended above the drinking pumps.

In the corner, Sam shovelled the last of the peanuts into his mouth. He paused, remembered something, and reached into his pocket, retrieving Dr Adams's pills. He popped one and washed it down with his shandy.

"Blasted things," he muttered, burying them in his pocket once more. He hardly needed reminding that he wasn't as young as he used to be. He'd been to this pub when he was just a boy with his father. Or, at least, he'd stood outside while his father ducked in for a thirst-quencher. Now he was even older than his father had been when he died. Funny how the tumbling years chipped away at a person's perspective.

He found himself missing Judith more than ever. He thought about her every day. It was impossible not to. Everything reminded him of her. Even Nicholas, whom he'd come to think of as part of his own family. The son they'd never had, perhaps.

Sam realised that memories of Judith had been surfacing more frequently as he spent more time with Nicholas. Guilt wriggled through him and he mentally shook himself. Now was no time to fill his head with sappy reminiscing or secret regrets. It was all just a distraction from the task at hand.

Judith couldn't have known what was going to happen. It was a horrible tragedy, and the injustice of it haunted him still.

He peered down at the *Bury Free Press*, but the paper held nothing that might help with Snelling or Laurent. He read every story nonetheless, scouring every article for anything unusual. The press was an invaluable tool in a Sentinel's investigations; though it was rare for Sentinels to have contacts at the papers, there were often stories that helped. Like the arson attack that was actually an occult sacrifice gone wrong. Or the traffic accident caused by a rampaging hellbeast, later reported as a mad deer.

Sam wished he'd kept in contact with the Bury police, but after moving to Cambridge, he'd let those old connections slip.

What did he have to go on? The odd markings on the floor of the basement in Snelling's house. That was it. That, and the gauntlet Nicholas had seen Snelling use. It unleashed electrical charges that Nicholas said nearly knocked him unconscious. What did that have to do with anything?

And then, of course, there was the matter of Laurent. Sam had already given Liberty a call and asked her to pay Nicholas a visit. She could help him with the seeing glass and perhaps even shed some light on what Laurent had planned. She was Sensitive, after all.

Sam scrunched up the empty packet of peanuts. Aileen had mentioned that the pub's landlord, a Sentinel called Harold, was away, but his son was still in town. Sam eyed the man behind the bar. He was big and bald and certainly looked like Harold. He would probably be good in a fight if the occasion arose, too. Hopeful, Sam approached the bar.

"I don't suppose you're Harold's son?" he asked.

"You want Merlyn," the bartender answered as he unstacked the dishwasher. "That's Merlyn with a Y. He's funny about making sure people know that." He nodded at somebody across the pub and Sam followed his line of vision. Among the patrons he spotted a boy who looked about sixteen. Only slightly older than Nicholas, but just as lean. He was arm-wrestling another youngster at one of the tables.

Sam frowned. That couldn't be him, surely. "The—" he began doubtfully.

"Yeah, the skinny one," the bartender nodded.

Disappointed, Sam thanked him and decided to leave. He'd hoped Harold's son might be able to help, but he couldn't imagine the boy in the corner being any use, even if he was another Sentinel.

As he went to the door, a jubilant roar filled the pub. Merlyn had conquered his friend at the wrestling match. He beat his chest like an ape.

Certain that he was making the right decision, Sam went out into the street.

"Hey, Bogart," a voice called.

Sam turned and found that Merlyn had followed him. Soft hairs sprouted from the boy's chin and a honey-coloured mane was swept back to settle over angular shoulders. Sam caught his breath when he noticed fang-marks and a trickle of blood at the youngster's neck before realising it was a grisly tattoo.

"You looking for me?"

"You're Harold's son?" Sam asked.

"Unfortunately," Merlyn said. "You know him?"

"Once upon a time. Back in the Dark Ages."

"Cool." Merlyn had the scruffy, unkempt look of a student. His crumpled T-shirt was emblazoned with a winged skull. Some colourful rock band, Sam presumed.

The boy laughed. "Didn't know they made them like you anymore," he said. At Sam's questioning look he added: "You were like an old Humphrey Bogart sat over here. Solitary and all that. On the job. Serious as a bloodhound. Could've picked you out of a crowd. Don't worry, to anybody else you're just another old sod with nothing better to do than drink away his pension."

"I'm beginning to understand why Harold needed a holiday," Sam commented.

Merlyn didn't notice the dig – or if he did, it didn't rankle him.

"What brings you to Bury, then?"

Sam considered him. He was having trouble deciding who to trust these days. Liberty was an old acquaintance and always dependable, but people he didn't know? Richard's face flashed in his mind and Sam inwardly recoiled. Even Sentinels couldn't be trusted now. Whoever was responsible for turning Richard and the others had made sure of that.

He became aware that Merlyn was still staring and wondered how long he'd let his thoughts take over.

"That sensitive, is it?" the youngster asked, his eyes alight with curiosity. He chewed a fingernail and spat a bit onto the ground. "Follow me."

Merlyn drew Sam back into the pub. He ducked behind the bar, beckoning for Sam to follow through another door into the house at the back. They stood in a dingy hallway that stank of old beer.

"So?" Merlyn urged.

"It's a difficult time," Sam said gently. "I can't go spilling my troubles to everyone I meet."

"Doesn't stop most people," Merlyn commented brightly. "Seriously, though. You can trust me." He paused, as if mulling over what he'd just said. "Which, I realise, is exactly what the bad guy always says before he stabs some poor prick in the back. But I'm knifeless." He held his arms wide. "See?"

Sam couldn't help smiling. The kid was spunky. Odd, but spunky.

"Besides, I know how to keep a secret. I turned sixteen last week, but Dad's had me tending bar for months." Perhaps noting Sam's unimpressed expression, Merlyn hastily added: "And I know three of the thirteen secret names the Trinity used for Esus. That's one more than Dad. He's been trying to get it out of me for months. I told him I'd give it him if he gave me a raise. Which means I'll probably be taking it to my grave."

"How do you know those names?" Sam asked.

"Picked them up here and there. The first one my dad told me, but only because I found the videos he hid in the loft and was going to tell Mum. How many do you know?"

"All of them."

Newfound respect flooded Merlyn's face. "You must be a bad-ass," he breathed.

"A bad-ass who's at something of a dead end," Sam said, immediately regretting his choice of words.

"What you looking for?"

Sam contemplated Merlyn and sighed. No Harvester was this good, he decided. And so what if he was? The things Sam had to say were probably common knowledge to any Harvester. It was worth a shot.

"I need information," he said.

"About?"

"Harvesters."

"No kidding," Merlyn marvelled. "What are the chances that you, a lone wolf who's lost the scent, would come here, to the very place where somebody's got exactly the kind of connections you need to pick that scent up again?"

"Fate's got nothing to do with it."

"Right." Merlyn was unabashed. "Still, you've come to the right man. I know everybody in these parts, and a few more than that in the neighbouring counties. Just call me The Centipede – I got feelers everywhere."

"What I'm looking for is extremely sensitive," Sam said, suddenly nervous that Merlyn was the sort of person who would shoot his mouth off to anybody. "*Extremely*," he stressed, just to be sure.

"Tact's my middle name," Merlyn grinned. "No, seriously, I hate it. Can't believe my mother lumbered me with it. But then her first name's Pernicious, so what can you do?"

Sam's head was spinning. Partly from Merlyn's babbling and partly because he was on dangerous ground. Could he really trust somebody called 'Merlyn'? He realised he didn't have much of a choice.

"Two names," he said eventually. "I need you to see if anybody can help me with them."

Merlyn nodded, growing serious. He looked even younger than ever. Sam couldn't fault the kid's confidence, though. He wondered what he'd seen in his time. Bury was even sleepier than Cambridge. Merlyn couldn't have encountered much demonic activity. The smooth, scar-free skin of his bare arms suggested as much. The best Sentinels all seemed to have jigsaw-like battle scars under their clothes. Sam had his share. What Merlyn lacked in experience, though, he clearly made up for in talk. And optimism.

"Tell me the names," Merlyn said. "And I'll see if I get any hits."

It was now or never.

"Raymond Snelling," Sam said. He hesitated before he spoke the second name, as if the mere act of uttering it out loud could bring its owner rampaging through the door. "And Laurent Renault."

CHAPTER NINE
Aledites

Nicholas opened the front door and promptly collided with somebody. A girl. She had slivers of purple in her hair and wore a purple hoody, which did nothing to hide the fact that she was larger than the average teenager.

Her eyes widened with surprise.

"Uh, hi," Nicholas said.

The girl averted her gaze.

"Dawn, right?" he asked.

She seemed pre-occupied with the front step. Her hair fell to cover her face and she nodded almost imperceptibly.

"Sorry, I'm in the way," he said. Dawn's nervousness made him nervous, too. He squeezed to the side and Dawn hurried into the house. He heard her climbing the stairs in the main house, and then the click of a door shutting.

"Strange girl," Isabel murmured from his shoulder.

As he prepared to shut the front door, Nicholas noticed another figure coming down the alley. A tall black woman in her thirties. She had braided hair and wore a calf-length green skirt with a sleeveless top. Gold bangles caught the sunlight.

Their eyes locked and the woman smiled warmly as she approached him.

"You must be Nicholas," she said.

"Who are you?" he asked, immediately suspicious. Isabel's claws spiked his shoulder.

"Sam's taught you well," the woman observed, her dark eyes twinkling. "Never trust anybody. My name's Liberty, I'm a friend of Sam's."

This is Liberty? Nicholas thought. Sam had mentioned that she'd be stopping by, but he hadn't pictured the woman who'd turned up. She was slender like a boxer, or a dancer, and Nicholas could easily imagine her going ten rounds in the ring despite her bohemian attire.

"He's not here," Nicholas said. "He went out an hour ago." He could swear the woman was giving him the same curious look that Jessica had the first time he met her. Just who was she?

"Actually, Sam wanted me to talk to you. As part of your *training*." Liberty grunted the last word like a sulky teenager, as if she'd been through it herself and considered it a total bore. "Where you off to?"

"Just for a walk." He'd been planning on going to the Moyse's Hall Museum; Aileen had suggested it might be a good resource, and Nicholas vaguely remembered it as an old, double-peaked building he'd visited once as a child. He'd spent the last few hours in Aileen's study poring over her *Sentinel Chronicles* collection. There was no mention of the word Tortor, though, and he was hoping the museum might be more useful.

The one ray of hope came when he typed '*Tortor*' into a search engine on Aileen's clunky computer. The results chilled him.

Tortor was Latin. It meant executioner or torment.

At first the thought of heading out alone made him nervous. What if Laurent was waiting for him? Nicholas decided that Laurent was the kind of guy who preferred lurking in the shadows over stalking people in broad daylight, though. Besides, he had his trusty guard cat with him. Whatever powers Isabel had possessed as a human seemed to be returning. The way she'd tackled Miss Fink had been impressive.

"Walk sounds good. Want company?" Liberty asked.

"How do I know you're really Sam's friend?" Nicholas was still wary. *Harvesters have many faces*. He couldn't just go off with anybody who appeared on his doorstep claiming to be a friend of a friend.

"You could read my mind if you'd like."

Nicholas jumped. Liberty hadn't moved her mouth, but her voice had vibrated in his head. For a moment he was confused, but then he realised what Liberty was and why Sam wanted her to talk to him.

"You're a—"

"Sensitive. The noun *and* the adjective, but only on good days. Shall we?"

Nervous energy fizzed in Nicholas's belly, as if he'd licked a battery. He'd never met a Sensitive before and Liberty seemed, for lack of a better word, *cool*. For some reason, he'd always pictured psychics as old and shrivelled. Card-readers who huddled in dark tents and smelled like wet dog. Liberty was the total opposite.

They left the alley and wandered toward the Abbey Gardens. Happy shrieks resounded through the park and they strolled along the path between two large flowerbeds.

"This must all seem pretty new and scary," Liberty commented.

"Bury?"

"Oh yeah, Bury's terrifying," Liberty joked. "The grey army's taking over with its battalion of knitting needle-wielding pensioners."

They found a bench that overlooked the kid's play area and sat down. Isabel spread herself out in the shade beneath them. Nicholas wondered how much Liberty knew. She was a Sensitive, but did that mean the secrets of the universe were hers for the taking?

"Don't be nervous," the woman said, as if reading his mind. It didn't put him at ease and she laughed good-naturedly. "You tell somebody you're psychic and they immediately start thinking about all the things they don't want you to know. You can relax, I'm not the prying type."

Nicholas released a breath he hadn't been aware he was holding. "Can you really sense what people are thinking?"

"Thinking, feeling, *not* thinking, you name it. Everybody's different, though. People transmit signals twenty-four-seven, but some are less obvious than others."

"Have you always been able to do it?" Nicholas felt the questions bubbling up from the pit of his stomach, erupting from the place he'd crushed them ever since he'd become aware that he could do things other people couldn't.

Liberty smiled kindly. "It's a gift passed through blood. My father was Sensitive, and my grandmother. Some people inherit big noses or perfect abs. I got something else."

Through blood. Nicholas wondered if his grandparents had been Sensitives. His parents didn't seem like the type.

"And..." Nicholas tried to order the questions, stop them burbling out in a confused mess. "When did you find out how to control it?"

Liberty hissed through her teeth and chuckled. "Too late," she said. "My father tried to advise me, but I was a shy, moody teenager. School was miserable and the more secluded I became, the more I could sense how much of a freak the other students thought I was."

"Sounds familiar." Nicholas had felt like a freak for weeks.

"It will get better," Liberty assured him. "It just takes time. You have to train. Learn how to control it rather than the other way around. How much training have you done?"

Nicholas felt a blush creep into his cheeks. "Uh, some. I used the seeing glass."

"How was it?"

"Horrible."

Liberty laughed. "The first time always is. It'll get easier." She squinted at him through one eye, as if trying to suss him out. "Let's see what you can do."

"That man over there, tell me about him."

Liberty's voice echoed in his head again. He followed her line of vision to a bedraggled man picking cans out of a bin by the play area.

"What do you sense from him?"

Attempting to settle his nerves, Nicholas trained his attention on the bin-raider. He thought of how the seeing glass had made him feel. The calm that flooded through him like fresh water. His muscles relaxed and the park noises became muffled, fading into the background.

Hunger. Fear.

"He's afraid of something," Nicholas said in his mind, wondering if Liberty could hear him.

"Good. What's he afraid of?"

Nicholas squinted, attempting to peel away the invisible layers that shrouded the man. To see inside. An image flashed before his eyes.

The man wears a business suit and holds his head in his hands.

Nicholas pushed harder, attempting to understand what the image meant.

He's lost all of his money and his wife has run off with his friend. He's bankrupt and alone and his house is being reclaimed...

The image faded and the park sounds returned. Nicholas blinked, emerging from the trance, his head fuzzy.

"He lost everything," he said, still reeling over the fact that he'd managed to read the man. It was almost easy, and he hadn't felt nauseated like before. "His job, his wife, his home."

Liberty was looking at him strangely.

"What?" he asked uncomfortably.

"You're a natural," Liberty murmured. "You have a powerful gift."

"I can't always do it. Sometimes it hurts. Sometimes I feel sick. And I can't–" He stopped himself. He'd almost said: *I can't find the girl Esus wants me to find.* His power was fickle, unpredictable. The Sentinels had so many secrets, he wasn't sure if he was expected to keep them, too. Could he tell Liberty why he was in Bury?

"That will pass," Liberty said. "Like any talent, you must take time to hone it, focus it, and learn from your mistakes. Use the seeing glass. The man you just read has few barriers, little protection against us. Reading him is easy if you know how. The same doesn't apply to the agents of the Dark Prophets. They don't like to share their secrets and they have ways of hiding them."

"Something bad is happening here," Nicholas said. "Can you help?"

"I can try."

"I need to find somebody. A girl. But I don't know where to start."

Liberty's eyes were kind. "Finding people's the hardest. Ever heard the phrase 'needle in a haystack'? Try 'needle in a field of haystacks' and you're halfway there. You can't just throw your thoughts out there and hope they land on the person you're looking for. You have to be more specific. You'd need to know something about them. Their name. Or you'd need one of their possessions."

Nicholas sagged. "So basically it's impossible," he said.

"Nothing's impossible." Liberty winked at him. "Use the glass. Keep trying until you can't try any more. Then try again." She checked her watch. "I should see if Sam's back at Aileen's. Coming?"

"I'm going to stay here for a bit," Nicholas said. "See what else I can do."

"Look after yourself, Nicholas. Make your own barriers, protect yourself. Build a wall. You don't want the Dark Prophets in your head, trust me."

He spent another hour in the park, dipping in and out of people's lives. By the time he'd tapped into a fifth person's memories, he could do it almost without thinking. But he began to feel guilty. Even though the things he sensed were surface-level, everyday problems, he was intruding on people's privacy. He knew he had no right to.

Nicholas watched kids frolicking through the park. Was this what the Dark Prophets wanted to destroy? Any semblance of happiness? He had to find a way to prevent that from happening.

Liberty had said he needed something of the girl's to find her. A name or a possession. He had a name. Lydia Green. Esus had said she wasn't called that anymore, but it was a start.

Closing his eyes, he held the name in his head. He tried to imagine what she might look like, or where she might be. Supposedly, she was here in town. But where?

He tried until his head began to pound again and sighed in annoyance.

The museum. He'd go to Moyse's Hall Museum and research the Tortor. The Market Square was just a five minute walk up Abbeygate Street and he might be able to sense something about the girl on the way. He just had to keep trying.

He became aware of snuffling snores coming from beneath the bench. He prodded Isabel with his toe and she shot up as if she'd been electrocuted.

"What? Where?" she hissed, unsheathing her claws.

Nicholas laughed. "Come on," he said.

He wandered through town with Isabel on his shoulder. The images from the seeing glass continued to flicker in his mind. The burning red triangle. The bowler hat. The raven pendant. Were they connected to the girl?

Every girl he passed in the street caught his attention. Could she be the one? He really had nothing to go on. He didn't know what she looked like or how old she was, let alone what name she was going under. Unless the girl at the school really was the one he was looking for. He should be so lucky.

Five minutes later, he was inside Moyse's Hall Museum. It was an unusual place. The floor of the long, low lobby was an uneven patchwork of stone. Sand-coloured columns supported an odd ceiling that swooped and fell in shallow arches.

On his shoulder, Isabel sneezed and Nicholas was glad that there were no museum workers about; they'd surely throw the cat out. Their absence struck him as odd. Were they all on a break? He seemed to be the only person in the building.

The collections were equally odd. The further he went into the museum, the more gruesome surprises it divulged. When it was built in 1180, Moyse's Hall was used as a gaol, and a gibbet still swung from one stony ceiling – a man-shaped metal cage used for displaying the rotting cadavers of criminals and pirates. This gibbet was created in the 1700s for Jonathan Nicols, a man who had butchered his sister.

The contents of one particular glass cabinet gave Nicholas further cause to shiver with revulsion. Inside rested a shrivelled-looking brown book. It was an account of the trial of William Corder, who was found guilty of the infamous 'Red Barn Murder'. The barn itself was in Polstead, Suffolk, and was the meeting place of Corder and his lover, Maria Marten. When they met at the barn one night in 1827, Corder shot Marten dead and fled. After his death by hanging, the record of Corder's trial was bound in his own skin.

"A ghoulish curio," Isabel observed quietly. "Imagine your skin being used to bind a book recounting your death."

The placard said that after he'd been hanged, Corder's body was cut down and taken to the courtroom at Shire Hall where five-thousand-strong crowds were permitted to look in as his corpse was carved open.

"Sick," Nicholas murmured.

"Who's the sicker man – the man who commits a devilish crime of passion, or the man who watches as another is put to death?" Isabel mused.

There was nothing in the museum about the Tortor. He hadn't really expected there to be. Nothing was that easy.

As evening drew in, Nicholas paced through the town, increasingly frustrated that another day had passed and he was no closer to finding the girl.

On Angel Hill, he peered at the Abbey gate; a squat tower with a portcullis and weather-worn statues. He felt a gentle pull toward the park and wandered back inside. His parents had brought him here as a child. Grief spasmed his stomach. He hadn't realised how fresh it still was. The Sentinels and their enemies had been a distraction ever since his parents died, but the pain was still there, needling under the surface.

Isabel hopped from his shoulder and scampered through the bushes. She was growing wilder every day, succumbing to her animal instincts. He was sure he'd spotted her eyeing a bird with a hungry glint in her eye earlier.

They were the only two left in the park. Dusky light washed through the gardens, lending them a magical air. Nicholas's thoughts returned to the images from the seeing glass and frustration moiled in his chest. He kicked a stone that almost hit Isabel.

"Careful, boy!"

"I can't do this," he grunted, slumping against a tree.

"Do what?"

"Any of it, it's useless. All I have to go on is a load of pictures I saw in my head and some vague orders from a guy whose face nobody's ever seen."

"Now now," Isabel tutted. "Feeling sorry for yourself isn't going to help anybody."

Nicholas grit his teeth and kicked the tree. People were counting on him. A lot of people. And Esus had made it sound so easy. *"The knowledge resides dormant in you. It is your duty to unlock it by any means necessary."* But how? And what if he was too late? What if he never figured it out?

"Breathe, boy," the cat said. "We'll tackle one thing at a time. First the girl, then the Trinity."

A chill crept into the air and the sky darkened. Something was wrong. Isabel's mirror-like eyes brightened with concern. What had she sensed? Around them, the trees rolled in the wind, their soft *'shhhhh'* sounds a warning that they shouldn't be there.

A mournful shriek echoed through the park.

Nicholas froze. The hairs on the back of his neck stood on end.

"What was that?" he whispered.

An answering howl reverberated through the air. It was a haunted sound, like a creature in pain, high above their heads. It couldn't be the shadowy murklings, though. They hadn't made sounds like that at the school.

"We must get away from here," Isabel urged, her tail puffing up.

A shadow tumbled out of the sky and rushed past Nicholas. He threw himself to the ground instinctively, dodging sharp talons. The creature – a solid, living thing, not a shadow at all – swept up into the sky again and became lost in dark clouds.

"What the hell was that?!" he exclaimed.

"Something that doesn't seem to agree with us."

He'd seen it before. It was one of the visions from the seeing glass. A swooping monster.

"Great," he muttered. "Thanks for the heads-up."

Another plaintive cry shivered above them, and more winged shapes plunged from the evening sky, soaring toward them. Nicholas raced out of the way, running for the trees. A gust of air blasted at him, accompanied by the flap of large, leathery wings beating just over his head.

His foot jammed into something and he collapsed awkwardly to all fours – just in time for the creature to whorl overhead, screaming in annoyance. It looked like a gargoyle brought to life.

Nicholas looked back and saw that he'd tripped over a branch. He snatched it from the ground and brandished it like a sword.

A winged beast flew at him, yellow eyes piercing the unnatural murk that had descended on the park. Nicholas drew the branch back and buried it in the creature's chest. It emitted a piercing shriek and toppled to the ground. Nicholas tentatively approached, and the monster unfurled its coriaceous wings, turning a squashed, diamond-shaped face in his direction. Slick fangs were bared and the creature hissed. The sound made the hairs on his arms prickle.

Nicholas hit it again and again until the beast lay still.

Enraged whoops battered him from the skies and Nicholas was under attack again. He couldn't tell how many there were, it was impossible to see as the winged things swooped toward him. He wielded the branch in front of him like a sword and took down another.

"There, boy!" Isabel yelled. "To your left!"

Nicholas struck out again, slashing at a third monster's wing so that it tore and the creature toppled awkwardly from the air.

The furious screeching gave way to another sound. Slow, deliberate clapping.

"Not bad. Not bad at all."

The voice came from the side. Nicholas whirled about.

A man stood at the centre of the path. In the gloom, his skin was like ice.

"Who's there?" Nicholas demanded. "Who is that?"

The man smiled.

"The aledites have a very distinctive cry, don't they? They originally hail from the stormy wastelands of the demonic Eld Regions. I believe you've already encountered a demon from that domain. Nasty, boiling hell pit of a place. Small wonder they're so eager to reclaim our world."

The branch felt heavy in Nicholas's hands. Laurent. The Sentinel traitor. He attempted to hold the branch steady in front of him, but he wasn't sure how much longer he'd be able to. Sam's training echoed in his ears.

Hands up. Hands up!

"I had to see for myself the boy who fought Diltraa and lived. Not many can attest to that." Laurent's blond hair was slicked back and he wore a fitted navy jacket. He stood so still that he could be one of the Abbey gate's statues.

Something brushed Nicholas's leg and he almost jumped out of his skin before realising it was Isabel.

"How do you know about that?" he demanded.

Laurent bared perfect white teeth. A row of bleached gravestones.

"I know a great many things about you, Nicholas Hallow. Your mother was a nursery worker; your father a publisher. Both perished in a train crash. Tragic, tragic accident. At school, you received average grades and you were predicted a 'B' in Maths. Not bad, but hardly what one might expect from a boy of your intelligence." The man paused. "Were you distracted at school? That's one thing I don't know. Was it girls? Boys? Or perhaps the sense that you were meant for something bigger than classroom studies. That certain... abilities were going to waste."

The branch drooped in front of him. Nicholas couldn't hold it up any longer.

"Alright, you've read my bio, big whoop," he said. He had to get away. Laurent had killed his entire family. Nicholas didn't want to think about what he might have in store for him.

The man's smile hardened. "Been toughened up by recent events, too. You have such potential, if only you were open to what I have planned."

"You're a monster," Nicholas spat.

"You think you're better than me?" Laurent sighed coolly. "Something tells me we're not all that different, you and I. How well do you really know yourself, Nicholas? Are you kind? Thoughtful? Or are you bull-headed? Brazen?"

"You don't know me."

"I know enough," the man drawled. "The Trinity chose you. You, out of countless others." At Nicholas's look, he sneered. "Oh, yes, I know all about that. The Trinity made you their Earth-bound emissary. Here's a little secret. The Trinity chose you, but the Dark Prophets chose me."

Freezing ice coursed through Nicholas's veins. The Dark Prophets had picked this man to do their bidding? Esus had said that Nicholas was the only one who could resurrect the Trinity. Was Laurent the opposite of that? Did he know how to raise the Prophets?

"They've whispered their secrets in my ear since birth," the man leered. "They're here with us, even now, watching in the night. When they return, I shall by their General, and nobody – not even Samuel Wilkins – will stand in my way." He snorted. "There are only three things in the universe that cannot stay hidden for long: the sun, the moon and the truth. You know, secrets between friends can be deadly."

What was he talking about now? Nicholas was so thrown by the stranger's words that he didn't hear the monster coming. It glided up behind him on silent wings and then steely claws clamped his shoulders.

The ground fell away.

Nicholas yelled as he was dragged up, kicking and flailing, away from solid ground, up into the vaporous nothing of the sky. The branch he'd used as a weapon clattered to the ground.

Below him, Nicholas saw another aledite seize Isabel and wrench her into the air.

"Let's see what your insides are made of," Laurent called up from the path. "Let's find out just how well you really know yourself. Enjoy the view while it lasts."

Within seconds the park was so far beneath them that it looked like part of a toy village. The whole town spread out just beyond his feet. He couldn't help thinking it was lucky he wasn't afraid of heights. He peered up. Large, powerful wings thrashed. Where were they taking him? The monster just seemed to be climbing higher and higher without actually going anywhere.

The question was answered a moment later when the claws at his shoulders slackened.

With a sickening lurch Nicholas knew what was going to happen next.

He was going to be dropped to his death.

CHAPTER TEN
NALE

THE WIND SCREAMED IN HIS EARS. Panic boiled through him and Nicholas couldn't catch his breath. There didn't seem to be any air up here. He kicked his legs and tried not to imagine what it would be like when he hit the ground. Would he feel anything? How many bones would shatter on impact?

"Unhand me, foul beast!"

Isabel's voice rang over the wind and Nicholas saw that she was squirming in the second aledite's grasp. The creatures carrying them were about fifteen feet apart; too far for Nicholas to reach Isabel, but close enough for him to see the cat's eyes were almost entirely black.

Above him, the creature whooped and chittered, revelling in its deadly task.

"I said unhand me!"

Nicholas watched as the cat sank her claws into the monster's clutching mitts, and the aledite shrieked. It faltered and dropped lower, and Isabel scrambled into its face, slashing ferociously at the creature. The aledite flapped lower still, though it remained dangerously far off the ground.

With a final angry scream, the creature seized Isabel, peeled her from its face, and hurled the cat away.

"NO!" Nicholas cried.

She plummeted twenty feet into the Abbey Gardens and crashed into the branches of a tree. Nicholas saw a tiny black shape tumbling limply and then he lost sight of her.

"ISABEL!" he shouted, fear bursting through him.

The aledite that had been carrying Isabel shrieked jubilantly and dive-bombed the park, rippling into the shadows.

Fresh panic tore through him as the claws loosened around Nicholas's shoulders.

"Don't you dare!" he yelled up at the monster.

The aledite peered down at him and bared its fangs in a low hiss. Its breath reeked of rotting meat.

The claws opened and for a second Nicholas was airborne.

Time stopped.

He hung in the balance, supported by nothing more than dying sunlight and rushing wind. For a horrible moment, he was resigned to his fate. In his mind, he saw the ground welcoming him and only hoped it would happen quickly.

Then he snapped to his senses. Instinct took over. In a final act of desperation, he thrashed upwards and grabbed hold of the aledite's barbed feet. The barbs scratched his palms and the creature bellowed furiously, trying to shake him off. Nicholas held on, seizing the creature as tightly as he could despite the stinging in his hands.

The aledite weaved and dove, trying anything to knock him loose.

But Nicholas wouldn't give in. He squeezed tighter still and the aledite roared in outrage. Talons flashed and claws snatched at him.

"Come on, then!" Nicholas shouted. "You ugly, flea-bitten piece of..."

A talon raked through his hair and Nicholas gritted his teeth. He wouldn't let go, not for anything. The aledite could slash at him all it wanted. He wouldn't. Let. Go.

They were over the town now. Nicholas could see the market square far below.

"We need... to go... lower..." he muttered to himself, as if the words alone could steer him to safety.

Escape plans raced through his mind. Maybe if he aimed for one of the rooftops it would break his fall. It was preferable to hitting the ground directly.

A crazy thought struck him and Nicholas knew what he had to do. Looking up, he stared into the sickly yellow diamonds in the centre of the creature's demonic face.

"Come on, then," he murmured under his breath. "NOW!"

He lunged, grabbing one of the aledite's outstretched wings and yanking, hauling downward with all of his strength.

Together, they pitched sideways, half flying and half falling. The aledite caterwauled so loudly that Nicholas wondered if he'd be left deaf. But it was working. They were losing height by the second. The town rushed up to meet them.

Nicholas gasped as a sharp pain exploded in his shoulder and he saw that a talon was buried in it.

His grip on the creature slackened.

The aledite kicked out with all four of its limbs.

Suddenly there was nothing left for Nicholas to hold on to.

He fell.

He stared down as a roof grew larger until all he knew was crunching, smashing pain and the sound of tiles splintering under his weight. The momentum carried him over the edge of the rooftop and Nicholas sailed into the air once more.

The cobbled street below him beckoned.

Then it was all around him.

Then there was nothing.

*

The skies were clear tonight; a dark canvas studded with stars.

Benjamin Nale contemplated a swallow as it zipped back and forth across the sea. He squinted and drew on the last of his cigar, then dug the stub into the sand with his boot.

The sea was as still as the heavens. A hush had fallen over it, as if a siren's song had lulled it into a glassy slumber. Across the water, Nale glimpsed distant, twinkling lights. The Wash was a square-shaped cove and Snettisham locals often remarked that this portion of The Wash was where "Norfolk stares at Lincolnshire". It was a drowsy, enchanting place full of birdsong and merfolk murmurs.

"Zeus!" Nale barked.

A dog trotted obediently away from the water's edge. Its shaggy silver coat shimmered in the moonlight and its considerable frame loomed larger as it approached. Nale patted the dog's head and it nuzzled his hand wetly. The Irish Wolfhound almost came up to Nale's waist, which was impressive given the man's own height. They trudged over the beach's sandy peaks until they were back on firmer ground and the dry marram grass crackled underfoot.

Nale was a man of goodly dimensions. Pushing fifty, he towered over most people. He walked with a perpetual hunch, as if attempting to diminish his size, and scratched at his bushy beard, the smell of nicotine still strong, trapped under grimy nails. Despite his size, Nale barely made a sound. He seemed to always be walking on cotton wool.

Zeus darted ahead, having spotted the caravan in the distance. It rested in an isolated part of the coastal lands, away from the holiday trailers and out of sight of the main tourist roads. A long hedgerow shielded most of the wagon from sight, and if the lights were out it was almost invisible in the dark.

It had been home for half a decade. An old traveller's wagon with large wooden wheels and fragments of carnival posters forever engrained in its ribcage. A pipe poked out through the caravan's roof and three suspended steps led up to the crooked front door. It was a ramshackle old thing from another time, but Nale was more content here than he had been anywhere else.

Zeus was scratching eagerly at the door, whining softly by the time Nale strolled up.

"Enough," Nale told the dog. It fell silent.

Inside, Nale lit a gas lamp and fed Zeus. The dog ate noisily in the corner, then flopped onto a mound of blankets, watching its master contentedly as he boiled a beaten-up kettle over a camping stove.

Nale had never been a big sleeper. The night-time hours were his favourite. The world was at peace, then. The insatiable squawks and spasms of civilisation ceased, and the silence was blissful. At this late hour, you could almost feel the earth breathing.

Nale tapped the gas canister of the stove. It resounded hollowly. Time to buy a refill. Next time he ventured into town he'd pick up a couple.

The inside of the caravan twitched in the lamplight. Puppets dangled from the ceiling, grinning grotesquely at one another, and a samurai sword was strapped to the wall above a row of coffee tins. It was part Geppetto's workshop, part knick-knack repository, all home; a crammed, unrestrained mess that spoke of Nale's many collected interests.

He rifled around in a box of old records. Retrieving a battered LP, he blew dust from it. He'd not listened to music for a while. The return of the summer sun must have affected him more than he would ever admit.

The record cover was a montage of black and white photos, over which was scrawled in red: *The Rolling Stones – Exile On Main St.*

Nale showed Zeus the LP. The dog barked and Nale nodded.

The speakers crackled as he dropped the pin into the record's first groove, and the unmistakable thrum of 'Rocks Off' set the caravan's lighter knick-knacks rattling. Nale moved around the inside of the caravan, wiping a mug clean with a faded dishcloth and foraging about in the old coffee tins, scooping teaspoons of dried powder into the mug. He kicked a boot to the beat and Zeus barked in appreciation.

Nale eased himself into a beanbag chair with an old-man sigh, the steaming brew clasped in thick, hairy fingers. His head bobbed and Zeus closed his eyes.

Only a handful of years ago, Nale couldn't have told anybody what contentment felt like. It was an alien, abstract concept that he couldn't believe existed in the realm of experience. Life had been a grind. An endless routine of hunting and slaying with no thought for his own life beyond those inherited duties. He was glad he'd escaped.

The guilt never left him, though. No, not guilt. He didn't feel guilty at all. Escaping was the first choice he'd ever made that was entirely selfish; a choice to better his circumstances, to live free. It wasn't guilt that haunted him. It was the sensation that now he was the hunted.

Zeus raised his head, ears cocked. In a flash, the dog was at the door, an uncertain grumble in his gullet.

Nale stiffened. He ambled over to the record player and flipped up the needle.

Silence.

Nale listened. Had they found him? Were they here to take him away? Or worse, punish him? He wriggled free of those nipping worries. It had been years, and he'd been careful.

He went to the caravan door, pushing Zeus back.

"Bed," he told the dog. Begrudgingly, Zeus obeyed him.

Nale pushed open the door.

Hands lunged from the darkness and Nale was dragged outside.

He heard the caravan door slam shut, muffling Zeus's frantic barks.

A fist went into Nale's gut. Once. Twice. He coughed and swung in retaliation, but it was too dark. He saw shapes gathered around the caravan. Men. A blinding blue light flashed and something barrelled into Nale's chest with such force that he was lifted off his feet. He rocketed backwards, crashing against the side of the caravan. He landed face-first in the mud.

Another flash and Nale heard a strangled cry. He realised it had come from his own throat. He squirmed in agony.

Hands dragged him to his feet. The Earth tilted on its axis. Nale resisted the urge to vomit. He stood groggily, held up by two men, one on either side of him. Their grip was unrelenting.

In front of him, a gathering of six other men stood unmoving. The one at the centre was different. He wore some sort of metal glove on one hand.

"Benjamin Nale."

The men parted and a woman slithered between them.

Red fabric wrinkled like raw flesh.

Nale couldn't move. He was transfixed by snow-white skin, blood-red lips, a slender neck...

"Good evening, Benjamin."

The woman's voice was lazy and smothering, dripping with a deadly kind of venom.

In the caravan, Zeus barked wildly, throwing himself against the door.

Through the grogginess, Nale felt something probing at the edge of his mind, where his thoughts met infinity. He stared defiantly into that pale face, resisting whatever charms the beautiful newcomer was weaving.

"Why is a strapping man of your moral fibre hiding in the wilds of Norfolk?" the woman teased.

He didn't answer.

Her lips ruptured into a smile. "Who keeps you warm at night?" she massaged. "Surely not the dog?" She trailed a finger across her exposed breast bone.

Nale spat at her feet.

"Malika—" one of the men said, but she raised a hand to silence him.

"A man of few words," the woman called Malika observed. "That won't be a problem."

She slunk closer, raising a hand to brush his boulder-like shoulder.

"Strong, vital man," she noted. "The fresh air has built you up. It has a tendency to do that. You're a difficult man to find, Benjamin. The search was justified."

Nale struggled against the hands holding him, but his captors wouldn't yield. *Harvesters*, he thought as the fog in his brain began to clear. They couldn't be anything else. But... Harvesters working for somebody? That was unheard of. He'd been out of the loop too long, evaded that world to his own detriment. He had no idea what was going on. Self-serving Harvesters working for this woman? It might as well start raining frogs.

"Not difficult to understand why you fled here," Malika added conversationally. "Look at the stars. How beautiful they are. Don't they just make you want to dance?" She twirled and her dress fanned out around her. "'Twas noontide of summer, and midtime of night, and stars, in their orbits, shone pale, through the light,'" she quoted, coming to a standstill. "A shame they'll soon all be blotted out."

Nale's head was clearing and he was tiring of this.

"Just do what you're going to do," he snarled.

Malika gasped theatrically. "He speaks!" she exclaimed, rushing at him. "The man mountain has a tongue. What other uses has he for such a defiant instrument?"

Zeus's barks grew hoarser by the minute. The door shuddered as the dog pawed at it.

Malika clapped her hands and clasped them before her.

"You're right," she said. "Let's move along. I have an offer. It's quite simple really: you do as I say and Sebastian here won't kill you." She gestured at the Harvester wearing the gauntlet. "Join us," she cooed.

"And you'll become part of a formidable army. An army that will have this world on its knees."

Nale squinted at her wearily.

"Tried that," he grunted. "Didn't work out."

"That's right." Malika nodded, unsettling her auburn curls. "You defected. You're a traitor; a filthy runaway. I wonder what the Sentinels would do if they found you here? What's the bounty on a runaway nowadays? Last I heard it was a princely sum. Perhaps we'll just cash in."

She gave him a look – the kind a snake gives a small animal before it swallows it whole.

"You have no loyalty to them; what did the Sentinels ever do for you?" she asked. "You abandoned your family, severing all ties with your unique lineage. Join us and they'll be cowering at your feet. It'll be like stepping on snails."

Nale hung his head. He couldn't look at her.

Malika pressed a hand to his chest.

"Trust me," she lulled. "It hurts far less if you consent. Join me at the beach. I'll be waiting."

The hand left his chest and Nale heard the woman's footsteps softly retreating. He was alone with the Harvesters.

Boots approached and the one called Sebastian stood a few feet away, pointing the gauntlet at Nale.

"She lied," the Harvester uttered unsympathetically. "This is going to hurt. A lot."

Sparks burst around the gauntlet. Electrical currents that burned blue in the dark. They gathered between the device's fingers and the Harvester grinned, his face lit up as he aimed the lethal charge at its target.

The gauntlet erupted. Blue energy crackled through the air.

Nale let out a howl and flexed, dragging one of his captors off his feet and into the path of the blue lightning.

The Harvester let out a strangled scream and slumped to the ground, steam boiling off him.

Nale clutched at his other captor and wheeled him about, tossing him like a shot-put.

The man crashed into Sebastian and they landed in a heap on the ground.

NALE

As the other Harvesters charged, Nale ripped open the caravan door. An angry, salivating mass of gnashing teeth and bloodshot eyes flew out. The Harvesters yowled as Zeus tore at them, maiming and ripping, lunging for arteries. He was nimble enough to dodge their blows and savage enough to kill with a single bite.

The Harvester with the gauntlet got to his feet and aimed it at Nale. Not giving him the chance to ignite it again, Nale bowled into the Harvester, crashing into him with his full weight. Sebastian shrieked furiously and Nale heard the wind rush out of him as his back struck the earth. Nale went to hit him, but a hand grabbed his balled fist and somebody dealt a blow to the back of his head.

Stars exploded in Nale's vision, and he slumped forward, almost crushing Sebastian. The Harvester was still opening and closing his mouth silently, attempting to draw breath.

From behind him, hands came. They clamped around Nale's thick neck, attempting to squeeze.

A growl rumbled nearby and the hands snapped away from him, were followed by a gurgling scream.

As the stars cleared, Nale saw that Sebastian had almost recovered. The Harvester raised the gauntlet and went to shove it in Nale's face, but Nale reacted too quickly. He swung a massive fist into Sebastian's jaw.

Teeth and blood splattered the ground.

Sebastian lay unconscious. Or dead. Nale couldn't tell.

Sucking in great lungfuls of air, Nale stayed where he was, crouched over the Harvester.

A stillness settled over the clearing. Nale peered blearily around and saw that the other seven Harvesters all lay dead or unconscious, defeated by Zeus. The dog stood panting among them, muzzle red with blood, tongue lolling from his jaw.

"Good dog," Nale muttered.

Zeus went to the caravan and collapsed by the stairs.

Recovering, Nale inspected the gauntlet still attached to the Harvester's hand. He prodded it gingerly. When nothing happened, he pulled at it, wrenching it free. It was heavy, made of metal, intricately crafted. Nale peered at it, holding it up to the moonlight so that it glinted coldly. The light caught in five amber stones affixed to each finger and thumb.

"Its powers remain a mystery."

Nale's head whipped around at the voice.

A figure stood beside Zeus. The dog lay still, barely breathing, eyes fixed on Nale.

"You're the first to lay hands on one." Esus's voice throbbed in the clearing. "The first to overpower anybody in possession of one."

Nale simply stared at him, still on his knees in the dirt.

"You may stand."

Cautiously, Nale got to his feet. He cradled the gauntlet in his hands and stood facing the masked entity.

"Your whereabouts have been known to us for years," Esus's voice rumbled, as if he had read Nale's mind. "That choice was yours to make. There will be no reprisals."

The phantom gestured at the gauntlet.

"This, however, is another matter. You will take the instrument to Cambridge. To a woman named Liberty Rayne."

When Nale offered no reply, Esus added: "Consider it your final duty as a Sentinel."

Nale contemplated him for a moment. Then, slowly, he nodded.

CHAPTER ELEVEN
Detonation

He was falling again. All he could see was the road below, the cobbles looming larger as he plummeted. He couldn't do anything to stop it. Wind howled, distorted by inhuman shrieks. The cobbles span. He threw out his hands...

There was a flash of red and Nicholas jolted upright.

Pain split his head open and, weak with nausea, he collapsed back onto something soft.

A beeping sound tapped out morse code nearby. A sigh of gas. Somebody calling out meekly.

Nicholas blinked through the grogginess and realised he was in bed. The blankets were bound tightly around his legs and he was propped up on funny-smelling pillows. The row of beds opposite him were all occupied by people in various stages of illness, all of them far older than him.

Hospital, he thought. *What happened?*

He felt like he'd been hit by a bus. Or ten buses. A bus the size of ten buses, perhaps. Massaging his throbbing temples, Nicholas attempted to lift his right arm and found that he couldn't.

It was in a sling around his neck, encased in plaster.

"What the—?" he began, and then he remembered.

The man in the park. The flying monsters.

The fall.

"Christ," he muttered. Luck wasn't on his side. In the past two weeks alone he'd been in a bus crash, fought a demon, nearly died in a collapsing house and now this. Still, he was alive. Which wasn't something he felt particularly positive about at this moment in time.

"Oh, you're up. I just came to wake you – can't be too careful with a concussion."

A young man in a nurse's uniform strolled up to Nicholas's bed.

"How you feeling?" he asked.

"Annoyed."

The nurse laughed. "You had quite a fall," he said, taking a clipboard from the foot of the bed and scanning the notes. "It's lucky you didn't crack your skull open."

"Feels like I did."

"Naw, just your common, garden variety ulnar fracture." The nurse seemed to notice Nicholas's blank face and winked, adding: "You've broken your forearm. Or at least fractured it. Only in one place, though. Hardly worth the bother."

Nicholas cursed under his breath. He'd never broken anything before. It didn't feel how he imagined it might. Rather than jagged pain, it just felt... *wrong*. Like his arm had been turned inside out. The broken arm was hot and uncomfortable, throbbing under the plaster. He attempted to wiggle his fingers and they moved sluggishly, transmitting a twang of discomfort. Sweat broke out on his forehead.

"What exactly were you doing on that rooftop? Pretending to be Batman?" the nurse asked.

"Something like that," Nicholas muttered. "Who are you?"

The nurse put the notes away. "You really were out of it last night if you don't remember that. I was here when they brought you in. You were in and out of consciousness while you were treated." He paused. "I'm Alastair, staff nurse." He took the hand in the sling. "You getting much pain?"

"A little."

"How about the head? Any dizziness? Nausea?"

"Not really."

Alastair nodded, releasing his hand. "I'll get you some water. You need to stay hydrated."

"Can you call somebody for me?" Nicholas realised that Sam probably didn't know he was here. He didn't have any ID on him and he wasn't a local. He probably had 'John Doe' written on the whiteboard behind his bed.

"Nicholas?"

Sam appeared at the end of his bed and Nicholas had never felt more relieved. The old man was clutching his fedora, face drawn tight with worry. He hadn't shaved, and sharp little silver hairs needled across his jawline.

"That's him." Sam nodded at the woman accompanying him. "Thank you, nurse."

The woman beside him nodded back and left.

"What's happened here, then?" Sam asked, strolling into the cubicle. Relief replaced the anxiety on his face. The worry lines settled back into their usual wrinkles as he appraised Nicholas's broken arm; the cuts and bruises he could feel on his face.

"I..." Nicholas began, but he fell silent, aware of Alastair the nurse.

Sam seemed to understand. He reached a hand out to the other man. "Samuel Wilkins," he said. "Nicholas's legal guardian."

"Trouble always finds its way home, eh?" the nurse joked. "I'll leave you two in peace."

When he was gone, Sam sat at the bedside. He looked oddly small to Nicholas, who was spread out on the raised mattress.

"Legal guardian, huh?" Nicholas said.

"It's the truth," Sam replied. "Your parents signed you over to me in their will."

"And you didn't think that was something I should know about?"

"You were under the care of the *Vaktarin* within days, what difference did it make?"

It made all the difference, Nicholas thought. He had a choice. Legally, he was Sam's responsibility. He needn't be cooped up in that big fusty house.

"How did you know I'd be here?" he asked.

"Process of elimination. Lad, what happened?"

Nicholas wiggled his plastered fingers at the old man. "Laurent. He was in the Abbey Gardens. Then these *things* came and..." He stopped. Something was niggling at him, but he couldn't think clearly through the throbbing in his arm.

All the colour drained from Sam's face. "Laurent," he said softly. "I'm sorry."

"Not your fault."

"It's my job to protect you."

"I think that's more of a two-man job," Nicholas said. "Anyway, I'm here aren't I? Even if Laurent did want me out of the way." He shifted uncomfortably in the hospital bed. At some point, he had been put into a gown, though he couldn't remember when, and it was tangled up around his legs. He felt trapped.

"Esus told me that the Trinity chose me," he continued softly, almost thinking out loud. "Apparently I'm the only one who can bring them back. Laurent knew that." He checked Sam, seeing that the old man's face had sagged, though he wasn't sure why. Concern? Horror? Nicholas continued anyway. "Laurent said that the Dark Prophets had chosen him. I think... he wants to raise the Dark Prophets."

They stared at each other for a moment, neither knowing what to say.

"That is something we'll have to find out for ourselves," Sam breathed finally. "You get your rest now, and when you get back to Aileen's, she'll have cooked up something extra tasty, I'm sure."

Nicholas smiled, but his smile slackened as that niggling feeling returned. With a sickening lurch he realised what was bothering him.

"Isabel!" he cried. "Where's Isabel?"

★

Soft footfalls rustled nearby. A shriek stabbed, wrapped in unfamiliar giggles.

The darkness receded momentarily, just long enough for her to see hands reaching through the undergrowth. She was too weak to resist and Isabel surrendered as she was bundled into rough fabric that reeked of damp.

What must have been some time later, it was darker. The stink of damp remained and she was still wrapped up snugly. Everything ached when she tried to move.

A bowl rested nearby. The smell of warm milk turned her stomach.

In the gloom, a shape moved. Isabel tensed.

There was a ripple of movement followed by quiet footfalls.

A hand scratched behind her ear and Isabel slipped into darkness again.

*

It was dark in Retro Threads. It was always dark. With the windows boarded up, the summer sun couldn't find its way inside and Rae was grateful for the coolness as she clambered through the latch window.

In the shop corner, Twig lay on a mound of blankets. Despite the heat, he had one pulled up to his chin. Even in the gloom, his black eye stood out and his lip was cut from the fight with the teen from the marketplace. Damon. Rae had always thought Twig possessed a wiry resilience, but now he looked tiny and vulnerable.

"Here," she said, handing him a half-drunk bottle of Coke. It was crazy what people threw away. Twig took it and gulped it down. She sat beside him, leaning her back against the wall. Her plan to leave town had been delayed a whole night thanks to the fight. She didn't know what to do. Leaving Twig now would be heartless, a quality she had always prided herself on. So why couldn't she just go?

"Don't leave me."

She rested her head back and stared at the ceiling. "I'm not."

"You are," Twig said. She peered sidelong at him. He didn't look feral anymore. He looked like a scared little boy. "You've wanted to for ages. I can tell."

Rae didn't know what to say.

"Tell me a story," Twig said.

"I'm rubbish at telling stories."

"Tell me about Kay."

Rae reacted as if she'd been punched. "How you know that name?" she snapped.

"Heard you when you were asleep. Who is she?"

Rule number two. *Don't talk about your past.*

"Nobody." She closed her eyes and Kay's face was waiting for her. Eyes bulging in fear. Rae jumped to her feet and went to the counter. She sorted through the scraps of food, though for once she wasn't hungry.

"Was she your friend?"

Rae slammed her hand against the counter. A familiar, anxious energy throbbed in her chest. She tried to force it down. Crush it into nothing. But it hurt. It didn't want to be suppressed.

"She's dead."

"How did she die?"

I killed her.

"Accident," Rae said. "I'm not talking about it."

The air had been sucked out of the shop. Her insides tingled. Heat sizzled through her; spiny, angry, insistent. She couldn't control it. She had to.

Her head snapped toward the latch window. Somebody had lifted it up from the outside and a face appeared.

"What you doing in here?" a voice asked. Somebody sniggered, then a shape clambered awkwardly through the window and dropped to the floor. Two more gangly shapes followed.

"Rae?" Twig asked.

"Rae, is it?" asked one of the shapes. She'd recognise him anywhere. Damon, the pock-faced teenager from the market. Except he wasn't blushing and puffing his chest out anymore. He jeered at her. "Nice place you've got here. Cosy."

They must have followed her. Rae inwardly kicked herself. She was getting sloppy. There was too much going on and now they'd found her home.

Home. It was all she'd ever wanted. Somewhere safe. Every new place had the potential, but none of them were ever home. She had to keep moving.

"Get out of here," she said.

"Careful guys," Damon said to his friends. "She can do stuff. Why don't you show us what you can do?"

"What kind of stuff?" his friend asked. He was stocky with greasy black hair.

"Show 'em," Damon ordered. "Or maybe you really are just a thieving rat."

Rae was about to throw herself at him, but Twig beat her to it. Warbling, he pounced from the pile of blankets in the corner and hurled himself at Damon. The teenager was taken aback, but he recovered quickly. As Twig clawed at him, Damon seized him around the neck and held him in a choke hold.

"You could work on your hosting skills," the teenager growled. Twig wriggled in his grip but it was no use.

"Leave him alone," Rae shouted. Anger roiled inside her like a living thing. The mannequins trembled beneath their plastic sheets.

No, she thought. Kay's face came to her and Rae felt her grip loosening on the thing festering inside. *Don't*, she told herself. *Don't do it.*

"She's nuts," Damon's friend said. "Let's get out of here."

"Not until she shows us," Damon said coolly. He shook Twig and the boy yelped.

"Stop it!" Rae cried. Her hands were in her hair. The pounding in her skull was unbearable.

Breathe. Breathe.

But she couldn't breathe. All she could feel was the fury.

"She's a freak," Damon continued. "A filthy freak."

"She's not!" Twig cried, squirming in the teenager's arms.

The light in the shop was dimming.

Breathe. Breathe.

She couldn't let go. If she let go, it would all be over. She couldn't let what happened to Kay happen again.

Kay. That look on her face.

It was burned into Rae's memory. That look of surprise. Then everything had gone black and she'd heard screaming. Rae had come to in the street. She'd passed out. And there was Kay. Broken by a bench. The impossible angle of her neck…

"No!" Rae sobbed.

Pain squeezed her heart. Anxious, pumping. She hated everything and everybody. But most of all she hated herself. If she just let go…

Twig roared and sank his teeth into Damon's arm. Howling, the teenager tossed him to the floor.

"Get him," Damon ordered. His friends grabbed Twig and hoisted him off the ground.

"No!" Rae yelled. She groped at one of the boys, but Damon forced her back. She tried to get past him and he threw a punch. Rae reeled back, her cheek stinging.

"Stay back, freak," Damon warned.

The air simmered. Queasy energy pulsed through her.

"Hold him," Damon ordered his friends. He raised a fist, ready to lay into Twig.

"NO!" Rae shouted.

The last thing she saw before the shop exploded was Damon's face contorting in surprise.

★

Fuzzy darkness retreated. Where was she? What had happened?

"Rae," a voice said.

Rae blinked through the daze, sat up. She was covered in dust. No, not dust. Ash. It rained down on her, fluttering and feather-like. The air smelled burnt. She was sitting in a crater of cinders. Burnt wood and smashed things.

For a moment, she was five years old again. Had awoken in her burning bedroom with her foster parents screaming on the other side of the door. Then she remembered.

The shop.

She gazed around, shock and disbelief coursing through her.

The shop was blackened and burnt. It had collapsed in on itself. And there, half-buried in the debris, was Twig. He wasn't moving. He looked...

"No!" she cried.

"Rae."

She turned at the sound of her name. A man stood amongst the rubble. Pale, blond, worried.

The museum man.

"Rae, it's time you came with me."

CHAPTER TWELVE
THE GIRL

NICHOLAS WAS RELIEVED TO BE BACK at Aileen's. After a restless night's sleep filled with thrashing gargoyles, Sam had fetched him from the hospital and driven him back to the safehouse. The landlady crushed him to her bosom and made a great fuss before she let him trudge wearily up to his room.

Isabel's absence was a yawning hole. He was surprised at how much he missed her and blamed his vulnerable state. He needed to get back out there and find out if she was okay. He had to know that she wasn't dead.

He remembered her limp body tumbling through the tree and shuddered.

Laurent was planning something. The attack in the Abbey Gardens had been an act of war. It couldn't have been a coincidence that he had found Nicholas in the park. Nicholas was quickly coming to the conclusion that coincidences didn't exist. He was lucky to be alive.

A wave of tiredness made him dizzy and he shuffled toward the bed, catching his reflection in the mirror as he went. His face was a patchwork of scratches and an ugly bruise coloured his jaw. He drew his T-shirt up to expose his belly. More bruising. A watercolour blend of blue and green. No wonder he ached.

He got onto the bed and propped himself up, unable to find a comfortable position with his arm in the sling. After a while, he finally drifted off. He slept dreamlessly. But then…

The woman in red was dancing. She stared at him as she swept the crimson folds of her dress in silky ripples, swaying to some unheard music.

Nicholas couldn't move. Thorny restraints snared his limbs, and though he battled against them, they refused to yield.

The woman sashayed closer and he could smell her. The fresh tang of blood. And something else that he couldn't place. A scent so familiar it made his arm hairs bristle. The woman stretched out long fingers and stroked his cheek. Sharp pain cramped his stomach, but he couldn't resist her. Blood trickled over her face and her hot breath caressed his lips...

Nicholas awoke with a gasp. He was slick with sweat and he had a crick in his neck. And he wasn't alone. Startled, he sat up, quickly regretting the sudden movement. He'd forgotten about the broken arm and the bruises. He cursed under his breath and the girl sitting in the chair in the corner fidgeted nervously.

"Uh, Aileen wanted me to bring you these," Dawn mumbled. She spoke so quietly he could barely hear her. She couldn't hold his eye for long, either. The purple mascara twitched agitatedly and she looked down at the tub in her hands, which she placed on the bed beside him.

"Brownies," Nicholas said appreciatively, peaking under the lid. "Nice."

"She said you could use some sugar," Dawn murmured. She was skittish as a mouse. Everything about her was purple, too – her hoody, her trousers, the colour in her brown hair. Even her rosy cheeks looked vaguely violet as she blushed.

"Cheers for bringing them up," Nicholas said, the girl's obvious unease fuelling his own. "Er, you want one?"

She shook her head. Contemplated the floor.

"I know who did this to you." Her lips barely moved as she spoke. The words seemed to whisper straight from her mind into the air.

"You do?"

"He calls himself Laurent." Dawn shrugged and pulled at the sleeve of her hoody, staring at the frayed threads.

Nicholas had to stop himself lurching upright for a second time. "What do you know about Laurent?"

She blinked at him and Nicholas saw something in her face that surprised him. Pain.

"Did he hurt you, too?" he ventured. She didn't look physically injured, but he had a feeling Laurent enjoyed toying with people in a lot of different ways. Eventually, Dawn nodded and the hair fell across her face. Her voice came out between the mousy fringes and she picked at her chipped nail polish.

"It started with my parents," she said. "They're, um, not around anymore, but when they were, I went everywhere with them. They were sort of crazy about travelling, exploring, experiencing different cultures. They didn't think a Sentinel should stay in one place. Dulled the senses, they said." She shook her head. "Anyway," she continued, as if struggling to stay on point. "We went everywhere. Tibet. Rome. Australia."

"I still don't—"

"There was this guy," Dawn cut in, her voice rising only slightly. Nicholas smiled; maybe Dawn had a backbone after all. "We were in Cambodia with the Khmer Loeu people, a hillside tribe. Mum wanted to study their spiritual rituals; they were pretty radical. The leader of the tribe had met somebody who called himself Samnang. It means 'good fortune'. He'd travelled up from New Zealand. He was a wanderer. I... didn't like him." Nicholas saw her shudder. "Neither did Dad. There was something cold about him. He didn't seem right, like he thought he was better than everybody else. But the leader of the tribe let him in; he was desperate. A young woman was showing signs of possession and nothing had worked. Samnang performed a ritual and the woman seemed to recover. Samnang left and that was that. A week later, all the men in the tribe were gone, including Dad."

"Gone?" Nicholas asked.

Dawn nodded, but didn't look at him. "There was only ash left. In their beds, on the street, wherever they had been when... Nothing but ash. He burned the village to the ground. Mum and me, we... Well, she's not been the same since."

"When was this?"

"Six months ago."

"I'm sorry." He didn't know what else to say. He remembered one of the images from his vision. Fire and people running in fear. Had he seen that Cambodian village? He remembered the other images. The burning red triangle. Elvis Presley. The raven pendant. Three objects like pods. The well bathed in moonlight. And Malika drenched in blood.

"So... who was the man?" he continued. "Who was Samnang?" He asked, but he already knew the answer.

"Now, he calls himself Laurent," Dawn said softly. "After what happened in Cambodia, Mum was brought back to England. She's still in hospital. She... kind of lost it. Before Nan forced me to stay here, I stole Mum's credit card and tried to find out who Samnang really was and why he'd targeted the Khmer Loeu tribe. I went to the museums in London, even caught a few flights to Europe."

Nicholas was surprised that somebody as quiet as Dawn was so resourceful. She'd probably seen more of the world than he had.

"And?" he asked.

"He had different names everywhere he went, but people always remembered him. It was difficult to forget him after the things he did. He wanted power, that's the main thing. Whatever he did to people, he did it for power."

She broke off for a moment, seemed to attempt to gather the story back into a coherent form. "He let something slip one night when we were with the Khmer Loeu people. Before he killed them all. He'd drunk something the tribal leader had brewed and it seemed to loosen him up. He told us a story he'd heard on his travels. There would be a boy and a girl and they'd bring about the end of the world."

Nicholas frowned, unnerved. The way Dawn looked at him, it was clear that she thought *he* was that boy.

"He... Later that evening, I was walking alone and he came up to me. I think he thought... Well, I don't know what he thought. Maybe I was the girl from his story. He put a hand on my head and then walked away. I had a headache for days."

"What does he want?"

"The Dark Prophets," Dawn whispered. "Everywhere I went, there were folktales similar to the one Laurent told us; the boy and girl who would destroy the world." She snuck a curious look at Nicholas. "The more I looked, the more I realised Laurent had twisted the story's meaning. Maybe to scare people, maybe because he was delusional."

She became animated suddenly, reaching into a backpack on the floor beside her chair. She drew out a battered laptop and brought up a photograph of an old scroll.

"This was in the Kolkata Museum in West Bengal." The soft paper bore faded, beautiful images. A star being delivered to Earth, and from the star emerged two figures. "Ancient Indians told that the heavens would deliver two children to the Earth, and they'd save mankind." She clicked open another image, this one of hieroglyphs chipped into golden stone. "The Egyptians said that the children would wipe out humanity and usher in a new beginning."

Nicholas felt lightheaded. Could this really be about him? Civilisations all over the world seemed to have foretold his birth centuries ago. He'd think it was ludicrous if he hadn't become accustomed to such bizarre developments.

Dawn brought up a final image, this one of runes on a crusty stone tablet. "The Anglo Saxons give the clearest telling of the story," she continued softly. "Two children will enter the world and bring with them destruction."

Nicholas thought of Orville.

Dawn continued, "Then they say that the children will be responsible for a resurrection; for bringing the ancient gods back into the world. That's the bit Laurent was most interested in."

"He wants to bring back ancient gods?"

"The Prophets. The boy and girl in the stories, I think they're meant to revive the Trinity. But Laurent wants to use them to bring the Dark Prophets back. I figure he thinks they can do both."

"You think I'm the boy," Nicholas said. "Why?"

"Laurent only turned up when you did," Dawn said softly, though she blushed again. He wondered if she wasn't telling him something.

"There's a flaw in the theory." He raised his cast arm. "Laurent tried to kill me. He obviously doesn't think I'm any use."

"If he wanted you dead, you'd be dead," Dawn said. The certainty in her voice chilled him. "Besides, in all the stories, the children had different gifts. The boy always had vision, emotion. The girl had fire and strength. I wonder which one Laurent values more."

"This girl, who is she?" Nicholas asked. This was what Esus wanted;

it had to be. He couldn't believe that Dawn had already stumbled onto the information that he needed. His coincidence theory was already being put to the test.

"I have an idea," Dawn murmured.

She opened another file on the laptop. It was a blurry collage of primary colours.

"I have a thermographic camera," she explained. "Er, heat-sensing. I was messing around with the settings a few weeks ago, just filming people in the park, and then..." She pointed at a bright red outline. "That's a girl in town. At first I thought something had gone wrong with the camera, but then I kept filming and it was always the same. She runs hot. Dangerously hot. She's, uh, pretty mean, too..."

She clicked something and the colours of the image reversed, became a paused shot of a teenage girl.

"I've seen her, she was at the school before," Nicholas said, recognising the dark-skinned girl who had been watching them.

"Only one other person looks like that when I use the heat-capture setting," Dawn said. She looked sheepish as she opened another photograph. It was a high shot, possibly taken from her bedroom window, of Nicholas walking through the town. She must have taken it the afternoon he'd bumped into her outside the house.

Without a word, Dawn clicked something and the image turned into a blur of colours. Nicholas became a bright red blob, just like the girl.

He couldn't help swearing.

"There's one other thing," Dawn said. She opened a new browser window and showed him a news page on the *Bury Free Press* website. The headline read: *BOMBER IN BURY?* It was accompanied by a picture of a burnt-out building with its front wall missing. It looked like somebody had let off an explosive device inside.

"What's this?" Nicholas asked uneasily.

"This happened yesterday. Or, I think *she* happened to it."

"The bomb site?" Nicholas peered at the photograph of the shop with renewed interest. "She did this?"

"Fire and strength, remember? She obviously has some kind of power. I'd say she doesn't know how to control it yet – the shop was probably an accident. The police found a couple of bodies in the wreckage, they're still trying to ID them."

"That's one hell of an accident. You think she survived the explosion?"

Dawn shrugged.

Nicholas suddenly understood Esus's urgency. If the girl was capable of this kind of destruction, she needed to be found and isolated as soon as possible.

"She's a ticking time bomb," he murmured. "We have to find that girl. And Isabel."

"Isabel?"

"My cat. Sort of. It's a long story." He eased himself off the mattress, wincing at the pain, and went to the door.

"You're going out?" Dawn asked.

"Didn't you hear what I just said?"

"Um, but you're sort of a wreck."

Nicholas opened the door. She was right, he *was* a wreck, but he was a wreck capable of walking. He couldn't give up.

"Wait," Dawn called, hurrying after him. "I'll come with you."

★

Sam had just settled Nicholas into his room when he found Liberty in the kitchen. The Sensitive leaned against the doorframe, her black braids trailing almost to her waist.

"Liberty," he uttered in surprise.

"Ah, here he is, dear," Aileen trilled. She was sitting at the kitchen table polishing knives. A selection of daggers were spread out before her like doctor's implements and the landlady tended to them the way she might her posh crockery.

"Dinner at Aileen's is always eventful." Liberty winked at him, squeezing his arm affectionately. "Good to see you. How's Nicholas?"

"He'll mend." Sam noticed two other figures in the kitchen. A bearded, thick-set man sat with Aileen at the table. His sinewy shoulders were hunched as he brooded over a cup of tea, and his heavy brow considered Sam momentarily before he checked on the monstrous dog at his side.

"Sam, this is Benjamin Nale," Liberty said. "The dog's Zeus."

"It's been a while since I met a Hunter," Sam murmured, instantly curious. Hunters were elite Sentinels; the Olympic fighters of the community. They operated in packs — strange that this Nale fellow was alone.

Nale didn't say anything. He wore a khaki green jacket despite the heat and Sam wondered what his story was.

"Nale has something for us," Liberty said. She gestured at the man, who reached for a bundle off cloth on the table that Sam hadn't noticed before. Thick fingers untangled the cloth and Sam glimpsed silver. He took a step closer. The breath caught in his throat.

A strange metal device rested on the tabletop. A gauntlet. He'd seen the Harvesters using them in the temple beneath the cemetery.

"My goodness," Sam breathed. He kept his distance, half expecting the gauntlet to twitch to life and go for his throat. "Where did you find it?"

Liberty nodded at Nale. "Nale here took it from a Harvester. A good thing, too. It's ridiculously powerful."

"Took it?" Sam murmured.

"Malika attempted to, shall we say, engage Nale's services," Liberty said. "She tracked him down, tried to turn him."

I should have known she'd be involved somehow, Sam thought.

He contemplated the shaggy-haired man at the table. "A personal visit from the snake-haired witch. I wonder how many others can attest to that."

Nale didn't move. He merely returned Sam's stare until the old man blinked and considered the gauntlet once more. The Hunter hadn't uttered a single word. Was he hiding something? Sam hoped Aileen had already used her 'bad egg' test on him.

"Do you know what it is? Who made it?" Sam asked.

"I attempted to read the gauntlet," Liberty sighed. "It's protected. There's a barrier around it. But I have a lead." She crossed to the table and bundled the gauntlet up. "Aileen, do you have somewhere safe for this? We wouldn't want it falling back into the wrong hands."

"Just a moment," Sam said, tapping his chin. "This thing's a weapon of sorts, no? Would it not be advisable to use it? For protection, at the very least?"

"Dangerous." Nale's voice grumbled like thunder. The dog – an Irish Wolfhound, Sam thought – began panting and its ears pricked up.

"He's right," Liberty said. "This thing is seriously juiced. I wouldn't want to risk it until we know what it's really capable of."

Sam nodded. He really was desperate if he was considering using a weapon crafted by the agents of the Dark Prophets. If it levelled out the playing field, though...

"Aileen?" Liberty said.

"Nowhere safer than a safehouse, dear," the landlady said, easing herself up from her chair. Under her breath, she added, "Or that's how it used to be." She hugged the bundle of cloth containing the gauntlet to her bosom and disappeared into the pantry.

"I was hoping to take you for a drive," Liberty said to Sam.

"Anywhere nice?"

"That's open to interpretation."

They were on the road within five minutes. Liberty's Volkswagen was old and she drove in the same way she did everything. Calmly and with humour, swearing casually at bad motorists but never getting angry. Gusts of stifling summer air came in through the open windows.

Sitting up front with Liberty, Sam snuck a look in the rear-view mirror. Nale and his dog filled the entire back seat. The man's head bumped the roof every time they hit a pothole.

"We're going to Cambridge, by the way," Liberty said. "Sorry to disappoint you."

"I trust it's important."

"Dr Adams got in touch with me when she couldn't find you. Remember our friend Dr Snelling?"

"I wish I didn't."

"He posed as a doctor for years," Liberty said. "Dr Adams never met him, but a colleague of hers did. She did some digging and managed to get her hands on his list of patients. It wasn't that difficult; Snelling's been missing for weeks, somebody has to take up the slack. Turns out he was a very bad doctor. Loads of his patients died over the course of his career, but he was clever. Just a couple a year, and most of those were heart attacks."

Sam attempted to suppress the poker-hot anger that Liberty's words ignited. He clenched his fists.

"Only a few of them were Sentinels," Liberty continued. "I suppose Richard Walden and his family were a lucky find. There was one other name that stood out on the patient list, though. A man called Thomas Gray."

Sam didn't recognise the name.

"He was a well-respected young scientist in the 1990s, but then he stopped working. He became a recluse. Nobody's seen him in twenty years. Nobody except Snelling."

"How interesting," Sam mused. "I wonder what use Snelling had for him."

"Here's hoping Thomas can tell us."

They drove in silence for a while, the tarmac rolling under them in a dark stream.

"Tell me, Benjamin," Sam said into the rear-view mirror. "How did you escape Malika's clutches?"

Hooded eyes bore into him.

"Nale's not much for talking," Liberty said.

"Still," Sam persisted. "Not many have been so lucky. What did you do differently?"

"Zeus." Nale's voice was a bark. He petted the dog. "He's very loyal."

Sam squinted at the Hunter and tried to quiet his suspicions. If Liberty trusted this man, that should be enough. He'd never heard of a Benjamin Nale, though. Hunters were elite, elusive and few in number. Odd that he'd never come across this stoic giant before.

"It's getting scary out there, Sam," Liberty murmured. He noticed new crinkles at the corners of her eyes. It looked like she hadn't been sleeping properly.

"What have you heard?" he asked.

"Hellfire, demons, Harvesters, the usual." There was less humour in her tone than usual. "A swimming pool in Diss filled itself up with blood and bile yesterday. No explanation. And a cemetery in Leeds was smashed to bits. Every grave was emptied, every gravestone destroyed."

"Trinity spare us," Sam breathed.

"They found the corpses arranged in a pyre in the city centre. The Prophets are sending a message. Mum spoke to a friend who saw it himself. Apparently Esus is flying from town to town, finding, well, you get the picture."

The sun beat through the windscreen but Sam couldn't feel it.

"There have been rumours, too, about her," Liberty said. "Malika."

Sam looked at her in suprise. "Rumours?"

"That she's working with somebody. She was spotted in Cambridge with some mystery man, apparently. All unconfirmed, but where there's smoke..."

Laurent, Sam thought. *It had to be. Laurent and Malika were two powerful players. They must be working together.*

Twenty minutes later, they arrived in Cambridge. Liberty parked on Tennis Court Road, which was located in the city centre, and they all got out onto the pavement. Sam peered up appreciatively at Pembroke College, then let Liberty lead him down the street. Nale followed with Zeus at his heels. For a large man, he moved disarmingly quietly.

"How are things at home?" Sam asked Liberty, hoping to turn the conversation to happier things.

"Fine. Though Francesca's idea of an adult conversation is hurling paint at the wall and then blaming the dog."

"You have a dog now?"

"Nope."

Sam chuckled. He was glad to have Liberty at his side again. Though he generally liked to work alone, he was coming to the conclusion that he couldn't do everything by himself. Not at his age. Besides, Liberty was a useful person to have around. She should be able to pick something up from this Thomas Gray, even if he couldn't.

"How is the little cherub?" he asked.

"More wilful by the day. My mother has the patience of a saint. This looks like it." Liberty stopped by a row of terraces.

Sam noted the assortment of scientific oddities cluttering the cramped, overgrown front garden. Shiny metal devices were everywhere, some of them spinning and winking in the sunlight, others pumping water through silver tubes and into miniature jugs in an endless cycle. He was surprised he'd never noticed the house before.

At the front door, Sam pulled an unusual lever suspended at one side – he assumed it was the doorbell.

A desolate bell rang through the house.

They waited.

Zeus began to whine softly and Nale shot the dog a look that silenced him.

"Somebody's coming," Liberty said a heartbeat before the door opened.

The man who blinked out at them was in his early fifties. He wore a woolly hat despite the weather and he was shorter than both of them, drowning in a lifeless brown jumper punctured with holes. The sun appeared to hurt his eyes because he couldn't stop blinking, and Sam noted the grey pallor of his cheeks, the dry-looking lips, the sickly, yellowish pigment around his pupils.

"Yes?" the man said.

"Thomas Gray?" Sam asked.

The man nodded unsurely.

"Might we come in for a moment? If it's no trouble? We won't keep you long."

"What you want?"

"It's about Dr Snelling."

Thomas held Sam's gaze meekly for a moment. "Not the dog," he rasped as he turned and shuffled back inside, leaving the door open.

"Wait out here?" Liberty suggested to Nale. The man nodded and reached into his jacket, retrieving a cigar.

Liberty stepped inside and Sam went after her, pushing the front door to.

The house smelled like old cigarettes and there was a sharp metallic scent that Sam couldn't put his finger on. Burnt copper, perhaps. Every curtain was drawn closed and it took him a moment to get used to the gloom after the brightness of the afternoon sun. The house was old and creaky, the carpets threadbare. Thomas was already sitting in the living room just off the entrance hall, absorbed into a chair that seemed to have moulded to his form.

There was an air of tragedy about the whole place. Blankets had been thrown over what Sam assumed were mirrors above the hearth and hanging by the door, and all of the photo frames were empty. Unease heaved in his chest.

"You knew him?" Thomas sparked up a cigarette. His hand trembled, fingers twitching as he took a drag. "Snelling. You knew him?"

Sam removed his fedora and wondered how best to handle the situation. He'd had time to think it over in the car, but now that he was here, he found it difficult to focus. There were too many questions, and the state of the man before him threw him for a loop. Thomas Gray was ill, that much was clear. Sam wondered what it was. He eyed the woollen hat.

Cancer. Has to be.

"Dr Snelling is missing," Liberty said, taking a seat on a beaten-up sofa. Sam sank down next to her. "We were wondering if you'd had any contact with him in the past few days."

Opposite them, Thomas took another drag of the cigarette. The orange glow jabbed momentarily at the surrounding murk.

"Not seen him in months," he said.

"But he was your GP."

Thomas didn't say anything.

"The garden out front, did you build all of that?" Liberty continued. Sam wondered if she'd sensed something.

Thomas nodded. He didn't seem interested in them at all. Had he let them into his home merely out of boredom? Something to break up his day? He certainly didn't seem to want them there – but he didn't *not* want them there, either, or he'd have slammed the door in their faces.

"You're good at making things," Liberty observed. "Did it take long to create them?"

"Nah." Thomas exhaled. The smoke hung around him in a ghostly haze. "Not done anything like that for years."

"Your father was a physicist," Liberty said. She must have researched Thomas before she picked Sam up. "The physics apple obviously didn't fall far from the tree."

In other circumstances, Sam would have chuckled, but he couldn't, not in this heavy atmosphere of misery.

"He was obsessed with the cosmos," Thomas said finally, wearily. "He wanted to know what made the stars move, what existed between the matter we could detect. He wanted to know more about the invisible matter, the stuff that kept everything tied together up there." He seemed to emerge from his coma, his yellow eyes offering a hint of life. "I was always more interested in things closer to home."

"What sort of things?" Sam asked.

In an instant the spark was extinguished, as if Thomas had lost interest now that the topic had turned inward on his own life. "Atomic physics," he muttered. "Same as him, but I never cared about the rest of the universe."

Sam noticed something strange about the cuff of Thomas's jumper. Some material was poking out beneath the fabric – white gauze. A bandage. Thomas's wrist had been bandaged.

Thomas became momentarily lost in the smoke haze. His eyes grew unfocussed.

A floorboard creaked upstairs and his yellow gaze snapped to the ceiling.

"Old house," he muttered under his breath. "Creaks like a damn barn all day long."

The uneasy feeling welled in Sam's belly and he cast Liberty a look. Her expression was unreadable, though, and he couldn't tell if she'd sensed anything from Thomas or his home.

Thomas retched suddenly, coughing loudly. Finally, he calmed.

"You're not well," Sam said.

Thomas wiped the spittle from his lips.

"Docs at the hospital don't know what's wrong with me," he grunted. "Got bones like glass. They tried testing me, wanted to put me in a lab and poke me with sticks. I told them to go to Hell. I know what's done this to me."

"What has?" Sam ventured.

Silence.

"Why don't you tell me why you're really here." Thomas's eyes glowed like the tip of his cigarette. He knew they were lying. He'd known all along. Their cover story wasn't exactly the stuff of undercover genius, but it had gotten them through the front door.

"You want to know about Dr Snelling?" Thomas continued. He paused, coughing painfully once more. "He came here five months ago. Last time I saw him. He wanted something and I gave it to him."

"What did he want?" Sam asked.

"One of my creations."

It was as if somebody had slipped a cold blade into Sam's gut. Thomas's creation? Was he talking about the gauntlet? Snelling had possessed one. Could they be in the company of the man who had created those terrible contraptions?

"She'd be upset I said that," Thomas muttered. He took on a faraway look, distracted by the cigarette smoke.

"Who would?" Liberty asked.

"She turned up when Dad died. At his funeral. I was eighteen and alone. She gave me a project, something to busy myself with. I thought she loved me."

Sam resisted the urge to find an excuse for them to leave. This didn't feel right. The house creaked and bowed around them. Thomas had started rambling and Sam began to doubt the man's state of mind. He seemed to weave in and out of lucidity. Before he could say anything, though, Thomas was on his feet. He tucked the cigarette into the corner of his lips.

"Hurry," he urged quietly, beckoning them into the hall.

Uneasily, Sam followed. He found himself in the grubby hallway. Thomas lingered outside a door under the stairs, his skeletal frame hunched. Sam shuddered, recalling the basement in Snelling's house.

Thomas cast a glance up the stairs, then drew the cellar door open.

The scent of burnt copper rose up a set of cement steps. Thomas gestured at him and disappeared inside.

Without hesitating, Liberty went after him. Heart hammering in his chest, Sam followed.

The basement was full of strange gadgets. A single strip light illuminated an industrial-size chemistry set that monopolised a large work bench. Metal machinery proliferated every other surface. Jars held pickled body parts. Potted plants slumped.

Sam noticed an object covered in a white sheet on the work bench.

"Look if you want," Thomas wheezed. He leaned against a chair, clearly struggling to stay upright. Walking downstairs had taken it out of him. What was wrong with the man?

Shakily, Sam drew the sheet back.

A metallic device like a glove rested in a wooden cradle. It was pristine, shimmering in the fluorescent light. Overpowered with dread and curiosity, Sam reached for it, his hand hovering over the gauntlet.

A floorboard creaked above him and Sam froze.

"Should've got out when I could," Thomas muttered. He seemed to grow paler and more ghoulish with every passing second. He inspected his bandaged wrist. A speck of red stood out against the white material.

"You're hurt," Liberty observed, reaching for his wrist.

Thomas clutched his arm. "No," he warned. He peered down at the speck of red, his gaze distant. "I thought she wouldn't stop, but she did. She always stops."

"Who are you talking about?" Liberty asked.

He glared at her. "She comes and goes, but she loves me. When she needs shelter, I give it to her." He shook himself, appeared to become more lucid. "I knew you'd come eventually. Somebody has to know what we did. Somebody has to stop her."

"You made this?" Sam asked, referring to the gauntlet.

The look on Thomas's face was awful. Pride and guilt and horror mixed into one.

"It was meant to be used to separate atoms," he murmured. "A tiny reactor that blasted particles apart to be studied. But... it did something else. It unleashed an electrical current that peeled back the very fabric of existence..."

"What do you mean?" Sam asked.

"I'm the scientist, just the scientist," Thomas murmured. "She's the alchemist. She completed it. She completed me."

"What does it *do*?" Sam demanded, desperation knotting his stomach.

"It lets the darkness in," Thomas whispered.

"Demons," Liberty said. She hovered by the wilted plants in the corner, the strip-light catching in her dark eyes as she contemplated the gauntlet. Sam knew that look: she had sensed something. "It opens a portal *inside* a person. Lets a demon claw its way in."

A noise. The shriek of a door opening. Or the lid of a coffin.

Thomas's sallow gaze snapped to the ceiling.

"You have to stop her," he hissed.

It was too late. Even as Sam started for the steps, he found a figure blocking his path. He felt her before he saw her. His skin began to hum and his arm hair bristled.

"Thomas, you should have said we had guests," Malika purred.

CHAPTER THIRTEEN
Sickness

Sam imagined a spider after it had discovered an insect wriggling in its web. Despite the gloom of the stairwell, Malika radiated an icy vitality. Her auburn hair was coiled atop her head, her wiry form clad in a berry red dress that was square at the neck and cut off at the knees.

"I'm beginning to think you can't get enough of me." The velvety quaver of her voice sought to smother him. They were trapped in the cement-walled lab. She was blocking their only way out.

"So many people interested in my whereabouts," Malika murmured, idling at the foot of the stairs. "How blessed I am."

She knew. Of course she knew. Sentinels across the country had been dispatched to track her down, to contain her, and she was here, under all their noses, making a mockery of them once more. How many had found her? How many had been killed as a consequence? Sam recalled what Nicholas had glimpsed in the seeing glass. Malika drenched in blood.

A chuckle spilled from the woman's throat.

"I do believe I have rendered you speechless," she teased. "Old man, is it possible you fear me now? Do you finally understand that I cannot be stopped?"

"You will be stopped," Sam grunted. "If not by me, then somebody else. There is only one end for you."

"You seem so certain." Malika's teeth flashed ivory white. "Even the most certain of men can be proven wrong." Her attention turned to Liberty. "Still following this old goat. Surely you've learned by now? Or perhaps you're a glutton for punishment."

Liberty. Malika had used the Sensitive to gain access to Hallow House. She'd wormed her way into Liberty's head, tapped into her powers and exploited them. It had left Liberty bed-ridden and Sam had feared she'd never recover.

"Stay back," he warned the thing by the stairs. He pressed the satchel to his side. "What's he got you doing? Laurent never liked getting his hands dirty. You on the other hand..."

"Such suspicion," Malika drawled. Her attention bent to Thomas. The blood had drained from his face. His eyes were wide with – what? Adoration? What spell had Malika cast over him? She was the one responsible for his sickness. She'd manipulated him, just as she manipulated everybody. His brilliance had been twisted, wrecked, and he'd forged an abomination in her name.

"Thomas," Malika murmured softly. "Do it."

The man's lower lip trembled and spit dribbled from his chin. He started toward the work bench; toward the gauntlet.

"Thomas, no," Sam said firmly, standing in his way.

"Would you keep a man from his creation?" Silver sparks danced in Malika's cat-like eyes. "I owe Thomas everything. We're changing the world together. Such loyalty is rare these days. Why do you think we created the gauntlet? People don't want to be recruited, they want to be ruled. Commanded. Controlled."

"Spoken like a true dictator," Sam spat. His hand crept up the side of the satchel, feeling for a way in.

"What is a dictator if not an agent of change? A driving force. Somebody who confronts the world with itself and sets a new order in motion." She fixed him with an unflinching glare as he slipped his hand into the satchel. "I wouldn't do that if I were you." Her gaze intensified. "Tell me, how's the ticker?"

Crippling pain crushed his ribcage.

Sam's skin prickled and flushed. His vision swam and he choked aloud as something beneath his ribs contracted painfully. His heart. It was gripped in steel claws.

Malika's expression hardened. "Doc warned you against hunting, didn't she? You should've listened. You shouldn't be poking around where you don't belong."

"Sam." Liberty's voice.

He gripped the work bench, sweat beading his brow. Through the unnatural fever, he saw that Liberty had become very still, her gaze fixed on Malika.

The red-haired witch raised a finger and wagged it. "Uh-uh-uh," she reprimanded, turning to face the Sensitive. "Stay out of my head, or I'll snap that pretty neck of yours."

"Liberty," Sam croaked. "No."

"Thomas," Malika commanded. "Take his bag."

Sam felt hands at his side and attempted to push them away. Blood throbbed in his ears and pain locked his limbs. He clutched at his satchel, refusing to let Thomas take it. The other man grunted and wrenched. Sam balled his fist and swung. Thomas shrieked and released him.

"Men," Malika spat.

A rustle of red fabric, and he sensed her approaching, but then there was movement. Liberty flew from the corner of the basement. She and Malika crashed against the work bench, Liberty scratching at the woman's face.

The pain vanished. The relief was a cool tonic in his veins. Sam shook his head, his pulse returning to normal. He wiped his forehead and focussed, seeing that Thomas was cowering against the wall.

"You have to stop her," he gibbered, and even as he said it, his gaze lingered lovingly on Malika.

Liberty struck the ground with a thud and Malika clutched for her with blood-red nails.

"I tire of this meddling," she hissed.

"Here!" Sam barked. Malika turned and he didn't waste a breath, hurling the pouch that he'd retrieved from his satchel. It seemed to sail out of his hands in slow-motion. It cleared the work bench and exploded in Malika's face.

Her scream blistered the air.

Sam winced at the spit of sizzling flesh. Malika's hoarse screams made the apparatus on the bench shudder and the stench of singed flesh violated the air.

SICKNESS

"Hurry!" Sam yelled as Liberty scrambled to her feet. They staggered over to the steps and Liberty began upward. He paused, casting a look back at the gauntlet. Malika was in the way and he daren't attempt to retrieve it.

Thomas howled and hurried to Malika on all fours. In one swift movement, he unravelled the bandage at his wrist and crouched by her, prying her hands from her scarred face.

Malika's lips leeched around the bloody gash in Thomas's wrist. Sam heard ravenous suckling and fought the urge to vomit. He dashed up the remaining steps, bursting into the dingy hallway. Liberty was waiting for him and they clung to each other as they bound toward the front door, emerging into the garden.

The sunlight was blinding. Nale stomped his cigar into the ground and appraised them uncertainly.

"Inside," Liberty told him. "The basement."

Without a word, Nale bowled into the house with Zeus at his heels.

"You're hurt." Liberty motioned at Sam's arm.

Surprised, he looked down and found blood smeared from his elbow to his wrist. Wooziness sapped his energy in an instant; he must have lost a lot of blood without even noticing. A small wound pumped red liquid. Thomas had cut him and he hadn't noticed, lost in Malika's icy grip.

Liberty tore off his ragged sleeve and wrapped it around Sam's arm, so tightly that he had to grit his teeth against it.

"We need to close that quickly," she said.

Nale reappeared at the door, Zeus at his side.

"Gone," he gruffed.

"They can't be," Sam uttered. "We have to check—"

"I checked. They're gone."

Liberty drew Sam away from the house. "Come on. We'll summon Esus on the way to mine, he'll send others to sweep the house. You're in no fit state."

Sam cursed. She'd evaded them again. But where had Malika and Thomas disappeared to? He'd hoped the pouch would see her off, but he was beginning to accept it would take even more to eradicate Malika. Snelling had been a ruse all along. A puppet. Somebody to do

Malika's bidding and bow out early. Sam had been chasing the wrong monster. Snelling's story ended here with Thomas Gray. Malika's, it seemed, was only just beginning.

Nale helped Sam over to Liberty's car. As she unlocked it, the old man leaned in to the Hunter.

"Stay with her," he told Nale, nodding at Liberty. "Don't let her out of your sight." If Malika survived the day, Liberty might be next on her list.

★

Everything was so confused. It was as if somebody had taken a stack of papers and hurled them into the air. Now all Rae could do was watch them flutter to the floor.

She'd awoken on a camp bed in a strange room, her tongue dry, her body aching. Then the events of the previous evening returned in a smothering rush. The fight with Damon. The explosion. *Twig.* Rae wanted to scream. Pull her hair out. Instead she sat and balled her fists.

The moments after the explosion were a blur. The man from the museum had taken her to Moyse's Hall Museum. She'd heard fire engines but nobody had seen them. They'd moved quickly. She vaguely recalled the museum man ushering her into the office and showing her the bed. She didn't remember falling asleep.

Were they all dead? Twig and Damon and the others? Just like Kay? Retro Threads was a singed, shattered shell when she left it. And Twig had been lying in the rubble not moving.

Rae wanted to throw up.

The museum man had woken her after what felt like five minutes, given her food, water. His name was Laurent, he'd said, and he needed her help. Then he started talking about monsters. She should have laughed at him, but she'd glimpsed things. At night, the cities came alive with things that didn't want to be seen. She'd seen them. Glowing green eyes and claws that clattered over tarmac. They were rule number five. *Don't let the monsters see you.*

Am I a monster?

He left her to sleep again, arguing that she needed her rest. Rae had resolved to escape as soon as she got the chance, but she was so exhausted. Her body betrayed her and she'd succumbed to sleep almost immediately.

What was the time now? The clock on the wall said nine. Was that morning or evening? She couldn't have slept an entire day, surely. But... the wrecked shop. The explosion was the biggest she'd ever caused, which explained the deep ache in her muscles and the fuzziness between her ears.

She had to go. The police would be after her. You couldn't incinerate a building in a town like Bury St Edmunds without getting noticed. She had to disappear again. Find somewhere else, even if it meant going back to the street. Where hadn't she tried? The north, perhaps. She could sneak through the barriers at the train station and pretend she'd lost her ticket. In five hours she could have a new life.

Rae listened at the door but didn't hear anything. She drew it open.

A man with a buzz cut and thin lips stood outside. She closed the door before he noticed her. She was being guarded? Who was Laurent and what did he want with her?

Rae scoured the office for another way out. The room was windowless, though, and the bookcase against the wall looked too heavy to shift, even if there was a window behind it.

She scanned the desk and her eye was drawn to a postcard. It was a painting of a man in a bowler hat. The man had no face.

Rae shuddered.

The door opened behind her and she jumped.

"Rae," Laurent said. "You're awake. Do you feel rested?"

Rae crushed her back against the wall. He was relaxed, pushing the door to and observing her calmly. His expression betrayed no judgement, no fear, despite what he'd seen her do.

"What you want?" she demanded.

"I know you must be very confused," Laurent said. A single lamp illuminated the room and he was disarmingly attractive in the soft light. "Let's talk about the abilities that turned your home into a crater."

"Wasn't my home."

Laurent didn't seem fazed. "Nevertheless, if you wish to learn to control your abilities, I can help."

Rae looked down at her hands. Her fingers were knotted together. She didn't want to talk about what she'd done. What she could do. But she'd never met anybody who wasn't afraid. Did Laurent really want to help her?

"Can't," she muttered. "I can't control it."

"Nonsense." He strode to a drinks cabinet, plucking an expensive-looking decanter from it. He set the decanter on the desktop. "Sit," he said, pulling a chair out. She eyed him, then relented. Laurent strode in circles around her.

"You have a switch, everybody does. All you have to do is locate the switch and flip it. First we'll nudge it, just enough to ensure that you don't black out as you did before."

Rae hoped he couldn't see her trembling.

"No," she said. She couldn't let anybody else get hurt.

He paused on the other side of the table, hands clasped behind his back.

"This is for your benefit, not mine. Do you really want to wake up in a bomb site again?"

"What's wrong with me?"

She hated how she sounded, but Laurent's confidence caused her guard to lower.

"Nothing," Laurent soothed. "There are others with similar abilities, though I've yet to meet anybody with your sort of fire power. No pun intended."

"I start, I won't be able to stop. You'll get hurt."

"Trust me, I can handle it."

Rae doubted that. But, then, Laurent had seen the shop and he didn't seem scared. Could she really do this?

"Concentrate," Laurent instructed. "It's going to take all the concentration you've got."

Rae balled her hands in her lap.

Laurent stepped back into the shadows. "Concentrate on the decanter." His voiced floated out of the darkness. "Ignore everything else around it. Pay attention to the beat of your heart, your breathing. Feel the pulse in your chest."

She attempted to do as he said, staring at the decanter until her eyes itched to blink.

"Now think back to last night; what set you off?"

I'm a murderer.

"I can't–"

"You don't need to tell me," Laurent interrupted her. "Simply remember where you were, what you were doing. Try to build a picture in your mind, pretend you're back there."

Rae imagined the shop. Damon and his friends cornering her.

Twig.

Her pulse quickened. Her palms were clammy.

"You're a freak!"

She recoiled in the chair. Her stomach was alive with snapping scorpions.

"Good." Laurent's voice rippled from the darkness. His eyes were pinpricks of light beyond the desk. "Hold on to that feeling. Pull it deep within you, let it boil and charge."

Rae felt like she was on fire. Her skin burned. Her insides juddered. Something was wrong. She couldn't control it. She was going to lose it just as she had with Kay and Twig.

Her head started pounding. An axe had been buried in her skull. It was being withdrawn and slammed back down again. Over and over.

"Yes." Laurent's voice shivered in the dark. "Hold on to it, make it yours. Don't let it control you."

Her hands fused into fists, nails slicing her palms. Every muscle felt like it was being torn in two. Prised stickily from her bones. She was coming apart.

"I can't!" she objected through gritted teeth.

"Now, Rae," Laurent insisted. "Let go now!"

With a gasp, she unclenched her fists. It was as if something physically left her body. A pulse or blast of energy. It shot invisibly out of her. The desk and decanter exploded in a fiery blaze that sent shards of glass spearing upwards. Smoke engulfed the office and glass tinkled as it rained down.

As the vapours thinned, Laurent's face became clearer and clearer.

He was grinning triumphantly.

"Come," he said, opening the office door. Her body twitching, Rae stumbled to her feet. She'd done it. Nobody had been hurt and she hadn't passed out. Relief and a strange kind of euphoria flooded through her. She drifted after Laurent, climbing a staircase at the back of the museum.

It's not enough.

Like the vapours, the euphoria evaporated. The secret didn't belong to her anymore. For the first time in her life, somebody else knew. The thought filled her with dread. What did Laurent want with her? Laurent who wasn't afraid. Laurent who understood.

I have to get out of here.

Laurent went ahead. Sunlight carved apart the shadows in the stairwell as he opened another door and Rae followed him out into the fresh air. They were on the museum's roof and Rae could see streets away. Below them, people milled about like ants.

"When was the first time you became aware of what you could do?" Laurent asked, staring off into the distance.

"Dunno," Rae said. She couldn't help being cagey. *Don't talk about your past.* She'd learnt the hard way that knowledge was power.

"You don't need to keep anything from me," Laurent said.

True. She'd be gone the first chance she got. It didn't matter if she told him. She wasn't sticking around anyway.

"I was five. I woke up and the house was on fire..."

She hadn't understood why her foster parents were so scared after that. Paul and Elizabeth had looked after her since she was a baby, but after the fire, she caught their nervous glances. The house creaked with tension. A year after the fire, Elizabeth fell pregnant and they gave her up. She was taken in by an elderly couple who didn't know the first thing about kids. She'd run.

"You were scared."

Rae nodded.

"You've run ever since."

It wasn't a question. How did he know? She found his perceptiveness unnerving.

Run, the voice in the back of her head urged. After she'd fled the couple in their sixties, the authorities had caught up with her and she'd ended up with another foster parent, Karen Stone. Another three years slipped by, but one night, she'd woken up and the house was on fire again. She was ten and she knew she was to blame.

She ran again, and this time she didn't stop.

Run, run!

"You're safe with me," Laurent said. "But other people, they won't understand. Man always destroys what he can't understand. If you were discovered, you'd be destroyed. You understand that, don't you?"

Damon. He'd come to the shop with his friends to taunt her. Humiliate her.

For the first time since they had gone out onto the roof, Laurent looked at her. His blue eyes were shards of ice. Cold but beautiful.

"You're weak," Laurent said. "I can make you strong."

Rae forced herself to stare back.

"With my help, you'll never have to fear those who would seek to destroy you."

He seemed so sure.

Later, she was back in the office. Laurent said she needed to rest, but she couldn't sit still. She'd killed Twig and the others. She was a murderer. She had to get as far away from Bury as possible. It didn't matter that Laurent wanted to help her. The only person she could trust was herself.

The buzz-cut guard lingered outside her door ("For your protection," Laurent had assured her). Anxiously, Rae paced the room. There had to be another way out. She attempted to drag the bookcase away from the wall, but it was too heavy. With growing desperation, she knocked on the walls, searching for a weak spot.

After five minutes, one of the knocks resounded hollowly.

Plasterboard. There was something behind it. Casting a wary glance at the door, Rae punched the wall, her fist disappearing into it. She pulled, tearing away the plasterboard to reveal an old-fashioned door. Her breath caught in her throat and Rae gave the door a shove. It opened stiffly. She glimpsed another room filled with display cabinets. Another of the museum's rooms.

Not pausing, Rae pushed her way through, hoping her guard wouldn't hear.

Covered in dust, she emerged into the other room. Not wasting a moment, she crossed the room quietly and peered out into the hall.

The guard remained outside the office. He hadn't heard a thing.

Opposite her lay the lobby and beyond that the market square. In five seconds she'd be free.

Not breathing, Rae listened. The building was quiet. Keeping her eyes on the guard, she hopped across the hall into the lobby. Blood thundering in her ears, she hurried to the front door and threw it open.

Breaking into the searing afternoon light, she ran.

CHAPTER FOURTEEN
Ashes

THERE WAS NO SIGN OF ISABEL in the Abbey Gardens. Nicholas and Dawn searched the whole park, but she was nowhere to be found. Nicholas's shoulder twinged and he hissed through his teeth. He was still getting used to the sling. It dug into his flesh and he swore he'd get rid of it as soon as the throbbing in his arm subsided. There were far more pressing matters for now.

The last time he'd seen Isabel was when the gargoyle hurled her from the air. She'd crashed into a tree and vanished. Nicholas steeled himself against the possibility that she was dead. The memory of her body toppling limply made his stomach flip.

She's got to be okay, he thought. *When has death ever stopped her?*

They scoured the area for an hour before they gave up. It was useless. Nicholas kicked a tree and cursed.

"If she's not here, that means we have a limited number of possibilities," Dawn reasoned softly.

"What do you mean?"

"If she died, either somebody found her body or an animal took it."

"Took it. Ate it, you mean."

"If she's alive," Dawn continued in a more optimistic tone, "she's either crawled off somewhere or been discovered by somebody and taken."

A trio of shrieking under-fives bowled past and Nicholas jumped. He massaged his aching shoulder. What had Laurent been doing in the park that day? Had he followed Nicholas? Or had he already been there when Nicholas turned up? A very unfortunate coincidence?

The school had been desecrated for something and was being guarded by Sentinels to make sure nothing came out. Laurent had been there. How did it all fit together? And was Laurent really intent on raising the Dark Prophets?

"Laurent," he murmured, knowing what he had to do. "Come on."

They hurried back to Aileen's. On the way to his room, they came across the landlady in the kitchen. She was wearing her usual flowery dress and pinny. She had one foot braced against a chair and was polishing a long sword, which rested on her generous thigh.

"Oh, it's you, dears!"

Nicholas stared blankly at the strange sight. The Sentinels were full of surprises.

"Hey Aileen. Can't stop," he said, pushing into the pantry with Dawn behind him.

"You have fun, dears!" Aileen called after them.

In his room, Nicholas drew the curtains and set the seeing glass out on the carpet, which was considerably more difficult with only one working arm. Dawn folded herself up in the chair in the corner and watched, chewing on her sleeve.

Nicholas tried to remember what Isabel had said. Deep breaths and follow the amethyst. It shouldn't be too difficult. Sitting cross-legged, he tapped the crystal and it began to swing. It caught the light and flashed intermittently.

He tried to conjure an image of Laurent, then held it in his mind in the hope that he could force the glass to show him what he wanted.

"Laurent," he commanded.

The floor fell away beneath him. The walls evaporated and darkness clouded his vision.

The girl sits dazed and covered in ash.

The image changed.

A symbol burning fire. A triangle. A man in a bowler hat. An inhuman screech blasts through the night and then there are the Abbey ruins.

"Come on," Nicholas muttered. His voice echoed strangely in his head.

Cobbles. A passageway lit by buzzing electric lamps. The odour of dry earth.

Whoops and cheers filled his hearing and his pulse quickened with excitement, but the feeling didn't belong to him. He was sensing somebody else's emotion. A huge swell of exhilaration left a taste like blood in his mouth.

Nicholas emerged from the trance.

"What did you see?" Dawn asked.

"It was weird. Like I was underground." He sat up with a start. Sam had told him about the rumours of tunnels beneath Bury St Edmunds – an ancient network he'd read were once used by the monks.

"The tunnels," he said, grinning triumphantly at Dawn. "They're in the tunnels!" His grin slackened as he remembered the exhilaration, the bite of blood on his tongue. "But something was happening... Or it's going to happen. I think we're running out of time."

*

A loud clanging interrupted Isabel's sleep. Drowsily, she came to. It was dark, but her feline sight probed through the gloom. She was in a dank room. Water trickled down the walls and the air reeked of damp. Barrels were stacked in one corner. Another housed a great heap of blankets.

Isabel realised she was lying in an upturned crate. It was stuffed with musty bits of fabric that once seemed to have been used to clean floors. Somebody had made a bed for her. How had she come to be here? What had happened?

She struggled to recall and then the memory struck her like a blow. The park. The swooping gargoyles and the leering man from the school.

Nicholas!

Where was the boy? Panic prickled her fur and Isabel attempted to get up, but her limbs spasmed and she curled back up dejectedly.

A phlegmy cough reverberated through the chamber and Isabel froze, unsure where the sound had come from.

The blankets in the corner moved and Isabel realised they contained a person. Somebody struggled up from the floor. Isabel glimpsed sallow, saggy flesh and a pendulous bosom that a stained brown dress struggled to restrain.

The figure coughed and retched, wiping her nose on her bare arm. Grey eyes pivoted through the murk, focussing blearily on Isabel.

"Pretty kitty," the woman slobbered, shuffling across the floor. She extended a grimy hand and scratched the top of Isabel's head. "Pretty kitty's awake."

Isabel shrank back in revulsion. Tiredness overcame her and she closed her eyes.

"Pretty kitty!"

The woman's angry shrieks shook the crate, but Isabel couldn't fight the tiredness. The yells faded into the distance and she welcomed the darkness of sleep.

Some time later, Isabel awoke again. She listened. Still curled up in the crate, she heard guttural snores and wondered if the scraggly woman who was both her nurse and warden was asleep.

She had no idea how much time had passed since the incident in the Abbey Gardens. It could be a day or a week. There were no windows in the room and Isabel didn't know how long she had slipped in and out of consciousness. She reasoned that a considerable amount of time must have passed because she felt better than previously.

The cat extended a front paw, testing it. No pain. She stretched the other and then eased upright, her tail kinking into a question mark. One of her back legs twinged slightly, but otherwise she felt fine. Weak, but fine.

She had to escape this cell. Nicholas needed her.

If the child survived the attack.

Isabel refused to think otherwise. The boy was strong-willed, if tempestuous in his behaviour. How peculiar that those qualities often went hand in hand.

More snores rattled from the bundle of rags in the corner and Isabel padded warily across the stone floor. She ignored the wooziness and attempted to move silently as a shadow. If her captor discovered her there was no telling what she'd do.

The door was solid wood and shut tightly. Isabel peered up at it, her whiskers trembling. She had no idea if she had the strength to do what was necessary, but she had to try.

Blocking out the sound of her captor's nasal grunts and ignoring the fusty air that tickled her nostrils, she attempted to centre herself. This would be a true test of the power she suspected still resided within her.

Focussing on the door knob, she imagined a human hand reaching for it. A five-fingered shadow detached itself from the floor and strained upward. It closed around the handle. Turned.

The door vibrated faintly and Isabel squinted, doubling her efforts. With a squeak, the handle rotated.

Seizing her moment, Isabel swiped a paw under the door and yanked it open.

"Kitty?" a tired voice mumbled.

Isabel darted into a gloomy hall.

No, not a hall. A tunnel. Refusing to acknowledge the weariness that sucked at her resolve, she cantered down the tunnel. Even that tiny incantation had exhausted her, but if she succumbed to the weariness she'd never escape.

Her insides quailed as the door crashed open behind her.

"KITTY?" a voice warbled.

Isabel's heart leapt. She couldn't be captured again. Racing on, she followed the tunnel round a bend. There had to be somewhere to hide. The few doors that lined the passage were closed and Isabel didn't have the strength to prise them open.

"PRETTY KITTY?"

The voice shrilled behind her and Isabel couldn't be sure if she'd been spotted. She daren't cast a look back, scampering further down the tunnel, blind to what lay ahead.

Bare fleet slapped the stone floor and she realised the woman was giving chase. Isabel had no idea where she was, but she guessed it was enemy territory. The man who had attacked them in the gardens must have allies, and the woman was one of them. She must have found her after the attack.

Isabel darted round another corner and spotted a rusted grate where the wall met the floor. It must lead to old ventilation shafts. She sprang toward it and squeezed between the bars into the darkness beyond.

"KITTY NO!"

A hand groped between the bars and Isabel saw that the woman was on the floor, slobbering and sobbing as she stretched for the cat.

"KITTY!"

Isabel's tail lashed in irritation.

"Have some dignity," she spat, turning from the prone woman and padding into the darkness of the ventilation shaft. The shrieks soon died away, but she crept quietly, aware that there could be other openings.

She wandered for what felt like an age. The air was just as stuffy here as it was elsewhere in the tunnels. Perhaps this wasn't her way out, after all. Perhaps there was no way out. If she was in a network of tunnels, it stood to reason that she was underground. But where?

Isabel's ears twitched, picking up a distant sound.

Voices. Or one voice, at the very least. It sounded familiar.

Unable to suppress her curiosity, Isabel followed the sound. She spied another grate ahead. Flickering light probed her hiding place and she edged closer to the bars.

The room beyond was bathed in candlelight. A bare-chested man cowered in the centre of the floor, which was scrawled with peculiar lines and circles. He was shackled to the floor and his youthful face was tight with fear. A blood-smeared symbol had been carved into his chest.

"For your sacrifice, you will receive a great reward," a deep voice murmured. "The Dark Prophets welcome all who surrender to their divine embrace."

Robes swept past the grate and Isabel ducked back, her ears flattening against her skull. She knew that voice. As the robed figure circled the floor, she caught sight of blond hair and darkly glittering eyes.

It was the man from the park. Laurent.

"What is he up to now?" Isabel murmured to herself, suppressing the growl that wanted to be unleashed.

"Please..." the chained man sobbed. "Please..."

Laurent looked down his nose at him, hooded eyes devoid of compassion. He reached out a hand and placed it on the chained man's head. He murmured something under his breath and even Isabel's hearing couldn't pick out the words.

The man on the floor writhed in agony. His mouth opened as if he wanted to scream, but only a terrible croak escaped his throat. His eyes became bloodshot. His entire body tensed; every bone protruding; every muscle hardening.

Isabel wanted to throw herself upon Laurent, but she resisted, knowing he would easily overpower her in her present condition. She watched in horror as the shirtless man's face grew gaunt. All life drained from it and his features grew more skull-like with each passing second.

Then he was on fire.

Flames roared over his skin, surging up Laurent's arm. Laurent threw his head back as if in ecstasy.

A flash lit the chamber and silence fell.

Isabel peered through the bars and her hackles raised in horror.

Where the chained man had been, all that remained was a crouched figure of ash.

Laurent's exultant pants echoed in the chamber and he stretched his arms out, his back cracking. Cheeks aglow, he went to a cabinet and unlocked it with a key attached to his wrist. Isabel craned through the bars.

She heard Laurent cooing at something in the cabinet, but what? He took a step back to admire the cabinet's contents and Isabel caught sight of two objects – an ugly vase inscribed with strange symbols and a crude stone carving in the shape of a woman.

A wave of nausea caused Isabel's stomach to do slow somersaults. She couldn't pry her gaze from the objects in the cabinet. They drew her in the way a snake bewitched its prey. She was certain she could see the vase and the stone carving vibrating. All strength left her body.

Wrenching her gaze free, the cat crawled lethargically away from the grate. If she didn't get out of here soon, she was doomed.

★

The platform at Bury train station was rammed with people, but that's how Rae wanted it. Easier to slip unnoticed onto the train when it arrived. She squeezed through the crowd of commuters – kids her age who must live in nearby villages and shop-workers who were finished for the day – looking for the perfect spot. If she hung out near some teenage girls she should escape notice.

A few boys shot her lazy glances that made her gut quiver as she passed. What if one of them came over? She fired a warning look at the nearest one and his friends howled with laughter, slapping him on the shoulder.

Rae slipped away, stopping by a group of girls. They ignored her, staring at something on one of the girls' phones. Their shrieks split the air.

Just get away, she told herself. She forced herself to take a breath. If they checked tickets on the train, she'd hide in the toilet until the conductor moved on.

The monitor suspended above a field of heads announced that a train to Cambridge would arrive in three minutes. She'd go there, then switch to another. Whichever left quickest. She was desperate to see the countryside zipping by the window and count the miles between her and Bury St Edmunds. The town where Twig had died.

The town where I killed him.

She stared at the opposite platform, the beginnings of panic clutching at her. Bury station was tiny, consisting of just two platforms that faced one another over twin tracks. The other side was equally busy. For a second, she thought she glimpsed a tall blond man watching her. The crowd shifted and the man was gone. Laurent couldn't have followed her. She was being paranoid.

Rae noticed people jostling about nearby and wondered what was happening. Her shoulders tensed. Two policemen in bright yellow reflective gear eased their way through the crowd, scanning their surroundings flintily.

Rae's pulse quickened.

They're not after you. Stop being paranoid.

What if they had those cameras in the town centre? The ones that watched people? What if the police had seen her leaving the crater of Retro Threads? They could be after her.

She imagined how it probably looked to them. A building exploding and some kid – *some homeless nobody, a trouble-making out-of-towner* – running away, leaving behind half a morgue's worth of dead bodies. They'd think she did it on purpose. That she'd *wanted* to blow the shop up.

Her head pounded. There were too many people. She'd never get away if she ran. She couldn't run if she tried.

She cursed her own stupidity and chanced a look down the platform. The police were closing in. Her eyes locked with one of the officers and his face changed. His jaw hardened into a line and he shot a glance at his partner. They both stared at her.

No.

Rae tried to push her way through the crowd, away from the officers.

"Move! Out of the way!" a voice shouted. Confused mumbles rippled along the platform and Rae was afraid. There was no way off. The police were between her and the exit. All she could do was hurry to the other end and hope there was another way out.

"Move!" one of the officers shouted. He sounded close.

Rae shouldered between people, mutters and tuts following her. And another sound. A faint vibration. The train was approaching. She'd never make it aboard now. Even if she managed to clamber on, the police would follow. Then she really would be trapped.

A hand clenched her arm. A man wearing a baseball cap. One of the passengers.

"I think they want a word with you, love," he said.

"Leave off me!" Rae yelled, wrenching her arm free.

"Hey–" the man protested, but Rae elbowed past him.

"Stop her!" the officer hollered.

Rae heard the train approaching. The tracks shuddered and she was only halfway along the platform. It was impossible. She'd never escape. The crowd parted to let the officers through and they closed in, now barely ten feet away.

The tracks.

Rae teetered on the edge of the platform, watching the train rattle closer.

The officers were almost upon her.

Steeling herself, Rae knew there was no other option.

She jumped onto the tracks.

Horrified gasps fizzled above her and Rae ignored them, staring down the train as it thundered toward her. The vibrations shook her bones and she braced herself on the tracks.

"Get off there!" one of the officers cried.

Rae ignored him. Heat raged through her, but she couldn't let go. She'd controlled her power with Laurent, she could do it again. But she didn't trust herself here. Not with so many people around.

Stand your ground.

She had to wait for just the right moment. If she jumped onto the other platform as the train arrived, it would block the police. By the time they made it to the other side, she'd be long gone.

The train's whistle screeched and the boys on the platform whooped like gorillas. Were they cheering her on or desperate to see her steamrollered into a gory mess?

One of the officers clambered down onto the tracks and Rae knew she had to move now.

As the train bore down on her, she hopped out of the way and breathlessly clambered onto the other platform. The crowd stood dumbfounded. Mouths hung open. Others sobbed.

Rae pushed into the throng, hustling people aside, but a hand snatched at her and she found herself staring into the exasperated face of one of the officers. He'd followed her across the tracks.

"That's enough," the policeman huffed, sweat pouring down his face.

"Let me go!" Rae yelled.

Don't do it. Don't.

The heat raged. Molten lava coursed through her veins. The roof above the platform shook and Rae tried to calm her pulse, but everybody was staring at her and the officer's grip was iron.

Freak.

People peered nervously at the roof as it shook more violently.

No. Don't.

The people on the platform backed away from her. She was contagious. Dangerous. She might as well have a bomb strapped to her chest.

The roof rumbled like thunder. The metal supports shrieked.

"Get off me," Rae warned the policeman. He began dragging her through the crowd.

The roof peeled open like a tin can. Debris rained down and the officer released her. Terrified howls reverberated through the station and Rae seized her moment. She barrelled down the platform, shoving anybody who got in her way, blindly tearing away from the officer. A din of shouts buffeted her from all sides.

She didn't stop until she was out on the street, pausing only to scan the car park for more police officers. There weren't any, so she ran.

She ran, ran, *ran*, her breath catching in her throat, the screams of the people on the platform deafening her, even though she'd left them far behind.

Finally, she was forced to stop. Rae crouched in a side street, hiccupping up sobs. The faces of the people she'd almost killed filled her vision. Their derision turning to fear. The wails as she tore away the platform's roof.

She hadn't wanted to. She hadn't meant to.

Were they hurt? Dead?

Rae forced herself to breathe deeply, to curb the sobs.

It had been a glimpse of the future. If she didn't get herself under control, she'd become even more volatile. She'd already killed, and she'd kill again. She couldn't let that happen.

Run, the familiar voice urged.

No.

She couldn't run anymore. She'd run her whole life and where had it gotten her? She had to find a way to control whatever it was that churned inside of her. It's what Twig would have said. He'd seen what she could do in the alley and he hadn't run away. But he was dead, and there was only one person left in the world who wasn't afraid of her.

In a daze, Rae staggered up the street. The museum wasn't far. Filled with resolve, she hurried into the Market Square and finally reached Moyse's Hall. Sweaty and bleary-eyed, she careened into the lobby.

A man looked up from the desk and relief washed through her. He was still here.

"You're back," Laurent smiled.

*

An hour later, Rae sank onto the edge of the camp bed in the office, her hands wedged under her legs. She'd told Laurent everything. She hadn't cried again. She felt more clear-headed than she had in years.

"I'm going to help you," Laurent said softly, his arms crossed as he leaned against the wall.

She stared at her lap, broken, sapped of any defiance. "Thanks."

"You have a powerful gift, Rae. You can help people."

She caught the scoff before it blurted out. *All I do is hurt people.*

"I killed Kay," she whispered, unable to keep it inside anymore. "She was my friend. The only one... She taught me how to get by on the street. I killed her."

"Tell me what happened," Laurent said. There was no judgement in his voice.

"She wouldn't stop going on. She wanted to know how I ended up on the street and she wouldn't leave it alone." Rae's throat constricted. Her rules for survival fell apart before her eyes.

Don't make friends.
Don't talk about your past.
Don't tell anybody what you can do.
Don't show weakness.
Don't let the monsters see you.

They were useless now. They'd been useless all along. All they'd done was cause her pain.

"She kept pushing and *pushing*... I got angry..."

Laurent crouched before her. "The world is sick," he uttered mellifluously. "There are things out there far worse than you, believe me."

"They sound terrifying."

He laughed. "You have no idea. What I said about monsters is true. They're everywhere and they're multiplying. If you directed that power at them, there would be no stopping you."

Laurent wanted her to become a fighter? Rae didn't know what to think. She was so tired. She'd fought before – the streets were a breeding ground for petty squabbles – but never using her power. She didn't think she'd ever want to. She'd seen the monsters that scrabbled about at night and they were hideous, stinking, terrifying. She couldn't possibly face them.

If Laurent helped her control the churning, though...
He didn't need to know that she couldn't fight.
"What do we do?" she asked.

CHAPTER FIFTEEN
BREAKING IN

николаs examined a wall in dawn's purple bedroom. It was plastered with more documents than he could count. Posters. Maps. Newspaper clippings. Photographs. Star charts. There were pins and bits of string zigzagging in determined lines. It was exactly like the walls he'd seen on cop TV shows where the movements of serial killers were tracked in desperate, meticulous detail.

"Do you believe in fate?" he asked.

"I didn't used to," Dawn said, seated at her desk, bathed in the glow of her laptop. She was so quiet, but he didn't mind. He sensed that Dawn only spoke if there was something important to say. She wasn't like other teenagers, most of whom seemed to spend their time making as much noise as possible.

"But you do now?"

Dawn took a swig from a can of fizzy drink. "I don't want to. It's stupid and sentimental. A way of explaining something we don't understand."

"Like?"

Dawn shrugged. "Vikings rationalised things that couldn't be explained by creating the *norns*; they were mythical beings that wove the fate of men and gods like it was a grand tapestry, a story in cloth." She paused. "I don't believe in fate... but how do you explain the fact that I'm here at the same time as Laurent and you and that girl. We all ended up in the exact same place for different reasons, but we're all connected somehow."

"Maybe it's like a mathematical equation," Nicholas suggested. "Probability or something. No matter how improbable something seems to be, there's still a probability, no matter how tiny, that it could happen."

"I like that."

"Or Laurent's here because he wants to throw me the goriest birthday party ever."

"It's your birthday?"

"In..." Nicholas counted in his head. "Two days. Wonder what he's going to get me."

Dawn fiddled with the can. "At first I thought he'd come for me," she admitted softly. "I saw him for the first time last week and I thought maybe he'd come to finish me off."

Nicholas didn't know what to say. He couldn't offer any comforting words, so he inspected one of the newspaper clippings tacked to the wall. "That why you didn't talk to me when I got here?"

Dawn picked at her nails. She shrugged. "Scared, I suppose."

"Of me?"

"No. That it was time to fight again. I didn't want to be part of it."

"You don't have to be."

"Like I have a choice anymore."

Nicholas understood. The stage was being set for a battle that would affect everybody. Dawn had as much right to fight as he did.

"What's it like?" he asked. "Growing up knowing about all of this stuff?"

"What's it like not knowing?"

"Good point. Your nan know you've done that to your wall?"

Dawn shrugged again. Nicholas leaned in closer to one of the newspaper articles. It reported a robbery at a rich bureaucrat's home in France. An expensive Chinese vase had been taken.

"What's this?" he asked.

Dawn swivelled her chair. "Oh, just something I thought might be relevant."

"How?"

"Well, you know I tracked Laurent after Cambodia? Or, tried to. Paris was one of the places he stopped off at. I don't know how long he was there, but nothing particularly interesting happened in that period. No bombs, no strange deaths. But that vase was stolen from Andre Bisset's home. He's some important art collector. The vase is old and valuable, but nobody's seen it since."

"You think Laurent took it? Why would he do that?"

"I'm not sure yet," Dawn said, returning to the laptop and typing. "But it has a strange history. Ah!" She slumped back in her chair, apparently defeated by something. Nicholas ambled over. Dawn had hacked into the local council's database and was attempting to find the entrances to the catacombs beneath the town.

"Find anything?" he asked.

"Nothing," Dawn said, sounding annoyed. "I think the tunnels were built before anybody ever heard of a blueprint. The monks used them."

Nicholas lowered himself into the wicker chair by the window. So much for Sentinel training. He couldn't even find something a layer of tarmac away. And Esus thought he was capable of raising the old gods. With his broken arm, he could barely even tie his shoelaces. They had looked online for anything about the word 'Tortor', too; the word the hideous old crone at the school had uttered. All that came up was that same Latin definition: Tortor meant executioner or torturer.

"Do you think it's possible? Raising the Dark Prophets?"

"Nobody's succeeded so far," Dawn said.

"Laurent thinks it can be done."

"Laurent's nuts."

"And Esus thinks I have the power to wake up the Trinity. How does that even work? I mean, do I ring some sort of supernatural alarm clock?"

"If we knew that, we wouldn't be here."

"How much do you know about the Prophets?" All Nicholas knew was that they were the baddest of the bad. They'd been banished by the Trinity to a hell dimension, but they wanted back in.

"Nobody knows exactly what they are," Dawn admitted. "There are illustrations of them as dragons, as men with horns, as goat-footed monsters. There are always three, though. That's the only consistency between any of the theories."

"Three Prophets. Three members of the Trinity."

"That's generally how it works. The universe loves symmetry. Matter and anti-matter. Yin and yang."

They heard the front door go.

"That might be Sam," Nicholas said, hopping to his feet. What he'd sensed about the tunnels made him anxious. The whoops of excitement and the bitter tang of blood. Something big was happening down there – it could be happening right now. "Come on," he said.

They went downstairs and into the lounge. Sam sat in one of the armchairs. His arm was bandaged and he rubbed his forehead wearily.

"You okay?" Nicholas asked.

"Long day," the old man said. "How's the arm?"

"Annoying. What happened to yours?"

"Malika."

Nicholas felt winded. "You saw her? What happened?"

"She's the one responsible for the gauntlets," Sam said. "We found one of her dens. We escaped, but by the time other Sentinels arrived to apprehend her, she was gone. Burned the place to the ground."

"So she's still out here?"

"I'm afraid so."

Nicholas chewed his lip. It was bad enough that they had Laurent to go up against without Malika out there scheming, too. Was she still after him? She'd tried to make him kill Jessica when she broke into Hallow House. Would she try again? He envisioned a vulture hovering over a wounded animal. If Malika was working with Laurent, she probably wasn't breaking much of a sweat. She'd observe the world's dying spasms, then pick its bones clean.

He wanted to know more, but he had to tell Sam what he'd discovered. "We figured out where Laurent's hiding. He's using the tunnels."

"Tunnels?" Aileen asked apprehensively, coming into the lounge with a tea set.

"The ones under the town; the ones you told me about," Nicholas elaborated. "He's using them to get around. Or at least we think he is. He must have the girl down there, the one Esus wants me to find. The seeing glass... I think something's happening down there right now. Something big."

"The Bury tunnels," Sam breathed, straightening in the chair. "I thought they were a myth. Do you know a way in?"

Nicholas shook his head, frustrated. What if Laurent had already started whatever he'd planned? What if they were already too late?

"There are entrances all over town," Aileen chimed in, setting the crockery down on the coffee table. "If the old wives' tales are to be believed. That reminds me of old Mr Pearson. I used to help out at one of the cafes on Abbeygate Street and my boss, Mr Pearson, he used to talk about a funny trapdoor in the cellar that led into some tunnels. Used to joke they went all the way to Australia. Wasn't known for his sense of humour, Mr Pearson..."

"Which cafe was that?" Sam asked.

"Now let me think," Aileen mused. "Yes, it's called Abigail's now. They changed the name when Mr Pearson died. I don't know anybody there these days, though."

Nicholas recognised the glint in Sam's eye.

"We're going out again, aren't we?" he asked.

Sam got to his feet. "Aileen, call as many Sentinels as you can. Tell them where we're headed. I'll phone Liberty."

The landlady bustled quickly from the room and Nicholas noticed Dawn moving for the hall.

"Thanks," he said, stopping her in her tracks. "For, you know, today."

Dawn looked embarrassed and nodded, then disappeared.

Sam paced into the hall and picked up the phone. Nicholas heard him talking and replacing the phone into its cradle.

"Liberty knows where we're going," the old man said as Nicholas joined him. He popped the battered grey fedora on. "You can never be too careful, especially where people like Laurent are concerned." He didn't question what Nicholas had sensed about the tunnels. Sam was trusting him completely, which made Nicholas jittery. What if it was a trap? What if his vision was wrong? They could be going to their deaths.

Before he could talk to Sam about his uneasiness, though, the elderly man had stepped out the front door. Nicholas hurried after him, their footsteps ringing in the alley. Sam clasped his satchel and rifle,

Nicholas squeezed the Drujblade at his hip, reassured by its presence.

"What if it's bad down there?" he asked. He thought of the whoops and cheers. "What if Laurent isn't alone? *She* could be down there."

"Remember what we talked about, the different types of battles? This is pure reconnaissance. We're gathering information only."

"And if we're caught?"

"We fight. You know how to use that dagger?"

Nicholas nodded. He couldn't tell if he was being cowardly or canny by questioning Sam. This was what Sentinels did, after all. They had to stop Laurent. But Sam looked desperate. So far, Laurent had eluded them and this was the first break they'd had. Nicholas understood Sam's urgency, but that didn't quiet his nerves.

"You sure you're alright?" he asked. He dreaded to think what the bandage on Sam's arm was hiding.

"Fine, lad."

For the first time, Nicholas was worried for him. Sam seemed to have forgotten he was seventy-one years old. He had to be more careful. Nicholas was glad they were investigating the tunnels together, though he wasn't sure how much help he'd actually be if they had to fight.

What if Malika really is down there? he thought.

Anger trembled beneath his ribs. He'd hoped he'd never see Malika again. He'd been naïve to think she would simply retreat, though. She was a vicious monster, and he was learning that those sorts of things wouldn't stop until they were put down.

How could they defeat Malika, though? She was wily and resilient. Nicholas had watched Sam burying two bullets in her, neither of which stopped her for very long. If she was working with Laurent, or worse, the Prophets themselves...

Nicholas realised he was clenching the Drujblade at his side so tightly that his knuckles hurt.

"Ah, here we are," Sam breathed.

They were halfway up Abbeygate Street. Abigail's cafe was quaint with an old-fashioned hanging sign. A hand-drawn cup of coffee emitted tendrils of steam that spelled out the business' name. Net curtains were pleated neatly in the window.

The street was quiet as they approached the door. They were lucky

– there were no restaurants at this end of the street. A murmur of voices floated from a few hundred metres away as diners chatted over their evening meals. Nicholas and Sam were tucked out of sight by the door.

"Eyes, lad," Sam said. Nicholas nodded, standing with his back to the cafe and watching the street. He heard the old man using his lock-picking kit for the third time in almost as many days. The moon peeked interestedly over the chimneys above them.

Nicholas heard the door open and hurried into the cafe with Sam. A curtain on the back of the door shielded their activities from the street. The moment they began walking between the tables, which were stacked with upside-down chairs, an ear-piercing shriek filled the cafe.

They had triggered the alarm.

"Blast," Sam yelled over the noise. "I'd hoped there wouldn't be one. We need to move quickly." He hurried to the back of the cafe and Nicholas followed. They found nothing more than a small kitchen, so they returned to the shop front.

Had Aileen been wrong? Nicholas didn't want to doubt her, but with the alarm wailing, he began to panic. Any second now the police would arrive. He felt sick. He'd never had a proper run-in with the police – the night he'd been found sleepwalking in the snow in the wake of his parents' deaths didn't really count – and there would be no way of talking their way out of this.

The alarm screamed at him.

Out, out, out, it shrieked.

"Here," Nicholas called, spotting a square in the floor by the coffee machine. He tugged at a metal ring with his free hand and lifted the trapdoor. Steps led down into the cellar.

"Good lad," Sam said, descending first.

Nicholas hesitated, recalling the basement at Snelling's. He didn't have a choice, though, and Sam hadn't exactly blanched at the thought of another basement. Gulping down his uneasiness, Nicholas clambered down the steps, finding it difficult to squeeze through the cramped opening with his broken arm.

At least the alarm was muffled down here. The cellar was cramped and stacked full of boxes illustrated with coffee beans. A door at the back led to another stock room.

"Where is it?" Nicholas asked, his desperation mounting. "Where's the trapdoor?"

"Move those boxes," Sam ordered evenly, setting his rifle down and heaving one of the cardboard obstructions out of the way.

Ignoring the complaints of his broken arm, Nicholas used his good one to shove a box across the floor. Sweating from the exertion and struggling to breathe in the airless stockroom, he moved box after box, the thought of the police spurring him on. They *had* to find a way into the tunnels.

Finally, they had cleared a space at the back of the stockroom.

An unremarkable round metal plate was set into the stone floor. It looked like a manhole. Old and ordinary. Nicholas supposed the more mundane the entrance to the tunnels was, the less conspicuous it would seem. Still, he couldn't help imagining that they were about to open up a sewer.

"How do we open it?" he asked. He doubted if this entrance had been used in decades. What if it had rusted shut?

Sam tapped his nose and retrieved something from his satchel. Nicholas watched as he unravelled a thin wire and dug it into the grooves around the edge of the manhole.

"Step back," the old man said, striking a match. He lit the end of the wire and blue sparks fizzed along its length, wreathing the manhole in smoke. When the sparks met, a muted WHUMP resounded through the stockroom and the manhole jumped in its stone seat.

Nicholas wondered what else Sam had hidden in his bag. He looked up, sure he'd heard somebody moving above their heads.

The alarm continued wailing.

"Give us a hand," the old man entreated, crouching over the metal plate. "Just the one," he added with a wink. Nicholas helped him heave the plate up and together they slid it across the floor. The old man motioned him back again and pointed a torch into the hollow. With a satisfied sniff, he looked at Nicholas.

"Ready for a little sight-seeing?" He packed everything back into his satchel and drew some of the boxes back around the hole to hide the entranceway once more. Sam went foot-first into the ground, lowering himself down into the tunnels.

Thump, thump, thump.

Nicholas looked up. He'd definitely heard something that time. It sounded like boots stomping across the floor above.

The police.

Heart hammering, he hurried over to the hole in the ground. Sam peered up at him.

"It's safe. Come on, lad."

Suddenly the thought of confining themselves to the catacombs beneath Bury St Edmunds seemed foolish. If this was where Laurent had made his nest, they'd be trapped with the most dangerous man imaginable. The man responsible for killing Dawn's dad and having her mum committed to a psychiatric ward. The man who wanted to turn the world down-side up.

"Yeah, let's just offer ourselves up to Laurent in his underground lair. That sounds like a great idea," Nicholas grumbled to himself. He swung his legs over the side of the hole and attempted to lower himself into the tunnel with his good arm. He lost his grip and fell, hitting the dirt floor hard.

"Easy there, lad," Sam said.

Nicholas coughed and wrinkled his nose at the fusty air. Above him, Sam reached through the hole and Nicholas heard the metal plate scraping across the stockroom floor. It clunked into place and they were sealed inside the tunnels.

CHAPTER SIXTEEN
UNDERGROUND

Nicholas eyed his surroundings apprehensively. There was no going back now. The walls curved around him, as if carved in the wake of a giant worm. Bricks knitted together over his head and unlit gas lamps lined the bibulous swerve of the pathway. A pungent reek of damp faeces made him purse his lips. A pale blue light glimmered somewhere further into the tunnels and the silence was unnerving.

He clutched the Drujblade at his belt.

"Remarkable," Sam said, peering around the tunnel. "Some myth. People used to say they were used by the monks when the Abbey was still standing. Supposedly there's a network of them under the entire town. If the stories are true, you could cross the whole of Bury without ever seeing a soul. Apparently they were sealed off at some point. Forgotten about."

"Somebody remembered," Nicholas said.

"Let's go. And, lad—" Sam tapped his nose. Nicholas nodded his understanding. Cautiously, they worked their way through the catacombs. It felt like they were foraging through the dried-up arteries of the Earth itself. Nicholas wondered where they were in relation to the town. Were they heading toward the Market Square? Or nearer to Aileen's safehouse? It was impossible to tell as the tunnel wove on.

"Do you think he'll do it?" Nicholas whispered when he couldn't bear the blood thumping in his ears any longer.

"What?"

"Raise them. The Dark Prophets."

Sam's shoulders stiffened and the pounding in Nicholas's ears quickened.

"No," the old man whispered gruffly. "He'll fail just like the rest."

"Other people have tried it?"

"Course. Any adept or Prophet worshipper worth their weight has tried to resurrect the Prophets; or at least claimed to. Fools. It's nothing more than an arrogant endeavour to inspire awe in those around them."

"And they all failed?"

"We're still here, aren't we, eh?"

The thought reassured him until Nicholas thought of Laurent. No matter what anybody said, he didn't seem crazy. An extremist, definitely, but not a madman. Not somebody with a convoluted plan that served only to set him apart from the other servants of the Prophets. He was deadly in his intelligence. You could tell that from his predatory glare and the way he carried himself, as if the secrets of creation were in his keeping.

And Laurent wanted the girl. Possibly had her already. That was the most important part. Laurent had searched for her just as, Nicholas presumed, Esus had. How long had Esus looked for her? Ever since he chose Jessica as his successor? That was almost five-hundred years.

Sam made a hushed sound and came to a standstill before him.

The passage divided into three. They could carry on straight ahead, follow it to the right, or go left. The final option seemed the least likely; the tunnel appeared to make a U-turn and run parallel to the one they were already in.

Nicholas paused. A familiar, uncomfortable prickling stirred in the pit of his stomach and he felt drawn to the tunnel on his left. Cautiously, he peeked around the corner.

His grip on the Drujblade tightened.

Two figures stood on either side of a circular door. A man and a woman. The passageway was short and unlit, ending in a dusty round door with an ornate, hammered-iron lock. Nicholas was thankful that he and Sam weren't visible from this angle. The odd couple must be Harvesters. They were festooned in weaponry. Daggers hung from their belts and the woman had a sword mounted on her back. The man clenched a blood-stained whip.

There's something in there, Nicholas thought.

He stared at the cobwebby door that the Harvesters were guarding. It was fashioned out of black wood with large, dull rivets. Neglected. Something important resided inside. The prickling in his stomach confirmed it. Nicholas's skin crawled, as if snakes were slithering all over him.

Sam tapped his shoulder and jerked his thumb to the side. Nicholas nodded. He followed Sam's back down the tunnel to the right, out of view of the Harvesters. This one was brighter. There was a glow ahead and the drone of voices. Nicholas thought he was imagining it at first, but the sound grew louder as they walked. His insides shuddered with dread.

What now? he wondered.

Sam raised the rifle, which Nicholas took as a sign of impending danger. He drew the Drujblade from its sheath. If only he didn't have his stupid arm in a cast. When he was younger, he'd thought kids with casts were cool. Now he understood how annoying they really were. Potentially life-threatening, too, in his case. He was a one-armed fighter and not by choice.

He snapped to as the hum of voices was replaced with a sharp tone that whistled through the catacombs.

There was no mistaking the voice. It was Laurent.

The tunnel was deserted, though. Where was he?

Nicholas and Sam edged further toward the voice. Nicholas couldn't help feeling they should be turning around and running in the opposite direction. They were here now, though. Why had they come into the tunnels if they were just going to retreat when they found Laurent? They had to find out what he was up to. Nicholas hoped it wouldn't hurt. He glimpsed the end of the passage. Dark red curtains obscured whatever lay beyond. There were no guards, which only served to increase Nicholas's unease. What was going on?

Sam went ahead. He turned to the side, rifle raised, and put an eye to the gap in the drapes. His expression was as unreadable as ever. Nicholas crouched next to him and Sam raised his finger to his lips before letting Nicholas peek inside.

A sickly radiance struggled to illuminate a congregation of people.

Not people. *Harvesters*. The chamber had a low ceiling but it was large enough to fit at least fifty of them – and a stage to the back. The figure on the stage surveyed his audience down his long, straight nose, bright eyes glittering. The soupy light was cast by mottled bronze lamps that Nicholas imagined had once held candles, but were now hooked up to a power supply. There was a dull buzz in the air. The crackle and moan of electricity.

"This night belongs to us."

Laurent's voice swept over the audience. Variously scarred and blade-bearing, each Harvester sneered or hunched against his or her neighbour. Nicholas realised this must be why only two Harvesters had been spared to guard the peculiar door they had passed – nobody wanted to miss Laurent's address.

"We were born into the night, and it is the night that we shall reclaim," Laurent called. He wore a dark red jacket and he looked just as Nicholas remembered him from that day in the Abbey Gardens. Sharp shoulders were drawn back arrogantly, blond hair swept up from a brooding brow. "We shall be the first to succeed where others have failed. We are the children of the Dark Prophets. Blades, fire, poison. None shall stop us, for we are the undying things of night and nightmare. We are possessed of enough might and wisdom to raise the Prophets in all their majesty."

The Harvesters jostled together in eagerness, heads craned, nostrils flaring.

For a moment, Nicholas glimpsed what they must see in Laurent. A man of such confidence that it seemed he could achieve anything. Nicholas shivered. Laurent's words were as purple as his lips, but every Harvester appeared to have fallen under their spell.

"The Tortor will rise," Laurent said. "The Tortor will rise and the skies will rain blood and ash."

A cheer arose. Blades jabbed the air and Nicholas wished he was far, far away from here.

Tortor, he thought. Just what was it? Whatever it was, it appeared to be crucial to Laurent's plan.

Laurent surveyed the crowd. He tipped his head, appearing to listen to something other than the adoration of his assembled devotees.

"They whisper to me," he said softly when the cheering had subsided. "They see each and every one of you. They are the disseminators of every dark thought that was ever turned into action. It is Their desire that stabs and strangles and drowns. You are Their fists. You have been chosen."

He stopped again, listening to something that nobody else could hear. The sneering grin that split his face made Nicholas shudder.

"We have guests," Laurent called over the collected Harvesters. He looked right at the gap in the curtain where Nicholas was peeking through. "Welcome, Nicholas and Samuel."

Nicholas's knees almost buckled. Every single head swivelled toward where he and Sam were listening.

"Nicholas, run!" Sam hissed. He tore the curtain aside, pointing the rifle into the room and firing at the first Harvester that lurched toward them.

"Seize them," Laurent commanded calmly.

There was an explosion of smoke and blood as Sam fired again, followed by the peal of angry shrieks. Together, Nicholas and Sam hurried back the way they had come. The old man paused a moment to fire once more. Bricks erupted violently.

Still the Harvesters surged forward.

Nicholas staggered down the tunnel. He glanced over his shoulder and saw a large Harvester swing a leather-strapped fist at Sam. The elderly man ducked out of the way and the knuckles scuffed his temple.

"Sam!"

Nicholas's voice echoed in the passage. A sea of eyes flashed in his direction.

"Run, boy!" Sam yelled, fighting a raging tide of fists and blades. He was caught. The Harvesters closed around him and Nicholas couldn't see him anymore. Gritting his teeth, he charged at the mass of bodies, slashing blindly with the Drujblade. He heard muffled grunts and felt something hot and wet. The blade was stuck, so he wrenched it free.

Then his feet left the ground.

He was in the air, gripped by one of the Harvesters. The large one who had struck Sam.

"NO!" Nicholas cried. Pain ricocheted through his broken arm as it was crushed to his chest. He felt bone scraping bone and weakness engulfed him, rendering him useless.

"Come, come," Laurent's voice drawled. "Welcome to our gathering."

Through a bright haze of pain, Nicholas saw that they weren't in the tunnel anymore. Sallow light ebbed from the bronze lamps and Nicholas found himself on the stage. The Harvester set him back on his feet. His arm throbbed, felt boneless and heavy. Then Laurent's bright blue eyes loomed closer, scrutinising him coolly, and Nicholas knew there was no escape.

"Young Nicholas, how wonderful to see you again. You're still recovering. Funny how cumbersome a broken arm can be. You must feel so fragile. A cub with an injured paw."

Sam. Where's Sam? he thought.

"You survived the aledites." Nicholas couldn't tell if there was admiration or annoyance in Laurent's tone. "Few would have; fewer still in such fine form. You have mettle, boy."

The nausea began to subside, overtaken by fear, and Nicholas saw that Sam was standing a few feet behind him. His hat was missing and his arms were behind his back, held fast by a woman with dark, curly hair. She hissed something in Sam's ear.

Laurent reached a hand out, fingers splayed.

"Stay back," Nicholas growled, fumbling at his belt. The Drujblade was gone. What had happened to it? He must have dropped it during the scuffle. He was utterly defenceless. A mouse in a nest of rats. All he could do was hug his broken arm and push his chin out defiantly.

Don't show the fear. They'll eat you alive.

Laurent laughed. "Bravery eh?" he said. "The size of the fight in the dog is what matters. You're an example to us all."

"You're sick," Nicholas spat. His head cleared as the throbbing in his arm dulled.

Laurent's amusement only seemed to increase at the insult. He reminded Nicholas of a swarthy gameshow host – there to entertain the audience no matter what.

"Sickness," Laurent said firmly, "is nothing to trivialise, young man. Take the Sentinels. The corruption there is quite something. If you knew anything about your own history, you'd understand a thing or two about sickness. Did you know that certain Sentinels drill holes in their foreheads? They believe it will open their third eye and a direct line to the Trinity."

A few of the Harvesters spat on the ground and heckled.

"They—" Nicholas began.

"Others hack off their ears and cut out their tongues, believing it will enable them to hear the Trinity's secret whispers," Laurent interrupted with all the importance of a world-weary teacher. "And that's just the self-mutilation. What they've done to those you might consider 'innocent' is even more disturbing."

"Lies." Sam's voice gruffed over Nicholas's shoulder.

"Samuel." Laurent regarded the old man with undisguised disdain. "Still fighting after all these years. You just don't know how to die, do you? You must tell me your secret."

Secrets. Nicholas found himself thinking back to the night he'd encountered Laurent in the Abbey Gardens. *"Secrets between friends can be deadly,"* he'd said. What had he meant by that?

"Bury St Edmunds is fascinating, don't you think?" Laurent continued. He seemed to like the sound of his own voice. "The power emanating from the Abbey ruins is remarkable. It's one of the most powerful sites in the country. Which is, of course, why we're here. Surely you can feel it?"

Sam didn't answer.

"Nicholas? No? A pity. It really is invigorating, especially here in these catacombs. You can practically hear the earth's heartbeat."

He turned to address the Harvesters.

"The Prophets have surrendered a gift this night," he called over the crowd. Nicholas imagined he could see black thoughts polluting the space above their heads. Their eyes were on him and Sam. A young Harvester wet his lips and pressed a thumb-ring with a spike to his cheek.

They want us dead.

"The Prophets," Laurent continued, "have rewarded your unwavering faith with a gift. Two gifts, in fact. This old fossil and this young cub are emissaries of the Trinity. They seek to destroy you, but tonight it is they who shall we destroyed."

"Split open their veins and let us bathe in their blood!" one of the Harvesters snarled.

"The child! Give us the child!"

A female Harvester shoved the man at her side, the whites of her eyes ablaze with bloodlust. "The child is mine!" she growled, unsheathing a dagger with a serrated edge.

Laurent's laughter curdled the air.

"Esmerelda," he said. "You wish to claim the cub? Then come for him."

Nicholas looked from Laurent to the woman with the dagger. She was skinny but solid, muscle rippling under bleached, freckled skin. Her head was shaved, her skull etched with tattoos. She clambered up onto the stage with the agility of a leopard, leering at him, her eyes shining with a mad hunger. He'd seen that look before in Snelling.

He couldn't breathe.

"Lad," Sam said.

"Silence him," Laurent uttered. Sam grunted and didn't speak again. Nicholas couldn't tear his gaze away from the Harvester called Esmerelda. She flipped the dagger in her hand as if it were nothing more than a small coin.

"Let us measure the size of the fight in this dog," Laurent drawled, his face filling with the same crazed expression as Esmerelda's.

Esmerelda barked and Nicholas jumped. She snickered and slashed at him with the dagger. Nicholas flinched before realising that she hadn't come close enough to cut him. She sniggered again. She was toying with him.

They circled about on the stage. Nicholas peered at Sam over Esmerelda's bony shoulder. The curly-haired Harvester holding him captive clamped her hand over his mouth and Sam's eyes bulged.

"Yap yap!" Esmerelda shrieked, slashing the air with the dagger.

"Stick him!" one of the Harvesters yelled.

"Slice him! Cut him!"

Where was the Drujblade? Nicholas tried to come up with a plan, tried to remember what Sam had taught him in Aileen's garden. *Hands up.* It was impossible with all those eyes on him. Angry voices baying for his blood. And he only had one hand to work with this time.

Anger. He had to get angry. It was the only way he could fight the fear. He thought back to Snelling; how Snelling had tricked his way into Hallow House. How the anger had pumped through him hotly, instinct taking over.

Forget the arm. Fight.

Esmerelda struck out with the dagger again and, without thinking, Nicholas snatched at her. He clasped the hand clenched around the knife's handle.

She tugged. Attempted to pull the blade free, but he held tight. Her forehead crinkled with annoyance and she seized his shoulder, smashing her forehead against his.

Crack.

A cheer went up. A shiver of cackles.

Bright lights exploded in front of him and Nicholas staggered back, grabbing his head where a sharp pain pulsed.

That was stupid.

The lights popped and faded and Esmerelda remained, fired up, urged on by the crowd. Laurent lingered behind her, his fingers steepled together, drinking in every detail of the scene. Nicholas had the feeling he was being tested. Just as the aledites were a test. Did Laurent really want him dead? Would he step in if Esmerelda found a home for the dagger? Was that the real test?

Silver flashed before his eyes and Nicholas only just dodged out of the way in time to evade the dagger. A fist came at him. Esmerelda was advancing her attack.

Nicholas ducked away again. A fist struck his jaw and he didn't feel pain, only rage. An eruption of fury.

Yes.

He retaliated, imagining the cushions he'd jabbed during Sam's training. He hurled a punch that cuffed Esmerelda's right cheek. He thrust again and winced as his knuckles struck bone. Esmerelda staggered slightly. Exhilaration set his heart racing, but Nicholas didn't have time to celebrate.

Seething, Esmerelda flew at him, thrashing the blade at him.

Slash. Punch. Slash. Punch.

Nicholas dodged every deadly jab, but only just.

Enraged, Esmerelda lashed once more and Nicholas cried out as the dagger bit his shoulder.

Just a cut, he told himself. *It's not deep.*

He grabbed Esmerelda's hand once more. Holding it tightly, he hooked his foot behind her nearest leg, found the back of her knee and yanked.

Esmerelda shrieked angrily as her leg gave beneath her and she collapsed to one knee.

The dagger was his.

Nicholas wrenched it free. As he went to kick the Harvester in the face, Esmerelda seized his foot and dragged it out from beneath him.

His back hit the floor and the breath huffed from his lungs. Gasping, Nicholas found himself staring up into Esmerelda's crazed face as she threw herself on him. A haze of panic smothered him.

And then Esmerelda's eyes were wide with shock.

Hot wetness slid down his arm and Nicholas peered down to where the dagger was buried between Esmerelda's ribs. He hadn't meant to. Blind instinct had driven his hand up and now the blade was in her.

Get it out. Get it out.

He twisted and pulled and the blade came unstuck. Esmerelda made a strange sound. Blood spurted his T-shirt and the Harvester toppled to the floor beside him. She retched and floundered and finally lay still.

Nicholas was paralysed with shock.

I killed her.

A cacophony of hisses and boos erupted from the Harvesters and the crowd thrashed into motion. Bodies clambered onto the stage.

I killed her.

He was only vaguely aware of the Harvesters closing in. Bile burned his throat. He'd killed somebody. She lay next to him, dark liquid pooling around her, sliding towards him.

Then Nicholas noticed the unnatural quiet. The Harvesters had stopped in their tracks, mere feet away from where he lay, propped up on his elbows. Their eyes weren't on him anymore.

Nicholas followed the Harvesters' united gaze.

The girl.

She was on the stage with Laurent. He didn't know where she had come from, how much of the fight she had seen, but she was looking at him. Cold and detached, but intrigued. Wary. Gold buttons winked on her velvet green jacket. Her hair was pulled tight in a bun at the back. She looked smart. Different.

"You," Nicholas wheezed, fighting the rising bile.

"You know Rae?" Laurent asked innocently.

Rae. She has a name.

"You're her," Nicholas said. The adrenaline made his lips fat and clumsy. His tongue tripped over the words. "Rae. I've seen you. You have to come with me."

Laurent crowed loudly and rested a hand on Rae's shoulder.

"And where do you think you're going, Harvester slayer?" he implored patronisingly.

"Cut him! Kill him!" The Harvesters roared again and fists beat at the stone ceiling.

"He's using you," Nicholas told Rae urgently. "He doesn't care about you. All he cares about is death and pain. He wants to destroy everything."

She didn't blink, held his gaze.

"You're wrong," she said simply.

CHAPTER SEVENTEEN
SMOKE

NICHOLAS WANTED TO LAUGH, BUT HE knew it would come out as a hysteria-pinched shriek. He was losing his mind. Or she'd lost hers.

Laurent. It's Laurent, he thought. *He's done something to her.*

"Whatever he's said to you, he's a liar," Nicholas entreated desperately. He was still on the floor, staring up at her. He didn't trust himself to get up. If he moved too quickly, he'd throw up. His limbs were jelly. A wobbly mess.

Shock, he thought. *Must be*. The combined shock of killing Esmerelda and the throbbing discomfort of his arm.

For a moment, he'd forgotten about the body lying next to him. As he contemplated getting to his feet, though, he remembered Esmerelda and fresh nausea coursed through him. Cold sweat broke out over his top lip.

Rae's eyes became slits. What had Laurent told her?

"Dear boy," Laurent snarled. "If you continue to insult me, I may be forced to do something I'll later regret."

"Regret, ha!"

It was Sam who spoke this time. He was still behind Nicholas, though Nicholas couldn't see him from where he lay.

"Regret only comes with humility, humanity," Sam's voice said. "You're about as human as a reptile."

Laurent's features hardened. His cheekbones were razors, his eyes mercurial.

"Lies," he mused, his gaze returning to Nicholas. "Interesting that you speak of lies. I would suggest that you direct such accusations at your companion here, Nicholas. You might be surprised at what comes *slithering* out."

Nicholas didn't understand. Laurent was accusing Sam of lying to him? He twisted about on the floor and peered at Sam. The old man was still in the grip of the curly-haired Harvester, but he stared at Laurent with an unsettling mixture of hatred and fear.

"Sam?" he asked uneasily.

"Don't listen to him," Sam said curtly, though his eyes didn't leave Laurent.

"Your parents," Laurent said coolly. "Why don't you ask Sam about your parents, Nicholas?"

"My... what about them?"

The nausea evaporated and an icy chill flooded his veins. Sam looked so different. His face was a mask. Taut and tired.

"Or how about his wife? Why don't you ask Sam how his wife really died?"

A bellowing cry rang through the chamber as Sam struggled in the Harvester's grip. He wrenched his hands free and threw his elbow into the curly-haired woman's face. Blood sprayed from her nose and she collapsed backwards. Sam charged toward Laurent, but the other Harvesters descended, quickly subduing him.

Sam twisted in their hands but they held firm and the elderly man sagged, panting and exhausted.

"She was a midwife," Laurent said softly, undeterred. He seemed to be feeding on Sam's misery. "In fact, she was the only midwife in the village of Orville, which is why she was assigned to your parents, Nicholas. She was good at her job. Everybody liked Judith Wilkins. 'Jolly Judith' they called her, and not just because she was generous in her dimensions. She helped every mother in Orville safely deliver their precious, pink little parasites. Until, that is, your mother gave birth to you."

Nicholas was transfixed by Sam. His arms were held aloft either side of him by two Harvesters and his head sagged to his chest. He resembled a broken scarecrow.

"Your birth was magnificent," Laurent cooed. "A poem to

destruction. The entire village was obliterated. Judith, of course, bore the brunt of the explosion. She and your loving parents were killed. Even as you wriggled out of your mother, your first shrieking breath incinerated the three of them – and the rest of Orville."

Nicholas couldn't speak. Couldn't breathe.

Laurent lies, he told himself. *Laurent lies.*

As he looked at Sam, though, Nicholas knew this was no lie. Tears streamed down the pensioner's face. The fight had left him.

My parents weren't my parents.

Fresh nausea burned through him and, with it, Nicholas felt a familiar rage igniting deep in his chest. The same rage that had burned uncontrollably when his parents died. Anger at the world, at himself, at them. His parents.

Not my parents.

The floor tipped beneath him and he felt dizzy, as if an invisible rug had been pulled. Nicholas rolled onto his side and Esmerelda's dead eyes locked with his. He wanted to be sick. He retched and felt angry tears spiking.

This is what Laurent wants.

The thought brought him to his senses in an instant. Laurent was toying with them. Even if he was telling the truth, he was doing it to hurt him. To weaken him.

"Rae," Nicholas said, looking imploringly up at her. "You should leave. Get out of here."

"And you know what's best for me?" she snapped. She was so cold. Even colder than Laurent. There was no compassion in her face. She observed him as she might a wiggling worm. He imagined her crushing him under her boot.

"He's dangerous," Nicholas said.

"So am I."

"Nicholas," Laurent said softly, as if addressing a nephew he was fond of. "I fear your words fall on deaf ears. And you've outstayed your welcome. Perhaps you should take Sam and leave."

Nicholas slowly got to his feet, not believing what he was hearing. Laurent was letting them go? At Nicholas's distrustful expression, Laurent merely nodded and Nicholas traipsed over to Sam, careful not to turn his back on the Harvesters and their leader.

"You can't—" began one of the Harvesters holding Sam. Laurent raised an eyebrow and Sam was shoved into Nicholas's arms.

"Nicholas—" the old man began, his watery gaze meeting Nicholas's.

He couldn't say anything. He shouldered Sam's weight and began to make his way to the front of the stage, but a tall Harvester stepped into his path. Nicholas bumped into him and the Harvester pushed him roughly to the side. He almost stumbled over, but caught himself, steadying Sam beside him. Undeterred, he tried again, but the Harvester with the talon ring blocked his way.

The Harvester hissed at him. A low hiss that never ended. It was taken up by the others.

Laurent's laugh rolled up into the rocky ceiling and Nicholas shot him a look. He was still toying with them. Laurent wasn't letting them go.

The talon-wearing Harvester shoved his shoulder and Nicholas stepped back, steadied himself. He clenched his fist, fresh anger rising.

"Sam," he said.

At the sound of his name, the old man emerged from his torpor. The renewed danger seemed to have jolted him back into the present, made him momentarily forget the awful truth that had been revealed.

"Nicholas," he said, grabbing Nicholas's arm and pushing him behind him. "Stay back."

"No," Nicholas said, attempting to get around him, but Sam wouldn't have any of it. He squared up to the tightening pool of Harvesters, keeping Nicholas behind him.

"My bag," the old man whispered over his shoulder. "Where's my bag?"

Nicholas couldn't remember. The struggle in the tunnel had been so confused; he couldn't even recall being dragged to the stage. The pain in his arm had been so debilitating.

"Slash them, cut them, kill them," the Harvesters spat, slashing their blades through the air.

"BOY!"

A new voice entered the chamber and Nicholas's insides leapt. He scanned the Harvesters, not trusting his own ears. But then he saw her.

A black shape streaked through the chamber, using the Harvesters as stepping stones. The cat leapt from a head to a shoulder, moving so swiftly that the Harvesters didn't have time to react until it was too late. Finally, the cat had crossed the entire chamber and landed on the stage.

"Isabel," Nicholas uttered in disbelief.

The cat prowled in front of him, hissing at the Harvesters encircling them.

"You're alive," Nicholas said, still unable to believe it.

"Back!" the cat hissed at the Harvesters. "Back you brutes!"

The Harvesters looked down at her in confusion. Then one of them laughed. The laugh was taken up by the others and the cramped space rocked with the sound.

Laurent opened his mouth to speak, but a blinding flash lit the chamber and the ground shook. The laughing ceased abruptly.

Nicholas held on to Sam. Was this another of Laurent's tricks? The light seemed to have come from the entrance to the chamber. All heads pivoted in that direction and for a moment, Nicholas imagined he saw smoke. With a start, he realised he wasn't imagining it. Thick smoke spewed into the cavern. A small object sailed through the air and struck the floor.

Another flash blinded him and the Harvesters were engulfed in smoke.

"What's happening?" Nicholas coughed, his vision clearing. "Isabel?"

The cat flattened herself to the floor, apparently as surprised as he was.

"Cavalry," Sam murmured hopefully.

A startled cry sounded somewhere in the smoke. The Harvesters stared about in confusion and figures toppled, wrenched by some invisible force, surrendering to the smoke.

No, not the smoke. Something in it.

Nicholas frowned. He thought he saw something moving in the vapour. The shadow of a dog. An impossibly large dog. It flickered and vanished before reappearing in a different place, jaws snapping, drawing blood.

Screams and angry yells littered the cavern.

More figures rippled through the smoke. Their faces were obscured by breathing apparatus and they wielded swords, which they used to slash at the Harvesters.

Rae.

Nicholas searched about for her, but both Rae and Laurent had vanished.

The smoke curled up around him and he coughed. Sam pushed him back, away from the all-consuming cloud, away from the Harvesters. He attempted to resist. He wouldn't go down without a fight.

"Sam–" he began.

The edge of his vision blurred. He couldn't see through the smoke. Sam stumbled and they both fell to the floor.

Nicholas looked up as an enormous man loomed through the smoke. A breathing mask concealed most of his face, but not his massive shoulders.

Lash? Nicholas thought, wondering what Jessica's bodyguard was doing here. *No, not Lash. Somebody else.*

The man reached down and pressed something to his face.

"Breathe," a deep voice rumbled.

Nicholas gasped in a breath of clean air, finally able to see properly. He watched as the man fitted Sam with the same apparatus. Sam blinked and drew in lungfuls of air.

Without another word, the stranger lifted them both to their feet as if they weighed nothing and shrugged at them to follow.

Nicholas grabbed a hold of Sam and together they staggered after. He felt a weight at his shoulder as Isabel joined them.

"Swiftly," the cat hissed. "Move."

Her presence spurred him on, inspired a warm swell of hope. Through the curtains of smoke, he saw fallen Harvesters everywhere, bloodied and beaten.

A number of figures emerged from the smoke. About five, Nicholas guessed. One of them, a woman with braided hair who wore the same breathing apparatus and carried a dagger, kept step with them.

With a start he realised it was Liberty.

"Sam," she said. The giant dog that Nicholas had glimpsed cantered alongside her, panting.

"Liberty," Sam replied. "Your timing is impeccable, as always."

"Want to get out of here?" she asked, winking at Nicholas. She swiped an object from the floor and handed it to Sam. His fedora. Pushing his satchel into his hands, too, Liberty led them back through the tunnels. The air was clearer here but Nicholas still felt light-headed, as if he was only half awake. They went down a part of the tunnels he didn't remember, the battle cries receding into the distance behind them, and climbed a short ladder.

Liberty pushed open a circular manhole in the ceiling. She disappeared through it. Sam went next, then Isabel.

Nicholas clambered up through the hole, ignoring the twinge in his shoulder, and was surprised to find himself crawling onto grassy ground. He tugged the breathing apparatus free and got to his feet.

The ruins towered above them and the trees rustled.

They were in the Abbey Gardens.

The mountainous man who had saved them lifted the dog through the hole and then climbed up into the moonlight. He was even more imposing out in the open. He pulled the breathing apparatus off, shaking out his shaggy brown hair. The dog, which came up to his waist, nuzzled his hand.

More figures emerged from the hole and Nicholas realised that Aileen had done what Sam had asked; she had gathered together as many local Sentinels as she could. Silently, Nicholas thanked her.

Liberty nudged the manhole closed with a dull THUNK.

"Let's get you back to Aileen's," she said.

★

It didn't take long to reach the safehouse. The seven newcomers surrounded Nicholas and Sam the whole way back, some going ahead to check the way was clear, others hanging behind to ensure nobody followed them. Nicholas found it fascinating watching the Sentinels in action. It took his mind off what he'd learned in Laurent's hellish warren.

Isabel was a comfort; something Nicholas had never thought possible. She perched on his shoulder, her tail hugging his neck, and for a brief moment it felt like the world wasn't about to end.

When they reached Aileen's, the landlady showed them all into the living room and brought warm cloths so they could clean themselves up. She didn't say anything about the dog, though Nicholas glimpsed a grumbling tabby blur as Rudy darted toward the kitchen.

Isabel hopped onto the windowsill as Nicholas mopped at his face. The cloth came away stained red with Esmerelda's blood.

The thought of her lying next to him on the ground made his insides convulse.

My parents, he thought.

He shoved that thought away as well, attempted to crumple it in his mind as if it were a bit of paper.

"What happened to you?" he asked the cat. "How did you end up down there?" Like everybody else, Isabel looked like she'd been sleeping rough for the past few days. Her fur was matted in places and she was scrawnier than usual. Her eyes remained sharp as ever, though.

"I was consigned to that wretched warren," the cat replied.

"You're not hurt, though?"

"I am well enough. But look at you." She scrutinised his cast. "You can't be trusted on your own, can you?"

"It's good to have you back," he said softly.

Sam sat on the other side of the room. He looked exhausted. Even the subdued lamp light couldn't hide his drawn expression, nor the way his limbs seemed to weigh him down. He reclined in the chair and Nicholas noticed Liberty shoot him a worried look.

The other Sentinels stood about wiping the grit and blood from their faces and hands. Two women and four men, counting the giant who had helped him and Sam.

"That's what I call action," one of them joked. He was skinny, about the same age as Nicholas, and had floppy blond hair. Nicholas noticed a tattoo of a winged devil on his arm.

"Merlyn," Sam sighed.

Funny name, Nicholas thought.

"Sorry we got to the party so late," Merlyn said, winking at Nicholas. His grin was warm and lopsided. Nicholas couldn't help liking him. "Liberty here wanted to wait."

Liberty merely looked at the youngster.

"It's difficult to sense anything from above ground," she said, putting her cloth on the tray Aileen had left on the coffee table.

"Sense schmense," Merlyn shot back. "We almost didn't make it in time."

"I'm very grateful for your assistance," Sam said. His voice scratched tiredly and it silenced everybody in the room. "I hadn't anticipated quite so many. Nor so well-armed." He contemplated the fedora resting on his knee.

Nicholas was sure Sam was avoiding his gaze on purpose.

"I suppose introductions would be a good idea," Liberty said. She went round the room one by one. "Ginger, Frank, Steph," she said of the three people by the fireplace. "They're all Waddells. Bury born and bred. Obviously you know Merlyn. And that's Harry," she said of a dark-skinned man in his forties who had an earring. Finally she looked at the tall man who had rescued them in the cavern. "And this is Nale," she said. "Benjamin Nale. The mutt's Zeus."

Nale merely nodded at them and then began inspecting the dog for injuries. It was almost as big as he was – a shaggy grey titan. Zeus was the perfect name.

"My head's pounding, too." Merlyn grinned at Nicholas, his cheeks glowing rosily. Nicholas realised he was staring and glanced at Sam. The old man looked how Nicholas felt. Numb. As if he was underwater. He couldn't process what Laurent had said in the cavern. He didn't *want* to process it; not if it was true.

Finally, Sam told the other Sentinels their story. It was nothing new to Nicholas; he'd lived it. His ears perked up, though, when Sam started talking about somebody called Thomas Gray. The man who invented the gauntlet.

"We believe that Laurent isn't working alone; he has Malika with him," Sam finished. "Diltraa's Familiar. And his plan to raise the Prophets appears to be predicated on the young girl he currently has in his company."

"Rae," Nicholas said, though he hadn't meant to speak.

Everybody looked at him. He shivered, recalling the way the Harvesters' eyes had swivelled at him in the tunnels, but no hatred was being directed at him this time.

"This is Nicholas Hallow," Sam said, still not looking at him.

Not my parents.

Who were the people who had raised him if they weren't his parents?

His stomach rolled unpleasantly and Nicholas swallowed, refusing to give in to it. He forced himself to look at the other Sentinels. They gazed back with varying degrees of pity, sadness and understanding. They must have known his parents, or at least that Sentinels by the name of Hallow had died in a train crash. They were probably unaware that Jessica and Esus considered him special. All they saw was a young, battle-tired Sentinel whose parents had been taken too soon.

The only one who looked at him differently was Liberty. Her large, dark eyes locked with his for a moment and the hairs on his arms tingled. She'd said that people transmitted thoughts and feeling all the time. Nicholas dreaded to think what he was transmitting. He attempted to build a wall around himself as she'd suggested.

"This girl, what does she have to do with it all?" Liberty asked Sam.

"She's powerful," the old man replied. "That's all we know."

"Oblituss."

A quiet voice came from the door. Dawn had appeared. She kept her timid gaze levelled on Nicholas, as if afraid to look at anybody else.

"Dawn?" he said.

"I've, uh, been looking into the tunnels," she murmured softly. "This word keeps coming up. Oblituss... But I can't find what it means."

"Anybody?" Sam asked. He put a hand to his forehead tiredly. Nicholas felt sorry for him. No, not sorry. Angry. He was angry at him. Angry for keeping more secrets. Nicholas wrestled with his insides. Everything Sam had ever done was to protect him. Sam only wanted to preserve Nicholas's memories of his parents. To keep him from the pain and confusion he was currently feeling. For the first time, Nicholas realised that some secrets are too awful to reveal. It was Laurent he hated. Laurent who deserved his anger.

"Oblituss," Nicholas murmured to himself. He'd never heard the word before.

Across the lounge, Liberty stiffened. She became very still and she didn't blink for a long time. Nicholas began to worry, but then Liberty's eyelids fluttered and her muscles relaxed.

"Laurent intends to open the oblituss," she said firmly.

"Which is?" Sam asked, apparently as lost as everybody else.

"I see a door," Liberty said. "It's old, guarded. It's locked, but Laurent knows how to open it."

"You know the door, you've seen it."

A shiver rippled down Nicholas's spine. Liberty's voice was in his head again.

"*Yes,*" he thought, recalling the ancient doorway that the Harvesters had guarded. "*It's in the tunnels.*"

A flicker of a smile toyed with Liberty's lips and then she addressed the other Sentinels.

"It's in the tunnels," she said. "We need to stop him opening it."

"Man, I wish I could do what you do," Merlyn said to Liberty, tapping his temple. "I'd make so much *deniro*."

That thought had never occurred to Nicholas. He wondered how many lottery winners were secretly psychic.

"What's in the oblituss?" asked Harry, the dark-skinned man who hadn't spoken yet.

"All I'm getting is white noise," Liberty said with a shake of her head.

"Chances of it containing frisky kittens are pretty low, though, huh?" Merlyn said.

"It's high time this young man got his rest," Aileen said, bustling into the living room. She patted Nicholas's shoulder and smiled. "There are rooms for anybody who needs them. I know the Waddells and Merlyn are local, but you're all welcome to stay."

Though he was exhausted, the thought of going to bed made Nicholas fidgety. He didn't want to be alone with his thoughts. He knew he wouldn't get any sleep; he'd just doze restlessly until the sun came up. Which was – he checked the clock on the mantelpiece – in about four hours anyway.

"Time's running out," Liberty said sombrely. "We've all heard about what's going on in the rest of the country. It's spreading to Europe."

"What's spreading?" Nicholas asked.

"Chaos," Merlyn said. "Cows giving birth to demons, snakes raining from the sky... The Dark Prophets are reaching up from whatever hellpit they're in, and the world's starting to, well... Ever heard the song 'Highway to Hell?'"

Nicholas's gut trembled.

"We're all tired," Liberty said to the room. "We need rest. We'll meet again in the morning."

Heads bobbed cheerlessly in agreement and the Sentinels began moving toward the hall. The Waddells and Harry decided not to stay.

"Nice meeting you, Nick," Merlyn said, shaking his hand enthusiastically. His grip was warm and strong. Nicholas frowned, noticing a strange bite mark on the boy's neck. He realised it was a tattoo.

"See you on the battlefield," the other boy added. His gaze lingered and then he left with the others. An odd lonely sensation wormed through Nicholas. He'd felt a burgeoning kinship with the other Sentinel. They were the same age, but Merlyn had apparently been raised fully aware of the Sentinel life. Nicholas wanted to know more about his experiences fighting demons.

Nale took Zeus out to check the area, leaving only Sam, Isabel and Liberty. Nicholas stayed where he was, resistant to the thought of bed.

"Get some rest," Liberty told Sam. "There's a lot to catch up on in the morning."

"Meet me in the garden."

Liberty's voice echoed in Nicholas's head and he welcomed a distraction from sleep.

"I'm going to get some air," he said to Isabel. Before she could reply, he went into the kitchen and opened the back door. The sky was already hovering somewhere between night and day. It became a deep, inky blue and the stars twinkled a bright farewell.

He settled into a pristine garden chair flush against an ivy-smothered wall. What did Liberty want with him? Was she worried about Sam? The way she had looked at him with those marble-like eyes made him nervous. It was as if she could see right into him.

Nicholas became aware of another presence in the garden and spotted a fluffy shape lounging on the wall. Rudy. The cat looked grumpier than ever.

Finally, Liberty joined him. She handed him a steaming mug.

"Here. It'll help you sleep." At his hesitance, Liberty added: "Don't make me force you like I had to force Sam."

Nicholas peered into the mug. The contents were a deep purple and little green leaves floated on the surface. The steam that curled into his nostrils smelled delicious, though, and he sipped the drink. It tickled his throat pleasantly.

Liberty sat in the other chair. She drew her braids to one side, letting them hang over one shoulder so she could look at him.

"You've been through a lot, both of you," she said. "And not just tonight." She observed his arm in its sling. "Sam should have waited for us before going down there."

"We were doing alright," Nicholas murmured. His tongue felt fluffy. He contemplated his mug and wondered if it was to blame.

If you consider failing to find Rae alright. And then basically letting Laurent do whatever he wants.

"Nobody's saying any different," Liberty said. "There comes a time, though, when it's okay to call for help. Speaking of, here." She handed him something else. Nicholas took it with the hand poking out of the sling. It was his Drujblade.

"How did you..?" he asked.

"Found it on the way into Laurent's tea party," Liberty explained.

"Thanks. I must've dropped it."

He clutched the dagger, relieved. He'd grown attached to it.

"So much responsibility at such a young age," Liberty mused. He met her gaze and wondered for the second time since meeting her just how much she knew. "The Trinity," she continued kindly. "You've been told about your part in all of this, right?"

He nodded slowly.

"Must feel like you're balancing a dump truck on your shoulders."

That's exactly what it felt like. "Esus says it's up to me," Nicholas said. "I'm the one who has to figure out how to bring them back."

"And then you discover the truth about your parents," Liberty breathed. "Nobody ever said life was fair. You blame Sam. That's okay. People are complicated; sometimes they don't know what drives them. They're urged on by some caveman instinct. Sam, all he's ever wanted is to protect you. I think you know that."

Nicholas didn't know what to say. He should be feeling something. Some kind of heartache, maybe. A different ache to the one he'd endured since his parents died. But he was numb.

"Keep drinking," Liberty said.

He sipped more of the purple brew. The world grew hazy, as if somebody was puffing smoke into his eyes. He almost felt like he was hovering above the ground.

"Did you try the seeing glass again?" Liberty asked.

He nodded, his head heavy.

"What did it show you?"

"Load of stuff I couldn't understand," Nicholas grunted drowsily. "Triangles and the raven pendant. Some guy in a hat. Random rubbish."

She touched his hand. It didn't feel like it belonged to him anymore. She could be touching somebody else's hand.

"You have to trust what you saw," Liberty urged him gently. "Embrace that power. Somewhere in there is the key to all of this."

Nicholas didn't care. "Sam's wife," he murmured despondently. "His family... You have family?"

"I have a daughter. She's six. And my mother and my brothers."

"Where are they now?"

"In Cambridge."

"You're from Cambridge?"

"You and this girl, Rae, you're connected," Liberty continued, steering the conversation back to things he didn't want to talk about. Her voice began to sound distant, as if it was coming through a radio, and he had to focus to make out what she was saying.

"Yeah," he murmured. "We're going to destroy the world together."

"Hardly. But it's important that we find her, and soon. Laurent's plans won't wait, and it seems she's integral to them."

"I tried... I can't..."

"We'll try again. I'll help you."

"She's so angry, she won't let you."

"She's hurting, too." Liberty's voice was an echo.

"I think we're all going to die..."

Drowsiness overcame him and Nicholas drifted into the petrol blue sky. The stars flashed around him and then there was nothing.

CHAPTER EIGHTEEN
The key

Rae leaned in to the wall and studied the sky. There was no wind. Peculiar shapes darted through the air, gibbering inhumanly as the morning sun blazed. They were bat-like but almost man-sized and their shrieks tore at the sky.

Rae stifled a yawn. Her limbs were heavy and tired after a long night of training with Laurent. He'd forced her to engage her power again and again, until she could shatter things on command.

It was exhilarating. Laurent had taught her how to catch the power in her fists, stop it from scorching destructively through her. It was so easy she couldn't believe she'd never figured it out for herself. All she had to do was breathe and focus; not let her feelings get the better of her.

She felt strong already. She'd wanted to keep training through the night, but Laurent urged her to rest. Four hours of snatched sleep later, he roused her again. It was morning and he had a task for her. Something that would require her to combine her skills as a runaway with those she'd spent all night honing.

"There's something we need," he'd said. "After our visitors last night, I've had to step up my plans. This will help us in the fight against the monsters. Once we've succeeded, we can continue your training."

Rae ignored the wails above her and focussed on the flint-stone cottage across the patch of grass before her. It was just one in a craggy row that kneeled at the borders to the Abbey Gardens. They were the oldest homes in the town. Priests lived there once, but not anymore.

She had to break into one of them. That's what Laurent had trusted her with. A tingle of unease buzzed through her. Was it too soon? Could she really break into somebody's home and steal something? She'd thought her days of stealing were behind her.

Rae approached one of the cottages and listened at the door. It was quiet inside. She'd watched the residents, a couple in their fifties, leave twenty minutes ago. The cottage should be empty. Still, she'd move quickly.

Breathing evenly, Rae pressed her palms against the door and summoned the power as Laurent had taught her. It spiked queasily through her and the wood blistered immediately, warping under the heat that she poured into it. The wood blackened, as if rotting before her eyes, and when she shoved it, the door disengaged itself from the frame, wood splintering around the lock, which remained in place.

The heat subsided and Rae hurried into a dark hall. There were no windows and the light was hazy. She wondered briefly if people would call her a witch. She could do things that other people couldn't. Things that would terrify them. According to the definition in a book she'd found in Moyse's Hall, a witch was a woman 'thought to have evil magical powers'. Was she evil? Was she the same as the women who were executed in Bury St Edmunds in the 1600s?

No. She'd seen evil. Tramps being kicked to death in the streets. Helpless nobodies who nobody would miss. She wouldn't become one of them. She'd do whatever it took.

An image of the boy flashed through her mind. Nicholas had said Laurent was evil, but what did he know? Doubt slowed her. Laurent had introduced her to the demon hunters in the tunnels beneath the town. *Harvesters*, he called them. They were scarred and savage and reminded her of the Cronies, the London street gang she'd fled from with Twig. They made her nervous, scared even. If they were demon killers, though, it stood to reason that they were vicious.

A pang of disquiet stilled her. Something didn't feel right. Rae wondered if Laurent was being completely honest with her. How much did she really know about him? What did Nicholas know about him?

Shaking off the doubts, she retrieved a small silver disc from her pocket. It looked like a ten pence piece, except it was inscribed with rune-like symbols. She held it in the flat of her palm and spoke a word in her mind; the one Laurent had taught her.

"Expiscor."

The disc darted through the air and vanished through a doorway. She heard a dull thunk and hurried into what turned out to be the kitchen. It had a flagstone floor and potted herbs nestled on the windowsill. But where had the disc landed?

Then she spotted it, buried in the brickwork above an old-fashioned stove. Beneath the disc, one of the bricks bore a chiselled cross.

Rae silently thanked the priests for the ancient marker. The current occupants had been naïve enough to turn it into a feature, leaving it where it had been for centuries.

She reached out and touched the stone.

Something bright barrelled into her and Rae yelled in surprise as she hurtled backwards, landing in a heap. She cursed, quickly clambering to her feet.

The cross in the stone glowed gold.

It can protect itself? she thought. *How can a stone do that?*

Rae clenched her fists. Even if the stone could defend itself, it had made her angry, which was a good thing. She embraced the anger and pooled it into her fists. Her heart pounded and heat coursed through her. She felt as if she were about to burst into flame. Her fists shook as the scorching energy amassed. When she couldn't hold on to it any longer, she threw her hands out, aiming at the stone.

A fiery charge exploded away from her.

Gold sparks fizzed around the stone as it fought her, battled to keep hold of its secret charge. She wouldn't be beaten, though. Rae grit her teeth and poured everything she had into the flames.

The stone exploded. Fragments rained down on her, but Rae smiled weakly to herself, lowering her hands. She felt drained, but triumph overpowered the exhaustion.

On the hob, something winked in the sunlight.

A golden key.

Rae seized it and pocketed it as she left the kitchen.

She crashed straight into somebody. It was the middle-aged man who lived in the cottage; the one she'd seen leaving earlier.

"Who are you?" he demanded, eyes wide behind rectangular glasses.

Rae didn't notice the heat gathering in her fist, it had become so normal. Without wavering, she buried her fist in his jaw and the man collapsed against the wall, propelled by her power. He lay on the floor, out cold, his jaw pink and raw.

They probably would call her a witch, Rae decided as she stepped over him and left the cottage. And they should definitely be afraid of her.

Whatever it takes, she thought.

★

Nicholas jolted awake as the screech of an aledite blasted in his ears and he discovered, relieved, that he was in the safehouse, safe in his bed. He'd been dreaming. Whatever Liberty had given him, it had done the trick. He'd slept through until nine am.

Something hopped onto his bed.

"Still lazy as an idle cow," a crisp tone rang.

Nicholas sat up with a start. Golden eyes gleamed at him. Isabel stood on the bed peering at him.

"You know I'm a teenager, right?" he mumbled, wondering if she could tell he was pleased to see her. He'd never admit it.

"And while young fools slumber, the world comes apart at the seams."

"Has anybody ever told you to dial down the melodrama?" Nicholas shoved a hand into his curly hair. He realised she wasn't being melodramatic. The world really was coming apart, one stitch at a time. It wouldn't be long before everything unravelled completely.

"Pish to melodrama," Isabel spat. "Come, the girl has information."

"You mean Dawn?"

"*Somebody* around here is taking recent events seriously. I spoke with the girl while you slept."

Nicholas changed his T-shirt and splashed some cold water on his face in the bathroom, and then hurried downstairs.

"Breakfast, dear?" Aileen called as he darted from the larder. He grabbed a piece of toast from the kitchen table and shoved it into his mouth.

"Thanks," he mumbled, making his way quickly up to Dawn's room. Isabel had already nosed her way inside, leaving the door open a fraction. Dawn sat at her desk peering at something on her laptop screen.

"Morning," Nicholas said, wiping crumbs on his T-shirt.

"Hi." She didn't look at him.

"This may sound weird, but have you spoken to any cats lately?"

"She came up earlier," Dawn said.

"You seem pretty okay with the fact that she can talk."

"Sometimes cats talk."

Nicholas couldn't argue with that. It must take more than a talking cat to freak Dawn out. She had grown up as a Sentinel, after all, and knew all about the things that went bump in the night.

"Right," he said, sinking onto Dawn's bed. Despite the sleep, he felt exhausted. The heat was a succubus, leeching the life from him. His tongue sat like a slug in his mouth and his hair felt double its normal size. He daydreamed about standing under a freezing cold shower and remembered what Jessica had said when he first met her.

"The weather is a sign. Balances are shifting; the equilibrium is becoming distorted. The seasons do not remember where they belong – already a manner of madness is slipping into the world."

Was the sweltering weather another sign that things were coming undone?

"I've been looking into that word, oblituss," Dawn murmured. Isabel hopped onto her desk, squinting at Dawn's computer screen with interest. "It's an old one."

Nicholas wondered how much the Internet really contained about demons and Sentinels. Were there special Sentinels who monitored the 'net for demonic activity? Dawn was good with technology. Perhaps she'd end up becoming an online specialist. Assuming they survived Laurent, of course.

"Listen, boy," Isabel spat, whipping her tail across the desktop.

"Right, oblituss." Nicholas straightened up to show he was paying attention.

"It's a demon word," Dawn continued quietly. "The demon Obliett used to kill people by warping their memories. It made them forget. Each victim was different, but mostly Obliett would make people forget what danger was. So they'd walk in front of moving vehicles, go into dodgy areas at night, do stupid things like smoke around petrol…"

"Creepy. So this door has something to do with the demon?"

Dawn shook her head. "There's nothing to indicate that the demon Obliett was ever in Bury," she said. "I think the priests borrowed the name to scare people off."

"Priests?"

"They used the tunnels under Bury. Back in the day, it was only the Abbey monks who used them. Then the priests. But at some point, the tunnels were sealed off and forgotten about. Because of the oblituss."

"Which is what, exactly?"

"A jail."

"A jail?"

"The priests incarcerated something deep under Bury, something so awful that history doesn't remember what it is." She gave Nicholas a shy smile. "Not even the Internet knows."

"Well if the Internet doesn't know…" he joked back.

"Whatever it is, if Laurent wants it, it's bad. That's why…" Dawn grew serious. "I never understood why he destroyed the village in Cambodia. But after tracking his movements, I'm pretty sure he was collecting totems. He used the fire as a distraction. The Khmer Loeu had something; a carving of an idol. They called it The Slaughter Stone. It made children feral – they turned on their parents. The chief of the Khmer Loeu tribe hid it, kept it close for safe-keeping. After Laurent, the stone was gone."

"What would he be collecting totems for?" Nicholas asked.

"I don't know."

"I heard talk of such a stone many years ago," Isabel mused. "It is older even than I. And I have looked upon it with these very eyes."

"What do you mean? You've seen it?" Nicholas demanded.

"In the brute's lair," the cat said, her features sharpening. "Beneath the town last night. I saw the Slaughter Stone and a lacquer vase. Two totems, both vibrating with a formidable power."

"The Èyùn vase," Dawn murmured. Nicholas glanced at her bedroom wall, where the article about the stolen vase was tacked.

"You said it has a weird history," he said. "What kind of weird?"

"There are stories about it, but most of it's hearsay. Nothing solid. It dates back to the Ming Dynasty, where there's an old legend about a broken-hearted woman. She gave the vase as a gift to the man who had jilted her. A few days later, his body was found at the foot of the Tianmen Mountains. He'd thrown himself off. And everybody who's owned the vase since has suffered some sort of misfortune."

"Totems tap into primal energies," Isabel mused. "Laurent could be using them for any number of reasons."

"We have to tell Sam and the others," Nicholas said.

Sam.

He felt as if he'd been punched in the chest. He couldn't face Sam. The anger was fresh as a new wound yet to scab over, but guilt overpowered even that. Sam's wife... Nicholas had often wondered what actually happened to Judith Wilkins, why she wasn't around anymore and hadn't been since he was born. Nobody ever talked about it, and eventually he'd accepted that he shouldn't either. Now he knew why.

I killed her, he thought.

Not just her, but his parents, too. His real parents. He'd killed them all. It didn't make any sense. People had always commented on how much he resembled his mother. Anita. He could even see it himself sometimes, if he caught his reflection when he wasn't expecting to. How could he look like her if he wasn't her son?

We were still related. Somehow. Even if they weren't my parents.

It was an obvious answer, but it offered little comfort. He still didn't know who his birth parents had been and he felt like it shouldn't matter. Anita and Max had raised him. They were his parents. But it did matter. It mattered for reasons he couldn't even begin to understand.

"Boy." Isabel scrutinised him, her whiskers trembling. "What preys on you?"

He got up from the bed. "Nothing."

Out of nowhere, Tabatha Blittmore's words came to him. *"Can't keep stuff pent up for long, it goes bad inside."*

He didn't care. He needed to do something. Anything. Now that he was fully awake, he felt jittery and anxious.

Stop Laurent. Save Rae. That's all that matters.

"Come on," he said. Isabel hopped onto the shoulder not encumbered by the sling and they all went downstairs. In the hall, Nicholas bumped into Sam. The old man looked better than he had the night before. Clearly Liberty's potion had done the trick. He gave Nicholas a glance that made him uneasy, though. He couldn't tell what was glimmering in those pale blue eyes.

"Lad," Sam said softly.

Nicholas found he couldn't meet his gaze. Unexpected anger threatened to explode out of him and he clenched his teeth so that it couldn't escape.

"I'm sorry," Sam said. "What happened that night in Orville…"

"What's happened?" Isabel asked in her usual brisk manner.

"Nothing," Nicholas said. He went into the living room. He couldn't stop moving. If he stopped, he'd have to confront the things that were writhing in his belly. He barely had time to think about everything happening in Bury in the present, let alone what had happened fifteen years ago when he was just a baby.

When I killed my parents.

In the lounge, Zeus was stretched out on the rug in front of the fireplace. The monstrous dog nearly took up the entire floor, his bear-like paws disappearing under the coffee table. His ears pricked up when Nicholas entered. Spotting Isabel, Zeus barked and leapt to his feet.

Isabel scooted quickly onto the nearby sofa as the dog made a beeline for her. He shoved a curious snout into the cat's face and she lashed out with a claw.

"Remove this witless creature at once," she snapped. Zeus scooted backwards, snorting in surprise.

"Zeus, here." Nale's gruff voice resounded commandingly and the dog went quickly to the man's side, though he continued to stare at the cat, head cocked. If Nale or Liberty were surprised by Isabel's ability to speak, neither showed it. Nale could barely fit into the armchair he was occupying, while Liberty sipped tea on the sofa. Aileen fanned herself with a newspaper in the remaining armchair.

"Yo," Merlyn said, punching Nicholas's arm – thankfully the one that wasn't in a cast. He looked as tired as Nicholas felt. "Ready for another day of fighting the forces of evil?"

"Just tell me where they are," Nicholas deadpanned.

"Morning," Liberty said. "Nicholas, Sam, Merl."

Nicholas stood by the window with Merlyn as Sam sat beside Liberty. Dawn lingered in the doorway, as if she didn't want anybody to see her.

"What a lot of sour faces," Aileen marvelled. "Not surprising, I suppose. Who'd have thought Bury would play such an important role in the apocalypse? Wouldn't have put my money on it."

"We're not quite in apocalypse territory yet," Sam said gently.

"Not far off, though," Liberty commented.

Nicholas scratched his shoulder where the sling dug into his flesh.

"What are we going to do?" he asked.

"We have to stop Laurent from opening the oblituss," Liberty said. "Whatever it contains."

"Dawn says it's a jail," Nicholas said. "The priests... They put something down in the tunnels. Hid it away."

Dawn shrank further away from the doorframe, as if the group's surprised stares caused her physical pain.

"To that end..." Liberty set her tea cup down and picked up a bundle of sacking that had been resting at her feet. Carefully, she unwrapped it and held something up for everybody to see.

The breath caught in Nicholas's throat.

It was a gauntlet just like the one Snelling had used.

"Where did you get that?" he asked.

"Nale stole it from a Harvester," Liberty explained. Nicholas regarded Nale with renewed respect. He massaged his chest, remembering the blast of energy the gauntlet had unleashed. It had nearly rendered him unconscious.

"The gauntlet itself is a complex hybrid of science and magic, fit for one purpose," Liberty said. "Turning Sentinels."

"Turning them?" Aileen asked.

"Corrupting them," Sam explained. "Transforming them into servants of the Dark Prophets."

"It opens a portal within the host," Liberty said, "lets a demon inside. The host is killed in the process, but the demon takes possession of the corpse."

"I fail to see how possessing such a thing can possibly help us," Isabel said from the windowsill.

"I sort of lied when I said it has one purpose. It's also a weapon," Liberty explained. "It releases powerful electrical charges. Enough to subdue someone."

"So what's the plan?" Nicholas asked. "We use it to fight Laurent?"

"In a nutshell," Liberty said. "Nale has agreed to guard the oblituss until we've stopped Laurent and his followers."

"That could take weeks, months," Sam scoffed.

Nale remained silent. Nicholas wondered why anybody would agree to such a thankless task. Nale merely sat in silence. Zeus licked his hand, as if understanding the seriousness of the situation.

"We move now," Liberty said firmly, wrapping the gauntlet up once more. "All of us. Nicholas, if Rae's down there, you're the only one who can get through to her."

"She didn't seem that bothered last night."

"You'll find a way. You have to keep trying."

Isabel hopped onto the coffee table and surveyed them all. "I was down in the bowels of Laurent's domain," she said. "I saw what he's capable of. I hope you're prepared for what is to come."

"What did you see?" Sam asked.

"He feeds off the living," Isabel revealed dourly. "He leeched pure energy from a man, leaving behind nothing but ash."

Nicholas thought he saw Dawn recoil in the doorway. The same thing had happened to her dad.

"That's not all," Isabel continued. "He has been collecting perverted totems. I saw two, the Èyùn vase and the Slaughter Stone. Their dark energies were dreadful. If he has further totems and they're united in one place, they could amass a devastating charge of power."

A nervous silence filled the living room.

"We need everybody," Liberty said finally. "Aileen, contact as many Sentinels as you can."

"There's, uh, one more thing," Merlyn said. "Sam asked me to look for information on Laurent. I have a contact in Ipswich. He's a nut, but he says he knew Laurent."

"Is he trustworthy?" Sam asked.

"He's solid."

"Is it likely he'll know anything useful?" Liberty asked.

Merlyn shrugged. "Just the messenger," he said. "But... Solomon's a rare one. It might be worth a punt."

"I should go, then," Sam said.

"Not alone," Liberty replied. Nicholas thought he sensed scorn in her tone. "I'll go with. Everybody else is tunnel-bound."

Nicholas grimaced. They were going back into the tunnels? It seemed like a suicide mission, especially considering how many Harvesters had been there the previous night. There didn't appear to be any alternative, though. And on top of it all, he had to convince Rae to join them.

Now it was his turn to unpick things. He'd have to unpick the lies that Laurent had stitched around her.

Aileen bustled from the room. "And I thought running a safehouse would make for a quiet retirement," she sighed.

"Nicholas." Sam was by his side. The elderly man nodded his head at the living room door and disappeared through it. Butterflies in his belly, Nicholas begrudgingly went after him, joining Sam in the garden. The air was thick with heat and Nicholas struggled to think clearly. The unnatural warmth fogged his brain and he wasn't looking forward to whatever Sam had to say.

"Take a seat, lad," Sam said, contemplating the ground.

Nicholas complied gladly. His knees were practically knocking together. Sam remained standing, his features cast in shadow by his fedora.

"I wish I could tell you that what Laurent said about your parents was a lie," the old man said finally. "But I can't."

Nicholas had known that anyway, but hearing Sam say it opened a sucking pit in his chest. His palms became clammy.

"I had hoped to spare you that painful truth, but I see now that I was naïve. I should have known it would be used against you, if not by Laurent, then by somebody else."

Nicholas's tongue stuck to the roof of his mouth. Questions cemented his throat closed. He knew that if he tried to voice them, they'd spew out in an idiotic torrent.

"Anita and Max loved you, but you don't need to be told that." Sam's voice creaked, his expression wooden. "They were your parents. They were your family. You know that. Their love for you was never in doubt, especially as they chose to take you in. They wanted you in their lives. They accepted that responsibility gladly."

"Who–" Nicholas tested his voice. "Who were they?"

"Anita was your sister."

Nicholas's skin prickled. He hadn't expected that. At the very least, he'd expected to be told that the people he thought were his parents were actually his aunt and uncle. That would make sense. But this...

"My... sister?"

"She was nineteen and already engaged when your parents died. Relatively young for a mother, but not unheard of. Your parents died the day you were born. Whatever it was that came into the world with you, it claimed them, like the other residents of Orville. Your mother's name was Alice. Your father was Daniel."

Nicholas had never heard those names before.

"They were so excited..." Sam broke off, his voice wavering. "Anita was staying with Max out of town when you were born. When Alice died, Jessica wanted to take you in. Raise you herself. Esus wouldn't allow it. He knew that it was too dangerous. Too obvious. So you were hidden with Anita and Max. They became your parents."

"But why pretend that she wasn't my sister?"

Sam shrugged. "The more you resembled a traditional family, the better. If the Dark Prophets were aware of your birth, it stood to reason that they'd dispatch their agents to look for you. The more you blended in with the rest of society, the more easily you could hide."

"And they never told me." He didn't know how he'd have reacted if they had told him. Would he have been angry? Upset? Now, he just felt numb, like his body wasn't his. Just as his parents weren't his.

Had Anita ever tried to tell him? He wracked his brains, but he couldn't think of a single occasion. There hadn't been any hints, any broken sentences, any cross words that threatened to spill the truth.

That was why they'd looked so alike. They were siblings.

"They kept everything from me." He fought the threat of tears. "Everything."

"Never maliciously," Sam said. "They only ever wanted the best for you."

Nicholas rubbed his eyes, willing the tears away. "You kept an eye on them. That's why you were always around."

"They were young and they had nobody. I was there for them if they needed me." Sam rubbed his forehead, whether in frustration or weariness, Nicholas couldn't tell. "Lad, whatever you're feeling, it's normal. Who can say if what they did was wrong? They kept things from you, and I was complicit in that, but they cared for you. They loved you."

Nicholas had the feeling Sam was talking as much about his own feelings as Anita and Max's.

Anita. It felt wrong referring to her as anything other than 'mum'. His thoughts were muddled and he didn't think he'd ever get over the raw feeling of betrayal. How could he trust anything anybody said? It seemed everybody had their secrets; destructive secrets that could tear a person's world apart in a heartbeat.

And under the mist of confusion, far more disturbing thoughts huddled. *You're a murderer*, they whispered. *You're no good.*

He tried to block them out, but they wouldn't be ignored. He remembered what Malika said to him when she cornered him on the bus.

"You're dangerous. A threat to the world."

She was right.

"There's something you should know about the girl," Sam said.

Nicholas looked up sharply, plucked from his thoughts. "Rae? What about her?"

"She was born that same night in Orville."

Suspicion bit into him. "What else aren't you telling me?"

Sam sighed. "That's all I know. And I only know that because of Judith. Laurent was right; she was a midwife. She was run off her feet with two pregnant ladies in the village. Then you both arrived on the same night and changed everything."

Nicholas couldn't believe Sam had kept so much from him. Anger scorched his veins and he felt like shouting, aiming every rage-filled resentment at Sam. But he couldn't. His parents, Anita and Max, hadn't kept things from him out of malice, and neither had Sam. From the start, everybody had simply tried to protect him.

Or protect the world from me.

Rae had destroyed the shop in town. Nicholas had decimated an entire community. Could they really be agents of good? The Trinity had chosen them, or at least that's what everybody thought. What if they were wrong?

"There's something else," Sam began, but he stopped when a gangly figure materialised at the back door.

"Liberty's asking for you," Merlyn said. "She wants to hit the road."

"Thank you," Sam said distractedly. He hesitated, meeting Nicholas's gaze at last. His eyes were an overcast blue. "We'll talk later. I'm sure you have many questions. I'll answer them if I can." He turned stiffly and left.

"You could cut the atmosphere out here with a chainsaw," Merlyn commented, joining Nicholas in the garden. He was wearing another of his heavy metal T-shirts, this one for a band called 'STIGMATA'. The picture was of a skull-faced angel. He was such a contradiction, Nicholas thought. Merlyn's goth style clashed with his tanned skin and golden hair.

"Chainsaw? Don't you mean knife?" Nicholas said.

"Normally, but the atmosphere out here is pretty damn thick."

Nicholas almost laughed, but it stuck fast in his throat like a pill.

"That bad, huh?" Merlyn mused, one corner of his mouth drooping. "Whenever I get yelled at or somebody pisses me off, I go out and kill something."

"You know that makes you sound like a serial killer?" Nicholas said. Already the mood in the garden seemed lighter, as if Merlyn had punctured it with a pin.

"Serial killer of *monsters*!" Merlyn declared, thumping his chest. He jabbed a thumb over his shoulder. "What was with Bogart?"

"Bogart?"

"Sam," Merlyn said. "Somebody die?"

Yeah, his wife, Nicholas thought. *My parents. Because of me.*

And my sister raised me and we're all part of a supernatural soap opera that will probably end with Sam revealing he has an evil twin working as an undertaker in Transylvania.

Nicholas shrugged. "A while ago, but I'm only just finding out about it."

"Harsh. Want to fight? I'll keep one arm behind my back to even the odds."

"Fight?"

"Yeah."

"I'm no good at it."

"I'll train you up," Merlyn insisted. "I trained with my dad. He's not the best, but he has some moves. Others I learned online. There's this guy called Hung Lu. Sounds like a joke, but he's like Bruce Lee's cooler brother."

"You really like fighting?"

"I guess I got a taste for it," Merlyn said. "You do something long enough, it sort of becomes hard to stop." Nicholas recalled how swift Sam had been on his feet during training, a result of a life spent on the demon front-lines. He couldn't believe that only a few days had passed since Sam trained him in the garden. It felt like months. So much had happened. So much had changed.

"You fought many things?" Nicholas asked.

"Bury's pretty sleepy, but some of the villages round here are nasty. Ever hear of a krypost?" Nicholas shook his head. "Two heads, six legs, and more teeth than I've ever been able to count. They're attracted to farmhouses, no idea why. This one time, Dad took me out to Ixworth. We fought three of them. I killed one and its mate took a bite out of my thigh. Wanna see?"

Merlyn began unbuttoning his jeans.

"I'm good," Nicholas said, waving his free arm and laughing.

"Knew I could break you out of that mood."

They exchanged a look that Nicholas couldn't quite understand. Something flickered in his belly and he got to his feet, trying to ignore it.

"What was it like when it bit you? What were you thinking?" he asked.

"I don't really like thinking. I like doing. So, fight?"

Nicholas didn't think he had the energy for more training. He looked up as a shadow fell into the garden, finding Nale in the kitchen doorway.

"Time to stick pointy things in bad guys?" Merlyn asked.

Nale nodded.

And just like that, training was the least of Nicholas's worries.

CHAPTER NINETEEN
On The Water

Gulls chattered above the water, painting rippling white reflections across the surface as Sam pulled the Morris Minor up to the docks. He and Liberty got out of the car, and Sam took a breath of the salty air, surveying the moored boats. He felt heavy. Weighed down by ghosts.

Attempting to focus on the task at hand, he pushed the memory of Nicholas's sullen face from his mind. Pitying the boy wouldn't do him any good. Nicholas was tough, but he'd need to toughen up even more if he wanted to survive the coming days.

Sam strolled beside the water with Liberty, looking for the boat that Merlyn had directed them to.

"What do you think?" he asked.

"Pretty place," Liberty commented.

"I meant about this wild goose chase, and you know it."

Liberty flashed him a smile. "I don't mind chasing a few geese if it brings Laurent down."

"Well said."

Sam tugged at his shirt collar. The midday heat was unbearable. He attempted to brush his natural suspicions aside. He hated that it had come to this: questioning the intentions of other Sentinels. Malika's plan to corrupt them had worked, even without the gauntlets. Paranoia was slithering through the community, infecting it with disquiet and fear.

He clutched the satchel at his side, reassured by the pouches huddling inside. They may not have stopped Malika, as far as he knew, but her screams had been sign enough that they inflicted horrendous pain. He'd use them against her again without hesitation, and this time he'd make sure she didn't have anybody to feed on to replenish her strength.

"That Nale chap," he said. "What do you know of him?"

Liberty took a moment to answer. "He's tough to get a read on," she said eventually. "I've only caught snatches. He's got a strong mind. You know how he doesn't say much? That's what his head's like."

"But... snatches...?"

"Just images, really. A few feelings." Liberty glanced at him. "Something scared him."

"A Hunter? Scared?"

"I know. Look out for the flying piglets. But he was scared. And there was an image of a well. Sort of half-glimpsed, though, like one of his eyes was sealed shut."

"What do you think it means?" Sam asked.

"I'll ask him," Liberty said, her eyebrows arching mischievously.

"You think he'd mind? Considering how you got that information?"

"About as much as I'll mind when he crushes my skull with his bare hands."

Sam was about to reply when he spotted a narrow boat set a little apart from the others. The chipped silver paint bearing its name gleamed against the surrounding maroon panels.

Darling Cassandra.

Lights came through the windows. Thin curtains glowed. Plants cluttered the roof. It looked cosy; almost like somewhere a gnome might live. *If gnomes existed*, Sam thought.

They approached gingerly and Sam rapped on the door.

It burst open immediately. A small, mole-like face blinked out at him. The man's eyes were a little too far apart and surprisingly dark. His nearly-hairless head gleamed in the sunlight and his round face quickly split into a bucktoothed grin.

"Gosh, is it that time already?" the man said. "You forget, don't you? How short the days can be. Even in the summer. Not that we've had much of a summer this year, eh?"

Sam was taken aback. Who was this odd-looking gentleman and what could he know about Laurent?

The man on the boat craned through the door to peer briefly at the sun.

"Helios," he greeted cordially, before turning to Sam. "I'm sorry, you'll have to come back later, I'm very busy."

"Solomon?" Sam asked before the man could disappear back inside. The dark eyes scrunched up in contemplation. Sam could swear there was uneasiness there, too, as if the man had been caught in headlights.

"I really am very busy," he said.

"It won't take a moment. Please."

The man relented, vanishing into the boat. His voice sailed through the doorway: "Tea? I only have herbal, caffeine'll rot your gut. Come on inside, then! Keep the door open too long and the sun himself will try to join us, and he's terrible company on a hot day like this."

Pausing a moment to gather his wits, Sam reminded himself that first appearances could be deceiving, especially nowadays. He ducked through the tiny door, Liberty close behind.

The boat was narrow, and the interior was a veritable mare's nest. Sam was struck by the light. Coloured handkerchiefs were draped over lamps and the effect was part jazz bar, part carnival. Small mirrors and figurines all crowded onto perilously narrow shelves.

The man's head appeared from behind a partition where Sam assumed the kitchen lay.

"It *is* Solomon, isn't it?" Sam called.

"Take a seat," the man said, ignoring his question. "Kutu will keep you company for the moment."

Sam hoped he wasn't referring to the stuffed rabbit on the table, though there was nothing else in the vicinity that seemed appropriate. Eyeing the animal, he had barely sunk into a rickety wooden chair before the stranger bustled into the room with a tray. Liberty lingered by the door. Her keen gaze roved from one odd trinket to the next and Sam hoped she'd sense any imminent danger.

"Kutu does witter on a bit, but his heart's in the right place," the man said conversationally, setting the tray down and pouring them each a handle-less cup of something hot. "Rabbits," the man tutted. "They do make a fuss. Marvellous at keeping secrets, but *skittish*, you know."

Sam could sympathise – he suddenly felt twitchy himself. Why had Merlyn sent them here? Though the stranger didn't appear dangerous, it was becoming increasingly difficult to tell. Sam's hopes for a lead on Laurent were rapidly fading, and he resolved to sip the tea (or whatever it was) and then be on his way.

"There," the man sighed. Sam noticed for the first time that he was wearing a bow tie. It was turquoise and paired with a shiny silver trouser suit. The cuffs of his orange shirt glittered. "It's Jasmine, by the way. The tea. Night-blooming, which always struck me as rather lovely. A flower that comes out in the dark. I can appreciate that sort of quirkiness, can't you?"

Sam nodded. "Yes, I suppose I can," he admitted.

"Sam," the other man said. "Samuel. A Hebrew name, originally, if I'm not mistaken. You're a good judge of character, aren't you? And though you have power, you'd much rather share it with others. Funny how names can dictate who we are."

"I didn't realise I'd come here to be read," Sam murmured. So this man was a psychic? A Sensitive, perhaps? Or, by the looks of his outfit, a one-time fairground worker who'd sufficiently honed his natural observational skills to convince people he had mysterious powers.

Oh, Merlyn, Sam thought. *Have you been duped by a talented con artist?*

He couldn't help feeling disappointed. Liberty could probably tell him more about Laurent than this man.

"You're the judge, why don't you tell me what you read in me?" the man said.

He gave him an encouraging smile, buckteeth protruding more than ever.

Sam drew a breath. "You like animals."

The man shook his head. "No, no, no," he reprimanded. "Too easy. Something else. Go on. Something that actually *means* something."

Sam's patience was dwindling. He cast around the boat, looking for clues about this odd little man. There was a framed magazine cover. *Paranormal Times*. This man beamed from the cover, a silly magician's hat on his head. It wasn't the only frame, either. There were more, most of them photos of the little man with bleach-teethed people who looked famous. The one of him with Prince William stood out.

Sam frowned. Had he seen this man before somewhere?

He looked at Liberty. Amusement played on her lips and she shrugged at him.

"You like to collect things," he suggested, noting the accrued paraphernalia.

"You're not even trying," the man berated him softly. "No matter, we'll come back to that later."

"I'm sorry, Solomon. Your name is Solomon?"

"Would you feel that you knew me better if you knew my name?" the man asked.

"It would be a start."

The man nodded. "Solomon," he said. "That's the name I chose for myself, oh, thirty years ago. I won't tell you what it replaced." He winked. "The secret name of things is what gives them their power. Surrendering your name is like surrendering your sword. Anybody could use it against you."

"What do you mean?"

Sam sat up a little straighter. It was the first thing the stranger had said that seemed to be of any value. The Trinity had many names, and in the Sentinel community, those names were often closely guarded. He wasn't sure why. Perhaps it was to protect their power.

"If you can name something, you can control it," Solomon explained, as if he had read Sam's thoughts. "A name confines something, sets it in stone. Makes it fallible. We throw words around every day, unaware of their value. And a name is the most valuable thing of all."

Sam realised he was staring at the other man, shocked by his sudden insight. He attempted to cover his surprise by drinking some of the tea.

"My case in point," Solomon commented, apparently aware of how Sam had judged him. "You discover a man who thinks stuffed rabbits can talk and you make certain assumptions. It's no bother." He looked over Sam's shoulder. "Is he always this jittery?"

"Only when there's an apocalypse on the horizon," Liberty said.

"Can you help us?" Sam asked. Those were four words he rarely strung together.

"There's a darkness around you," Solomon said, his mole-like features sharpening. He studied Sam's face. "You're troubled, but anybody with eyes could tell you that. Why else would you be here? You have a name for me."

Sam squeezed his hands together under the table, rubbing his weary knuckles.

"Laurent Renault."

Solomon spluttered, nearly choking on his tea. "No," he gulped, slamming his cup down. "Not him. I won't talk about him."

"Why not?"

"Dangerous. Very dangerous," Solomon said. "Ask me something else. Anything."

"Laurent Renault," Sam repeated sternly. "You obviously know something."

Solomon's eyes crinkled and he looked torn. He fussed with his orange cuffs and polished his glasses. Finally, he peered at Sam. "I knew Nathan," he said quietly. "We were both masquerade ball fans. We met at one in Cambridge a few years ago. Then Nathan fell in with Laurent. Oh, it was all roses at first. But Laurent was using him."

"Using him?" Sam asked, wondering who Nathan was and how he fit into Laurent's plans.

"Physically."

"Ah. I see."

"Nathan got worried. He was no fool; he was a Sentinel. He told me that Laurent got violent and he had strange visitors. One of them was a woman, or she pretended to be. Red hair."

"Malika."

Solomon stroked the stuffed rabbit and contemplated the ceiling.

"It didn't take long for Nathan to find out about Laurent's history. The murder of his family. You know how many of them he killed? Twenty. His four brothers, his parents, three cousins and more besides. Everybody. Some of them, only body parts were found."

Sam stiffened. He remembered that time. He'd spent the last twenty years trying to forget it.

"Why?" Liberty asked. "Why'd he do it?"

"Lots of reasons," Solomon murmured. "Pride. Jealousy. But I suspect the real reason was that it made him immune from a blood attack."

"Blood attack?"

Solomon looked like he wanted to spit. "If anybody ever wanted to, shall we say, take Laurent down, they'd have a fighting chance if they got a sample of blood – from him or a relative. Blood ties us all. Laurent's family made him vulnerable. He couldn't take that risk. Of course, obliterating his bloodline had other benefits."

"Such as?" Sam asked.

"He mixed demon blood with his own. Injected himself. Corrupted himself."

Sam's stomach turned in on itself. Was that even possible? He'd encountered awful things over the years, but could a man really survive such a thing?

"I don't see how killing his family made it easier to do that," Liberty said.

"As the last in his lineage, Laurent became an *ensamblod*. Separate from everything, stronger. An island. Ever wonder why the human race is so obsessed with reproducing? An *ensamblod* is a dangerous, volatile thing. There are theories... Being the final member of a bloodline can cause a person to... change. Open him up to possibilities. I never understood it, but it's what Laurent believed. And I suppose he was right..." Solomon looked sad again. "Nathan turned up dead. Drowned in the bathtub. The police did nothing; what could they do? There were no prints, no sign of a struggle. They assumed it was suicide."

"I'm sorry," Sam said softly. He'd lost enough friends to know how Solomon must feel.

The psychic sighed and appeared to dislocate himself from the past. "Before he died, Nathan asked me to do a reading to find out what was in store for him and Laurent. He thought he could save him, make Laurent see sense. I couldn't turn him down. Nathan had never asked for anything; I knew how important it was to him. I wish I could take that reading back."

"What did you see?"

Sweat beaded Solomon's top lip. He twitched, starting to resemble the rabbit he was cradling.

"What did you see?" Sam pressed.

"The end of all things."

Solomon's hiss sent shivers down Sam's spine.

"The end?"

Solomon held his gaze and Sam dreaded to think what the psychic had glimpsed. He had to know.

"What is Laurent planning?"

"Aside from the destruction of everything and everyone you love?" Solomon puffed. "He's going to tear reality apart, rent the very fabrics of existence and let Hell in."

"How?" Sam urged, leaning in to the table. "How is he going to do it?"

"He's already begun," Solomon said mournfully. "He's allied himself with Malika. They have a Harvester army at their feet. The gauntlets are just the beginning. Next, Laurent is going to unearth the oblituss and with it the Tortor."

"The–" Sam struggled to keep up. "What are they? Why are they important to Laurent?"

"The Tortor... It's an agent of chaos. It's going to reduce that town to nothing."

"How can we stop it?"

Solomon tapped his lips thoughtfully. "The totems. Destroy the totems and you'll derail Laurent's plan."

"Will it stop him?" Liberty asked.

Solomon said nothing. Perhaps the answer was too depressing to say out loud.

Sam released a breath. "You knew all this and you did nothing. You knew Laurent was out there killing, scheming, and you told nobody."

"I'm no hero."

"You fled. Saved your own hide."

"There was one thing I could never understand," Solomon mused. He squinted at Liberty, then Sam. "During the reading with Nathan, I saw my own demise. I tried to avoid it. I got as far away from Cambridge as I could, but now I see it's unavoidable."

"Why do you say that?"

"The final thing I saw was you, sitting across from me and–"

The entire boat rocked. The wet crunch of splintering wood filled Sam's ears, mixed with the inexplicable sound of rushing water.

Sam looked down, unable to comprehend what he was seeing. A hole had been punched through the floor of the boat, right beside the table. Water gushed stealthily inside.

"What is this?" he demanded, the water already around his ankles.

Liberty steadied herself against the wall.

Solomon looked horrified. "No, no, no," he wailed. "Not now. Not yet!" He seized the stuffed rabbit from the tabletop and clutched it to his chest. Sam jumped to his feet, just as Liberty went for the door handle.

It was no good. They were locked in.

Sam whirled round to survey the interior of the boat. The dirty river water pumped into the little living room, spilling across the floor. Already it was creeping up to his shins. Filthy, smelly, everywhere. He saw something moving in the water and Solomon started screaming.

Dark shapes squirmed and Sam had to concentrate to keep up with them. They whisked by like lithe, sinewy lightning.

"Stay still," he hissed at Solomon, but that was the worst advice he could have given. They were trapped on a sinking boat with no hope of escape.

"The windows!" Liberty yelled.

Solomon tossed the stuffed rabbit aside and lunged at the window by the table.

His fingers barely scraped the steamed-up glass before he emitted a strangled shriek and crashed to the floor. Something was attached to his leg. A trunk-like, fleshy organism. It expanded and contracted as if it were feeding on him. Solomon reached down to scratch at it, but Sam yelled: "Don't touch it!"

He'd barely uttered the words when more snake-like creatures whipped from the water. Faceless heads that were nothing more than circles of gnashing teeth lunged for the psychic, who spluttered and splashed in horror on the boat's floor. The water was above his waist now, and the boat groaned alarmingly, as if it knew its fate.

Liberty waded over and attempted to drag the creatures free, but it was no good.

Sam reached down to his boot and extracted a hunting knife.

"Oh God!" Solomon choked. "Oh God!" He floundered about in the water and Sam realised the psychic's hands were moving with purpose. They were searching for something.

"Stay still," Sam warned him.

The psychic wasn't listening, though. Finally, his front teeth protruded in a triumphant grin and he raised Kutu the stuffed rabbit from the water. In one swift movement, he snapped the creature's head off and drew a blade from the body.

"There!" Solomon cried jubilantly. He slashed the knife at the creatures and black blood pooled around him. The monstrous leeches released him, slithering back into the water.

Sam reached down and heaved the man from the floor. Together, they clambered onto the table, which was only just above the water, and crouched in wait. Across from them, Liberty crammed herself onto one of the shelves, her boots tucked under her, away from the water.

Sam's mind raced. Had they been followed? Was this Laurent again? Or one of his minions? Malika? Were they outside even now crowing together as they watched the river devour the boat? He had to get out of here, if only to make it to the shore and wipe the smug grins from their faces.

"Can't... Can't stand the water," Solomon gibbered, shivering beside him.

"You could've fooled me, living in a place like this," Liberty said.

"Don't mind being on it. *In* it's another matter." The psychic eyed the turgid water fearfully. He clutched the table edge so tightly it seemed his knuckles would burst through his skin.

Not so smart after all, Sam thought.

"Keep an eye out," he told Liberty firmly. "If those things come back, well..."

He left the thought unfinished, swivelling round to examine the window. He'd have to smash it; that was the only way they'd ever fit through. He reached into his satchel and drew out a pistol. As he raised a hand to fire, he felt the air move and heard something splashing into the water.

"Solomon!" Liberty yelled.

There was no sign of the psychic. Sam was alone on the table. Before he could stop her, Liberty dove from the shelf, disappearing into the murky water.

Sam held his breath, despairing as the water rippled over the top of the table and threatened to loosen his grip. He felt something brush his leg and flinched, staying as still as he could.

"Liberty!" he called.

The water was too dirty; he couldn't see anything below the surface. Seaweed and muck from the riverbed had flurried in with the water, creating a grim soup. And still the water level rose.

Something tugged at Sam's leg and he had to fight the rising panic. Another tug. A nip. A yank. Sam took a great breath just in time as he was dragged under the surface.

His nose and ears flooded with grimy water and the shock of it almost prompted him to expel the precious air he'd gulped in.

Calm. Calm. Think.

Disorientated, he forced himself to open his eyes. They stung in the river water. Slithering black shapes skimmed by and he tried not to imagine those circles of razor-sharp teeth sinking into his flesh. Another tug. He shook his leg, attempting to loosen whatever it was that had a hold of him. The grip loosened and Sam shook the thing free. He tried to see what it was that had him.

Solomon's puffy face rose through the scum. Dead. Drowned.

Free of Solomon's dying grasp, Sam kicked his way to the surface. He broke into the air and his head bumped the ceiling. The boat was almost completely submerged.

Liberty gasped for breath beside him.

"I think... we're done here," she coughed.

"The window," Sam panted. "We have to break the window."

A snake-like form lashed from the water, lunging at Sam's face. He threw an arm up and fangs sank into his hand. The pain was incredible. Liberty grabbed the creature's tail, tearing it away. Without pausing, she beat it against the ceiling, where black liquid exploded violently from the monster's gnashing maw.

In an instant, the water came alive with thrashing black monsters.

"NOW!" Sam yelled. He gasped in another breath and sank below the surface.

They were everywhere. Swarming like river snakes, teeth glinting in the gloom. They darted at him in waves and Sam was glad for the protection that his thick jacket and trousers afforded.

The gun.

It was still clenched in his fist. Would it work underwater? He'd heard that some guns reloaded faster when submerged, but he had no idea if his would even fire. He had to try.

Locating the window amid the flurry of nightmarish shapes, he aimed and fired.

A spark lit the water and Sam heard a muted *WHUMP* as the bullet struck something. As the leech monsters slithered together against him, he kicked his feet against something solid and propelled himself toward what he hoped was the shattered window frame.

Alien noises echoed in his ears and the world became a swirling confusion of muddy colours. His lungs screamed at him to draw breath, but he knew that if he did that, it would be over. He jerked his legs, thrashing through the scummy water.

Light cascaded above him and he urged his body toward it, hoping it was sunlight.

Something gripped his shoulders.

He was hauled up out of the water.

For a moment, Sam thought he saw red curls, and he grunted fearfully as he was dragged from the water. Spluttering, he found himself on the docks. A hand patted his shoulder.

"Sir, are you alright? Can you breathe?"

Sam looked up at the woman. A police officer.

"Liberty," Sam gasped, struggling for air. "Where's Liberty?"

CHAPTER TWENTY
Oblituss

THE ABBEY RUINS RESEMBLED COLOSSAL ROCK giants. Isabel clung to Nicholas's shoulder and he peered nervously at the others, who were positioned around the manhole they'd escaped through the previous night. This time, they were heading back inside. It seemed like madness.

Nale. Zeus. Merlyn. Harry.

They were really doing this. And without Sam. Aileen was contacting every Sentinel she knew in the area, but time wasn't on their side. Neither were the numbers. Nicholas shuddered at the thought of how many Harvesters would be waiting for them in the tunnels. And here they were; two men, two teenagers, two household pets.

He squeezed the Drujblade. Despite the midday sun, he felt cold. Oddly detached from it all. He noticed Merlyn watching him from the other side of the manhole. The youngster winked and struck a pose like a battle-ready ninja. Nicholas couldn't help smiling.

"Everybody ready?" Harry asked. "Everybody know what they're doing?"

Nicholas's list was short. Find Rae. Stop Laurent. Try not to get killed. Should be easy enough.

Nale heaved open the manhole. He wore the gauntlet he'd taken from Malika and Nicholas eyed it warily until Nale hopped down into the tunnel. Nicholas saw a flash of blue light followed by the sound of angry grunting. Something heavy hit the ground.

"Clear." Nale's voice sounded through the hole and Nicholas went first, the Hunter helping him down. Isabel gripped his shoulder, but he barely felt her claws needling his flesh as he scanned his whereabouts. His body hummed, prepared for danger.

"Mind them," Nale grunted, gesturing at two bodies slumped to the dirt floor. The Harvesters who had been guarding the entrance. They probably hadn't known what hit them when the giant dropped into their space.

There were no lamps in this section of the warren. When they were all in, Nale drew the manhole closed. The tunnels were almost pitch black and the smell of dank was accompanied by a peculiar chill. Nicholas shivered. He felt something edging at the corner of his mind; a subtle nudge that he was getting used to.

It meant danger.

"Something's wrong," he said quietly. His voice resounded back to him in the enclosed space. "The oblituss."

Were they too late? Had it already been opened?

Nale used a flashlight to illuminate the way forward. The others did the same with their phones and their eerie lights darted over the walls.

It couldn't be anything else but the oblituss. The unnatural cold crept through the tunnels and curled around Nicholas's bones. He could see his breath in the gloom.

Nale went ahead ahead with Zeus. Nicholas followed, Merlyn at his side, while Harry took up the rear. Nicholas's shoulders ached and he realised he was already tensed against whatever might confront them in the darkness.

"Wicked dagger," Merlyn hissed at his side.

"Cheers."

"I'm more of a chain-lover," the other boy said, showing Nicholas his weapon; a heavy-looking chain attached to a short staff. He whirled it at his side and it buzzed. "Medieval but it does the job."

"You done this before?" Nicholas asked.

"Loads of times." Merlyn's eyes flashed at him. "We've pretty much jumped from the frying pan into the fire, y'know."

Nicholas nodded. "Try not to get burned."

Isabel's fur brushed his cheek. "The air is foul," she commented sourly.

They trudged on through the dank tomb, the coldness intensifying as they pressed on. When they reached another passageway, Nicholas realised Nale had stopped abruptly.

"Listen," Isabel whispered, tensing on Nicholas's shoulder.

A crackle of blue energy zagged through the air, smashing into a wall. Dust and chunks of charred brick blasted into them.

"Harvesters!" Nale bellowed.

Figures swarmed through the dust cloud and the next few moments were a choking, noisy confusion. Nale put himself between the Harvesters and Nicholas. Merlyn and Harry darted fearlessly ahead and Nicholas felt like a liability. He had to do something.

Blue lights flashed and bricks exploded. He coughed, the dust catching in his throat. Through watering eyes, he saw Nale pummel each Harvester that emerged. Bodies dropped limply at his feet, but there were always more forms jabbing into view.

"Nicholas, back!" Nale barked.

"No!" Nicholas yelled.

"The girl! We must find the girl," Isabel urged. "Let them fight."

Begrudgingly, Nicholas hovered where he was. Clenching the Drujblade, he determined to count to ten and then go after them.

Gunshots rang over the din of detonating brickwork.

"Merlyn!" Nicholas called, his voice getting sucked into the void ahead. "Nale!"

He couldn't wait any longer, he had to help.

"Boy!" Isabel yowled, but he didn't listen. He hurried forward, immediately crashing into somebody. A tall young man, barely older than him. The Harvester leered, raising a gauntlet. Before he had a chance to use it, though, the Harvester's eyes glazed over and he thudded to the ground.

Merlyn appeared behind him.

"Come on," he urged, but then he grunted as a figure bowled into him from behind. A Harvester clung to his back, a blade raised, ready to strike.

"No!" Nicholas cried, hurtling forward. Esmerelda's face loomed large in his mind and he balked momentarily at the thought of sticking the dagger into somebody else. Knowing he didn't have a choice, he thrust the blade into the Harvester's throat and then quickly removed it. The Harvester collapsed to the ground.

"Cheers," Merlyn grunted. Then he was gone again, swallowed by the dust. Coughing, Nicholas plunged into the flashes of blue light, trailing his free hand along the wall as he went. Gradually, the air began to clear, and he found himself in a new tunnel.

A door stood open at the end of it. It was the same door he had passed with Sam the previous night.

"The oblituss," Isabel growled.

It stood open.

The cat hopped down onto the floor, her whispers twitching.

Icy waves pulsed from it and an impenetrable darkness seethed beyond the doorframe. Nicholas frowned, squeezing his eyes shut. There was something else. The buzzy nagging in his head returned and he breathed through it, attempted to embrace it rather than push it away.

Rae. She steps into the oblituss. Laurent watches her enter, then turns to a pair of Harvesters, ordering them to keep watch.

His chest tightened.

"Rae's in there," he said. The guards were gone, though. They must have joined the fracas, leaving the oblituss untended.

"Nicholas!"

Merlyn staggered toward him, covered in debris and blood, a cut on his forehead. Nale and Harry weren't far behind.

"Goddammit," Harry cursed, staring fearfully at the doorway. "What's he done?"

"Rae's already in there."

Another flash of light blasted into the tunnel and a portion of the wall erupted in a hail of crumbled bricks. Merlyn, Harry and Nale rushed to confront a fresh wave of Harvesters, pouring into the tunnel and, knowing it was now or never, Nicholas hurried to the open door.

"Nicholas," Isabel cried. "Nicholas, no!"

Taking a breath, he entered the oblituss.

★

He regretted it immediately. This desolate part of the underground warren was far older. It was so dark he could barely see, but as his sight adjusted, he shuddered at the tortured roots groping from the rocky ceiling, as if curious about who had intruded upon their isolation. The craggy walls, hewn roughly from the rocky earth, bore painted symbols. Crosses and a bearded man with a halo. Winged soldiers, swords drawn, flaming blades pointing towards whatever evil was incarcerated in this part of the tunnels.

Nicholas noticed words, too. A Latin prayer or warning placed there by the priests. He saw the word Tortor inscribed alongside others he didn't understand.

"They mean business," Nicholas murmured.

Whatever they had hidden down here centuries ago had clearly terrified them to extreme measures.

He shivered. His arm ached inside the cast, as if nervous of what awaited him. And it was so quiet, he realised. He couldn't hear anything, not even the sounds of Merlyn, Harry and Nale fighting, though they were only footsteps away on the other side of the door.

Whatever resided down here had blanketed everything in an unnatural calm; a deadly drowsiness. It was a place to forget and be forgotten.

Rae, Nicholas reminded himself. He started tentatively down the tunnel. What if he was too late? What if something had already happened to her? He'd never forgive himself. Though he was new to the Sentinel ways, he was sure he knew more about them than Rae, which made it his responsibility to keep her away from the kind of things that were imprisoned here. In that, he had failed.

He entered a small cave. Little white rocks glowed sombrely, embedded in the walls; a constellation of lights that beckoned. He raised a hand to one of the rocks and it brightened when he drew closer to it. When he moved away, it dimmed. Intrigued, Nicholas waved his hand back and forth, captivated as the light ebbed and flashed.

Wait.

Wasn't he here for something? He scrutinised the glowing rock, as if it held the answer, and found he couldn't look away. The pulsing light drew him in and he felt his eyelids drooping.

Rae.

The name shattered the spell.

Nicholas staggered away, repulsed. The caves wanted to trick him. They wanted him to forget. He squeezed the Drujblade and shook himself, attempted to untangle himself from the spell. His head clearing, he noticed another tunnel and hurried down it.

The next cave was littered with bodies.

Neither human, nor animal, they were small, cat-sized, but spindly. Long, vicious-looking legs were singed and bulbous bodies had exploded, spilling their filthy contents across the ground.

Nicholas noticed the walls were blackened and the stench of burnt flesh flooded his nostrils.

She did this, he realised. This was why Laurent had chosen Rae. She could protect herself from whatever the caves threw at her.

"Coward," Nicholas spat. He continued on.

The next cave was similarly destroyed, a series of booby traps lying in ruin.

The next, though, was almost empty. Large boulders communed in a circle and the ceiling was remarkably high. Nicholas thought he glimpsed eyes watching him from above, but it could just be his imagination. Or another trick.

He paused. Something definitely wasn't right.

The air had become charged. The hairs on Nicholas's arms bristled and he felt clammy with fear.

Impulsively, he hurled himself behind a rock and crouched low, listening as feather-light footsteps approached. He tensed against the boulder, the electricity in the air unnerving him. He daren't breathe in case it gave him away. The footsteps continued.

Somebody was in the cave with him.

Some*thing*.

Overpowered by curiosity, Nicholas chanced a look over the rock – and froze.

A figure glided through the darkness, moving with elegant, unhurried steps. A man in a bowler hat and a black suit, a bamboo cane poised in one foppish hand.

Nicholas felt ill. The seeing glass had shown him this figure. For a horrible moment, reality and unreality collided and Nicholas didn't know where he was. If he was even awake.

His head started buzzing and he realised he was definitely awake. He grit his teeth against the pain and his heart hammered as he watched the man in the bowler hat.

The figure paused, turned slowly toward him, and Nicholas only just caught the scream in his throat.

The man didn't have a face.

There was nothing but smooth, pearly flesh. A gaunt mask that betrayed no emotion, no humanity.

It wasn't a man at all. It was something else. And it was responsible for this unnatural cold, the charged air, the twisting fear that had gripped Nicholas even before he'd caught sight of the pale, repulsive face.

Nicholas clung to the rock with his good hand, not daring to breathe in case the scream escaped.

The hideous, eyeless visage seemed to look right at him, but the figure didn't move in his direction. It paused. Cocked its head to one side. Listened; appearing to contemplate its surroundings. Then it was moving again, gliding the way Nicholas had come and disappearing from sight.

Isabel, Nicholas thought. *Merlyn.*

Before he knew why, he was on his feet and tearing in the opposite direction, away from the faceless man. He had to get as far away from that thing as possible. Some primitive instinct seized hold of his body and he ran, ran, *ran*, his broken arm throbbing painfully from the exertion.

It didn't matter how loud he was now, as long as he kept going. He stumbled over small rocks, swatting away limply-hanging roots, plunging further downward until it seemed he was about to reach the earth's own pumping heart.

Finally, he saw a light ahead. Flickering candlelight.

"Rae?" he called.

His echo taunted him, returning elongated and alien. It was the only reply he received.

Cautiously, he skirted around the wall and peered into a dingy cave. At first he didn't understand what he was looking at, but then he realised that the warped metal had once been the bars of a makeshift jail cell. It had been destroyed; broken apart. Beside the cell sat two grinning, cobwebby skeletons in clerical dress. Priests, still guarding whatever it was that had been in the cell.

Except whatever had been in there was gone, and something had replaced it. Rae was in the cell, crumpled to the floor.

"Rae," he said breathlessly, climbing in with her. She didn't seem to hear him. She was peering down at her hands. "Are you okay?" he asked.

She whirled to face him and he saw that she had been crying.

"Stay away from me!" she yelled.

Nicholas held his hands up, wincing at the shard of pain in his broken forearm. "Woah, okay. I'm sorry. I'm staying right here. Away."

Anguish was all over her face and she was shaking. "That thing," she trembled. "I didn't think... He said... What was it?"

"Something very bad," Nicholas said. "Which is why we need to get out of here."

"Not going anywhere with you," Rae spat. "Just leave me alone."

"That's sort of not an option," Nicholas said, trying to remain calm. "I've... been looking for you."

"Why is everybody obsessed with following me?!"

"If you just shut up for a minute and let me explain–" he began, his patience dwindling.

"You shut up."

Stay *calm*, he told himself.

She got to her feet and staggered out of the cage. As she stepped through the warped door, though, she wobbled and grabbed one of the bars. Nicholas imagined what it must be like to come across something like the faceless man alone in the dark. He'd been scared, and he'd already encountered his share of demons.

"Take it easy," he said.

"What was that thing?" she asked again, her voice shaking.

"A monster. Laurent wants it out there killing. He wants a whole world of monsters because he doesn't know how to get along with people."

"He didn't say that," Rae murmured. "He wants to fix things. Make them better... That thing... Why didn't it have a face?"

"Never come across a good-looking demon before," Nicholas shrugged.

She looked at him and the hardness had gone from her jaw.

"It looked different before. Then I felt it in my head and it changed." She shook herself. "What you mean, you were looking for me?"

"It's kind of a long story and I don't think you'd believe me if I told you..."

"That thing had no face."

Nicholas didn't know where to begin. He decided to keep it simple. "Laurent thinks you have this power. He's lied to you from the moment you met him because he wants to use you."

"He hasn't." She didn't sound certain.

"Where is he now?" Nicholas demanded. "Hiding somewhere; too much of a coward to come down here. He sent you to do his dirty work."

"It's not like that."

"It is. And it's not safe here. Come with me and I'll tell you everything."

"I'm getting out of here."

She turned to leave and, desperately, Nicholas grabbed her arm.

It was as if somebody had torn the lid off his mind. Images spilled inside.

Rae sleeps under a park bench; a homeless man and woman heckle her; Rae sobs in the rain, clutching something in her hand; a raven pendant; a young boy lies dead in the rubble of a decimated building...

Rae wrenched her arm free.

"What you doing?" she cried.

"I didn't mean... That's never happened before," Nicholas murmured. Not with a person, anyway. He'd seen her life, or snatches of it. He felt a rush of empathy. She'd had it tough. She was his age and she'd endured things he'd never dreamed of. The street was no place for anybody, let alone a kid.

The raven pendant. Rae had one, too.

Finally, he understand why he kept seeing it in his visions. Liberty had been right. It was the key.

"Look," he said. He pulled something from his pocket and held it up. The raven necklace his parents had given him. Rae's expression changed. She reached to her neck and tugged at a slender chain, revealing an identical necklace.

"How much do you know about all of this?" he asked.

She didn't answer, her attention captured by his silver raven. Perhaps she couldn't find the words. It was a lot to take in and Laurent must have been very convincing.

"You can still make it right," Nicholas said. "Come on."

The fight had left her. He walked ahead, listening for her footsteps behind him. She followed.

It was easier getting out. Whatever enchantments had been woven over the caves only seemed to work one way – they wanted to stop anybody entering, rather than leaving. The priests must have felt confident that nothing would ever escape the oblituss.

After what felt like an age, they finally stepped through the oblituss door, emerging back into the tunnels.

Merlyn grabbed Nicholas's shoulders.

"Nicholas," he gasped. "We were about to come after you, but that thing..."

"We have to stop it," Nicholas said. "Whatever it is. We have to stop it from getting out."

Merlyn looked crestfallen. Nicholas glanced over at Nale, who was on the floor, his back pressed up against the wall. He was staring down at his large hands, a look of disbelief on his face. The gauntlet must not have worked on the faceless man. An unconscious form lay in the rubble. Harry.

"It's too late," Merlyn breathed. "It's already out."

CHAPTER TWENTY-ONE
The Faceless Man

The figure walked calmly, its steps unhurried. It carried a cane in one hand, a bowler hat resting on a poised head.

The figure had no face.

In the market square, the clock began to toll. Five chimes. Evening was approaching. The faceless man observed the clock, then turned toward movement. Somebody had emerged from a shop and was busily locking up. A middle-aged man attended to the door so closely that he didn't notice the figure in the bowler hat coast silently up to him.

The faceless man extended a hand, stretched slender fingers toward the shopkeeper.

He tapped the man lightly on the shoulder, then stood silently, observing.

The shopkeeper stopped what he was doing. Clumsy fingers unlocked the shop again and ungainly feet shambled inside. As if in a dream, he plodded through the murk, passing rows of garden tools and merry-faced gnomes.

He took a bottle from a shelf. The label read: *petroleum*. Like a sleepwalker, the man popped the cap and stumbled back through the shop, slopping stinking liquid out onto the floor.

At the front of the shop, he stood in the window. Staring out at the market square, eyes unseeing, lips unmoving, the shopkeeper upended the bottle.

He doused himself in the petroleum.

He struck a match.

★

"Guys, we need to get out of here," Merlyn said, helping Harry to his feet. Blood stained the older man's sleeve and he held onto Merlyn for support. Nicholas went over and put Harry's other arm around his free shoulder.

Clumsily, they made their way through the tunnels. There wasn't a single Harvester to obstruct their way. Laurent's army seemed to have retreated.

Or they're off doing more important things, Nicholas thought.

The evening air was warm and anxious and Nicholas cast a worried look up into the sky as something squealed in the heavens.

Harry tensed beside him. The mournful wail swooped around them. It sailed over their heads, and though Nicholas couldn't see the winged monsters, he knew they were out there.

"Aledites," he murmured.

"You alright?" Merlyn asked on the other side of Harry.

Nicholas nodded and cast a worried look at Rae. She seemed to have retreated into her own private dream world. She looked wiped out. Ready for bed. Or the grave, whichever came first. Rae probably wouldn't mind which, going by her expression.

All he knew was that she was the reason he'd come to Bury. Rae was where the trail ended; the one that Esus had ordered him to follow. It was probably why Jessica had permitted him to leave Hallow House. Rae needed to be found. She was powerful – she had to be if she was coveted by the servants of the Dark Prophets.

The thing that really worried him was the fact that Laurent had abandoned her in the tunnels. Was he done with her? Was that it? Had she fulfilled her purpose? Nicholas was sure there was more to it. A sneaking suspicion formed in his mind and he resolved to keep a close eye on Rae.

"You did alright back there," Merlyn said.

"Cheers."

"Listen, if we get through this alive, we should go out and have fun or something. Forget about the bogies and drink something we shouldn't."

Fun. Nicholas had forgotten what that was.

"Yeah," he said. "That'd be good."

"What kind of music you into?"

Nicholas had a strange sensation of being split down the middle. It had been ages since he'd had a conversation that didn't revolve around monsters. He'd forgotten how to talk about normal things. Things that weren't trying to kill or manipulate him at every turn.

"Uh, anything that was recorded before the millennium," he offered, thinking about the CDs he'd inherited from his grandparents and his store of classic eighties rock albums.

Merlyn grinned. "We're going to get along just fine."

They made it to Aileen's in one piece. The landlady was waiting for them in the hall, already wearing a tabard and a pair of medical gloves. She must have been expecting the worst, and when she saw Harry was injured, she took him from Merlyn.

"Come on, dear," she said softly. "Let's patch you up." She and Nale shouldered the injured man's weight and took him into the kitchen, Zeus padding silently behind.

Nicholas was about to turn to Rae when somebody flew out of the living room. Liberty crashed into Merlyn, shoving him against the wall. She was soaked through and her eyes were gleaming black buttons.

"Why'd you do it?" she demanded, pinning Merlyn with her arm.

"Liberty–" Nicholas began, but she shoved Merlyn again.

"You knew, didn't you? You set us up. Who put you up to it?"

"I don't know what you're talking about," Merlyn choked.

"Tell me the truth!" Liberty yelled. Her eyes locked with Merlyn's and he cried out in pain. With a lurch, Nicholas realised Liberty was reading the teenager, just as Nicholas had read the people in the Abbey Gardens that day.

After a moment, the dangerous glint in Liberty's eyes faded and she let Merlyn go. Instead of retaliating angrily, he put a hand on the Sensitive's shoulder, the fear turning to concern.

"What happened?" he asked.

"They took him." She looked around suddenly, noticing Rae. Her features were pinched, dark bags under her eyes. The change in her set nervous butterflies skittering in Nicholas's belly. "Is everybody okay?

What happened in the tunnels?"

"We're fine. Mostly. Are you?" he asked. "Where's Sam?"

"Something happened in Ipswich. The police took him."

"The *police*?" Nicholas didn't understand. "What do they want with him?"

"There was an incident. Solomon's dead. I managed to avoid being spotted by the police, but Sam wasn't so lucky. The good news is that he's at the station here in town. Something about the Ipswich station being refurbished. I don't know." She sighed. "Merlyn, I'm sorry–"

"We're going to get him out, right?" Nicholas interrupted.

"I'm working on it," Liberty said.

"I think Harry could use one of your brews," Merlyn said. "He's in bad shape."

Liberty nodded.

"See you in a bit."

Her voice echoed in Nicholas's head as she and Merlyn disappeared back into the kitchen.

Nicholas felt at a loss. He'd found Rae, and now Sam was gone. He knew he should talk to Rae, try to understand her, find out which lies Laurent had filled her head with, but he didn't know where to start. He suddenly understood Jessica's evasiveness. What if Rae fell apart when he told her the truth? Or worse, blew him up?

"You're back." Dawn lingered at the foot of the stairs, half in shadow. She must have seen the whole thing.

"In one piece," Nicholas said.

"You?" Rae shot Dawn a dirty look. "What is this, some kind of stalkers fan club?"

Dawn avoided her gaze.

"You two know each other?" Nicholas asked.

"We met," Rae muttered.

An uncomfortable silence lay between them.

"Uh, you might want to come and look at this," Dawn said, turning and heading upstairs.

"Well, stop dithering," Isabel said impatiently. Rae shot the cat a surprised look.

"She's more verbal than most cats," Nicholas explained.

"And he enjoys stating the obvious," the cat added.

"Let's see what Dawn's found," Nicholas said.

The cat clambered up the stairs and Nicholas hurried after her, hearing Rae behind him. Dawn's bedroom door was slightly ajar. She looked up from the desk as they entered.

"Purple, wow, what a shock," Rae muttered, though she couldn't hide her curiosity as she peered around the room, just as Nicholas had done the first time he saw the wall crammed with photos and diagrams. She strolled over to it. Pictures showed tribesmen practicing strange rituals. A star chart was marked up with lines. The photos of Nicholas and Rae were pinned alongside an illustration of a boy and girl holding hands.

Rae glared at Dawn. "You've been following me, haven't you? Ever since I came here."

"It's a good thing that she did," Isabel interrupted from the windowsill. "Or we'd never have found you."

"Found me? I dunno know who you are, *cat*, but–"

"I will not be spoken to in that impertinent manner!" Isabel spat.

"You really don't want to get on her bad side," Nicholas warned Rae. "Trust me."

"She's a talking cat!" Rae laughed incredulously. "The dog read tea leaves?!"

Isabel emitted a low growl that vibrated in Nicholas's chest.

"Let's just... not," he said, eager to avoid any more drama. "Rae, yes, we've all been trying to find you, but Laurent got to you first."

She stared at him, but she no longer seemed on the verge of erupting. Perhaps she could tell that he was being truthful. Or perhaps she, too, still felt what he had in the oblituss – that crackling connection, like something had slotted into place. They fit. Two peas in a paranormal pod.

"What's special about me?" she asked.

"Apart from the fact you can blow up buildings on command?" Nicholas joked. A look of pain flickered across her face and he recalled the vision of a dead boy in rubble.

Great start, idiot.

"Seriously, though, you might want to take a seat," he said. Eyeing him warily, Rae leaned against the wall. Deciding that was probably about as relaxed as she was going to get, Nicholas began. He told her about the Sentinels, and demons, and everything else in between. He explained what Laurent was planning, how he wanted to resurrect the Dark Prophets and unleash hell on earth.

When he'd finished, Rae stood quietly, her expression barely changing. He wished he could tell what she was thinking. She'd grown up on the streets. She must have seen things. Was the truth really that much of a surprise?

Finally, she spoke. "And you need me...?"

"We're the same. We have... abilities, I guess. The Sentinels believe we can raise the Trinity. Which now I say it out loud sounds seven types of crazy. But that's what they believe."

"You blow things up, too?" Rae asked.

"I see things," Nicholas explained.

"*See* things?"

"He has the sight," Isabel snapped.

Rae bit her lip. "That mean your parents are..."

"*Were*," Nicholas corrected her. He glanced at Dawn. "And Dawn's were, too. Sort of."

"Welcome to the Orphans' Club," Dawn murmured. She wasn't quite an orphan, but she probably felt like it with her mum not around.

Rae pushed away from the wall, turning to look at it once more. Nicholas still couldn't believe he'd found her, that he'd managed to convince her to come with him. He remained wary. Had the faceless man really shocked Rae to her senses, or was this all part of Laurent's scheme?

"I don't believe..." Rae murmured. "How am I supposed to know who's telling the truth and who's a big fat liar?"

Nicholas was stumped. She had a point. It was naïve of him to think she'd simply accept everything he told her, especially after all the nonsense Laurent had filled her head with. He couldn't tell her. He'd have to show her.

"I have an idea," he said. "We'd probably have to hold hands, though."

Rae's stare was lethal. Nicholas was reminded of the way he'd acted when he first arrived at Hallow House. The anger and frustration. Not understanding anything; discovering himself at the edge of a forest of secrets. He felt sorry for her.

"Children," Isabel growled.

"Do you want to know the truth or not?" Nicholas demanded, holding his hand out.

Finally, Rae rolled her eyes and grabbed his hand.

This time, he controlled the flood of images. He showed her everything he'd experienced since Anita and Max had died in the train wreck. The secret study in their room. Malika. Jessica. Hallow House. Snelling. Laurent attacking him in the Abbey Gardens. The images poured out of him. His grief was a black ooze, and he shared that, too. He opened himself up, gave it all to Rae. It was the only way she'd ever understand.

He didn't ask anything in return. She'd show him when she was ready. For now, her mind was a brick wall again, and he wouldn't abuse her fragile trust by blasting through it.

She gasped as she released his hand. She looked at him differently, trembling.

"All that happened? For real?"

He nodded. There was nothing left to say.

After a moment, Rae sighed. She stared at each of them in turn, as if seeing Nicholas, Isabel and Dawn for the first time. Her prickly edges had been worn down.

"How do we stop Laurent?" she asked.

"I thought you'd never ask," Nicholas replied.

"Tortor," Dawn said softly.

"You find something?" he asked.

"It's Latin. Tortor means 'torment'."

Dawn clicked something on the laptop and an image of a piece of paper came up. It was singed around the edges.

"The only time 'Tortor' is used as a noun by anybody as far as I can tell is in this journal by somebody called Father Philip. He was a priest in Bury in the 1600s. This entry is from 11 April, 1608. I had to run it through a translation site, but basically, he says, 'The devil Tortor has been contained. Peace will return.' And that's all he wrote."

It was the Tortor that had been locked away in the oblituss. The faceless man. And now he was out.

"Is that all there is? Nothing more?"

"Well," Dawn said, "there was a fire. On 11 April, 1608. One-hundred-and-sixty houses were destroyed. If I was a gambler, I'd say the Tortor was responsible."

"It's not just a weird coincidence?"

"Thought we didn't believe in those," Dawn said.

"Right." As if on cue, the sound of distant sirens came through the window. Nicholas rushed over and watched red and blue lights dance over the rooftops a few streets away. Fire crackled in the distance. A great plume of black smoke rushed into the evening sky.

Nicholas squinted. He was certain dark shapes were swooping above the town.

The *aledites*.

"Looks like the Tortor's started," he said. He peered down. People were coming into the safehouse. More Sentinels. Back-up had arrived. He returned his attention to the room. "But... the Tortor destroys things. Sets fires. Big whoop. How does that help Laurent?"

"It must be tied to Laurent's plan," Dawn said quietly. "Whatever he's going to do, he's doing it tonight."

"Rae," Nicholas said, filled with urgency. "What did Laurent tell you? Did he say anything about what he was planning?"

She looked torn for a moment. He feared that her loyalties still weren't set.

"Please," he said. "People are going to die if we don't stop him."

Rae tugged at the slender chain around her neck. "Trikraft," she relented finally. "I heard him with somebody. They were talking in one of the rooms down there. He kept saying 'trikraft'."

"Isabel?" Nicholas ventured.

The cat's whiskers trembled. "The trikraft traps power," she said. "Three points are marked to form a triangle and a summoning incantation is spoken. They're often used to summon unquiet spirits. Strange, the trikraft is usually associated with female power."

A triangle. Another piece of the puzzle the seeing glass had presented.

"Could it be used to summon the Prophets?" Nicholas asked.

"If Laurent has discovered a way to channel dark magic through the trikraft, it is, theoretically, possible," Isabel mitigated sombrely.

Nicholas hurried to the wall and scoured a map of the town. *Three points.* He traced his finger from the condemned school to the Abbey Gardens to Moyse's Hall Museum. Three places Laurent had been seen. If he linked them all together, they formed a perfect triangle.

"He's going to use the whole town as some sort of gateway," he said.

"He will need to perform a ritual at each point within the hour of the incantation," Isabel said. "If he leaves it any longer, the power will dissipate and he'll have lost his chance."

"We're going to have to hit those three locations, then," Nicholas said, pulling the sling off and shoving it into his pocket. He raised his arm, stretching his shoulder out. It felt creaky but good. "Rae, do you know which one Laurent will be at?"

Rae shrugged. "No idea."

The window erupted in a hail of glass. Something thudded against the wall and dropped to the floor. A flaming rock. Stunned, Nicholas stared at the shattered windowframe. A dark shape was clambering inside.

"Harvesters!" he cried. He threw himself at the figure, forcing it back out the window. The Harvester shrieked and plummeted to the street below. Nicholas chanced a look outside. More dark shapes were hurling themselves at the front door, smashing their way through the lounge window.

"Downstairs!" he shouted.

They bowled out of the bedroom, hurrying down the stairs. Nicholas crashed into Liberty in the hall.

"Nicholas, everybody, hurry," she said.

He heard screams and shouts from the living room and rushed through the kitchen. Aileen stood in the pantry, holding open the door to the secret rooms.

"Inside," she urged.

Nicholas pushed Isabel and the girls through, hurrying after them.

"Where's everybody else?" he panted, climbing the stairs to the bedrooms. The landing was full of people. At least thirty of them were crammed into the tight space.

"Nick," Merlyn called. "You okay?" He pushed his way through the crowd to join them.

"We're fine. How did they find us?"

"That's what I'd like to know," Merlyn said. He shot Rae a suspicious look.

"She's been with us the whole time, it wasn't her," Nicholas said.

"Somebody must've been tailed," Merlyn said.

A boom resounded through the pantry door. Liberty appeared with Nale and Aileen close behind. Zeus shepherded them up the stairs and then the giant dog stood guard, his eyes trained on the pantry door below.

"Rudy," Aileen whispered. "Poor Rudy."

"We're locked in, should buy us some time," Liberty said.

"He's using the town," Nicholas told her. "The school, the ruins, the museum. Laurent's creating a…"

"A trikraft," Isabel drawled from his shoulder. "Have you noticed it's getting awfully crowded in here?"

"Right, trikraft," Nicholas said, ignoring her last comment.

Liberty nodded solemnly. "Everybody quiet!" she yelled. The Sentinels fell silent. Muted thumps came from the pantry door as the Harvesters attempted to force their way inside. "There isn't much time," she continued. "As soon as they get through that door, it's a free for all. Is everybody armed?"

Weapons of every variety jabbed at the ceiling.

"Nicholas, tell them," Liberty said.

Nicholas's knees went weak. He stared at the expectant faces, trying to block out the sounds of the Harvesters hacking at the pantry door.

"Laurent's released the Tortor," he said.

"Speak up!" somebody gruffed.

"Laurent's released the Tortor!" Nicholas yelled. "He's going to destroy this town and everybody in it. He has to be stopped." His voice rose. "We have to separate. When we get out of here, we have to get to the school, the Abbey Gardens and the museum."

"What is this Tortor?" somebody asked.

"It's a demon without a face," Nicholas said.

"Sounds like my ex-wife," one of the Sentinels deadpanned.

"Laurent's been collecting totems," Liberty said. "If you get close enough, destroy them. Trust me when I say it'll hit him where it hurts. Form three groups. Laurent wants to raise a little hell; let's show him how it's done."

The pantry door smashed open and a cacophony of rampaging Harvesters rang in Nicholas's ears.

★

The darkness of the oblituss welcomed him.

Laurent almost permitted himself a smile, then quickly suppressed it. Not yet. Not until he had what he needed.

He quivered as he moved through the dank caves. The vibes pulsing through this desolate wasteland were intoxicating. The power that had resided here, the combined might of the priests and the monster they'd buried, was potent as gunpowder. The two forces forever tussled in the atmosphere, even after both parties had departed.

Laurent approached the final cave and took in his surroundings. The twisted metal of the jail cell; the fallen priests, their skeletons grinning madly at him.

"Evening, chaps," he murmured, scratching his fingernails across the cranium of one of the skulls. It tumbled to the floor and rolled into a corner.

The girl was gone. They must have come for her. It didn't matter; his followers were on her trail even now. They'd bring her back to him. Everything would work out just as he'd planned. The old man was in police custody, right where he belonged. It was all falling into place.

Laurent stepped through the warped bars into the cell that had once housed the Tortor. He trembled, sensing the power that had festered within the cell, biding its time. He wasn't here for that, though. Striding purposefully, he went to the back wall and ran his hand over the rocky surface.

Here. Somewhere here.

He touched something cold and solid. A golden coin embedded in the stone. A seal, put there by the monks long before the priests turned this cave into a jail cell. The coin was meant to bless what lay within the wall; keep it from harming anything or anybody.

"Two crows, one stone," he muttered, punching the rock with his bare hand. His knuckles came away torn and bloody. He punched again and again, the rock collapsing into pieces. The golden coin chimed as it struck the floor, and there was a hollow in the wall.

"Yes," Laurent whispered, reaching in. He drew out a small wooden chest shrouded in black gossamer. Ominous vibrations travelled through his fingers and up his arms.

Finally, he smiled.

CHAPTER TWENTY-TWO
Holding Cell

Sam checked his watch and groaned. He caught his reflection in the interrogation room mirror, disheartened by his shrivelled, worn-out appearance.

He'd been waiting for almost an hour. Were they purposefully wasting his time? Was it a police tactic? Let him squirm for a while before the barrage of questions? Surely they understood that what happened on Solomon's boat was an accident.

The door opened and the female police officer who had apprehended him entered. Her features were severe; bleached hair, bloodless lips and a collar done up so that it almost wrung the life out of her. Wordlessly, she sat opposite him and placed a file on the table between them. A second officer, a man, shut the door and stood motionless in the corner.

"My name's Detective Sharp, this is my colleague, DC White. Please state your full name and date of birth for the record."

Sam realised they must be recording the conversation, though he couldn't see a microphone anywhere.

"Samuel Matthew Wilkins," he said before giving his date of birth.

"Do you know why you're here?" Detective Sharp asked.

He shook his head. "I can only imagine it's about what happened on that boat."

True to her name, Detective Sharp observed him precipitously, bright green eyes unblinking. Though there was no spotlight on him, Sam felt like a rat in a lab.

"How familiar are you with Solomon Skye?"

Sam blanched.

"I only met him once, today in fact."

The detective nodded, her expression unreadable. "And what was the nature of your visit with Mr Skye?"

Anxiety flushed hotly through him. Solomon was dead. He'd seen him in the boat, dead eyes full of river water. Did the police suspect he was responsible for the psychic's death? Had his body been found? The police couldn't possibly think *he'd* killed him. But then, here he was being questioned.

"I..." Now he was stumped. He couldn't tell them he required the services of a psychic. Then again, if they knew who Solomon was, they must also know he was a psychic. Sam recalled the framed photos in Solomon's boat. The cover of *Paranormal Times*. The cover line had read: *The Skye's the limit*. Strange the things that stuck in his brain, sometimes. Either way, Solomon's psychic activities clearly hadn't been a secret.

"He was recommended to me by a friend," Sam said. He affected an embarrassed expression. "I don't know if you're aware that Solomon was a psychic..."

This didn't seem to surprise Detective Sharp.

"Do you make a habit of visiting psychics?"

"This was my first," Sam said. "I... I lost some friends recently. I thought it might help. Nothing else has."

The green eyes narrowed. Assessing. He wondered if she could hear his pulse.

"What can you tell me about what happened today?"

"I went for a reading with Solomon," Sam said carefully. "We were interrupted by the sound of something under the boat, and then water started flooding inside. I barely escaped alive."

Detective Sharp handed him a photo. Solomon's boat, *Darling Cassandra*, submerged in the river. Only a portion of the boat was still visible, like a pale hand waving for help.

"At 12.15pm, the police received a call reporting screams in the Ipswich docks. When officers arrived on the scene, Mr Skye's boat was found submerged and a body was retrieved from the wreckage. We're waiting for a positive identification that it was Mr Skye."

Sam looked up from the photo.

"Did you have an argument with Mr Skye?" the detective asked.

Slowly, he shook his head.

"No."

"Do you know what happened to his boat?"

"No."

Detective Sharp stared at him, unblinking. She didn't seem angry or suspicious, but her cold manner suggested that she considered him a suspect. He'd consider himself a suspect if the positions were swapped.

"I wish I could help you, detective," he said, "but I'm afraid I don't know anything about what did this to the boat. I've told you everything I know."

The green eyes remained on him.

Detective Sharp gathered the photos up. Sam watched her hands and frowned.

Red nail polish. Had she been wearing red nail polish before?

He glanced up and his blood ran cold.

Red lips. Full lips, tugging into a smile. And the reflection behind her in the mirror – it wasn't Detective Sharp sitting there, but somebody whose snake-like red hair slithered over pale, bare shoulders.

Malika.

His gut twisted. Rage flooded through him and the next thing Sam knew, his hands were around her neck. Malika barely registered the attack. Her expression mocked him as he squeezed.

"Mr Wilkins!" a voice yelled, but he barely heard it.

She was behind this. It was all her doing. Sam wanted to crush the life from her.

The witch laughed, porcelain teeth flashing.

"Laurent sends his regards," Malika spat.

No, not Malika.

Sam faltered. The eyes had changed. They stared at him in shock. Green and hardening into a glare. Detective Sharp pried his hands from her neck, flipped him and shoved him hard against the table, gripping his hands behind his back.

"Mr Wilkins, get a hold of yourself," she said sternly.

"You alright, ma'am?" DC White asked her.

Holding Cell

Sam grunted into the table top and felt metal at his wrists. *What's going on?* He couldn't remember. Something about that hell-witch. Malika. She was here. Wasn't she?

Everything was fuzzy. He sucked in a breath, pain spearing his shoulder as Detective Sharp handcuffed him. Why was she handcuffing him?

"Take him to one of the cells."

"What?" Sam mumbled, his head beginning to clear. No. He couldn't stay here. Nicholas needed him. Laurent was out there doing who knows what, planning who knows what. He had to get out.

"I've told you everything I know," he protested. "I need to go."

"Easy," warned DC White, dragging him to his feet and shoving him toward the door.

The cell was bare but blessedly cool. It was just one of five that Sam glimpsed in a small corridor at the back of the station before he was ushered inside, handed a blanket and locked up. He sank unsteadily onto the edge of a metal-framed bed.

Peering down, he saw his hands were shaking. He felt dazed. What had happened in the interrogation room? Had Malika really been there? She couldn't have been. It was Detective Sharp.

And he'd tried to strangle her.

Sam put his face in his hands. In all his years as a Sentinel, he'd never landed in a spot like this. Then again, in the past he'd had connections with the police, which meant he was able to avoid situations like this one. Were there no Sentinels in the police force anymore? Were their numbers dwindling so rapidly? Or perhaps Sam really was too old for the demon-hunting game.

★

He didn't know how long he'd been staring blankly at the wall when the door clunked open.

Sam rubbed his eyes as the light from the corridor intruded upon his cell.

"Thank you, officer," a voice said.

Sam stiffened.

No.

He looked up at the figure who had entered. For a moment he thought he'd gone mad. But no, there he was, standing as plainly as if he had always been standing there.

"Good evening, Samuel," Laurent said. The door closed behind him and he stood with his hands clasped before him; a perfect portrait of a gentleman. Sam knew he was anything but.

"I'm sorry to wake you. You have my word that I won't keep you long."

Sam pushed the blanket off and gripped the bed frame.

"Don't get up, please," Laurent purred, and Sam sat still, hands clenched as he stared at the wall. He wouldn't do Laurent the justice of looking at him again.

"How did you get in here?" he asked.

Laurent smiled. "Friends." He shrugged, fixing the cuffs of his shirt. "It's amazing where one finds oneself if one simply makes the right connections. Why, just look at you."

What did that mean? Sam looked at Laurent; he couldn't help himself. The gloating expression on his face told him everything. He'd come here to boast. Laurent had done this.

"You... What have you done?" he asked.

"Oh, this?" Laurent stopped smiling. "How times have changed," he mused, peering up at the ceiling of the cell, his amusement and disdain quite clear. "There was a time I was on the wrong side of a set of bars and you sought to judge me." He sighed. "Makes this quite fitting, don't you think? Poetic, almost. You refuse to die, so you can rot here. By the time you figure out an escape, the world will already have been fashioned anew."

Sam clenched the bed frame, resisting the urge to launch himself at the other man. Just to land one good blow would be worth it.

"You killed your family," he said. "You deserve to be in a cell."

"They had to die."

"You wiped out your entire bloodline!"

Laurent's eyes twinkled.

"Blood," he uttered. "You're so busy trying not to spill it you completely overlook its importance. Destroying a bloodline is one of the most powerful acts on this earth. It was the only way to ensure nobody ever held that power over me."

Solomon had been right. Blood was often integral to black magic. Acquire a single drop of a man's blood and you could control him with dark enchantments. Laurent had protected himself from that in the most horrific way imaginable.

"You're a monster," Sam rasped.

Laurent said nothing.

"They'll soon realise they have the wrong man. That you killed Solomon. And who knows who else besides."

"Samuel, I've been playing this little town like a fiddle ever since I arrived." Laurent beamed. "It's making such a wonderful tune, don't you think?" He turned and rapped on the door. "It's a shame you'll miss the grand finale."

Sam knew that Laurent wanted him to ask, but he couldn't resist. "Finale?" he ventured apprehensively.

Laurent's cheeks glowed rosily.

"You think it's been bad this far? Old man, the fun's just about to begin."

★

The safehouse erupted into chaos. Nicholas was jostled down the landing, through the crowd, away from the Harvesters that had broken through the pantry entrance.

"Rae!" he yelled, scanning the faces around him. "Isabel?"

He couldn't see them. Elbowed forward, he stumbled through an open doorway and found himself in one of the guest bedrooms.

He whirled around breathlessly, fist raised as another figure stumbled in after him.

Dawn held up her hands and he unclenched.

"Where are Rae and Isabel?" he asked. He'd only just found them both. He couldn't lose them again.

"I don't know, but we need to get out of here." Dawn pointed across the room. "The window."

Begrudgingly, Nicholas hurried to it and peered out, making sure no other Harvesters were lying in wait, clinging spider-like to the outside of the building.

The coast looked clear so he pushed the window open.

"We'll have to go over the rooftops," he said. At least this time he wasn't being dashed against them by some shrieking gargoyle. "We should get the others."

He tensed as a third figure staggered in, but let out a relieved breath when he saw it was Nale. The man was enormous in the small bedroom, Zeus at his side. He no longer had the gauntlet he'd used in the tunnels. What had happened to it?

Nale gave them both a glowering stare, then blinked at the window. "Go," he said.

"You first," Nicholas said to Dawn. She swallowed nervously and gripped the window frame, easing her way out.

"Nicholas!"

Liberty lurched through the door. She slammed it shut behind her and pressed her back against it. "Take this," she urged desperately, thrusting a rucksack at him. Nicholas took it.

"What's in it?" he asked.

"Just don't lose it."

"What about the others? Isabel and Rae?"

"I'll find them," Liberty assured him. "We'll spring Sam and head for the school. You three get to that museum. Go!"

Nicholas didn't stop to think. He shrugged into the backpack and crossed the room as Liberty disappeared back onto the landing. Nale had picked Zeus up and was climbing through the window. Nicholas went after him.

Memories of the aledite attack burst in his mind and he grit his teeth, forcing himself not to think about the bone-crunching pain as he struck the tiles that evening.

It was difficult to stand on the slanting roof, so he crouched low and scuttled over it, pressing his broken arm to his chest protectively.

Molten lava roiled in the night sky. It bubbled and slithered, a hot soup that clung to the firmament usually studded with starlight. Nicholas wiped his forehead, already sweating. How were they supposed to get down? He hoped Dawn knew a way.

Ahead, she hopped onto the neighbour's roof and disappeared over the edge. Nale did the same with Zeus. Ignoring the twinge in his arm, Nicholas scrambled clumsily onto the neighbour's roof and peered over the edge. Another roof rested just below, nearer to the ground. Dawn beckoned to him.

"I hate roofs," Nicholas muttered, throwing a leg over the edge and jumping down. Nale helped him into the back garden. Nicholas had never felt more relieved to have his feet on the ground.

"Where now?" Dawn asked.

"The museum."

"This way." She led them to the gate at the end of the garden. It opened into the alley.

"This heat," Nicholas griped, his tongue sticking to the roof of his mouth. He paused, hearing screaming and shouting. "What's going on?"

They hurried to the end of the alley, emerging into Churchgate Street.

Nicholas couldn't believe his eyes. Houses were ablaze and the street was teeming with people. Shop windows had been shattered. Cars were on fire, their alarms shrieking. And people were fighting. Bare-knuckled. Seizing broken objects from the ground. Raising them.

Blood splattered the tarmac.

What could have done this?

Then Nicholas saw him.

The Tortor. The faceless abomination glided serenely through the bedlam, sidestepping each of the crazed townspeople. Nicholas spotted a tear-stained boy standing in the fragments of a window. He couldn't be any older than five. Helplessly, he watched the Tortor tap the boy on the shoulder.

The crying ceased. The boy's face darkened. He dropped his toy bear and disappeared back through the broken window. Within seconds, yet more screaming started.

Nale began to move in the Tortor's direction, but Nicholas grabbed his arm.

"No," he said. "We don't know what that thing's capable of." The boy in the window had changed after a mere touch. Who knew what the monster could do if it got its hands around a person's neck.

Battling with his conscience, Nale hung back, the dog whining at his side. Nale patted Zeus on the head.

The Tortor vanished down a side street.

A shrill cry echoed down the street and a woman wielding a hammer appeared. She charged at a man in a business suit, burying the weapon in his skull. It made a sickening crack and hot red spurted against the ground. The woman bared her teeth and bayed. Her eyes found Nicholas's and he saw only madness dancing in them.

"The museum," he said, his voice hoarse. "Hurry!"

Before the woman could make her move, they ducked into another street.

The whole town had gone mad. Barely an hour had passed since he'd found Rae in the oblituss, and already Bury St Edmunds was in chaos. No wonder the priests had incarcerated the Tortor so fastidiously.

"This is insane," he said, dodging out of the way as a snarling man threw himself at him. The man hit the tarmac, growled and staggered to his feet, only to be tackled by a woman in curlers and a dressing gown. She slipped a shard of glass between the man's ribs and he howled, gurgling up blood.

Zeus barked but refrained from entering the fray.

"He's trying to destroy everything, isn't he?" Nicholas said as they hurried on.

"Distraction," Nale offered gruffly.

"Laurent's keeping us from getting in his way," Dawn murmured.

His plan's working so far. How could they hope to stop Laurent when the townspeople had all lost their minds? The town itself was being gutted, turned into a smoking shell. Come sunrise, there would be nothing left.

"It's more than that," Dawn said. "Fire's associated with destruction *and* creation. Fires can be used for purification."

"So this isn't just for show?" Nicholas asked.

"I think Laurent's purifying the town. He's creating a nest for the Dark Prophets. An untainted site for their re-entrance into the world."

Nicholas saw the market square ahead. It was bathed in fire and smoke choked the air. He felt it worming its way into his skin.

"He's lost it," he coughed.

"He doesn't think like a man anymore," Dawn muttered. "Because he isn't one."

"What else did you find out about him?"

Fear shone in Dawn's eyes and she shook her head.

"What?" Nicholas pressed. "If it's important—"

"His power, it's all... acquired," Dawn said, not meeting his gaze. "He was powerless before, so he stole the power of others."

"What do you mean?"

"He used blood... Demon blood. Mixed it with his own. Now he has some of them in him."

Nicholas stared at her, horrified. He hadn't known anything like that was even possible. So Laurent was more than just a man, now; he'd corrupted his body in the pursuit of power. If he was capable of that, Laurent was even more dangerous than Nicholas ever imagined.

The market square was a bonfire. Flames roared in shop windows and bodies littered the pavement. The only building as yet untouched by the carnage was the museum. Its windows flickered with the reflected flames, observing the chaos like a patient old man, perhaps knowing it was only a matter of time until it, too, was set ablaze.

Nicholas nervously eyed the people prowling outside the museum. Twenty of them. Possibly more. It was impossible to tell if they were Harvesters or townspeople driven mad by the Tortor. They blocked the museum completely and Nicholas knew that they would put up a fight if he tried to get past them.

It wasn't a thought that seemed to bother Nale. He strode determinedly into the throng, towering above the sea of heads and knocking people out of the way. He wasn't using full force, Nicholas noticed. For the time being, he mostly shoved people, landing a blow if it was absolutely necessary.

He was clearing a path to the museum for them.

"What if he—" Dawn began, but Nicholas didn't want to hear it.

"Come on," he said, hurrying to the museum's door. It was locked. Undeterred, Nicholas seized a brick from the ground and hurled it at the nearest window. He shrugged at Dawn. "It's not like anybody'll know it was us," he said, clearing the shards of glass away using his cast.

He heaved himself up onto the window ledge and winced as pain shot spikily through his broken arm. Crying out, he tumbled headfirst into the museum.

"Smooth," Dawn said softly, squeezing through the window and dropping down beside him. She hauled him to his feet and Nicholas shot her a grateful look.

"If he's here, he probably heard that," he whispered, drawing the Drujblade.

"You, er... ever used that on anybody?" Dawn asked, eyeing it.

Nicholas nodded. Dawn didn't seem comforted.

The low lobby was bathed in the fiery glow pouring in through the windows. Other than the sound of people clashing in the square outside, the museum was quiet. Nicholas tried to reach out, feel his way through the building with his mind, but it was as if it was wrapped in invisible netting. Some sort of enchantment stopped him.

"What do you think?" Dawn whispered.

"I think if we were in a horror movie we'd be dead by now."

"Do we wait for Nale?"

"He's a bit preoccupied at the moment."

Though he knew it would be madness to go any further into the museum, Nicholas also knew they had to. If Laurent wasn't here, perhaps there was some clue that would lead them to his whereabouts. He shuddered, his arm throbbing in the cast, reminding him of the first time he'd gone up against Laurent alone.

Shoving the thought aside, Nicholas stole through the lobby. It was disarmingly peaceful. He tried to flex his thoughts through the building again, sense if there was anybody else here, but he came up against that same impossible webbing.

The ground floor was deserted. They mounted the spiral staircase at the back of the museum and entered the room with the gibbet, the man-sized cage that Nicholas had seen earlier in the week.

In the dark, the glass cases looked sinister, as if their contents were being held against their will.

Something was out of place. As Nicholas surveyed the room, he was drawn to a mannequin in the corner. A woman in a dress, her gaze brooding on the window.

As Nicholas watched, panic rising in his throat, he saw the mannequin let out a breath. Porcelain skin shimmered. Red lips ruptured into a smile.

"Nicholas," Malika cooed. "You've come at last."

CHAPTER TWENTY-THREE
Pandemonium

NICHOLAS COULDN'T MOVE AND HE HATED himself. In the corner of the room, Malika was swaddled in shadows, but the sight of her still made his stomach spasm. His heart raced. She was the reason he couldn't sense anything in the museum. She'd cast a dark net over the building, protecting it from the Tortor, and it had sucked the air from every room.

"You look different," Malika observed, as if they were old friends. "You've matured. And you've brought a companion."

"You ran off last time," Nicholas managed to mutter. "I had to find somebody else to hang out with."

Malika laughed and Nicholas shuddered. He noticed a collection of ancient spears just out of reach. If he could grab one of them, he might have a chance against Malika. He'd have to get by her first, though.

"I like this, Nicholas," she purred. "It's a shame how events transpired before, but now here we are again. I feel we should embrace."

Nicholas pointed the Drujblade at her. She raised an eyebrow.

"You're shy, that's understandable."

"Dawn, go," Nicholas said. "Get Nale."

"Girl, if you move, you'll never use your legs again." The threat whipped from the corner and Nicholas didn't doubt Malika could carry it out without so much as breaking a sweat.

"So, Nale's here, too," she mused. "I do enjoy an old-fashioned reunion."

"Where's Laurent?" Nicholas asked. "You're his dogsbody now, right?"

He could tell he'd struck a nerve. Her shoulders tensed and the amusement died on her lips.

"Careful with those assumptions, manchild," Malika spat. Nicholas felt there was more she wanted to say, but she restrained herself. "This was delightful, it really was," she sighed eventually. "But you've caught me at an awkward moment. I'm afraid I have other plans to attend to."

She uttered a peculiar-sounding word and Nicholas felt the atmosphere in the room shift. The netting withdrew like a gasped breath; the enchantment protecting the museum evaporated into the ether. It was only a matter of time before the building succumbed to the ravaging fires that crackled around it.

"Whatever you're doing, stop," he warned.

He barely saw her move.

Malika threw something at the ceiling. A flash of light blinded him and she was upon them. Any thoughts of seizing one of the spears was forgotten. With one hand, Malika snatched at Nicholas's broken arm and wrenched it upwards.

Pink stars exploded in front of his eyes. The pain was so intense that Nicholas forgot where he was. Who he was. His bones were jelly and he was only vaguely aware of Dawn hurling herself at Malika. There came the *thwack* of contact and Dawn tumbled backwards into the stairwell. Through the hot blanket of pain, he heard an awful thumping as she crashed all the way to the ground floor. Then silence.

"Children," Malika hissed in his ear. She twisted his arm again. Fresh stars erupted and his vision swam. He screamed bloody murder.

"Children shouldn't meddle in adult affairs," Malika whispered. She pulled his broken arm, dragging him across the floor. Battling to stay conscious, Nicholas heard creaking metal and then found himself shoved up against something hard. A vibrating clang shook him and Malika's grip released him.

He slumped against metal bars, resisting the urge to vomit as he cradled his broken arm. Panting, he wiped the sweat from his face. He was soaked through. As his vision cleared, the sharp pain in his arm dulled to a persistent throb and he became aware of where he was.

The gibbet. He was in the gibbet.

"A perfect fit," Malika smiled, clicking a padlock shut. She inspected something in her hand. *The Drujblade.*

Nicholas sagged against the side of the gibbet. There was barely any room to move, especially with the backpack still on. The metal cut into him, forcing him to stand upright. He could hear crackling fire and realised that the museum was already ablaze. Smoke roved up through the stairwell and he saw orange, flickering glows swelling.

And through it all his arm pounded like nothing he'd ever felt. If he could tear it from its socket to escape the pain, he would.

Dawn. Nicholas remembered the thumping sounds as she crashed down the stairs. He dreaded to think what sort of state she was in. If she'd landed awkwardly, she could even be...

No, he wouldn't let himself think it.

Malika's gaze drilled into him.

She's changed, Nicholas thought with growing dread. Before, she had been terrifying. Now, her eyes glinted with a cold, clear-sighted determination he'd not seen before. As if everything she had been planning was coming to pass exactly as she'd hoped.

Malika dripping with blood. The image from the seeing glass surfaced in his mind, but he still didn't know what it meant.

"What are you doing?" he demanded. He didn't want to give her the satisfaction of seeing that he was afraid. He wouldn't shake the cage or try to break it open. He'd remain calm. Show her he wasn't a child. That he wasn't afraid to die.

"You need me," he added. "You said before. If I'm dead..." He stopped short, cowed by the look that Malika gave him. It almost seemed to be pity.

"You could have been a powerful ally," she purred, stroking the Drujblade. "Laurent is foolish. He believes you will see the light when the Prophets arrive. I know better."

Hopelessly, Nicholas watched Malika handle the Drujblade. *His* Drujblade. His only defence, taken from him.

"This is the blade that you destroyed Diltraa with," she observed. "I owe you my gratitude."

"Gratitude?" The pain was still so intense that Nicholas couldn't be sure he'd heard Malika correctly.

Malika had served Diltraa, an Adept of the Dark Prophets. Esus destroyed the demon at Hallow House, tore the monster's head from its shoulders. And now Malika was thanking him for Diltraa's demise? It didn't make any sense.

"You freed me," she hissed.

"I saw you in the room, the pentagon room," Nicholas murmured, recalling his vision that night in the garden. He'd glimpsed her past. He couldn't remember it all, but one image stuck fast in his mind: Malika, naked, cowering in the corner of the pentagon room. He still didn't know what it meant. "What were you doing there? What happened?"

"Such things are of little importance."

"You wanted Jessica dead," Nicholas continued. In the days following the break-in at Hallow House, he went over and over what had happened in the gardens, attempting to make sense of it all. He'd assumed Malika simply wanted to eradicate the Sentinels' guardian, usurp Jessica and send the Sentinels into a panic. "There's more to it, isn't there? You wanted her dead for a reason."

Malika's gaze threatened to burn right through him.

"Manchild, there's so much you don't know. And you never will."

In a flurry of red she was beside the cage. A pale hand flashed through the bars and seized his free arm, yanking it forward. Her hand was like stone. The blade bit into his palm. Blood pooled and Malika collected it into a vial.

"Mind if I keep this?" she murmured, examining the Drujblade once more. "A souvenir. A reminder of the man you could have been one day. When the world burns, you'll be by my side; in spirit, at least."

He wanted to scream. Unable to help himself, he rattled the cage angrily, his bloody palm slipping on the metal bars, but it was futile. He was stuck in there.

Malika turned her back on him. She muttered something under her breath. A prayer or a spell.

Nicholas wasn't sure if the wooziness was making him imagine things, but the flames that lapped up the stairwell seemed to move slower, as if they'd grown tired.

Time stood still.

Malika shrieked a foreign-sounding word and hurled the bloody vial to the floor. A rush of energy blasted through the building. It shook on its foundations.

With a jolt, he understood what Malika was doing – she was performing the ceremony to open the trikraft. He'd walked straight into it. It was his blood. Laurent had used demon blood to empower himself. Whatever powers the Trinity had placed inside of Nicholas must be in his blood – and Malika was using it to summon the Dark Prophets.

"The knowledge resides within you," Esus had said. And his power resided in his blood...

A blinding flash of red light erupted from where the vial lay shattered and the ceiling came away.

Through the hole above their heads, Nicholas saw a glimmering red star burning above the museum. It stayed suspended in place like a beacon.

I have to get out of here, he thought.

He shook the cage, but it was no good. He eyed Malika. What had he done in the garden that night? He had broken through her defences, found a way into her mind. If he could do that again, perhaps he could find a way to escape.

"That is how you will fight," Esus had said. The phantom wanted Nicholas to fight with his mind, not his fists.

Attempting to shut out the thundering pain in his broken arm, he mustered his strength and focussed on Malika. He felt the vibrations in his skull and tried to direct them at her.

Fresh pain tore through him.

Nicholas screamed and his knees gave way. It was as if somebody had split his head open. He slumped against the cage, his vision swimming.

"Now, now," Malika tutted, wagging a finger at him. "You know it's rude to pry."

Through the agony, Nicholas watched her glide to the centre of the room. She had built new defences; ones that his feeble abilities couldn't hope to overcome.

Apparently satisfied, Malika went to the door. She paused, cast him a look. The flames from the stairwell bathed her in hellfire.

"I'll give your regards to Jessica," she murmured. Then she swept away and Nicholas watched in horror as, finally, the room succumbed to the fire.

*

Rae peered around the tree trunk at the police station. She watched as the police cars out front lit up one by one and tore off into the night, their sirens keening. Remorse stabbed unexpectedly in her chest as she realised that whatever was happening to the town was her fault. She'd let that thing loose from the tunnels. She was responsible for whatever damage it caused; whoever it killed.

A familiar nag filled her ears.

Run. Run away.

The time for running had passed. Perhaps her running days were behind her. She was part of this whether she liked it or not. She wondered where Laurent was. What he was doing. She'd trusted him, accepted that he had wanted to help her. Now she saw that he was one of the monsters he'd spoken about. Perhaps the worst one of all.

Twig. She'd let him down.

"Now what?" she asked the cat.

They had escaped the Harvesters and made for the police station. People seemed to have gone mad. They were fighting in the streets. Setting fire to things and smashing up buildings. Rae, the cat and an elderly woman called Aileen had moved quickly, heading for the station. The others were on their way to the school where the teachers had been killed.

Isabel was perched in a branch above her head, golden eyes set intently on the police station. Rae wondered what her story was. How was it possible for a cat to speak?

"We must locate Samuel's cell," Isabel said.

Rae chewed the inside of her cheek. "I blow things up. Could get him out."

"Too dangerous." Isabel dismissed her sniffily. "This is something that requires a touch of the old-fashioned."

"What do you suggest, dear?" asked Aileen. The landlady stood on the other side of the tree. With the sword strapped to her back and her bag full of weapons, she was an incongruous sight. A battlefield granny.

For a fleeting moment, Rae wondered if she was dreaming it all. The monsters, the talking cat, the sword-wielding old lady. She almost wished she was.

"Diversionary tactics," the cat said.

They listened as Isabel briskly outlined her plan. Rae had no choice but to go along with it, though it sounded crazy. Surely it would be easier to demolish the exterior wall of Sam's cell? She decided to stick with Isabel's arrangement, suspecting the cat would flay her alive if she refused.

A few moments later, Rae pulled open the door to the police station and walked into the brightly-lit reception.

"Sorry, love," an officer said, hurrying past her into the car park.

Rae remembered the cop shows she'd seen as a kid. The officers at the front desk were always simple-minded. Glorified office monkeys. She doubted she'd be as lucky, especially not with the town burning around them.

The officer behind the desk was probably in her early forties. She didn't look bored or doughy, as Rae had imagined; she was smart, her hair pulled tight in a bun, the sparest of make-up masking the odd wrinkle.

Rae surveyed the reception. A door beside the desk was open and she glimpsed a corridor that led to the rest of the station. They were lucky. This was a small, local facility – the most the Bury police probably dealt with was drunks and the odd thief. There was no need for Fort Knox-style security.

"Can I help you?" the policewoman asked as Rae approached.

"I can't find my phone," she said. "Think somebody pinched it."

A thief reporting a robbery. So long as it kept the officer distracted.

A framed poster on the wall behind the officer reflected the contents of the front desk. Rae saw two screens that showed CCTV footage of the rest of the station.

"Okay. Do you mind coming back in the morning? We've got a bit of a situation here at the moment."

This town won't be here in the morning, Rae thought.

Out of the corner of her eye, Rae glimpsed a black shape scampering silently through the reception. It disappeared through the door to the back of the station. Isabel was in. Now all she had to do was keep the officer from looking at the surveillance cameras.

★

Sam grasped the bars at the window and tugged hard.

It was no good. They refused to be forced either way.

"Blast," he groused. Through the mottled window he glimpsed distorted orange flickers. Laurent's grand finale was well under way and Sam was damned if he was going to sit in his cell and listen patiently as the world ended.

"Old man," a voice said.

Sam jumped. It sounded like…

"Isabel?" he ventured, going to the cell door. He peered through the rectangular window halfway down. The cat sat in the middle of the corridor.

"What are you doing here?" he asked.

"Saving the day, as is my lot," Isabel replied.

"You're getting me out of here?"

"Your faith in me is astounding." The cat's ears flicked and she looked off down the corridor.

"Somebody approaches," she hissed. "Step away."

Sam shuffled away from the door. Just how Isabel intended to free him was beyond his comprehension. She seemed to have forgotten that she was a cat. What use was a cat in a situation like this?

A sudden fizzing sound came through the door, as if a firework had been lit, and sparks spewed into the cell through the small window. He heard a peculiar humming and the edges of the door glowed gold, as if somebody had taken a blow torch to them. Sam's mouth fell open as the door collapsed inward.

It smashed to the cell floor, barely missing him.

Through the smoke, he saw two flashes of gold. Sparks sizzled in Isabel's eyes. Then they were gone.

"Come." The cat's voice punched through the haze. "Quickly!"

Sam hurried into the corridor. He heard footsteps approaching and two officers appeared.

"What the—" one of them began, but then a furry black shape flew at his face. Isabel attacked the officer like a thing possessed.

The other officer, in his thirties and built like a bodyguard, approached Sam stealthily.

"Come on, old man," he said. "Let's not make this into a—"

Sam buried his fist in the officer's face.

The officer staggered back, touching his jaw in surprise. Sam winced as his knuckles pounded. He no longer had the element of surprise.

"That's how it's going to be, then," the officer said, advancing again and drawing what looked like a stun gun.

"GET THIS THING OFF ME!" howled the other office, attempting to pry Isabel free. Unable to shake her off, he stumbled down a side corridor, taking her with him. They vanished from sight.

"You have no idea what's going on out there, young man," Sam said softly to the policeman who had the stun gun aimed at his chest.

"Don't make this any worse," the officer said.

Sam held his hands up.

"Alright, alright, I'm sorry." He made his voice tremble and was surprised at how convincing he sounded. Maybe he was getting better at lying. "Just don't shoot that thing at me. Got a bad ticker." He cowered, hoping he wasn't overplaying it.

The officer sized him up.

"Face against the wall," he said. "Hands behind your back."

Sam complied and the officer came up behind him. Before he could lay a finger on him, Sam dropped clumsily to his knees and turned, yanking the gun from the officer's hands. He aimed and fired.

The officer yelped and collapsed, spasming against the floor as the gun ticked.

Sam threw the weapon down.

"Sorry, chap," he muttered.

At the end of the corridor, he found Isabel sitting atop the other officer, who was sprawled on his back.

"Fool knocked himself unconscious running at the wall," she muttered, licking a paw and running it behind her ear. She hopped off and Sam followed her through the station.

A girl stood in the reception. Not just any girl; the one from the tunnels. The one Laurent had brainwashed.

"Rae, I presume," Sam said. She nodded.

"What happened to *her*?" Isabel asked, noting the unconscious female officer behind the front desk. An angry pink welt was swelling on her jaw.

"She looked tired," Rae said.

Sam went to the door. He shuddered, seeing the black smoke pouring up into the night sky.

"Where are the others?" he asked.

Isabel told him about the attack at Aileen's and Sam listened grimly. They were scattered, just as Laurent no doubt wanted.

"We need supplies," he said and his eyebrows arched in surprise when he spotted Aileen standing by a tree out front, a sword strapped to her back. He pushed the door open and went out, sounds of destruction clamouring in on him.

"Evening, dear," Aileen said, handing him his satchel.

"Aileen," he said. He rummaged through the bag, checking his stock. A raven feather, herbs, the deadly little white parcels he'd hoped he would never have to use again. "Thanks."

"Didn't have much choice," Aileen said. "The safehouse is gone."

"That bad?"

"Harvesters, dear."

Sam shook his head. "That mine?" he asked, nodding to the rifle in her hands.

"Here," she said.

He went to take it from her, but Aileen didn't release it. He found himself alarmingly close to her. Her eyes sparkled at the centre of her doughy face. She smelt like washing powder and apple crumble.

"We're tough old birds, you and I," she said. "Not as easy to pluck as one might imagine."

Bewildered, Sam nodded. Aileen's free hand was on his arm. It squeezed, gently but firmly.

"Let me..." she began softly. "Let me take care of you."

It was clear in an instant. The way she fussed around him like a mother hen. Clucking at his every movement. Fluffing pillows, filling kettles, primping and prattling. Sam didn't know what to think. How to feel. It had been years since anybody had looked at him that way. He was a doddery old man. Nobody looked at him like that anymore.

"Aileen," he began.

"I'm no spring chicken, I know that," Aileen said. "But that's no bad thing. We could be happy here." Sirens shrilled and Aileen checked herself. "Could be, after all of this."

With infinite delicacy she added: "It's been years since Judith, dear."

Judith.

He couldn't. Aileen seemed to notice something in him the instant he thought her name. Had his face changed? Did he look repulsed? Scared? It didn't matter. Aileen released both his arm and the rifle.

"No," she murmured as Rae and Isabel approached. "No, of course. Foolish of me. You still..."

"Aileen," he started.

"We best get going," she interrupted him, checking the sword at her back. "My, but your face is a picture," she chuckled, her old self returning in the blink of an eye. "Never seen a woman with a blade before? I doubt that. My granddaughter's somewhere out there, and I'll be damned if I'm going to let anything happen to her."

He knew better than to argue.

"I'd be glad for the company," he said.

He noticed that Rae looked worse than he felt. The dark bags under her eyes seemed to deepen with every second, as if the weight of everything that had come to pass was slowly squeezing the life out of her.

Shock, Sam thought. *This is all new to her.* And who wouldn't be shocked by what was happening in the town?

"Good, you're armed," Isabel said.

"You alright?" Sam asked Rae. She nodded.

"We must reunite with the others at the school," Isabel sniffed.

"You think Laurent will be there?"

"Even if he isn't, it's integral to his plan," Isabel said.

Sam's instincts told him that whatever was going to happen, it would happen at the Abbey ruins. That's where the tunnels were, and Laurent had talked about the primal energies pulsing there. But the school was important, too. It had been desecrated. He eyed Rae. They couldn't take her with them, surely. She was too dangerous. And how could they trust her after she'd allied herself with Laurent?

He felt claws sink into his shoulder and realised Isabel had clambered aboard.

"Go," she urged. "There isn't a minute to spare."

The town was worse than he'd imagined. Black smoke and fire filled the sky. Every building smouldered and the streets were filled with bodies and warring townspeople.

"Here," Sam said, handing out handkerchiefs and fastening one protectively around his face. Rae and Aileen did the same. They kept close to the buildings as they made their way down the street, attempting to draw as little attention to themselves as possible.

A car careened down the road and ploughed into a block of flats. A landslide of fiery rubble spilled onto the stalled automobile, cocooning it and its driver.

"Hurry," Sam called, taking up the rear, clasping the rifle tightly. He heard a strange noise and realised Aileen was singing softly.

"London's burning, London's burning," she murmured, as if to comfort herself. Sam appreciated the distraction, even if the location was wrong. "Fire fire, fire fire."

They made their way through the streets, meeting with destruction at every turn.

"The girl. She's fading." Isabel spoke quietly into Sam's ear. "Another hour and she'll be useless to us."

"Have a heart," Sam whispered back, his voice muffled by the handkerchief. He agreed, though, that things would be a hundred times more difficult if Rae became unstable.

"If the school's untouched, she stays there," Isabel said. "It's the only way. She's exhausted herself, or that brute has. Whatever she's been doing, it's not the way it's meant to be. She's abused her power."

Sam hadn't thought he could feel any worse about the situation, but Isabel's words proved him wrong. This wasn't good.

Royal Birch Primary School was located further out of town and as they cleared Bury's centre, they found that fewer buildings had fallen to the Tortor. The streets were quieter. They climbed a hill and Sam chanced a look back. His breath caught in his throat.

The town had become an inferno. Every rooftop flickered with hellish fire, belching ash and embers into the heavens. There were no more sirens. No shrieks. No screams. Bury was falling and there was nothing they could do about it.

"We'll lose them," Isabel warned. Sam shrank away from the town and saw that Rae and Aileen had gone ahead. He jogged to catch up with them, wiping sweat from his nose. He felt grimy with dust. The handkerchief over his mouth was already filthy so he pulled it free and tossed it to the ground. The others did the same.

At last, they reached the school. It seemed unaware that the world was ending. Somnolent behind a curtain of trees, its windows were peaceful, unperturbed by the mayhem of the town centre. The calm was a momentary tonic to the carnage they had battled through.

There were no people, though. No movement behind the blinds.

Sam eyed the building distrustfully. Was it possible that the sickness spread by the Tortor had yet to reach the school? Or was it being protected? Armies needed a base. Was this somewhere for Laurent to regroup? The quiet was alarming.

They stood staring up at the school. Sam didn't know what to think.

"Where are the others?" he said at last.

Sentinels had been sent to guard the school days ago, and Liberty should be here somewhere, too.

"We would be foolish to enter," Isabel said.

Sam knew they had to go in. It was their job. If the school was harbouring something insidious, who else would tackle it?

"Then we're all fools," he shrugged, ambling forward. "Stay close." Rae stepped in line with him, Aileen on his other side.

"I had forgotten how exciting this could be," the landlady said.

"I had forgotten what an adrenaline junkie you used to be," Sam commented. He kept his eyes on the school as they approached the entrance. There was no movement. Nothing that made him suspect an imminent attack. He pushed the door open and they all went inside.

The quiet hung like a veil. Something that smothered and obscured.

"I've never known a school so quiet," Aileen said. Despite the emptiness of the reception, her voice didn't glance off the surfaces. The atmosphere absorbed it hungrily.

"We should leave," Isabel hissed.

Sam looked at Rae. She swallowed nervously.

"We're here now," he reasoned. As he performed the protective ritual with the raven feather, Isabel hopped from his shoulder, padding silently across the polished floor, a four-legged spectre.

When Sam was done, he, Aileen, Isabel and Rae made their way down the main corridor. At the end, Sam eyed the staff room uneasily. It looked the same as it had earlier in the week. There was no sign of the hag who had set the shadow demons on them, though.

"Down here," he said, drawing everybody away from the staff room.

They went down another corridor. Sam paused, a vile stench assaulting his nostrils. He peered ahead. In the darkness, it was hard to see properly, but his heart thumped faster at what he could make out.

The corridor was painted with blood. It oozed thickly across the shiny floor and was splashed up the walls.

Sam pushed against the voice in his head that urged him to turn around. No matter how long he'd been doing this, that voice was always there, and it only got louder with age. When he was young, he'd found a way to ignore it; he'd imagine the worst thing he could, and that helped to diminish the horror of the things he had to face. All these years later, though, he'd seen enough horrific things to know that nothing good awaited them.

At the end of the corridor, a sign above a pair of double doors read: GYMNASIUM.

They approached slowly. Sam pushed the doors open. He nearly retched at the stench.

Rae and Aileen made disgusted sounds, shoving their hands to their mouths. Sam raised his arm to his nose but the stink of rot pressed in all around them.

"Rae," Sam grunted. "Stay here."

Steeling himself, he passed into the gym. The reek was overpowering and Sam blinked rapidly to stop his eyes from watering.

Bodies littered the gymnasium. Lifeless, heaped up against the walls. All dead. Left to rot. The Sentinels who had been sent to guard the school had been killed.

At the centre of the gym, Liberty and Merlyn turned to look at him.

"We just got here," Liberty said.

"What have they done?" Sam croaked. Fresh terror crashed through him. "We have to get out of here."

"But you've only just arrived." A silky voice roved into the gym and Sam's legs threatened to drop him. On the other side of the gymnasium, a shape detached itself from the shadows. Malika's smile was a wound-like slash of red and her eyes stabbed through the gloom. Sam gripped the shotgun tighter.

"You killed them," he muttered, not caring that he was stating the obvious. He had to find a way to stop her. What would it take to bring Malika down? Bullets had failed on the bus and she looked even stronger than ever. There wasn't even any facial scarring from the powder he'd used on her mere days ago.

"They all screamed and begged." Malika shrugged, rippling slowly through the shadows.

"Don't move," Sam warned, aiming the gun at her.

The mocking laugh that shivered through the gymnasium caused the hairs on his arms to bristle.

"Aren't you tired yet, old man?" the thing in the shadows spat. "You've aged at least a decade in the last week." She gave him a knowing look. "How's the blood pressure?"

Sam tried to ignore her. She wanted to get inside his head. That's what Malika did. If he let her in, he'd be finished.

"Stop." Liberty spoke. Sam noticed the Sensitive staring intently at Malika. Just a week ago, Malika had turned Liberty into a puppet, forcing her to participate in the spell that opened a portal into Hallow House. Sam's concern for her increased. If Malika had been in her head once...

Malika looked briefly troubled, then she arched her back, stretching out her spine as if in preparation of a fight.

"I'd like to see you try, hag," she said to Liberty.

"What do you want?" Sam asked.

"A good man to make an honest woman of me." She smiled coyly at Merlyn. "Are you up to the task?"

"Don't look at her," Liberty warned him.

"No," Malika purred, her gaze trained on the young Sentinel. "You love another."

Sam scanned the gym. The doors he'd come through lay behind him. Could they make it out before Malika made her move?

He frowned, noticing a metal structure against the wall. It was a freestanding frame about seven feet high, equipped with chains. Splotches of dark red stained the metal. It looked like a torture device. Sam was reminded of the racks that were used to punish wrong-doers in medieval times.

With a start, he realised he was looking upon the apparatus that had been removed from Snelling's basement. The marks scratched into the basement floor seemed to match the dimensions of whatever this odd structure was.

"Oh this?" Malika purred, having noted his inquisitive stare. "Just another of Thomas Gray's inventions. You met Thomas? Gifted scientist. Strong mind, in many respects. Unbelievably weak in others. I'm afraid he used up the last of his strength to ensure I survived our last encounter."

Sam didn't want to ask, but he had to. "What is it?"

"People will insist on struggling," Malika said sorrowfully, brushing the chains and making them rattle.

"You bled them," Liberty accused her, a mixture of awe and disgust in her tone. "You bled all of them. And then you left them to rot in here."

"Blood," Malika said, her teeth flashing. "Their blood was the only useful thing about them. Would you like a demonstration? It's really quite humane. No more barbaric than bleeding a cow."

"She bathed in it," Liberty murmured, flinching at whatever she could see in her mind's eye.

"So a literal bloodbath." Merlyn gulped.

Always blood. That's what had changed. Malika looked vital, refreshed, strong. Sam wasn't sure if the blood bath was a new development, but it was clear Malika had stepped up her game. Whatever she had planned, there would be no prisoners.

"You need more blood," Liberty mused. Sam wondered what else she might be sensing from Malika.

"I warned you before, witch," Malika cautioned her.

"But only from one more person, and for a different purpose," Liberty continued. "You need blood from..." Slowly, the Sensitive turned to peer over Sam's shoulder. He twisted, following her line of vision.

Rae stood in the door of the gymnasium.

No.

More shapes detached themselves from the shadows. Harvesters. And something else. Something he could only glimpse out of the corner of his eye, but vanished when he turned his head. Dark forms swelled over the walls, as if riding an invisible current. They seemed insubstantial, but that didn't mean they weren't dangerous. Quite the opposite. Sam recalled what had happened when he'd come to the school with Nicholas. The shadows had moved as if they were alive.

The murklings.

He cursed under his breath. Malika needed Rae, and they'd brought her without a moment's hesitation. They really were fools. He wouldn't let Malika take her. He had to stop her.

Without another word, and before Malika had a chance to make the first move, he pumped the rifle and fired a shot at the woman in red. Even if it didn't kill her, he could at least buy them some time.

Malika dodged it easily.

The gunshot heralded sudden chaos. Figures writhed away from the walls and spilled across the gymnasium floor. The Harvesters and the shadow creatures descended upon them ravenously.

Amid the creatures, Malika swept forward.

"Rae, run!" Sam bellowed, aiming the rifle at Malika once more. "Aileen, get her out of here!" He watched Aileen drag Rae back into the corridor and then hurried to Liberty and Merlyn. The three Sentinels stood with their backs together, tackling each Harvester that swung at them.

"Sam, down!" Liberty yelled, and the old man obeyed just in time, hearing the whir of a blade as it sailed over his head.

"We don't get paid anywhere near enough for this," Merlyn grunted. Sam heard him bury his dagger into something – someone – and then grunt again as he yanked it free. He fired at a stocky Harvester, who collapsed in a heap on the floor.

Sam heard a gasp and glanced over his shoulder.

Malika's hands were around Liberty's throat. She hurled the Sensitive through the air. Sam winced as Liberty crashed into the bleeding apparatus and hit the floor. Immediately, shadowy claws flew up from the polished floorboards, snatching at her.

"Liberty!" Sam gasped in horror.

Hands seized him, too, and he struggled to free himself from the Harvester at his back. Beside him, Merlyn was held back by two more Harvesters.

"Get off me, you slimy, bottom-feeding parasites!" Merlyn yelled.

"Time to say goodbye," Malika sneered.

Terror overwhelming him, unable to squirm free, Sam watched helplessly as dark, menacing shapes surrounded Liberty. They pinned her down, then the largest of them rose above her, talons flexing in preparation.

Sam became suddenly aware of the heat in the gymnasium. The temperature had risen sharply. The air crackled and Sam felt the Harvester's palms becoming slick with sweat, struggling to hold him down.

As the talons descended on Liberty, Sam managed to wrench himself free, taking advantage of the Harvester's clammy grip. He slipped to the floor and glimpsed Rae by the gym door. Crackles of electricity darted from her fingertips and the air wobbled around her, the way air sometimes looks in the desert.

Then the gymnasium exploded.

CHAPTER TWENTY-FOUR
Spears And Arrows

The fires blazed higher and higher. Nicholas watched helplessly as they roved into the museum, seeking out material to scorch and devour. He shook the gibbet with all his strength. He tried each of the bars, hoping to find one that was rusted and aged enough to pull loose. None moved and the padlock, though equally worn, refused to be pried open.

Rae. He had to get to her before Malika did. If she completed the trikraft, they might as well start digging their own graves.

Nicholas paused. Footsteps. He heard footsteps ringing up the staircase. Slow and resolute. His heart leapt into his throat.

"Dawn!" he called. "Are you okay?"

The Tortor emerged through the flames.

A wordless choke bubbled up in Nicholas's throat and wild panic clawed at him. He froze within the gibbet. If he stayed still, perhaps the monster wouldn't see him – it stood to reason considering it didn't have any eyes.

The bowler hat turned as the faceless man seemed to look around the room. Then it stopped, as if it had noticed Nicholas. The head tilted with curiosity.

Nicholas's resolve crumbled. How could he fight it? The Tortor was going to come over and lay his hands on him and Nicholas was going to die. He didn't know which death he'd prefer; being burned alive or succumbing to the devastation of the faceless man.

The Tortor took another step into the room.

Nicholas couldn't believe it. The flames actually flexed away from the creature. The Tortor was immune to the chaos he was so calmly disseminating. The fires set by those under his thrall wavered and bent away as the faceless man passed through them, as if they, too, were repulsed by the thing in their midst.

A clear path stood between them and Nicholas felt horribly cold inside, as if the Tortor's mere presence had frozen his heart. He shivered and pressed himself up against the back of the gibbet, straining away from the malevolence that stealthily approached, dispassionately closing the gap between them until Nicholas couldn't think clearly.

The only words that pounded in his head were: *You're going to die.*

"Stay away from me!" he yelled, though he knew it was futile. The Tortor wasn't listening.

Nicholas railed against the gibbet, attempting to rock it. It was chained to the ceiling, but maybe he could bust it open by swinging it against the wall. He swayed back and forth in the cramped space, throwing his weight against one side and then the other.

The chain creaked and Nicholas saw that the plaster where the chain was fixed was already succumbing to the fire. Maybe it would give with a little encouragement.

He jumped up and down in the gibbet, though there was barely room to move.

The Tortor continued his approach. He was mere feet away. His calmness only caused Nicholas's panic to increase and he refused to give in to it. Losing his mind would mean losing his life.

The chain in the ceiling creaked and Nicholas's struggles intensified. He pushed himself against the rusted bars and swung the gibbet wildly.

As the faceless man's skeletal fingers scraped the gibbet's bars, Nicholas felt the chain in the ceiling give way and the cage crashed violently to the floor.

Prone at the Tortor's feet, he wrestled with the gibbet, even as the monster's hands came roving.

Part of the cage had buckled and Nicholas dodged the Tortor's groping claws, prising the gibbet apart. He thrashed at the bars around him and rolled clear across the floorboards. He felt the air shift behind him as if a hand had swiped for his head and missed.

Breathlessly, Nicholas hauled himself to his feet.

The Tortor began another stealthy approach and Nicholas flew to the stairwell, raising an arm against the inferno. There was no way he could go down the stairs without being burned alive.

He whirled around. There had to be another way out. Over the Tortor's shoulder, he spotted another door on the other side of the room. It led into the rest of the museum. It was his only chance. He looked for anything that he could use to fight with.

The spears!

They were the only weapons in the room, propped up near the far door.

Ducking around a glass cabinet, he plotted a course across the room. The Tortor quickly adjusted his approach, weaving after him between the cabinets.

Nicholas felt something brush the hair on the back of his head and, with a cry, he hurled himself at the collection of spears. He landed on the floor mere inches away from them and threw his free hand out, wrapping his fingers around one of the weapons and yanking.

It came free just as the faceless man appeared, towering over him with hands outstretched. Nicholas dragged the spear free and, hardly daring to look, jabbed it at the monster.

The blade pierced the Tortor's chest and, finally, the monster's descent was halted.

There was no blood. No scream. No angry thrashing or flailing.

The faceless man contemplated the weapon buried in him. Then, with maddening calm, he clasped the spear in both hands, pushing the other end of the weapon against the floorboards so that he was propped up by the floor.

Nicholas's relief was fleeting. Something wasn't right. What was the creature doing? The Tortor slid its hands down the length of the spear. Then it pulled, dragging itself toward the floor. Toward Nicholas.

With a sickening lurch, Nicholas understood. The Tortor was shoving the spear further into its flesh, impaling itself like a hunk of meat on a skewer in order to get closer to him. To kill him.

He swallowed the rising bile and scrabbled across the floorboards on his back, hugging his broken arm to his chest. The Tortor turned to look at him and Nicholas knew that it wasn't over. He couldn't beat it.

He had to get out of there.

Getting to his feet, he ran for the door. The rest of the museum was ablaze and Nicholas didn't waste any time darting from room to room, searching for a way out. He knew there was a second staircase, if he could just find it.

As he charged through another doorway, he smashed into somebody.

"Get back!" he cried.

"It's me!" Dawn puffed.

"Dawn! I thought you were... Christ, are you okay?"

Blood streamed stickily down one side of her face.

"I'm fine," she said. "Come on, we need to get out of here."

"You think?"

She grabbed his hand and he staggered after her through the collapsing museum. How long did they have before the faceless man caught up with them? Nicholas swatted the thought away, hoped the spear would keep the creature impaled for long enough for them to escape the building. If they could escape it.

They reached the second stairwell and Nicholas cried out with relief. They took the stairs and found they were back in the lobby. Not wasting a moment, they both rushed through to the window they had come in by.

Nale's bearded face appeared. He nodded in greeting, reaching inside to draw Dawn out. Nicholas clambered after, tripping in his hurry. Strong arms caught him and set him down on the pavement.

"Cheers," he said. A wet nose nuzzled his hand and he found Zeus beside him, panting and blood-speckled, just like his owner.

The market square was eerily quiet. Bodies lay everywhere. Unconscious. Dead. Unmoving. It seemed that he, Dawn and Nale were the only living people left in town. Nicholas hoped that wasn't true.

"The others must be at the school," Nicholas said. "That's where Malika will be. She's opening the trikraft. But the Abbey ruins..." He stopped still. His head thumped, but it wasn't because of the suffocating air. He peered around, knowing exactly what the headache meant.

A raven flapped over their heads. It flew down the Butter Market and then, in its place, there stood a dark figure in a silver mask.

Esus raised a gloved hand and pointed down Abbeygate Street towards the Abbey Gardens. That confirmed it.

"Come on," Nicholas said.

Zeus cantered ahead of them. The raven wheeled above them once more. It caww-ed in what Nicholas thought was an encouraging manner. Was Esus going to help them? He'd killed Diltraa. Could Esus tackle Laurent, too?

"You feeling okay?" he asked Dawn. She wiped the blood on her face with the sleeve of her hoody and nodded. "You don't have to–"

"I do," she said and Nicholas knew the topic was closed. Dawn had as much of a reason to watch Laurent burn as any of them; perhaps more. Laurent robbed her of her parents. She deserved to be there when they took him down.

If they took him down.

When, Nicholas determined. There was no room for doubt.

Abbeygate Street was deserted. The buildings smouldered, fire-ravaged and spent. They hurried between them, down the cobbled street, wary that anybody could attack at any time. A grave silence had fallen over the town, though. There wasn't a living soul anywhere. The sky was black and burnt.

Nicholas's broken arm throbbed worse than ever. He pulled the sling from his pocket and slung it round his neck, fitting his arm into it with a sigh. The pressure lessened somewhat.

They emerged onto Angel Hill. The Abbey gate stood open like a mouth and Harvesters skulked in front of it, guarding the ceremony that Laurent must be performing inside.

Nicholas looked up at Nale, whose huge hands were already balling into fists.

"What do you think?" he asked.

"Be quick," Nale growled. He was going to clear the way for them again.

"Listen," Nicholas began. He felt like he should thank Nale for his help. It was impossible to tell what the grizzly man was thinking, and he spoke so little. But Nale needed to know that Nicholas appreciated what he'd done for them. Without Nale, he and Dawn would be dead by now – if not at the hands of the Tortor, then definitely by the citizens whom the creature had transformed into mindless monsters. "Thanks for... you know..."

Nale's gaze fell on him and it wasn't heavy as Nicholas had expected, but soft. Gentle. Nicholas wished he knew more about Nale. Malika had tried to turn him. Because he was strong? Or was there another reason? If they survived this, Nicholas swore he'd find out.

"Brave boy," the man rumbled. He placed a hand on Nicholas's shoulder, the other on Dawn's. "Girl." After a moment, he blinked and strode off, stomping toward the Abbey gate, Zeus clipping along at his heel.

Nicholas and Dawn ducked behind a water fountain on the hill and watched.

The Harvesters spotted Nale within seconds. They whooped and crowed, whirling blades that flashed with the same steely light that burned in their eyes. Nicholas almost felt sorry for them. Nale would cut them down like twigs.

Zeus was a grey blur and the Harvesters' whoops dissolved into angry howls. A wiry Harvester spun a mace above his head and Nale grabbed his enemy's head in one hand, slamming him to the pavement. Another Harvester replaced him, this one a thick-set woman with a machete. She licked her teeth and swung the blade. Nale caught her fist and the Harvester's grin sagged. He twisted the machete into the Harvester's gut and she collapsed with a cry.

One by one, Nale grappled with the figures at the entrance to the Abbey and each fell, crushed and broken.

"Now," Nicholas hissed. More Harvesters would replace those who had fallen. He and Dawn had minutes, if that, to get inside before the ranks were reinforced.

They dashed out from their hiding place and hurried toward the Abbey gate.

Something whizzed through the air. Nicholas felt it whisper past his ear, missing him by millimetres. An arrow embedded itself in the pavement beside him. He looked up. A figure was atop the Abbey gate.

"Run!" Dawn yelled, grabbing his hand.

They raced for the gate, faces upturned to watch as more arrows sailed down. They dodged them, one grazing Nicholas's leg as it descended. A horn sounded.

"Laurent knows we're here," Nicholas puffed as they tumbled into the shelter of the gate. "Hurry," he urged, pulling Dawn out the other side and into the park. Yet more arrows slashed down to meet them and only the trees prevented them from hitting their targets.

"Low," Nicholas said. "Keep low."

He had a strange feeling the Harvesters weren't even trying. Malika said Laurent wanted him alive. Was that still the case? Did Laurent really expect Nicholas to stand by his side as the Dark Prophets rose from the bowels of hell?

They went from tree to tree. A shriek echoed through the park. The aledites were here, too. Nicholas scanned the sky, but the trees were in the way and the heavens were too dark. The aledites were invisible against the tortured storm clouds.

The ground shuddered beneath them and Nicholas steadied himself against a tree.

"He's already started," he whispered.

"We have to get closer," Dawn said.

"You keep an eye out that side, I'll cover this side. If you see anything..."

"Scream like a girl?"

Nicholas grinned despite himself and they edged through the gardens, keeping to the shadows. He noticed a raven darting between the trees, swooping silently.

They came to a steep hill, which overlooked the ruins. Carefully, they clambered up, using the roots of an old oak tree like the rungs in a ladder. Above them, the raven settled in the oak's branches, hidden amongst the leaves.

With Dawn at his side, Nicholas lay flat and peered over the crest of the hill.

The ruins were bathed in hellfire. Shallow iron bowls contained flickering flames and there were more Harvesters than Nicholas could count. They perched in every rocky crevice, some sitting high up in the tallest of the ruins, others lounging over the broken flint-stone walls.

A figure moved in a part of the ruins that still had four low walls so that it resembled a room. Laurent wore a tapering, blood-red robe, like something a priest might wear. His skin was waxy in the firelight and he clasped something in his long, thin fingers. Nicholas couldn't see what it was.

An altar rested behind him.

Laurent murmured something under his breath and took a knife from the altar. He sliced open his palm. Then he held aloft the thing in his hands. Nicholas squinted. It was a black box covered in a shroud.

"The final totem!" Laurent declared, brandishing it above his head. The Harvesters whistled and shrieked, clashing their blades together.

Reverently, Laurent placed the box on the altar. He flipped the lid.

A hush rushed through the park. Fear inexplicably clutched at Nicholas's heart and he grabbed the tree, if only to have something to hold on to.

Laurent reached into the box and drew out a black object. He kissed it and raised it for all to see. An ugly carving of a three-headed beast. Was it a likeness of one of the Prophets' emissaries? Or perhaps a rendering of the Prophets themselves?

The Harvesters watched silently.

Laurent held his hand over the totem. Blood dripped onto it and a red light burst up into the sky, parting the gathered storm clouds. A crimson, star-like speck glowed. The second part of the trikraft was in place. In the distance, Nicholas saw the red light pulsing high above the museum.

"Sam," he muttered under his breath. "I hope you've stopped the third one..."

He heard Dawn's breath catch in her throat and followed her line of vision.

Laurent had glanced up, right at the spot where they were crouched. He must have known they were there the whole time. He bared his teeth in a triumphant grin and Nicholas knew they were out of time.

★

The ringing in Sam's ears threatened to go on forever. Somewhere in the part of his brain that hadn't been pummelled by the explosion, he attempted to count how many wrecked buildings he'd been in over the past week. Snelling's home, Solomon's boathouse... This time it was the school gymnasium.

He groaned and heaved himself up, finding that he was caked in debris.

Still standing, he thought. *The doc's pills must be working.*

"Isabel?" he murmured, coughing. "Aileen? Merlyn?"

A rustle came from nearby and a cat's head emerged from the rubble. Isabel spluttered and shook herself, a halo of dust scattering into the air.

"Damn and blast," she muttered. "Old man, are you injured?"

Sam checked himself over. "No," he sighed, scanning his surroundings. The ceiling had caved in and he could see the turgid night sky, veins of yellow lightning crackling through the clouds.

Liberty heaved herself up a few feet away, then pulled Merlyn free.

Where were Aileen and Rae?

Some of the debris shifted nearby and Sam turned in that direction, hope swelling in his chest.

Malika extricated herself from the wreckage and Sam knew he would have to move fast to subdue her. Even as he reached into his bag, though, Malika let out a high laugh and crouched down. What was she doing?

Other shapes drew themselves out of the wreckage. Harvesters. All of them bloodied and dust-speckled. Only five now. Others were still buried under the collapsed ceiling. Sam hoped they'd stay there.

The Harvesters surrounded Malika in a protective ring.

The red-haired woman drew something from the folds of her dress. It flashed briefly. A blade. She crouched down and then stood, the blade now wet with blood. Whose blood?

Rae? Sam thought with a lurch. He began to wade through the rubble, but then Malika said something and flicked the blade, splattering blood to the ground. A red light blasted up through the dashed ceiling, burning brightly in the sky. The clouds smouldered red and the ground shifted under his feet.

Sam staggered, regaining his balance.

Hot, crimson light pulsed in the clouds and the atmosphere grew even more troubled.

"What have you done?" he yelled.

Malika's cat-like eyes slid in his direction but she held her tongue. Her pale countenance read triumph.

"It's complete," Liberty said softly.

"The trikraft," Isabel uttered. "Hell-witch, you've doomed us all!"

Malika's reply was a coarse laugh and Sam quivered.

"Soon you'll all be ash," she spat. "Enjoy these final moments. Pray to your gods. They won't hear you. Tonight, the Dark Prophets rise and you'll all be condemned to the festering pits of their former prison."

She stopped, looked at Liberty. The Sensitive stood still, peering at the red witch in a way that Sam recognised. She was trying to read Malika again. Liberty blinked and breathed deeply. She must be searching for a way to stop her.

"You want to see inside my head?" Malika asked. "I'm not sure you'll like what you find."

Their eyes locked and Liberty's jaw clenched. Her body went rigid. Sam's gaze darted between them.

"Isabel," he murmured. "Do something."

"I cannot," the cat replied.

The two women were locked in a wordless, motionless battle. Sam thought he saw the air crackle between them, but he couldn't be sure. His heart lurched as a single line of blood trickled from Liberty's nose and she began to shake. Her eyes became bloodshot and blood oozed from her ears.

"Liberty," Sam gasped.

Liberty's expression crumpled with pain.

"S-Sam..."

Malika smiled, her eyes not leaving the Sensitive. She raised a hand and splayed her fingers, peering between them.

"Boom," she whispered.

Liberty's head snapped back with a sickening crunch and she collapsed heavily. Merlyn caught her just in time to prevent her crashing to the floor. He lowered her slowly down.

Sam didn't know what he was yelling; he was only vaguely aware that he was yelling *something* as he hurried to her, crouching at her side.

"Liberty," he breathed, pulling her gently onto his lap. With a shaking hand, he felt the pulse at her throat. Nothing. Liberty's bloodshot eyes were lifeless.

"We're done here," Malika said. She nodded at Rae's unconscious form. "Bring her."

"Black-hearted witch!" Sam roared. He threw himself at Malika, but a Harvester blocked his path. Fuelled by rage and grief, Sam beat at the Harvester with his fists, not feeling the pain as his joints complained. The Harvester went down, but another took his place.

Through the haze of pain, Sam watched two Harvesters pull Rae from the wreckage and go after Malika.

The next moment, Sam was on the floor, his ears ringing. He must have been punched, but he couldn't remember. A dull throb at his jaw, he looked up, searching for Malika.

Both she and Rae were gone. The Harvesters all turned and left.

An echoing snigger filled the gymnasium.

"*You're mine now,*" cackled the voice of the headmistress.

CHAPTER TWENTY-FIVE
Fire In The Sky

A CLAP OF THUNDER RESOUNDED THROUGH the heavens and Nicholas peered skyward just in time to see a red light blast up in the distance. The atmosphere sizzled and coloured lightning shot jaggedly between the three stars hanging in place above Bury St Edmunds.

The trikraft was complete.

Dawn muttered a curse word beside him and Nicholas looked at her in surprise.

"It's now or never," he said.

"We should wait for Nale and the others."

"You think *he's* waiting?" Nicholas gestured to Laurent.

The man's hands were stretched up to the sky.

"YES!" Laurent roared. The dark energies throbbing in the clouds deepened to blood red and Nicholas looked on, aghast, as a whirling hole opened above the spot where Laurent stood. Yellow light flashed in its depths and the ground fell away at Laurent's feet. A sucking cavity burrowed into the earth, a perfect mirror of the thrashing cyclone above.

"NICHOLAS!" Laurent bellowed. "Do you see?" A ferocious wind tugged at his robes, ruffling his blond hair. "The Prophets awaken!"

Nicholas got to his feet, standing defiantly atop the hill. To the watching Harvesters, all of them crouched within the ruins, he was probably nothing more than a spindly outline against the crimson heavens.

"What are you doing?" Dawn hissed.

Nicholas said nothing. He made his way down the hill into the ruins. Everything had become clear. This was what he had to do.

"Yes, come." Laurent smiled like a shark might, waving a signal at the Harvesters to let him pass. "Come, embrace the Prophets. Be the first to welcome them."

His heart thrummed in his chest and Nicholas felt empty. He was floating. Perhaps it was a way of coping with the fear. Of confronting Laurent without succumbing to the voices in his head that pleaded for him to turn around.

No, it was the clarity. If he had to die, that's the way it was. He couldn't let Laurent succeed.

A female Harvester snarled at him as Nicholas approached the room-like portion of the ruins, but she let him enter.

"Witness the beauty of destruction." Laurent's lips drew back into a skull-like grin, his eyes wide and wild.

A shape moved within the twisting pit in the earth and Nicholas froze. Claws thrust up, taking purchase of the ground. Something colossal hauled itself into the park.

"Welcome!" Laurent laughed. "Rise, foot-soldiers of the Prophets!"

The six-legged beast clambered into the ruins. Black scales glowed red in the light of the storm and enormous muscles flexed. A slithering tale whipped behind it and a face crowded with eyes swung about malevolently. Nicholas watched helplessly as the creature mounted the ruins. It drew in a great lungful of air and emitted a blistering shriek that threatened to burst Nicholas's eardrums.

Then, fixing its sights on the rest of the park, it stomped away.

"Stop this," Nicholas yelled, struggling to be heard as the wind howled between him and Laurent.

Laurent crowed. "Boy, it cannot be stopped! Nothing can stop it now!"

More creatures thrashed from the ground. Scuttling, wriggling monstrosities of different shapes and sizes, each more hideous than the last. Nicholas had thought Diltraa was repulsive, but these new hellbeasts were far worse. Some were elephant-sized and covered in porcupine-spears, others were as large as hairless mountain cats with rows of gnashing incisors.

Nicholas watched helplessly as they surged into the night, baying as they proliferated the park.

He saw something else dash through the Abbey gardens. Esus. The phantom wielded a sword, launching at the creatures.

Nicholas glared at Laurent. "I'll stop it," he pledged.

"You'll die! You're a spectator, Nicholas. You're no hero. The Trinity may have stored precious power inside you, but you're nothing more than a little boy with an inflated opinion of himself."

"Maybe we're not that different after all, then," Nicholas said.

Laurent shrieked with laughter. He'd lost his mind. Nicholas knew there was no reasoning with him. You couldn't reason with a mad man.

"You have darkness in you, boy. Embrace it!" Laurent urged. "Only something truly evil could do what you did in Orville!"

It wasn't true. Nicholas tried not to listen.

But there they were, those huddled doubts that waited for him in the darkest fog of his mind.

You're dangerous. You're a threat. You're no good.

He'd killed so many people. What if Laurent was right?

Laurent lies, he told himself. *Laurent lies.*

The aledites wheeled above their heads and Nicholas realised they weren't far from the spot where he had first encountered Laurent. This was where he'd been plucked from the ground, dragged kicking over the town and then hurled the way a bird dashes a snail.

"Stop the ceremony," he said, gritting his teeth. "Or I'll stop you."

"Itching for another one of those?" Laurent sneered, gesturing at his arm.

"One's enough," Nicholas said. He drew the sling up and released his broken arm.

The gauntlet was attached over the cast, fixed to his exposed thumb and fingers. It had been in the backpack that Liberty handed him. She must have seen this. She must have known that he'd be the one to get this close to Laurent.

Laurent's expression changed.

"You're too young for a toy like that," he growled.

"Make it stop!" Nicholas yelled.

Laurent held his gaze for a moment, then his eyes slid to the left and he nodded, signalling to a waiting Harvester. Nicholas understood. He was fair game now. He sensed a figure coming up on his right and turned, clenching his fist.

A flash of blue light flared before him and Nicholas's feet left the ground. He soared backwards and hit a rocky wall. He gasped for breath and shook his head. What had gone wrong? Struggling to sit up, he first saw Laurent's seething expression, and then a body on the ground, steam rising from it.

"WOO! YEAH!"

Groggily, Nicholas followed the voice. Dawn was atop the hill by the oak tree, pumping the air with her fist. She flashed an elated grin.

The gauntlet had worked!

"Seize her! Stop him!" Laurent screamed.

Nicholas would have whooped, too, but the ruins thrashed to life in an instant. As the Harvesters descended, he closed his eyes and thought about the seeing glass. It hadn't been useless. It had opened something in him that he'd been ignoring, and now he needed all the tools at his disposal. In his mind's eye, he saw the purple crystal swinging and the flash as it snared the light. The ground melted away beneath him and he felt strangely alert – more alert than he ever had in his life.

The earth. The quick heartbeats of birds. The angry, charged sky.

He could feel it all between his temples. And *them*. He could feel the Harvesters, too. Their thoughts were snapping teeth. They were coming for him.

He moved as if in a dream. Back on his feet, he wielded the gauntlet the way it was intended. He didn't lose his balance again, instead leaning in to the gauntlet as it blasted blue lightning.

Harvesters fell. Most of them didn't have time to scream. The electricity spun them violently where they stood, then dropped them like tired puppets.

Dawn!

Nicholas sensed her as well. Inquisitive, deer-like thoughts. He looked up at the oak tree, where Harvesters were already clambering toward her. She had a branch in her hands and whipped it before her, pale and daring. The Harvesters squawked and one of them seized the branch, snatching it from her.

Nicholas squeezed the gauntlet again and the Harvesters fell, tumbling back down the hill and lying still.

His eyes locked with Dawn's. Then her mouth sagged open in fear.

"Nich–" she began, but the winged forms had already tumbled raggedly from the sky, clutching for him. He ducked just in time as an aledite's claws flashed above him and Nicholas raised his broken arm, wincing as pain forked through it. He ignored the pain, squeezed the gauntlet and sent the aledite bowling backwards. It rolled into the sucking hole in the ground and was gone.

Another flew at him, and another.

The air around him was a thrashing mass of leathery wings and gleaming yellow eyes, and panic began to replace the calm. Nicholas flailed his arms, attempting to beat the monsters back.

A claw raked his scalp and he felt the warm pump of blood.

"STOP!" Laurent bellowed. In a fuss of coriaceous wings, the aledites left him and Nicholas panted for breath as Laurent glided forward. His expression was awful. "He's mine," Laurent declared, his fingers snatching at Nicholas's throat.

They clamped tightly and Nicholas gagged. He thrust his gauntleted arm forward, pressing it to Laurent's chest.

Laurent jeered at him. He twisted Nicholas's gauntleted hand away, forcing it to one side. Nicholas gasped in agony, feeling his broken bones grating against one another.

"You've impressed me, Nicholas," Laurent said coldly. "There's yet fight in this dog."

"You can't want this," Nicholas rasped. "You're going to destroy everything!"

Above them, the crackling yellow whirlpool in the clouds grew, vomiting noxious gasses that made Nicholas's head spin. Enormous shadows rippled over the ground as yet more hellbeasts scrambled free, gibbering as they seized control of the park. He caught sight of lithe, reptilian shapes with spearing fangs.

"Destruction is the way of the world," Laurent hissed. "Every era ripens and withers. It's *our* time. The Prophets have whispered their plans to me for years. They will rise and all you ever took for granted will be rendered ash."

"You can still stop it," Nicholas begged.

He saw movement behind Laurent and tried not to look, even though it meant staring into the man's manic eyes. He blinked away the blood trickling from his forehead.

"Now," he said.

He heard a dull crack and Laurent's head snapped forward. His face crumpling with confusion, he collapsed to the ground.

Nicholas found himself face to face with Dawn. She breathed heavily, a bloodied flint stone in her hand. She had pulled it free from the ruins and dashed it against Laurent's skull.

"Nice one," Nicholas said.

Dawn stared down at Laurent. She seemed to be considering smashing the rock over his head again. If she did, Nicholas wouldn't stop her. He touched her arm and she looked at him glassily.

"They'd be proud," he said.

Red lightning boomed through the heavens and Nicholas shuddered. Something was different. He turned and stared straight into cold, cat-like eyes.

"You're harder to kill than a cockroach," Malika purred. She idled by the ruins, no more than ten feet away. Two Harvesters came up behind her, carrying a limp body between them. They put the unconscious figure down on the ground and Nicholas was able to get a good look at her.

It was Rae.

"What have you done to her?" he demanded.

"She did this to herself," Malika said.

Laurent groaned on the ground and put a hand to the wound at the back of his skull. Dawn went to Nicholas's side and they watched as Laurent woozily got to his feet, adjusting his robes. His eyes flashed to Dawn.

"Young Dawn," he leered. His cheekbones jutted and the sneer made his attractive features ugly. "What would your parents say of such violent outbursts? Not much, I suspect."

Nicholas felt Dawn trembling beside him, but she didn't move.

Laurent dabbed at his head and peered down at his blood-smeared fingers. Then, as if he'd heard something, perhaps the voices of the

Prophets whispering to him again, he turned. His grin split slowly like a rupturing wound.

Nicholas followed where Laurent was looking and froze.

The Tortor swept through the Abbey gardens, the spear still embedded in its torso.

"Ah, now the fun really begins," Laurent purred.

★

Sam couldn't look away from Liberty. The tears spilled freely and he sank to the ground beside her body.

Not her, he thought. *Not Liberty.*

The girl he'd watched grow into a woman lay dead. The grief was a scream trapped in his chest. He could shout and cry all he wanted, but the scream would never dislodge. It squeezed his heart, smothered every thought in darkness.

"Francesca," he whispered. Liberty's daughter. She was only six. Another young Sentinel orphaned by the Dark Prophets. Another name to add to the list.

The grief blunted into blind anger and Sam seized a piece of the debris from the gym floor, hurling it across the room with a roar.

Weariness subdued him.

"Sam, we have to go."

He barely heard Merlyn speak, or the grim laughter that gurgled through the gymnasium. Miss Fink, the Harvester headmistress, was approaching.

He didn't care anymore.

"Nicholas needs us," Merlyn said.

The name struck him like a beam of light. It momentarily forced the grief to shrink back. For a second he saw clearly. Saw Merlyn, skinny and shaken; Aileen clambering to her feet while Isabel scanned their whereabouts. Liberty lying broken in the wrecked gymnasium...

"Liberty," he murmured.

Merlyn tugged his arm. "Come on, fella," he urged. "You can grieve later. We'll come back for her. But this place is screwed. We have to get out."

He knew he was right. As the initial shock receded, Sam wiped his face and cast about the gym. Already the shadows were threshing and coming alive.

"This way," Isabel called, at the gym door with Aileen.

Merlyn handed Sam his rifle and he squeezed it, clinging to it for dear life. He had to think clearly. This was exactly what Malika wanted. His wits cowering round his ankles. He wouldn't let her win.

"We have to be quick," he gruffed, stomping after Isabel, kicking the debris aside. Merlyn hurried after him, eyeing the moving shadows uneasily.

"What are those things?" the youngster asked shakily.

"Black manifestations," Isabel said as they entered the blood-smeared corridor. "Nightmare demons. In my day we called them murklings. Don't grant them access to your mind or they will turn your greatest fear against you."

As one, the four Sentinels hurried down the corridor. They rounded a corner and Sam skidded to a halt.

Miss Fink stood bent and buckled with age. The former headmistress of Royal Birch Primary School snickered through reptilian lips, her purple-white skin glowing in the gloom.

She stood in the middle of the corridor, barring their way.

"Much blood has been spilled in my playground," she hissed, clutching her mittened claws together. *"And yet more must be spilled."*

"The hag is mine," Isabel spat. "Samuel, go!"

In other circumstances, Sam might have argued, but golden sparks already spat and fizzed in the cat's eyes, and he knew this wasn't a battle he could win. The school had become a supernatural battlefield. Brute strength was nothing against the likes of Miss Fink.

"Boy," Sam said to Merlyn. "Aileen."

Aileen nodded and disappeared into one of the classrooms, Merlyn at her heels. Sam went to the door. He paused a moment to watch.

Miss Fink peered at the cat with sly curiosity.

"What jest is this?" she gurgled. As the golden sparks sizzled, though, the headteacher's expression hardened. A gnarled claw made a curious gesture and shadows spilled away from the walls, surrounding the cat.

For a moment, Isabel was lost. The flocking murklings blanketed her, swiping out with distended talons, their cut-out shadow mouths stretched open in silent shrieks.

Then an aurulent light erupted from the centre of the black mass and the murklings were cast off, melting back into the walls.

In a single, shambling step, Miss Fink was upon Isabel. She plucked the cat from the floor and Isabel shrieked. She writhed in the headmistress's grip, tail lashing furiously, but she couldn't free herself.

Miss Fink cackled.

The breath stuck in Sam's throat. Even as he pushed away from the wall, lunging for the headteacher, Miss Fink held Isabel aloft like some long-coveted prize and, crowing wickedly, she snapped the cat's neck.

★

As the Tortor made its way through the Abbey Gardens, trees combusted in its wake. Flames blazed where none had before, flickering eagerly to consume the sun-baked bark. Within minutes, the park had become an inferno. Even the grass burned, as if it had been doused with petrol.

"The totems," Nicholas hissed at Dawn. The altar behind Laurent was lined with the three totems – the three-headed beast; the female-shaped Slaughter Stone; the Chinese vase. Dawn nodded and clenched her fists at her side. Then, without so much as a cry, she hurled herself at Laurent.

The man was so taken aback, still recovering from the blow to the head, he nearly lost his footing. Dawn scratched at his face, thrashing wildly, diverting his attention away from Nicholas.

Nicholas seized his moment. He aimed the gauntlet at the totems and clenched his fist. Blue lightning forked toward the altar and an almighty flash briefly blinded him. When his vision cleared, he saw that the totems remained untouched. The air pulsed and recoiled, steam curling up from the altar.

The totems were protected.

Even as disappointment clutched at him, a bellow rang through the park. It was followed by a rallying cry. Nicholas turned to see a mass of bodies charging into the Abbey Gardens. There must be a hundred of them. Then he saw who was leading the charge.

Nale.

His clothes were ripped and his face was plastered in blood, but he held an axe aloft as he stormed ahead of the other Sentinels. He leapt onto the back of one of the scaly monstrosities that had emerged from the pit and buried his weapon in its skull.

The beast toppled.

The remaining Harvesters leapt into action, snaking over the ruins, spilling toward the Sentinels until they clashed messily at the centre of the park. Screams and yells rose above the battlefield.

Nicholas glimpsed Malika dashing among them. She wielded the Drujblade with deadly skill, slashing at exposed throats, revelling in the arterial spray that doused her in wet crimson.

He heard a cry and turned to see Laurent throw Dawn off. She tumbled over the ground and fell into the pit by the altar. She was gone.

"NO!" Nicholas shouted.

"Enjoy Hell," Laurent spat. He leapt at Nicholas and they tussled against the ruins.

"Rae!" Nicholas yelled. "Rae, wake up!"

"This is the end," Laurent sneered, gaining the upper hand. "Accept it."

Nicholas sensed movement and attempted to see past Laurent. He cried out as the man tore the gauntlet from his cast and smashed his broken arm against the flint wall. Screaming agony rendered him momentarily blind and Nicholas collapsed to the ground. A boot drove into his ribs. He tasted blood.

"What's this?"

Choking for breath, Nicholas looked up at Laurent's astonished tone. Hope surged through him. Rae was awake. She was at the pit, reaching in, pulling.

"Dawn," he croaked as Rae dragged a figure out. Dawn must have been clinging at the edge. She flopped onto the ground and Rae helped her to her feet.

"Still weigh a ton," she groused.

"Oh, Rae, don't tell me you've come over all heroic," Laurent jibed, gliding toward the two girls.

She looked at him and the air shimmered.

"After everything I taught you," Laurent oozed.

"Shut up," Rae spat.

Laurent made a strangled noise. He held his hands before him in shock and Nicholas saw boiling welts rising angrily. Rae. She'd turned on him.

Clutching his ribs, Nicholas attempted to stand. Pain tore through him and he thought he was going to pass out. No, he had to get to the altar. Gritting his teeth, he dragged himself across the grass.

"No, boy," Laurent gasped, but there was nothing he could do. His skin blistered and he was on his knees.

Nicholas seized the edge of the altar and attempted to prise himself from the ground. His ribs shrieked at him, as if they were tearing apart, but he had to keep going. Sweat beading his upper lip, he felt hands under his armpits and Dawn heaved him up.

Not wasting a moment, he seized the nearest totem. The Slaughter Stone. Nothing happened. No sparks. No flames. It hummed in his hands and his skin prickled, itching where it made contact with the stone, but he lifted it as easily as if he'd plucked something from a supermarket shelf.

"Stop!" Laurent yelled.

"Time's up," Nicholas said. He hurled the totem at the ruins. It smashed on impact.

"NO!" Laurent screamed. He threw himself at Nicholas, but he was too slow. Nicholas grabbed the Èyùn vase and the three-headed statuette, dashing them against the flint work, too. They shattered into hundreds of pieces.

Nostrils flaring, Laurent fell upon Nicholas. They toppled over and Nicholas's back struck the ground. Laurent clambered on top of him, swiping his face with his hands. Before he could do anything else, Dawn beat at the back of Laurent's head with the bloodied flint-stone.

The man grunted and sagged heavily to the ground.

"Something about doing that is too much fun," Dawn panted. She helped Nicholas to his feet.

Laurent lay sprawled. Unconscious or dead, Nicholas couldn't tell. He thought he saw a faint fall and rise of the man's chest. There was no time to find out, though. The Tortor had reached their part of the ruins. The monster paused on the other side of the wall, its feature-less face turned blankly toward them. The spear was still embedded in its chest.

Unnatural flames sprung up wherever the Tortor stepped, lapping almost as high as parts of the ruins. The heat was unbearable and Nicholas had to fight the wooziness.

"Rae," he said. Finally, he knew what they had to do. They were connected, and it was that connection that could defeat the Tortor. She hurried to his side and he grabbed her hand.

In a flash, he saw everything. Her anger flooded hotly into him, barbed and painful. He embraced it and lifted it away, drew it away from her and turned it into vapour.

They were linked. They were the same.

The flames closed in as the Tortor paced slowly toward them.

"That thing," Rae grimaced.

"Yeah, that thing."

There was new resolve in her face. She wasn't afraid anymore. She focussed on the faceless man and the air shimmered with heat. Nicholas's hand fused with Rae's and he could sense the power welling in her, becoming volatile, unstable. He attempted to give it borders, keep it from getting out of control.

Fire exploded around them, but it was directed only at the Tortor.

The blaze engulfed the faceless man. He began to shudder and twitch. The creature's skin bubbled, hardened, solidified into rock. The Tortor became rigid. A craggy statue. He reached for them, a quivering finger elongating, searching, before it, too, became solid and immovable.

Rae let out a breath at the same time as Nicholas.

They watched as the Tortor toppled, falling stiffly to the ground and thudding into the mud.

In an instant, the whirling cyclone above their heads closed. The pit directly below it filled in and the flames ravaging the Abbey Gardens extinguished, leaving behind scorched earth and little else.

The Tortor lay in a grave of cinders.

It was over.

"Guys, that was awesome," Dawn said.

Nicholas scanned the park. Nale stared back at him from the oak tree on the hill. There were no Harvesters left. He turned to where Laurent had fallen, but he was gone. There was no sign of Malika, either.

In the chaos, they had both escaped.

Other Sentinels battled the remaining monsters, and the mingle of human and inhuman shrieks made Nicholas's hair stand on end.

He pondered the tortured sky, which still roiled red and angry. Unnatural whoops and shrieks filled the air as the creatures that Laurent had unleashed made their way beyond the park, into the decimated town.

It wasn't over yet.

CHAPTER TWENTY-SIX
The Cat

The school was alive with deadly shadows. The foundations trembled, as if some immense creature was heaving itself up from the bowels of the earth, and Sam clung to a wall.

A shadow with teeth snapped at his face and he shoved himself away, staggering over to Aileen.

"What's happening?" she yelled, slashing the air with her sword.

"The shadow things," Merlyn said.

"Where's the cat?"

"Gone," Sam said.

He ignored the nip of remorse and dodged as a dark shape swooped for him.

"Hands up if you think getting the fudge out of here is priority numero uno," Merlyn yelled, slashing his own blade at the murklings. It passed ineffectually through them.

Sam felt a rush of heat as one of the murklings slithered through him.

Judith. He saw Judith. The last time he'd seen her, he'd kissed her on the cheek and left her in Orville. Left her to die so that he could attend a Sentinel summit in Cambridge. All that was left was ash. Not even enough to fill an urn.

"I didn't know," he gasped, attempting to free himself from the murkling. "I DIDN'T KNOW SHE WAS GOING TO DIE!"

The murkling released its grip.

Sam panted, planting his hands on his knees.

What were the murklings waiting for? They could kill them in an instant if they wanted to.

Fear, Sam thought. They wanted to bleed them dry of their fear. Even as he looked on, they were increasing in size, becoming swollen. Their cut-out eyes gleamed red.

A solid form emerged into the corridor. It hurled an object through the air and Merlyn cried out.

"Son of a!" He spun around, attempting to grasp at the round, cerated blade embedded just under his shoulder. Aileen came to his rescue, tackling the Harvester who had hurled the weapon. She moved faster than Sam ever thought possible. The sound of metal clashing rang over the din of murklings.

A wall exploded beside him and he saw that another Harvester had emerged, this one equipped with a gauntlet.

"That one!" he yelled. "Get that one!"

As Merlyn charged, Sam rooted around in his satchel. There had to be something to keep the murklings at bay. He'd never heard of anything like them. They were insubstantial. How could you fight something you couldn't touch?

His fingers closed around a box of matches.

Light.

It was worth a try. If they really were shadows, it stood to reason that they'd retreat from the light.

As Merlyn and Aileen fought off the Harvesters, all the while attempting to evade the murklings, he grabbed a chair from where it rested against the wall and smashed it. Seizing a splintered leg, he tore off a piece of his shirt and wrapped it around the end, dousing it in lighter fluid. He struck a match.

The murklings screeched and flashed away from him, melting into the walls.

"Aileen, Merlyn, this way!" Sam yelled, brandishing the torch.

Merlyn tugged his blade free from a Harvester's belly and hurried after Sam. Another wall exploded ahead of them. The remaining Harvesters were giving chase.

"Is this the way out?" Aileen puffed.

Dismayed, Sam realised they'd doubled back on themselves in the confusion.

"This way," he said, aiming for the doors that led out onto the playground.

As they staggered down the corridor, they came to a part of the school that seemed to have been subjected to a small explosion. A perfect circle of burnt linoleum. And the floor was littered with debris.

Sam squinted uncertainly.

Beside the debris lay the body of a black cat.

"What's this?" Merlyn said.

"Go," Sam urged, handing the young Sentinel the torch. Ahead, he saw the double doors that led to the playground. "That way. Go now."

"Sam," Aileen began uncertainly.

Merlyn took her arm and they hurried toward the doors.

Sam inspected the rubble more closely, confirming what he'd suspected. A body was half-buried in the mound of rubble at the centre of the blackened portion of the corridor.

It was Miss Fink.

She groaned, as if stunned, and attempted to move.

"You," Sam whispered hoarsely. Anger throbbed at his temples. He knew he should hurry after Merlyn and Aileen; get out of the building before it crushed him, but an uncontrollable rage drove him down. Before he knew it, he was crouching in the wreckage, going for the headmistress's scrawny neck.

As he dragged her up and shook her, the old woman thrashed to life.

Her eyes snapped open and they flashed briefly gold.

"Samuel," the old woman choked.

He couldn't believe his ears. His grip slackened.

"Isabel?" he murmured.

★

A grey dawn heralded a new morning. The light was cheerless, as if straining through dirty windows, and Nicholas squinted miserably at the remains of Royal Birch Primary School. He let the axe he'd taken from the battle-scarred Abbey Gardens rest against the ground.

"You think they're in there?" Dawn asked, eyeing the school.

"Hopefully not," Nicholas said. He didn't want to imagine what they'd find if they went into the school. Were Sam and Isabel alive? The last thing Rae remembered was blowing up the gymnasium. Aileen, Liberty and Merlyn had been with her, too. What if they were all dead?

The thought of Merlyn being hurt made him queasy. He wasn't sure why.

Attempting to shut out his trepidation, Nicholas focussed on the school and breathed evenly. The seeing glass had done its job. Within seconds he could see inside the building and was scouting the wreckage in his mind. He found only broken bodies. Harvesters littered the floors. Nicholas kept searching, attempting to find the gymnasium.

The breath caught in his throat.

A dead cat lay crumpled amid the ruins.

"Isabel," Nicholas gasped, emerging from the vision.

"Is she—" Dawn began.

Nicholas nodded, clenching the axe. After everything that had happened, Isabel was dead. He forced the sob down, ground his teeth together to keep the emotion at bay. "I didn't see anybody else. I think they're alright."

"Unless they've been taken."

"We should check inside, just to be sure."

"You go in if you want," Rae said. She sat on a bench facing the road. It was just the three of them. The other Sentinels, headed by Nale, were still in town hunting the monsters that Laurent had unleashed.

Nicholas peered up at the sound of wings. He turned in time to see Esus appear. The figure stood with the town burning behind him.

"They're on their way to Jessica," Esus intoned.

"They—" Nicholas began. "Sam and Aileen?"

"And the other woman."

Woman? Nicholas thought. *Liberty?*

"They left us?" he asked, shooting Dawn a look of disbelief. She picked at her nail polish anxiously.

"They were following orders."

"*Your orders?* You told them to leave us here?"

"Your journey continues without them," Esus said. "You must discover how to resurrect the Trinity."

Nicholas eyed Rae. He couldn't imagine where to begin.

"Cambridge," he said finally. It was the first thing that came into his head.

"This town has been compromised," Esus intoned. "It will not be long before Cambridge falls, too."

It was probably true, but Nicholas didn't know what else to do. Cambridge was home. Cambridge might have answers.

My parents, he thought. In the chaos, he'd almost forgotten. His parents hadn't been his parents. Perhaps there would be more answers about them at home. Morbid curiosity gnawed at him, but Nicholas wasn't sure if he wanted to know more. What if they had even more secrets? Sam would know. Sam and his wife had known his real parents. But Sam was gone.

He thought about what the seeing glass had shown him. There were still things that hadn't come to pass. Like the most incongruous part of the vision. Elvis Presley. And the moonlit well. He still had no idea how that fit into all of this.

"Go," Esus said. The spot where he stood darkened and then the masked phantom was gone.

Nicholas watched a raven whisk away, disappearing into the distance. He felt as if an impossible task lay ahead. They'd disrupted Laurent's plans and it still wasn't enough. The apocalypse was here and now. He wondered if Esus would only be happy when Nicholas was dead.

He squinted at the school. How long ago had Sam left? Could they catch up with him? With a sinking feeling, Nicholas knew they wouldn't be able to. Besides, he had no idea which way Sam had gone.

As the sun struggled through sombre clouds, he felt Dawn's hand at his shoulder.

"Hey," she said. "Happy birthday."

It was weird how she seemed to always say exactly the right thing at exactly the right time.

Nicholas grabbed his axe and hefted it onto his shoulder. "Cheers. Who fancies a walk, then?"

★

The Cat

A bird's coarse shriek shattered the stillness of Hallow House. A ragged black shadow tumbled down a hallway, and then, in its place, a tall figure strode purposefully. Dark robes dragged and a silver mask glimmered.

"Jessica?" Esus rumbled.

No answer. The walls flexed around him, bowing inward. It was too dark. The air a shroud. Esus strolled down the hall, making no more than a soft rustle as he moved.

There. A noise. The cowled head tilted. Listened.

A shivering breath and what might have been a sob or a gasp.

The black eyes behind the mask narrowed. On the wall. Something dark was smeared in a line. A sticky trail of something red.

Esus stiffened, shoulders curling up toward his ears.

Ahead. Another noise.

Esus reached a door. Blood pooled before it, oily black in the darkness. He reached out a gloved hand and opened the door.

A woman looked up from the closet floor. She was covered in red. Her hair hung in saturated strings. Her dress was wet crimson. On the floor between her bare knees rested a severed head. Dead teeth clenched. Eyes rolled back so the whites shone.

Lash. Her bodyguard.

"He wouldn't stop," Jessica said. "He wouldn't stop. So I made him. It's a game. Do you want to play?"

She grinned and her teeth were red.

EPILOGUE

A SICKLY MORNING LIGHT BROKE OVER the Abbey Gardens. The park was deserted but for two figures.

Malika sailed through the ash and cinders with deadly purpose, her dress trailing behind her. At her side, Laurent was pale with smudge-like shadows under his eyes, his jaw set determinedly. His hair was matted with blood at the back.

They entered the ruins and found the spot where Laurent had performed his ceremony just hours before. The grass was black. The ruins charred. And there, nestled in a bed of cinders, was the blackened form of the Tortor.

"They did well," Malika purred.

"They didn't know what they were doing," Laurent murmured, sounding satisfied. "The light show worked. They really believed that three powerless totems could revive the Prophets."

Malika watched him sink to his knees beside the faceless man. Then, seemingly unable to resist any longer, Laurent tore at the figure's stomach, ripping aside chunks of coal-like flesh. A faint green glow lit up his eyes, emanating from the cavity.

With a blissful sigh, Laurent rested back on his heels.

Peering over his shoulder, Malika's jaw became a hard line. In the recess of the Tortor's stomach rested three veiny pods the size of ostrich eggs.

"I can hear them," Laurent breathed.

Malika laughed, the sound high and mocking. His confused gaze only doubled her amusement.

EPILOGUE

"The Prophets," she whispered, her eyes narrowing into slits. "You still believe it's the Prophets who whisper their secrets to you."

Laurent got to his feet uncertainly.

"They always have," he murmured.

A flash of silver opened his throat. Hot wetness oozed over his collar. He clamped a hand to the wound, gulping, shock tugging at his perfect lips.

"Wha–" he choked, retching blood.

"The Dark Prophets have never spoken to you," Malika sneered, her fingers glistening red as she wiped the Drujblade on her dress.

Laurent sagged to his knees once more. What little colour his cheeks had held quickly drained from them. He grew ashen as the sky.

"We deceived them all," Malika hissed. "But nobody was deceived more than you. How happy you were to do my bidding. It was my voice that whispered in your ear. Mine that revealed the secrets of the Prophets. If you were chosen, it was by me alone. I know a loyal hound when I see one."

Laurent's eyes bulged and the blood pumped between his fingers. He grasped for her with his free hand, but she stepped out of the way and he collapsed on his front.

She contemplated his dying spasms and smiled.

She ran a bloody hand over her face, painting it red.

When he was still, Malika swayed in the sallow morning light and hummed a tuneless lullaby, peering down at the egg-like shapes in the Tortor's stomach.

The age of the Dark Prophets had begun.

The Sentinels will return.

"A great, imaginative, gripping read…"
Nev Pierce, Editor-at-Large, Empire

"Fast paced, surprising, and madly compelling."
Rosie Fletcher, Total Film

SENTINEL - BOOK ONE OF THE SENTINEL TRILOGY IS ALSO
AVAILABLE FROM PERIDOT PRESS, PRICED £6.99

PERIDOT PRESS LTD
E: INFO@PERIDOT.CO.UK   W: WWW.PERIDOT.CO.UK

Also Available

T-Shirt

Postcard Set

Peridot Press Ltd
E: info@peridot.co.uk W: www.peridot.co.uk

Litho Poster